THEIR FINEST

Lissa Evans

BLACK SWAN

TRANSWORLD PUBLISHERS
61–63 Uxbridge Road, London W5 5SA
www.penguin.co.uk

Transworld is part of the Penguin Random House group of companies whose addresses can be found at global.penguinrandomhouse.com

First published in Great Britain in 2009 by Doubleday
an imprint of Transworld Publishers
Black Swan edition published as *Their Finest Hour and a Half* in 2010
This Black Swan edition published as *Their Finest* in 2017

A CIP catalogue record for this book
is available from the British Library.

ISBN
9781784162610 (B format)
9781784163020 (A format)

Typeset in Bembo by Falcon Oast Graphic Art Ltd.
Printed and bound by Clays Ltd, Bungay, Suffolk.

Penguin Random House is committed to a sustainable future for our business, our readers and our planet. This book is made from Forest Stewardship Council® certified paper.

1 3 5 7 9 10 8 6 4 2

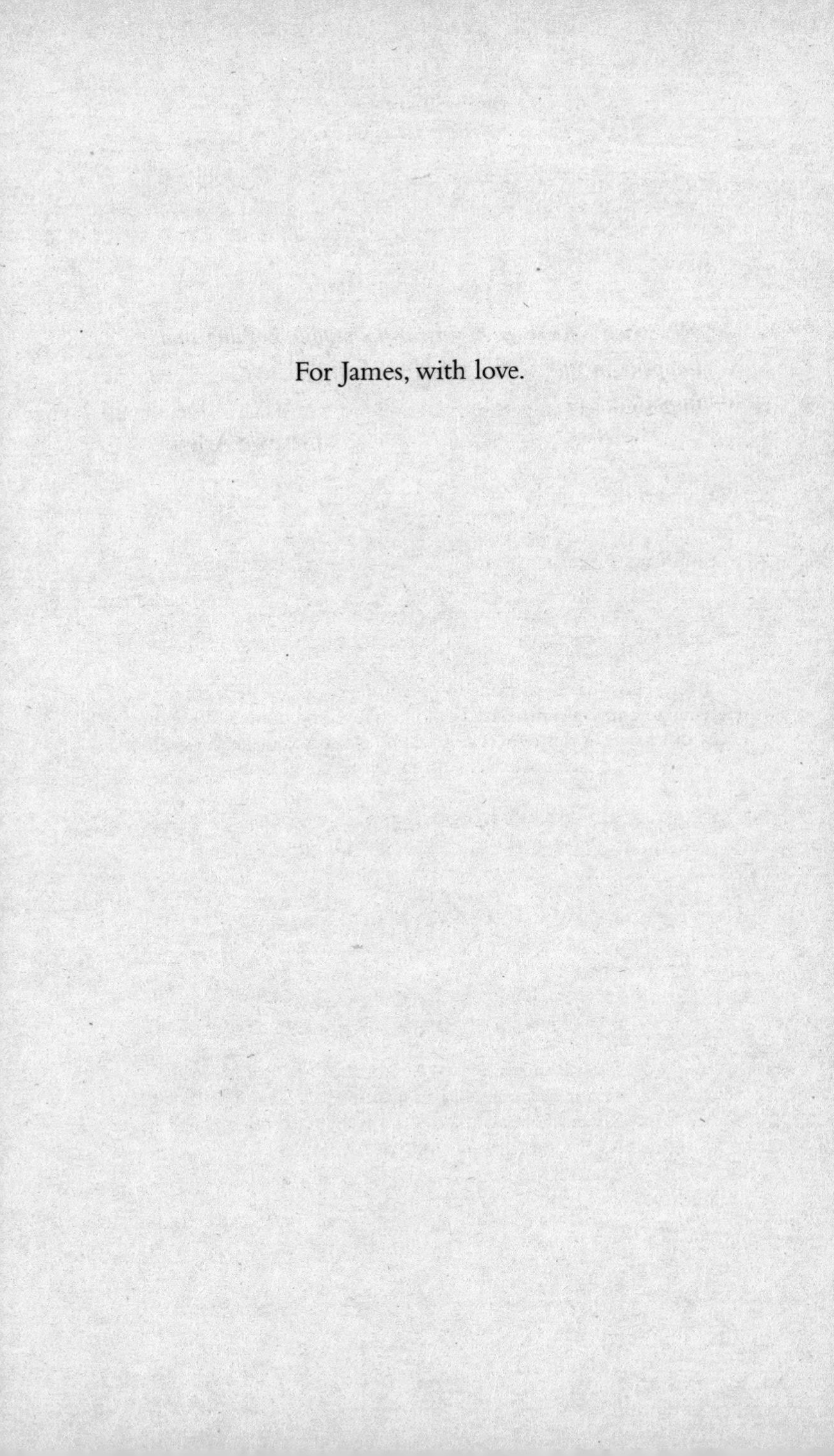

For James, with love.

. . . when once work begins in the studio, nothing that happens in the outside world is of any relative importance . . .

George Arliss

TRAILER

April 1940

'I was wondering,' Sammy said, tentatively, as they paused between courses at La Venezia, 'if you should think of getting a new photograph of yourself. Something just a tiny bit more up-to-the-minute, perhaps . . .'

Ambrose's first impulse was to dismiss the idea – after all, as he reminded Sammy, he'd had a perfectly decent set of prints taken not so long ago and they'd been bloody expensive, and it wasn't as if his current level of income allowed him to run to unnecessary extravagance. And surely the whole purpose of an agent was to increase a client's income, rather than spend it for him?

Sammy looked chastened, as well he might.

Back at home that afternoon, Ambrose dug the file of photographs out of the bureau, just to reassure himself, and yes, they were scarcely eight years old – taken in February 1932, not long after the highly successful kinematic release of *Inspector Charnforth and the Bitter Lemons Mystery* – and really, they were more than adequate: full face, chin on hand, a fine, frank gaze at the camera, a curtain draped artfully across the wall behind, a briar pipe and a volume of verse resting on a table in front. They spoke of depth and maturity, of vigour and yet also of a certain masculine sensitivity. Their invisible caption – unmistakably – was 'Leading Man'. He put the portfolio away again and gave no further thought to the matter until a fortnight later, in Sammy's office. Where he was being kept waiting.

'He'll be in any minute now, Mr Hilliard,' the typist kept

saying, brightly. 'He knows you're expected, only he's had to take his doggie to the vet, the poor little thing's ate half a tin of boot polish and it's been ever so ill.' And since the chaos of paper on Sammy's desk meant that it was impossible to discern which script it was that Ambrose was meant to be collecting, he was forced to sit and stew. The 1940 edition of *Spotlight* was on the office shelf, and he amused himself for a while by looking through the 'Character Actors' section – page after page of uglies, fatties, the once-beautiful and the never-handsome, each of them no doubt nurturing the hope that a browsing director, tiring of chiselled good-looks, might one day choose a more 'interesting' face for his next romantic lead. Poor deluded saps. He turned the page on the final gargoyle, and pointedly consulted his watch.

'Any minute now, Mr Hilliard,' said the typist.

It occurred to Ambrose that he ought to check his own entry in the volume, and re-opening it at the beginning, he started to leaf through 'Leading Actors', at first briskly, and then with a growing sense of unease. When he at last reached his own photograph, he stared at it for a while; it seemed, this time, somehow less than satisfactory. He glanced again at the portraits of his rivals, and it was like picking through a police file marked 'Dangerous Cases' – all was mood, spleen, sullenness, seething introspection. Here slouched Marius Goring, wreathed in shadow, here Jack Hawkins, peering shiftily from beneath the brim of his hat. Glowering presence succeeded glowering presence. No one stood upright. No one gazed directly at camera. No one smiled. It was clear that the fine, frank gaze had had its hour; nowadays it was de rigueur to look as if one were just about to cosh an old lady.

'I've been thinking about your suggestion of the other day,' he said to Sammy, when his agent at last arrived at the office. 'It's all a matter of style, of course. There are fashions in photography as in everything else, and one simply has to accept the fact. We are in a new and brutal age.'

Sammy nodded, a touch uncertainly. 'So, you'll have another picture taken?'

'If I must,' said Ambrose.

The photographer was a blue-chinned Hungarian refugee called Erno. He was trying to establish himself in London, Sammy said, and was therefore acceptably cheap. On the debit side, his English was rudimentary.

'Brooding,' said Ambrose, who had taken the precaution of bringing the copy of *Spotlight* with him to the room above a hat shop in D'Arblay Street. 'Darkly atmospheric.' He jabbed a finger at the picture of Leslie Howard (another Hungarian, come to think of it; Christ, they were *everywhere*). It showed the actor gazing dyspeptically off to one side, the dim lighting heightening the contours of his face.

'Like him,' said Ambrose, enunciating clearly.

Erno frowned, and looked from Ambrose to the picture of Leslie Howard and then back again.

'Like *heem*?' he repeated doubtfully.

Give me strength, thought Ambrose. 'Yes,' he said, trying to keep the exasperation out of his voice. 'I want you to make me look exactly like him.'

Erno stared at the photograph for almost a full minute, and then went away to a corner of the room and rummaged in a bag. He came back after some time with a piece of what looked like fine cheesecloth.

'Moment, plizz,' he said, and began, with painful slowness, to fasten the material over the camera lens.

'Will you be *very* much longer?' asked Ambrose. 'Only I have an awfully busy day ahead of me.'

ADVERTISEMENTS

May 1940

'Do you think I should wear my good shoes for the interview?' asked Catrin, still curled beneath the eiderdown. 'Not that they'll be looking at my feet, I suppose . . .'

There was no immediate response from Ellis. He was standing naked beside the window, peering upward between the opened blackouts in an attempt to gauge what the weather might be like at street level, and he scratched his knuckles, one hand and then the other, the skin between them permanently inflamed from contact with turpentine, before turning towards her. 'What was that?' he asked.

'Oh . . . nothing important, really.' She had learned that she talked far too much in the mornings.

She watched him scoop his shirt from the floor and begin to get dressed. He was tall, the skin very white beneath his clothes, his face high-cheekboned, almost Slavic. Not only handsome but *foreign*, she'd thought, with a thrill, when she'd first seen him, though he'd turned out, prosaically enough, to come from Kent.

'Are you back for supper?' she asked. 'Only I suppose I ought to use up the beetroot, it's starting to get little white spots.'

'What d'you say?'

'I was wondering if you'd be back for supper.'

'No, I'm on duty tonight.'

'Oh. Well, I could bring you something to eat at the studio, if you wanted.'

He was tying his bootlaces, and he looked up at her with an air of puzzled impatience, as if she *would* insist on speaking in Swahili; and it was impossible, as always, for her to gauge whether a scarred eardrum meant that he hadn't quite caught what she was saying or whether he simply wasn't listening.

'I could bring your supper to the studio,' she said again. 'After I get back from work. If you'd like.'

He gave a grunt and then straightened up, tugging at the sleeves that were always too short for his arms. 'I'd better be going,' he said.

She pulled on a dressing-gown and followed him into the kitchen. He was standing beside the table, frowning at the worn pocket-book in which he kept his notes, angling the pages in order to catch the light.

'Would you type these up for me, Cat?' he asked. 'One day soon, before the bloody thing falls to bits.'

'Of course I would.'

'Though you probably won't be able to read my writing.'

'I will. I'm sure I will. You should see Mr Caradoc's, it's all drunken spiders.'

He nodded, his thoughts already elsewhere. 'See you later, then,' he said. She stood barefoot on the doormat and watched him climb the basement steps two at a time, and it occurred to her as he disappeared from view that the 'see you later' must mean that he *was* expecting her to come to the studio with some supper, since otherwise he'd go straight from there to the warden's post at Baker Street, and she wouldn't see him again until the following morning. Though perhaps she was reading too much into the phrase.

She tended to do that, to pick through his speeches like a cryptologist, trying to elicit answers without having to actually ask him any more questions. And it was nearly always the boring-but-necessary things that he failed to catch the first time – meals and shoe-repairs and what to say to the landlord about the geyser – things that simply had to be sorted out before she left for work. She would hear herself pecking away at the same topic, phrasing and re-phrasing in an effort to dislodge a useful response, and it was dreadful to think of how dull she must sound to him.

She closed the front door and filled the kettle, and put the heel of a loaf under the grill. There was only margarine left, and nothing to spread on it but the carrot jam that she'd bought by mistake, thinking it was marmalade. She dabbed a spoonful of it on to the toast and ate it quickly, before the taste could catch up with her, and then went back in the bedroom and started to hunt for her good shoes. It was a long time since she'd worn them.

She shared an office at Finch & Caradoc with the junior copywriter, a good-natured boy, only a month or two younger than herself, but a tremendous talker, and since, this morning, he was away at his army medical, she was able to whip through Mr Caradoc's letters without disturbance. She had already moved on to her other work by the time that Donald flung open the door, lobbed his hat in the general direction of the coat-hooks and began to flap his elbows.

'Go on, guess!' he said, adding in some random footwork. 'Go on, guess what I've just been categorized. Go on, Catrin – guess.'

'A1?'

'No! I'm D2 and that means—' he stopped dancing long enough to fish a slip of paper from his overcoat-pocket and hold it triumphantly above his head. 'Unfit for *any* military service whether at home or abroad. *Any*.' He kissed the form and resumed dancing, adding a tuneless lyric to the patter of his steps:

> D2 – I love you baby
> Never let me go
> D2 – you drive me crazy
> Always . . . always . . . I need a rhyme, Catrin.

'Be my beau?'

'Excellent.'

'I can hear you wheezing from right over here.'

'Can you? Oh yes.' He stopped jigging and sat down, and then, as the exertion began to catch up with him, braced his hands on his knees and breathed effortfully for a while, neck sinews straining. 'Got a bit carried away . . .' he said, between inhalations. '. . . been dreading it . . . thought I'd get home duties . . . be posted to some lousy hole . . . brother's got asthma . . . C1, he's not so bad . . . in Caithness now . . . guarding an underwear dump.'

'Not really underwear?'

'Protective clothing . . . Underwear's a better . . . What's the word? Pay off.'

'I think perhaps you should stop talking for a while.'

'Sound bad?'

'Terrible.'

'Okeydoke.' He jerked a thumb towards the window. 'When's your . . . ?'

'Eleven o'clock – I'd better get on.' She glanced at her notepad again.

'New copy?' asked Donald.

'Yes.'

'Ivy and Lynn?'

'Yes.'

'Can I read it? When you've done?'

She nodded, and then, because it seemed possible that he would literally rather die than shut up for thirty seconds, she wound the carbons into the Underwood and began to type straight from her notes, changing the odd word as she went along.

IVY & LYNN #9. 'IMAGINATION'

Colin – this is set in Ivy's kitchen (already established

in I & L # 3, 4 & 7). I would be ever so grateful if Ivy could look a little less glamorous than usual (please – no corsage or hat, she's just doing some cooking).

Illustration 1

Ivy is sitting at the kitchen table, looking gloomily at a tiny chop, three potatoes and a parsnip. Lynn has poked her head round the back door.

Lynne: Out of ingredients?

Ivy: Out of ideas, more like.

Illustration 2

Lynn has approached the table and is holding up one of the potatoes.

Lynne: Surely even Bert likes casseroles?

Ivy: Loves them – but you try making decent gravy out of just one chop.

Illustration 3

Lynn has opened one of the kitchen cupboards and is rummaging around.

Lynne: He won't know it's only one chop if you add just a single delicious spoonful of—

Ivy: Don't torture me! I'm fresh out and there's none in the shops at the moment.

Illustration 4

Lynn, looking quizzical, is taking a full bottle of So-Bee-Fee All-Meat Extract from the cupboard. Ivy looks astonished.

Ivy: **Another bottle? But where on earth was it hiding?**

Lynne: **Somewhere you never look, you naughty girl. Behind the jar of carrot jam Bert's mother made!**

Colin, is it possible to put the final caption — 'So-Bee-Fee All-Meat Extract: Make Sure You Use Every Last Drop' — over an illustration of Ivy looking embarrassed, one hand over mouth, other holding product?

Catrin sat back and flexed her fingers. Six months before, when conscription had started to nibble away at the junior roster of Finch & Caradoc, her secretarial duties had been expanded – first to include sub-editing, and then copywriting – and she'd been handed the poisoned chalice of the So-Bee-Fee account, with its stolid pre-war emphasis on gigantic joints of meat and dim but eager kitchen maids.

'Try and come up with something more modern . . .' had been Mr Caradoc's vague brief, and she'd decided upon two protagonists not much older than herself: busy young housewives with too much to do and no time to do it in, the type of women whose beauty regimen would comprise a couple of hairgrips and a dab of powder. Colin Finch's prototype illustration had shown a pair of elaborately coiffured matrons, drooping languidly beside the kitchen table as if unable to support the weight of their Parisian daywear. 'But *no one* wears gloves to make pastry,' she'd protested, and Colin had shrugged and carried on drawing Lynn's diamanté stole-clasp. Since then, by a slow process of attrition (or 'nagging' as Colin called it), her creations had edged a little closer to reality, and she'd become quite fond of the pair of them – of Ivy, in particular, who was always stuck for dinner ideas and whose husband revealed a new, and irritating, food fad every other week. (*'Bert's told me he's never liked curly kale'*, *'Bert asked why we have to have potatoes quite so often'*, *'Bert's had enough of mince, he says.'*)

'Do the manufacturers mind that?' asked Donald, who had partially recovered, and was wheezing gently over her shoulder. 'Saying that there's no So-Bee-Fee in the shops?'

Catrin looked up at him. 'You mean you haven't had Mr Caradoc's little lecture yet?'

'Lecture about what?'

'About Haz-Tam? The wonder grate-cleaner?'

'Never heard of it.'

'Or Kleeze? Stain-remover?'

'No.'

'Or Effika? Brimmo? Kalma-tina?'

'You're inventing them.'

'No, really.' She slid the pages out of the typewriter and clipped them together with one of the six paper-clips still left in the office. 'According to Mr Caradoc they were in every housemaid's cupboard until the Great War and then the Kleeze factories stopped producing Kleeze and began churning out left-handed swivel-loaders or whatever-it-was and it didn't occur to anyone that, by the time it was all over, people would have forgotten they'd ever used Kleeze.'

'You mean they'd forgotten the ease that came with Kleeze?' said Donald, happily, sitting down again and swinging his feet on to the desk.

'So what Mr Caradoc says we have to remember is, that it's our duty to our clients to keep the memory of their products alive, whether or not they're available in the shops. Which, in the case of So-Bee-Fee, they're not. At least for a month or two.'

'Why not?'

'They've diverted the main ingredient into gravy for the forces.'

'And by "main ingredient" they mean . . . ?'

'Burnt sugar, Mr Caradoc says.'

'Not beef?'

'No.' She paused. 'There's no beef in So-Bee-Fee.' The thought still had the power to embarrass her, though it made Donald laugh. 'I'd better dash,' she said, getting up.

'Good luck, then. I suppose.'

'That's a bit half-hearted.'

'I don't want you to leave, do I? It's nice having a girl around.'

'Thank you.'

'Especially one like you.' He turned puce and made a great business of fishing in his pocket for a cigarette, and Catrin climbed the stairs to what Colin Finch liked to call his studio, and knocked at the half-open door.

'Come!'

He was standing in bulky silhouette against the window, gazing out at the plane trees of Fitzroy Square. 'Want your opinion, young lady,' he said, without turning, his voice stuck in a key of perpetual melancholy. 'The Female Viewpoint. Take a look at the sketch.' Catrin went over to the drawing-board and inspected the pneumatic blonde ATS girl straining her buttons at the wheel of a truck.

'Do you think she's attractive?' asked Colin.

She hesitated; although Colin always asked for opinions he never really wanted them unless they chimed absolutely with his own.

'Yes . . .' she said.

'Yes, what? Spit it out.'

'Yes . . . in a bit of an obvious sort of way.'

'Whorish, you mean?'

'No. Not as bad as that.'

'Tarty?'

'Well, maybe just a little. Who's it for?'

'McLean's. "Molly Brown's McLeaned her Teeth Today." Is she a McLean's sort of girl, I wonder?'

It took her a second or two to phrase a tactful reply. 'To be honest, Colin, I'm not sure that anyone's going to be looking at her *teeth*.'

He sighed. 'What bitches women are. You've brought your copy?'

She handed it over. 'I'll have to leave now, I'm afraid.'

'And why's that?'

'My interview. I'm sure I'll be back by early afternoon, though.'

He turned to look at her. 'What interview?'

'With the Ministry of Information. I showed you the letter last week.'

'Oh God,' he said, savagely, 'so you did, I forgot. Yet another conscript for the slogans department.'

'Do you think that's what I'll be doing?'

'More than likely. "Keep Mum and Eat More Prunes." Though you'll probably spend most of your time typing memoranda. "*Dear Cecil*," – he assumed a high, prissy voice – "*yours of the first inst, I shall look into the matter of the amendment to Clause 9 of Form 3/B7 just as soon as the international situation permits . . .*" 'He turned back to the window and laid his forehead against the glass. 'Soon there'll be no one left to write copy,' he said. 'Goods will be sold from giant cardboard boxes stamped "Rice" or "Hair oil". Buxom Molly Brown will be replaced by a label saying: "Clean Your Teeth by Order of the Minister for Hygiene." 'He sighed again, misting the windowpane in front of him.

'I really had better go,' said Catrin, after the moment of introspection had stretched out to half a minute.

'Best of luck, then,' said Colin, insincerely. 'Don't trip over any red tape.'

*

From a distance, the Ministry of Information looked almost elemental, a chalk cliff rearing above the choppy roofs of Fitzrovia. From the main entrance, where Catrin stopped to tweak one stocking so that the darn was concealed by her coat, it looked more like a vast mausoleum.

'Authority?' said the policeman at the door, and Catrin handed over her letter (*H/HI/F Division, Room 717d, Swain*) and was nodded through.

Room 717d had clearly been part of a corridor before three sections of plywood had transformed it into a space only just large enough to hold a desk and two chairs. Catrin had been waiting there alone for nearly ten minutes when a young man whose name she didn't quite catch poked his head round the door, checked that she was unoccupied, and proceeded to sit down, open a file and – without explanation or preamble – read her a series of jokes. Each time he finished a punchline he looked at her sharply, hoping, presumably, for laughter, but since his delivery possessed all the comic flair of a platform announcer it was hard to oblige, and Catrin could feel her mouth stiffening into a dreadful fake grin. 'Just one more,' he said, after the fourth. 'An ARP warden goes into a butchers and looks at what he's got on the slab. He's got liver, he's got kidneys, he's got sheep's hearts and he's got a lovely great tongue. "I'm going to get you summonsed," says the warden. "Why?" says the butcher. "I haven't done nothing wrong." "Oh yes, you has—"' The young man frowned, and there was a pause while he re-read the line, lips moving soundlessly. 'I'm so sorry,' he said, 'these are, of course, transcribed from actual conversations, hence the ungrammatical element which does tend to make them rather difficult to read. So anyway, the butcher says "I haven't done nothing wrong", and then the warden says, "Oh yes, you has, you haven't put your *lights* out."'

He sat back and gazed at Catrin expectantly. There was a long moment. 'Did you understand the pun?' he asked, frowning.

'Yes, I did.'

'You understood that "lights" is a synonym for some form of offal? Lungs, I believe.'

'Yes.'

'And therefore the warden's final comment is a play on the ARP's habitual call to "put your lights out".'

'Yes.'

'But you didn't find the joke amusing?'

'Not really, no. Perhaps . . . in context.'

'In a more jovial forum, such as a public house, you mean?'

'Yes, maybe.'

He made a note. 'And would you say that your opinion of the authority and/or ability of air-raid precaution wardens would be adversely affected by hearing this particular piece of humour?'

'I don't think so, no, but then my husband's a part-time warden.'

'I see.' He made another note. 'And if this particular piece of humour was broadcast on the wireless, do you think that would affect your opinion on the authority and/or the ability of the BBC to—'

The door from the corridor opened suddenly, admitting two men. 'Off you go, Flaxton,' said the younger and better-looking of the two, 'no one wants to hear your jokes.'

Flaxton slammed the file shut and stood up. 'We all have work to do, Roger,' he said, with something akin to a flounce. '*Morale* happens to be mine, whereas *undermining* morale appears to be yours.'

'No, telling rotten jokes badly is yours, and trying actually to get something done is mine. Heard the one about the junior under-assistant in Home Intelligence who got transferred to Reception and Facilities?'

'No,' said Flaxton, endeavouring to reach the door.

'You will.' The door closed, and the speaker turned back to Catrin, smiled charmingly and offered a hand. 'Roger Swain, assistant deputy sub-controller film division. I'm so sorry we were late and that you were subjected to Flaxton. His department's conducting a humour survey to examine public attitudes towards the civil defence services and he's run out of internal victims. Did you laugh?'

'Not much, I'm afraid.'

'Good.'

'*Film* division?'

'That's correct. It's Miss Cole, is it? Or Mrs?'

'Mrs.'

'Your husband's in the forces? Or is he another one of us pen pushers?'

'He's an artist.' She said the word with pride.

'An artist?' Roger raised an eyebrow. 'Would I have heard of him?'

'Ellis Cole.'

'Rings a bell. Pit wheels, belching chimneys, that type of thing?'

'That's right.'

'And is he keeping busy?'

'He's working on a short contract from the War Artists Committee – four paintings for the Ministry of Supply.'

It didn't sound much, she knew, but Roger nodded politely. 'Splendid. Well, we'd better get started, I suppose. This—'

'Buckley,' said the older man, laconically, seating himself on one corner of the desk and folding his arms across the shelf of his paunch; he had a slab of fair hair, a narrow ginger moustache and teeth that looked rather sharp. He was smiling, but the effect was more predatory than welcoming. 'I've been told I'm a special advisor,' he said, 'though not, it transpires, special enough to actually get paid. Welsh, are you?'

'Yes.'

'Can't be helped. *And* you're much younger than I thought you'd be. What are you, twenty-one, twenty-two?' His tone was accusatory; she felt herself beginning to redden.

'Nearly twenty,' she said.

'Saints preserve us. Here.' He slid a thin sheaf of paper across the desk top. 'Read it. Tell me what you think.'

She looked at him uncertainly. '*Read* it,' he said, with deliberation, and she hurriedly bent her head. It was a short script, carelessly typed on paper so that she could see the shadow of her fingers through every sheet.

BITING THE BULLET

I. EXTERIOR. BROWN'S ARMAMENTS FACTORY, EVENNG

Noise of machines etc.

2. INTERIOR FACTORY

Rows of production lines, women working away producing bullet casings. Close up of 2 young women in partic. Shouting at each other over the noise of the machines.

RUBY

Are you going out somewhere special tonight, Joan?

JOAN

Yes I am, I'm meeting Charlie at the Palais, he's got a weekend pass and I can't wait for a dance. What about you?

RUBY

No, I'm simply too tired, I've been working seven days straight. I'm staying in and going to bed early.

JOQN

I don't blame you, I could sleep for a whole wek. Roll on the end of the shift.

RUBY

There's only another five minutes to go.

JOAN

Just five minutes to go, girls!

The other women cheer and then carry on working.

3. INTERIOR GLASS-WALLED OFFICE TO ONE SIDE OF THE FACTORY FLOOR

A manageress is doing paperwork. The clock behind her shows one minute to eight. The phone rings.

MANAGERESS

Day manageress speaking. Oh, hello Mr Carr. Yes, yes, we had no problems making that order. Yes, that's right.

The clock hand moves to eight o'clock, and a bell rings.

4. INTERIOR FACTORY

The women on the production line start to shut down their machie.s and leave the floor, hurrying past the office.

5. INTERIOR OFFICE

MANAGERESSS

I'm sorry, Mr Carr, what was that you said? An emergency order? You need a hundred gross of bullets? By tomorrow morning?

Joan and Ruby, passing the open office door, overhear this and grimace at each other.
They wait to hear what the manageress says.

MAGAHERESS
I'm afraid that's simply imposssible. My girls have worked hard all day, they're dead-beat.

A whole group of girls are listening at the door now.

MANAGERESS
No, I can't ask them to stay on, even if it is for the sake of our soldiers.

Ruby bites her lip.

MAGANERESS
No, I'm sorry, Mr Carr, I know our troops are in desperate need, but you're asking me to push my workers beyond what is physically possible, and I can't—

Ruby makes a decision.

RUBY
Come on girls! The job's got to be done and we're the ones who can do it!

6. INTRIOR FACTORY

With a loud cheer, the women rush back to their machines and switch them on again.

7. INTRIOR OFFICE

MANAGERESS
(smiling) Mr Carr, you're not going to believe this,

but something quite wonderful has hppened . . .

8. INTERIOR FACTORY

Production lin going full pelt.

'What do you think?' asked Buckley.

Catrin looked up at him, trying to gauge the level of his question. 'You mean, what do I think of the patriotic message?' she asked tentatively, aiming high. There was no reply; she lowered her sights. 'The way it's set out, do you mean? I'm not familiar with this sort of thing, but I can see that it's inconsistent, I'm sure I . . . or do you mean the typing? There are lots of errors, I could go through it with a—'

'I'm talking about the script,' he said. His voice had a trace of northern accent, imperfectly concealed. 'Is it a good script? Would it make a good film?'

She shrugged, helplessly. 'I don't know anything about films. Are you sure—'

'Read it again,' he said. 'Pretend to yourself these are real girls having a real conversation and tell me exactly what you think of what Joan says to Ruby and of what Ruby says to Joan.'

Self-consciously, Catrin complied.

'Well?'

'I don't think they sou—' she began to say, and then stopped, mid-syllable, hit by an awful thought.

'*I* didn't write it,' said Buckley, reading her expression. 'Say what you like.'

'I don't think they sound as if they're in a factory. It says that they're shouting over the machines, but it reads as though they're somewhere quiet, talking over a cup of tea.'

'How would they talk in a factory, then?'

'In an abbreviated way, I'd imagine, to save their voices. Half-sentences. "You going out tonight?" That sort of thing.'

'All right. Anything else?'

She looked at the script again. 'The phone call.'

'What about it?'

'In real life nobody actually repeats what the person at the other end has just said – the emergency order, the hundred gross of bullets and so on. It sounds false.'

'Does it?'

Roger leaned forward. 'And the patriotic message, as you phrased it? If you were making bullets do you think it would inspire you to put in an extra shift?'

'I think . . .' Was there a correct answer? She attempted a tactful one: 'I think I might find it too unrealistic.'

'Too unrealistic to take seriously?'

'Yes.'

Roger nodded, and took a letter from his pocket. 'You're in company,' he said, drily, unfolding it. 'Let me read you something. Our current head of the films division receives regular reports from the field, so to speak, and this is from the manager of the Woolwich Granada. He writes: '*The MOI short* Biting the Bullet *was received by our audience, consisting of a very large portion of workers from the Arsenal (nearly all female), with satirical laughter and a chorus of "Oo's" and "Oh Yeah's".*' He re-pocketed the letter and folded his arms. 'Our current head of the films division has said that he requires more emphasis on a convincing and realistic female angle in our short films. Buckley, who's written a script or two—'

'Thirty-three features, fourteen shorts and a serial,' said Buckley.

'. . . has seen your work—'

'Gravy ads,' said Buckley.

'. . . and seems to think you have something of an ear for women's dialogue.'

'Might,' said Buckley, picking at one of his nails. 'Might have something of an ear. Might eventually learn, given time and a great deal of knowledgeable and patient coaching, how to turn out a line or two.'

'And, obviously,' continued Roger, 'as we would never ignore such an overwhelmingly enthusiastic recommendation from an expert of his calibre, we thought we might as well get you on board. We're working on a series of domestic shorts for Home Security, co-produced with an outside company. You can join the scenario boys on the fifth floor on Monday and see how you get on. Any questions? Mrs Cole?'

'No.' It was all she could manage to say. During her five-minute walk between the entrance and Room 717d, past walls of files and crates of folders, past meetings so short of chairs that participants were seated on upturned waste-paper bins, past typists whose hands were a pallid blur, she thought she had seen her immediate future: a shared plywood hutch and an infinity of shorthand. The new reality was too strange to assimilate.

Roger got to his feet. 'You'll need to see personnel before you go, we can point you in the right direction. I heard a new name for us yesterday,' he added, to Buckley, as they filed out of the office.

'What's that?'

'The Ministry of Malformation. Used seriously, by a woman on the bus.'

'Not bad.'

'My current favourite's the Mystery of Information. So apposite.'

'I heard Reith's gone.'

'Yes, last week, we're between ministers at the moment – this is public information, incidentally, Mrs Cole, so no need to worry about careless talk. I'm afraid it's like a fairground duck-shoot in here, we've had two ministers since September, and three heads of the films division in five months. The last but one came from the National Gallery – they thought they'd give us someone who knew all about pictures.' He sniggered at his own joke and then halted beside a bank of lifts. 'Take this to the sixth floor,' he said to Catrin, 'then ask again. And we'll see you next week.' He shook hands, and paused to wait for Buckley who was peering into another of the three-wall wooden shacks.

'Hell,' said Buckley. 'It's like an ant's nest.'

'No,' said Roger. 'Ants cooperate. Goodbye, Mrs Cole.'

She spent the afternoon at Finch & Caradoc fiddling with copy for a currently unobtainable face cream, thinking all the while about the occasions on which she'd seen the legend 'The Ministry of Information Presents' swim out of the darkness. There was a distinctive audience noise associated with its appearance, a vocal expression that was not quite a groan, more a release of tension, as if permission had been given to carry on talking and folding coats and settling in before the important business of the evening began. She could recall very little of the films themselves – the odd sweeping view of a field studded with hayricks ('this, then is Britain . . .'), a man in a stiff collar talking about war bonds, a demonstration of the correct way to use a garden fork – wholesome items all, but indigestible, the cabbage that had to be eaten before the meat. Dialogue, snappy or otherwise, had been minimal.

Going out tonight, Joan?

The Palais with Charlie. Can't wait!

By five thirty she had achieved nothing in the way of useful work, and Colin Finch told her to go home; instead, she caught the tube straight to Paddington, and queued for ten minutes at a chip shop before taking the familiar route along a narrow street that ran parallel to the railway lines, passing a succession of warehouses before reaching the disused garage where Ellis had his studio. 'Glass roof,' he'd explained when she'd first seen it, a virtue that apparently excused the seatless lavatory, the lack of hot water and the vicious cross-draughts that whined between the double doors. Blackout regulations had created yet another disadvantage, and at twilight, the occupants had to climb on to the roof and spend half an hour pulling a set of home-made shutters over the panes; Ellis was up a ladder doing just that when she arrived, and she passed unnoticed through the shadows towards the roughly partitioned corner where he worked.

It was neat, as usual, linseed and turps bottles wiped and capped, finished canvases stacked against each other and covered with a cloth, wood for framing tied in a bundle beneath a table. The only painting visible was hardly begun, charcoal lines and a greyish wash offering a ghostly view of a colossal cylindrical object, and a small figure peering into its interior.

Ellis's notebook was lying on the table. She picked it up and leafed through to the most recent entry, and found herself easily able to read the tiny, scribbled comments he'd made during his visit to an ordnance factory.

AA shells stored in rows on warehouse flr – after 10 mins there lost all sense of scale, shlls started to look lk rows of bullets.
Girders thrwing shadow grid across flr.
Man checking bore of AA gun, head rt in barrel like lion tamer.

She turned back a page or two.

White-wshd labyrinth, evry route nmbrd.
Maps so large on 1st sight lk like patterned wallpaper.

That had been his previous short contract from the War Artists Committee – two pictures of the subterranean ARP control rooms in Kensington. He had finished the commission and then enrolled as a volunteer warden. 'I should be painting this war from the inside,' he'd said, with his usual certainty.

Above her, another shutter banged to, and she heard his voice, indistinct through the glass. The first time she'd seen him actually at the easel, she'd expected dash and sweat and galloping inspiration and she'd been secretly disappointed; his technique was entirely without drama. He painted steadily and methodically, mixing colours with calm concentration and studying his preliminary sketches for minutes at a time. She had learned since then that if it were galloping inspiration she required, she had only to watch Perry, who worked in a cubicle on the other side of the garage, and who had recently, accidentally, painted over a fly that had momentarily landed on his canvas. His work wasn't a patch on Ellis's.

On impulse, she began to thumb through the little book from the beginning, looking for the point at which she'd seen him come through the door of the Rivoli Café in Ebbw Vale, two and a half years ago. She'd served him pilchards on toast and a cup of coffee, and had blushed scarlet when he'd caught her staring over his shoulder at the sketch-pad, at the bold, economical drawings.

'They're ever so good,' she'd said, shyly. 'It's the steel-works, isn't it?' and he'd nodded.

He was staying in Ebbw Vale for a fortnight, he said, making sketches.

And he was an artist, a proper artist, fourteen years older than herself, and he'd just come back, injured, from the civil war in Spain, and that evening he met her out of the café and kissed her in a doorway opposite the cinema and until that moment, she'd been hoping that a certificate in shorthand and typing from an evening course in Merthyr might be her ticket out of 12 Barram Terrace and away from a recently acquired step-mother, who was making it unpleasantly clear that there was room for only one woman in the house. She'd imagined a future in a place as far away as Swansea – a job in a typing pool, perhaps, a bed in a hostel for single girls – but when Ellis had left for London, ten days later, he'd said 'come with me if you want' and she'd done just that, she'd run off with him, and, oh, the *daring* of it.

'And I'll be useful,' she'd promised Ellis. 'I'll look after you ever so well.' Though, despite her best efforts, she wasn't much of a cook, and she could never seem to iron a shirt without leaving triangular scorch marks, and since she had never finished the shorthand part of her course, it had been hard, at first, finding a job that could make a decent contribution towards the rents for both studio and flat. She'd been lucky to find Mr Caradoc, who was deeply sentimental about his childhood in Wales, and who didn't mind a few errors.

Ebbw steelwks
Gouts of steam, evry single surfce black.
Filth & metallic purity, dkness & blinding lght, hvn & hell. Blake
Saw sheep looking thro yard railings. Unexpectedly white.

There was no mention of herself in the notes; it wasn't that type of diary, of course.

The last set of shutters slammed down and for a few seconds there was pitch darkness before the lights sprang on. Perry, over by the switch, shouted, 'Any chinks?' and there was an answering 'no' from the rooftop, and half a minute later Ellis squeezed between the double doors.

Catrin waved. 'I've brought you something to eat,' she called, and the two men strolled across, talking, and Ellis curled an arm around her waist and caught her close. 'You'll never guess—' she began.

'I wouldn't mind so much,' said Perry, continuing the conversation, 'if it weren't for the fact that most of the stuff – present company excepted, of course – that most of the stuff being bought by the Committee is so bloody anodyne, kiddies' nurseries, and bank clerks in tin hats, and pretty vapour trails over fields of barley and even when there's a chance to show war, actual *war*, who do they pick to send to France with the BEF? Bloody *illustrators*, that's who they pick. And who do they turn down, even though he offered his services? Only *Bomberg*, poor old sod.'

'They think he's too leftish,' said Ellis. 'Goes for those of us who went to Spain, as well.'

'They turned down Bomberg!' repeated Perry, incredulously.

'I've got some news,' said Catrin.

'And when the bombing starts in London,' added Perry, reaching for a chip, 'when there's death on every doorstep, who will they get to paint the devastation?' He paused, dramatically. 'Bloody *illustrators*, that's who. Bet they're kicking themselves Beatrix Potter's not available.'

Ellis shook his head. 'It'll change. New forms of war require new forms of art.'

'I should hope they do. I'm sick of seeing stuffy old portraits of generals, the sort of thing that chap Eves does – technique unchanged in twenty years. You know he's on a bloody *salary* from the War Office?'

Ellis released Catrin's waist and began to cut up the fish with the blade he used for sharpening pencils.

'I had my interview,' said Catrin.

'What's that?' asked Ellis.

'I had my interview at the Ministry of Information. And you'll never guess where I've ended up.'

'Slogans,' suggested Perry. '"Divide and Rule." "*Your* Courage, *Your* Cheerfulness, *Your* Resolution Will Bring *Us* Victory".'

'No, not slogans. They've seen the advertisements that I wrote for So-Bee-Fee and they're putting me in the film division. Helping to write scripts!'

She waited for a reaction; Ellis nodded a couple of times. 'Yes, I'd heard that they're starting to siphon money into film propaganda.'

'The transient arts,' said Perry, disparagingly. 'Next thing we know they'll be setting up a ballet division. And what are they paying you?'

'Three pounds a week. I'll be working mainly on women's dialogue. In short films. And they said I'd—'

'SHOWING A LIGHT!' shouted Ellis, suddenly, and the figure who had just entered the garage closed the door hastily behind himself and shouted an apology.

'Which is a reminder,' said Ellis, checking his watch, 'that I'd better get off to Post C. Thanks for the supper, Cat.' He kissed her on the lips and then crammed a last handful of chips into his mouth.

Catrin watched him go.

'Do you want the rest of that cod?' asked Perry.

'No thanks,' she said. She felt oddly flat. It was so seldom that she had anything of interest to tell Ellis.

'Three pounds a week,' said Perry, ruminatively, picking up scraps of batter with a damp finger. 'Wish I could write gossip for three pounds a week.'

THE MINISTRY OF INFORMATION PRESENTS . . .

June 1940

There was no chair with his name on the back. There was no dressing-room, and in any case there was no costume to be fitted. There was no car to collect him from home or to return him at the end of the day. The script was printed on what looked like rice paper. The sole water closet in the studio could be used by anyone, even electricians. The director was eight years old. The continuity girl was ninety. The pay was an insult.

'I really am grateful,' said Ambrose to the journalist from *Kinematograph Weekly*, 'to be able to do something for the war effort. Really – it's almost a privilege.' He took a mouthful of lukewarm chicory and smiled over the journalist's shoulder at the lady sitting at the next table. She looked startled.

It had been yet another disappointment to add to the catalogue accrued during the day so far that the journalist – a shabby, enthusiastic man named Heswell – was not interviewing Ambrose for a feature on Ambrose but for some article about Ministry-sponsored films, Ambrose acting as a mere conduit for information. There being – but of course! – no green room in the studio, they had adjourned to a café in the next street, taking advantage of the mid-morning break enforced by the striking of one inadequate set and the erection of another.

'I gather it's all very economical,' said Heswell, dabbing away at a tiny notepad. 'What is it – two films a day? Seventy seconds apiece?'

'Indeed.'

'And another two tomorrow?'

'For my sins.'

Heswell looked up at him enquiringly.

'That means yes,' said Ambrose, abandoning charm. 'I simply hope that the degree of economy being used does not transfer to the screen.'

'You mean, you hope it doesn't look cheap.'

'Your words, dear chap, not mine.'

'The designer used the word "simplicity" rather than "economy". He said that it was actually an exciting challenge to produce something stylish on a tiny budget – it made him think very hard.'

'Did it, indeed?' Made him think very hard, presumably, about painting a flat with taupe emulsion and then putting a table in front of it and calling it 'The Browns' Dining-Room'. Ambrose checked his watch; it seemed extraordinary that, despite the brevity of the scripts, the amount of aimless waiting around was, if anything, even greater than was usual in filming. It might, he thought, be worth using the extra time to go in search of some decent cigarettes, his tobacconist having last week fobbed him off with a Turkish brand called 'Pasha' which smelled of scorched wool and tasted of camel shit. 'So if that's all . . .' he said, pushing his chair back.

'No, not quite. I'd rather like to ask you about the challenge of acting in a propaganda piece.'

'Oh.' Ambrose lowered his buttocks on to the seat again. 'What about it?'

'Well . . . *is* it a challenge? Are new techniques required when you're attempting to convey a state-sponsored message rather than a simple story? Are you aware of a greater responsibility than usual in your interpretation of the text? Where does characterization end and didacticism begin?'

Heswell gripped his pencil and looked expectant, as if this cascade of nonsense deserved a considered answer. *Didacticism.*

Ambrose was unsure of what it even meant; it was one of those words that had suddenly appeared in the thirties, invented, presumably, in order to bulk out those long, dull political articles that nowadays dominated every magazine, even those supposedly devoted to entertainment. It was notable that *Film Fun Weekly* had never felt the need for questions like these. When Ambrose had been voted the third most popular British male star in their 1924 end-of-year poll, he'd been sent a list of 'things our readers want to know' and they'd included such queries as: '*What is your favourite flower?*', '*Which do you consider more important: truth or beauty?*' and '*What is your opinion of unmarried women who wear face "make-up"?*' Trivial, possibly, but at least the reader would actually finish the article in possession of more information than when they had started.

Heswell was still waiting. 'An actor *acts*,' said Ambrose. 'You may as well ask a river what it thinks of its name – Thames or Tiber, Rhine or Styx, it makes no damned difference – it simply goes on being a river.'

Heswell frowned, as if trying to recollect something. 'Wasn't that . . . ?' he began.

'I'm so sorry,' said Ambrose, getting to his feet, 'but I'm going to have to leave you, Mr Heswell. Business calls.' He tapped his watch, smiled and turned to find his path blocked by a short, entirely bald man.

'Come to get yer,' said the man, in a rusty monotone. It was like being addressed by an iron bollard.

'And you are . . . ?'

The figure lifted his head fractionally. 'Third assistant director,' he said, fixing Ambrose with a dead, grey stare. 'They've told me to tell yer that yer wanted on the floor straight away.'

'Very well, very well,' said Ambrose, slightly rattled. 'But please use my name in future. It's Hilliard, Mr Hilliard.'

'And mine's Chick,' said the man, catching the final sound on the back of his throat. It sounded like the unlocking of a safety catch.

'Chick?'

'Chick.' There was an unnecessarily long pause. 'I used to breed bantams,' he added, anti-climactically, and then turned – revolved, one might say, since the back of his head appeared no more human than the front – and preceded Ambrose through the café door. Ambrose found himself breathing again.

Where on earth, he wondered, were the studios finding the current workforce? Call-up had skimmed off the cream, and the industry was clearly awash with rancid curds. Of course, the third assistant director (the title was laughable, really, since the job was actually that of a messenger boy), came in many different guises, ranging from effete movie-mad youngest sons of the gentry to whom one had to remain courteous in case their next incarnation turned out to be that of director, all the way down to wizened ex-music-hall acts desperate for a crust, but it was usual for them to resemble human beings rather than items of street furniture. It was usual for them to have *names*. 'Chick' was the type of soubriquet Ambrose associated with electricians who, when not holding cast and crew to ransom with their private version of the Soviet manifesto, addressed each other by a host of oafish nicknames: 'Moose', 'Spud', 'Dixie'.

The commissionaire at the studio nodded him through, and Ambrose stopped just inside the double doors in order to light another cigarette. It was obvious from the amount of activity on the floor that the crew was nowhere near ready: the camera was in pieces, yet again, the electricians were still playing poker, and his fellow-professional, Cecy, was sitting on an upturned packing case at the back of the flat, drinking tea from a tiny spoon in an effort not to smudge her lipstick.

'Fun, isn't it?' she said, catching sight of Ambrose. 'Marvellous to be back in front of the camera. I've missed it dreadfully, I simply can't pretend I haven't, and when I hear that whistle blow – well, my *heart*!' She mimed a little flutter above her breastbone, and then returned to her tea-spooning, enabling

Ambrose to release his facial muscles from the polite smile into which they'd braced themselves. Cecy Clyde-Cameron. He'd almost turned round and left when he'd seen her sitting in make-up this morning, those great teeth clattering away as she recounted the lean theatrical years since her last celluloid appearance. She'd let out a great shriek of recognition at the sight of him, however, and he'd been forced to exchange kisses and pleasantries, and to sit beside her as she reminisced about their last professional encounter. How dreadfully she'd aged! She'd always looked like a horse, but in fifteen years she'd slid from racing stable to brewer's dray, everything wider, heavier, *lower* than before. Extraordinary to think that they'd exchanged a twelve-second screen kiss in *The Door to Her Heart* in 1925, and that he had actually suggested a second take because he'd enjoyed it so much. Extraordinary – hideous – to think that she'd now been cast as his wife. No kisses in the current script, thank Christ, just fatuous dialogue. He finished his cigarette and cleared his throat; his vocal chords felt coated with Turkish filth, and he spat discreetly into a handkerchief and strolled on to the floor just as Briggs, the first assistant director, was opening his mouth to call for the actors.

'Scenario Two, *The Letter*, Mr Hilliard, Mrs Clyde-Cameron,' said Briggs, who wore a coloured tie in lieu of a personality. 'Would you care to run through the lines before we light?'

'No,' said Ambrose, just as Cecy said, 'Oh *yes*, dear,' and he found himself sitting beside her in The Browns' Living-Room, a two-wall set papered with cabbage roses and furnished with what looked like the sweepings of a junk shop.

Cecy pressed her features into a simper and began to act.

'*I had a letter from April today*,' she said. '*A nice four-pager*.'

'*What's she on about this time?*' asked Ambrose.

'*She says she and Tony have made up ever such a clever code so that he can write to her about what he's doing without anyone being able to guess*.'

'*Oh yes?*'

'*They've thought of a word that means "overseas" and a word that means "leave" and a word that means "France" and another that means "England"*.'

'*I see.*'

'*And a word that means "troop train" and a word that means "regiment", and a number that means the date, and a word that means "embarking"*.'

'*Uh huh.*'

'*It's ever so clever.*' Cecy sat back and began some imaginary knitting.

'*And does she have a word for "careless talk"?*' asked Ambrose, '*and another for* – there's a dog on set, could somebody get rid of it, please – *another for "putting soldiers' lives in mortal danger"*?'

There was a long pause. 'You've thrown me there, darling, talking about dogs,' said Cecy, putting down her invisible knitting needles. 'I've lost my line.'

'It's *"Oooh, I don't know"*, said Briggs. 'And then Mr Hilliard says—'

'When I wish for a prompt I will ask for one,' said Ambrose. 'My final words are, "*Well, she'd better get thinking, then, hadn't she?*" That dog is still there.'

It was sitting quietly beside the boom, one paw resting on a cable.

'Sorry, Mr Hilliard,' said Briggs. 'That's our third AD's dog. It goes everywhere with him and it's never any trouble. Bit of a mascot, actually.'

'Look at this, Mr Hilliard,' called the sound recordist. 'Shake hands, Chopper.' The dog politely offered a paw.

'Oh, that's *killing*,' said Cecy. 'But, of course, the scene doesn't quite end with Mr Brown's line, does it? According to the script it ends with me putting a hand over my mouth in horror as I gradually and heartbreakingly realize the terrible consequences of gossip. Now, would it be possible for me to have a piece of knitting? My hands were aching for something to do during the end of the scene and it seems so right for the character. And the letter, of course – I feel I should have an actual letter in shot even if I'm not reading from it – oh, and is this standard lamp a practical, because I feel that if I was knitting I'd need a light on. Is it a practical, darling?'

There was a hiatus while Briggs went off to consult with the Bolsheviks about the lighting and Ambrose lit a cigarette and rested his head against the faded antimacassar. He had to give Cecy credit: thirteen years off-camera and her shot-grabbing tactics were as keen as ever. He could think of nothing that would enhance his own role apart from a greater number of lines; it had been the same with the first script of the day – Mrs Brown talking incessantly, Mr Brown nodding dumbly. He hadn't even been given his own close-up. 'No time,' Briggs had said, though they'd somehow had time for a vast and no doubt unflattering one of Cecy. And the quality of the lines! '*Oh yes.*' '*I see.*' '*Uh huh*'. There was no characterization in '*Uh huh*', no substance, no clay with which Ambrose could fashion a human figure. It wasn't even an English word; with '*Uh huh*' as a line he might as well have been dining on seal blubber in a remake of *Nanook of the North*.

He made a decision. 'Pippin,' he said, rising from the armchair. 'Might I have a word?'

The director looked instantly nervous. He was a little, pink-cheeked pansyish fellow who, like so many others in this terrible era, had clearly been promoted far beyond his ability and experience, and who had spent the entire morning so far crouched on a tiny stool beneath the camera, his voice a powerless bleat, his comments otiose.

'I wonder,' said Ambrose, 'if I might adjust a line or two. There's no question, obviously, of diluting the message – I fully realize the national importance of what we're shooting – but I simply feel that Mr Brown might react a little more strongly to the idea of a letter from this April character. Might I just see—'

Gracelessly, the continuity girl slapped a script into his hand;

she was long past the age of flirtation – one of the unmarried, angular types who ended up living in one room in a boarding house, solaced only by neat gin. 'Thank you,' he said, with a freezing smile. 'Now, if you look here . . .' he ran a finger down the page, 'this line, my character's second line, which at the moment is "*I see*" – instead of this line I could say: "*That'll be the first time April's ever done anything clever in her life.*" It would add a humorous element early on in the script, and then further down, instead of "*Uh huh*", I could perhaps say . . .' He was becoming aware of a figure hovering behind the director, a pretty young girl in a spotted blouse – nice clear skin, blue eyes, wavy brown hair, an air of gauche eagerness. With an effort, he switched his attention back to the script. '. . . instead of "*Uh huh*", I could perhaps say "*Embarking mad, more like*". As a pun on Mrs Brown's preceding line. D'you see? She says, "*. . . and a word that means 'embarking'*", and then I say, "*Embarking mad, more like*" . . .' He savoured the neat inventiveness of the line; of course, he wouldn't be paid for it. 'Simple changes,' he added, modestly, 'but, I feel, effective. Do you concur?' Pippin goggled up at him, indecision wobbling in every feature. He was clearly of the rudderless-ship school of direction, a hopeless, drifting wreck who required the efforts of a fleet of tugs to guide it to its destination. 'We're in agreement?' asked Ambrose, twisting the wheel.

'Er . . .' It wasn't Pippin who spoke, but the girl in the spotted blouse. '. . . I'm ever so sorry to interrupt,' she said, in a Valleys accent so thick that one could practically smell the coal-dust. 'It's just that I thought I should let you know that the final caption on the film is going to be "Careless Talk – Not So Clever". So if you were to say that new line about it being the first clever thing that April's ever done, then the caption might not work quite so well, and also Mrs Brown's next line won't make sense – and also, it was felt that Mr Brown's final lines would have more impact if he hadn't said very much up until . . .'

'Do we have a new director?' asked Ambrose, looking at Briggs with feigned bewilderment. 'I seem to be receiving notes from someone I've never seen before. Could you possibly clarify the situation?'

The girl had turned crimson. 'Sorry,' she said. 'My name's Catrin Cole, I wrote some of the . . .'

'Notes from here, notes from there,' said Ambrose. 'Perhaps this has become a *commune* – perhaps we're all allowed to throw in our comments. Perhaps there was a meeting at which this was decided, and I have only my own ignorance to blame.'

The girl shrank back behind the camera. 'I think . . .' began Briggs.

'Please, I've no wish to be the one dissenter to a glorious new regime. All I ask is to be kept informed, all I ask is that I'm allowed to pursue my craft in full possession of the facts. If the decision on lines is to be thrown open to the floor then simply let me know. Come one, come all . . .' He spread his arms wide, and Pippin pursed his little mouth, and looked anxiously at Briggs.

'A brief pause to marshall our thoughts?' suggested Ambrose. 'A chance for you to consult the new constitution of the people's collective of the Albany Road studios? I shall take ten minutes, then.' He stalked towards the heavy double doors, enjoying the silence, the singular, crackling, *theatrical* silence that invariably signalled the end of a powerful scene. Chick, standing beside the exit, opened one of the doors for him, and Ambrose inclined his head in thanks. Grace and power, he thought, grace and power, an invincible combination; there was no doubt who would win this fight, no doubt whose lines would be spoken when filming resumed. The door closed behind him with a dull thud, and he checked his watch. Ten minutes. Just about enough time to get to the tobacconist's on Clipstone Street and back.

Catrin's face felt like a great flaming disk, the skin emitting so much heat that she could almost feel her eyebrows crisping.

After the actor playing Mr Brown had walked out, she had been told off – in succession and in front of anyone who cared to watch (and there had been people hanging from the rafters) – by the plump actress, the man with the tie, and the director, who had given her a hissy little speech about undermining his authority. After that, the woman with the stopwatch round her neck had taken her into the dark canyon between the high wooden set and the studio wall and told her she'd been a damn fool to open her mouth on the floor.

'But what was I supposed to do?' asked Catrin. 'He's ruining the script.'

'If you had anything at all that needed saying, you should have spoken to the first AD.'

'The who?'

'The first assistant director – Briggs, the one with the ridiculous tie. You shouldn't even have come on to the set without asking him, it's not etiquette. And secondly, you shouldn't have been here at all. There's no point in the writer coming to the studio.'

'Why not?'

'Because no one takes any notice of you and you simply get in the way.' It was stated matter-of-factly and without malice. The woman was in her mid-forties, spare and dry-skinned, her sandy hair pulled back into a bun from which a fan of brittle loose-ends radiated like a sunburst. 'I'm Phyl, by the way,' she said. 'Continuity.'

'So most writers don't come to the filming?'

'They stick their heads in and wince and then go and drink tea somewhere. Occasionally they'll be called in to re-work a scene. That's if there's even a script in the first place. Half of these short films seem to be made up by the director as he goes along.'

'And by the cast?'

'Only if the director's the sort of wet lettuce we have today. And if the actor's a pompous old fool who doesn't realize that he should be grateful for any scraps that are flung his way. Do you recognize him?'

'I'm not sure. Did he play a detective in something? Quite a long time ago?'

'The Inspector Charnforth Mysteries. He didn't play Charnforth, he played the professorial type that Charnforth went to for advice – chin-stroking and so on. How old are you?'

'Twenty.'

'God, is that all? Well, when you were stumbling around in pinafores he was a bit of a matinee idol. Ambrose Hilliard. He was known as The Man with the Glint.'

'With the what?'

'With the Glint. In his eye, I presume. Now he's just a BF who hasn't grasped that the world has changed and that we simply don't have time for his sort of nonsense. Walking off set, I mean, *honestly* . . .' She rolled her eyes.

'So what's going to happen?' asked Catrin. 'Is he really going to alter those lines?'

'Absolutely not,' said Phyl, her jawline granite. 'If he starts on that before lunch on day one, then by tomorrow afternoon he'll think he's the producer. No, the director's backbone just needs a little reinforcement – I'll mention the words 'overtime' and 'budget' and 'Ministry money'. I suppose I'd better get on with it before the old goat comes back.'

Catrin watched round the edge of the painted flat as Phyl hurried across the floor towards the director. The space was full of people, and none of them, apart from Phyl, seemed to be doing very much. There were occasional bursts of hammering and the odd incomprehensible shout; a rope was lowered from the ceiling and left dangling; three men very slowly wheeled a colossal lamp from one side of the Browns' living room to the other, and then, after a short consultation, wheeled it back again; a man with a dustpan picked invisible bits of fluff from the upholstery of the two armchairs. 'Get yourself down to the studio,' Buckley had said to Catrin, 'take a look at the action.' In her excitement, she had missed the sarcasm.

There was a sudden movement over by the door, and she turned to see Ambrose Hilliard strolling back towards the Browns' living room, cigarette in hand, smoke wreathing the baggy, disdainful face. He was, she thought, no more than a decade older than Phyl – not actually old, but somehow *dated*, a piece of art deco in a utilitarian world. He skirted the brindled bull-terrier that was sitting directly in his path, paw outstretched, and gave a generalized and well-simulated smile that made him look almost handsome.

'Are we all ready?' he asked. 'Decisions made?'

Briggs and the director came to meet him, scripts in hand. Catrin stayed behind the flat, attempting – and failing – to eavesdrop, and watching the gradual drift of personnel towards the camera.

The serenity was broken by the blast of a whistle. 'Final checks, please,' shouted Briggs in a surprisingly manly voice. 'Going for a take on the first set-up of *The Letter*. Over shoulder single Mrs Brown.'

Briggs and the director took their places beside the camera; Ambrose remained where he was for a moment or two, his shoulders rigid. 'Make it Chinese,' bellowed someone, and there was the thud of a giant switch and a sudden buzzing blast of yellow light, turning the living room into a gilded tableau. Mrs Brown wound the wool around her fingers and picked up her knitting; Ambrose shrugged off the attentions of a woman with a powder-puff and seated himself opposite Mrs Brown. From his jacket pocket he took out what looked like a brand new pipe. The standard lamp in the corner flickered a couple of times and then steadied, and Catrin suddenly found herself staring at the opening image of the script – of *her* script, as she couldn't help but think of it, although she'd been allotted a pre-existing storyline and every draft of the dialogue had been tweaked and filleted, stuffed, carved and garnished by at least a dozen other people. 'Too many cooks,' Buckley had said to her during one of his fleeting visits to the Ministry. 'Too many cooks and most of 'em can't even boil an egg.'

'But what shall I do?' Catrin had asked him, clutching a copy of the fifth draft. 'Most of the notes I get are actually contradictory – it's impossible to act on them all.'

'Do nothing. That script's all right; it's not going to get any better. Write a memo. Tell them their comments are invaluable and that you've made all the requested changes and then enclose exactly the same script.'

'I can't.'

'Try it.'

'They'll notice.'

'They won't.'

And he had been right; the untouched version of draft five had passed from associate producer to script editor, from ideas conference to Home Security Propaganda Department Committee, subdivision 4/b (films) and it had been universally accepted as an officially-approved final draft. And here, now, were Mr and Mrs Brown, very nearly as she had imagined them (if a little too old), sitting together in the comfortably worn surroundings of their front room, a vision of suburban domestic harmony.

'Let's have some quiet,' called Briggs. 'Going for a take.'

'One moment.' Ambrose was packing shag into the pipe bowl with his thumb.

'Darling, you're not really going to, are you?' asked Cecy.

'What's that?'

'You're not going to smoke that filthy thing, are you?'

'I was going to, yes. I feel it's appropriate to the character. If someone as irrelevant as myself is allowed to have any opinions whatsoever about such an issue,' he added, glancing at the director.

'Couldn't you just mime?' said Cecy.

'I can mime smoking but I can't mime smoke.'

‘I suppose not. It’s just that my chest isn’t what it was.’

‘I’m using a bronchial brand.’

‘Besides, I always thought it was a continuity problem.’

‘In what way?’

‘Well, in the way that great puffs of smoke keep popping up at odd times.’

‘You may possibly be thinking of actors who don’t understand the concept of continuity, as opposed to actors who possess an innate technical awareness.’

‘I’m sorry, darling, I didn’t mean to . . .’

‘Excuse me, Mr Hilliard.’ It was Briggs, bending deferentially over the armchair. ‘The director says that he’d prefer if you didn’t have the pipe.’

‘Oh, does he? May I ask why?’

‘He feels it may distract the audience from the dialogue.’

‘Oh, how *ridiculous*.’

‘No, Ambrose, I think he has a point,’ said Cecy, jerking her needles for emphasis and knocking the ball of wool on to the floor. She reached out a hand, waggled it ineffectually in the general direction of the wool, and then looked around for help. ‘Could someone . . . *so* sorry to be a trouble.’

‘Everyone happy?’ called Briggs to the floor.

‘Perhaps I should read my dialogue from another room,’ said Ambrose, putting the pipe away. ‘I wouldn’t want to distract the audience with my presence.’

‘Settle down, everybody. Going for a take on *The Letter*, first set up. *Quiet* please.’ Briggs glanced over to the camera, where the clapper boy was standing, board in hand. ‘Rolling?’

‘Rolling.’

‘Speed?’

‘Speed.’

‘Sound?’

‘Yup.’

The clapper snapped shut.

‘And *action*.’

Mrs Brown clicked her needles for a moment or two, and then looked up with a wifely smile.

'*I had a letter from April today*,' she said. '*A nice four-pager*.'

'*What's she on about this time?*' asked Ambrose. The camera was behind him, shooting part of the back of his head and the whole of Cecy's face. She had angled herself towards the lights, as a sunflower swivels towards the sun.

'*She says she and Tony have made up ever such a clever code so that he can write to her about what he's doing without anyone being able to guess*.'

'*Oh yes?*' Of course, one always continued acting even if one's own face wasn't in shot, it was simple professional courtesy, but since Cecy was barely bothering to glance at him between phrases, he allowed his eyes to wander.

'*They've thought of a word that means "overseas"*,' said Cecy, '*and a word that means "leave" and a word that means "France" and another that means "England"*.'

'*I see*.' The garrulous young Welshwoman was standing in the shadows at the very edge of the set. She was looking down at her script and Ambrose treated her to a speciality glare, the one he liked to think of as 'twin venomous orbs that poison darts doth send'. He'd developed it during the silent era for long moments of speechless antipathy.

'*And a word that means "troop train"*,' continued Cecy, '*and a word that means "regiment", and a number that means the date, and a word that means "embarking"*.'

'*Uh huh*.' Catrin looked up at Ambrose as he uttered the syllables – it might possibly have been the tone in which he spoke them that attracted her attention – and catching his gaze, she flinched visibly and dropped her script. It was only a small noise, a whisper of paper across the cement floor, but a crew member glanced at her, accusingly.

'Sorry,' said Catrin. There was a horrible, extended silence and then the sound recordist took off his headphones and twenty-five faces looked in her direction.

'Cut!'

She tried to make herself very small, and then decided that she might look even smaller if she moved towards the exit.

'Oh dear,' said Ambrose, as he watched the doors close behind her. 'I do hope we're not going to overrun the morning session. I have an awfully important lunch date.'

Sammy had reserved their usual Monday table beside the window at La Venezia. He had specified one o'clock, but by ten past had still not arrived himself, and Ambrose ordered a second gin and stared out at the street. A sandbag from the pile on the corner had burst, the hessian rotted from a year of rain and dog urine, and one of the waiters was sweeping the grit into the gutter. Mario – or perhaps it was Angelo – applied himself listlessly to his task, stopping frequently to look along the road. A pigeon walked behind him, bobbing and halting and dodging, like a child playing at spies. Ambrose ate an olive and looked at his watch again. A minute had gone by.

It seemed to him that time passed very slowly at the moment. There was a war, of course, but so far all it had really meant was that he could no longer eat the food he preferred, or buy his favourite drinks, or drive his motor car whenever he wanted, or walk about after dark without barking his shins every ten yards, or travel abroad or even, for God's sake, keep a bloody housekeeper. Three in ten months! Mrs Parsons, who had been with him for years, had moved to Plymouth to be with her daughter; Madame Lefevre had started well, but since the invasion of France had developed the habit of breaking into bouts of loud weeping during the dusting and he'd been forced to let her go; and Betty Clive, a plain but strapping girl with a chin like a spade, had lasted eight days before announcing that she was off to join the FANYs in order to meet, drive around, and eventually marry an officer. Now he was scraping along with the help of next door's char and a washerwoman so old that he had to help her up the stairs. There had been times, lately, when he had looked back with something approaching nostalgia on the heel-clicking efficiency with which his ex-wife had run the household. It had been hell at the time, but at least he'd never had to cook his own breakfast or shine his own shoes – at least he'd never found himself sitting on the first-floor lavatory with nothing but the current copy of *The Times* with which to wipe his arse. Sammy, at least, had a sister for all that sort of domestic flim-flammery; he really didn't know how lucky he was.

Sammy, at this moment, rounded the corner opposite the restaurant, spotted Ambrose in the window and gave a little wave with the two remaining fingers on his left hand. His right was toting a large, stained canvas bag, the cloth straining over some ill-defined mass. He negotiated the curb (always difficult for someone of his bulk), gave the broom-carrying waiter a covert and obviously admiring glance, and squeezed himself through the door.

'I have to be back at two fifteen,' said Ambrose. 'I've already ordered.'

'Veal?'

'Off. Cutlets Milanese and semolina pudding.'

Sammy sighed, and leaned the bag against the table leg. One of the cloth sides drooped down, revealing a bloodied row of teeth and a lidless jelly eye.

'Sorry,' said Sammy, hitching up the side again. 'Half a sheep's head for Cerberus. I had to walk all the way to Beak Shtreet for it, but he simply can't live on potato peelings and bread shcraps, whatever this government may say. Sophie says she'll boil it up and make him some brawn, lucky fellow. Is this for me?' He took a sip of his favourite, loathsomely sweet dessert wine, then belched delicately, holding one finger in front of his mouth to stem the noise. 'I beg your pardon. How's the filming?'

'Slapdash. Amateurish. You realize that half of these shorts are played during the intermission and the other half when the only people in the cinema are the cleaners. Did you know that I'm co-starring with Cecy Clyde-Cameron?'

'No, really? Dear Cecy – how is she?'

'Fat.'

'She used to be shtunning. Didn't she marry poor old George Garamonde?'

'Did she?'

'I'm sure she did. And I *think* I heard that she had twins. Some years ago now, of course.'

'Looks as if she's still carrying them.'

Sammy tittered and looked around for service. Only two other tables were occupied and there were no waiters in sight. Sammy turned back and clasped his hands across his stomach. 'Lovely fresh sunny day,' he said. 'Shpring-like. Dogwood flowering in the shquare.'

Ambrose felt a twinge of irritation. It was a familiar accompaniment to his meetings with Sammy, a sort of indigestion of the soul provoked by the various imperfections embodied by his agent: Sammy's blancmange physique, for a start, that personified the flabbiness of his negotiating skills. Then there was the ridiculous name and speech defect. If you were trying to conceal the fact that your family were naturalized German Jews, then choosing the surname 'Smith' when you had never quite lost your accent and, moreover, lisped affectedly on every 's' preceding a consonant, might be perceived as a bad idea. The single statement – 'My name is Sammy Shmith' – would be enough to make the average Local Defence Volunteer reach for his wooden rifle. Then there was the fact that he was an obvious bum-boy, capable of uttering the phrase, 'I've simply never shpotted the right girl', while simultaneously eyeing up the nearest pair of fly buttons. Add to all this the fact that he had failed to find Ambrose a decent leading role for nearly six years, and it seemed astonishing that they were still associates – and yet, as a breed, agents were so short-sighted, so inflexible in their outlook, so lazy, so astoundingly and relentlessly unimaginative, that Ambrose had never found another who entirely suited his needs. He regarded these weekly lunches, therefore, as a way for him to keep a close watch on Sammy, to ensure that every thespian avenue was being explored for a role of suitable worth and proportions – and if, occasionally, the conversation strayed into reminiscence or gossip or topical comment, he was careful always to steer it back towards more important areas.

'Ooh,' said Sammy, veering off-topic immediately, 'did I tell you about Philip Cadogan?'

'Heroically joining the army? Yes, you did. More than once.'

'But did I tell you that he was evacuated with the BEF? Three days on the beach at Dunkirk dodging Shtukas and then picked up by trawler. He said he shlept for a solid twenty hours when he got back. I bumped into him in Black's and we had such a jolly talk. I think service life suits him, he's looking far more mature. I think that once this is all over he'll find that he's moved seamlessly from juvenile to leading man.'

Not unless he's seamlessly acquired a chin from somewhere, thought Ambrose, glancing over his shoulder towards the kitchen door. Still no sign of the cutlets. 'So what did you think of the new prints?' he asked, turning back. 'I have to admit he's clever, that photographer chap. All that business with shadows and filters. I thought the three-quarters profile with cigarette for *Spotlight*, and the full-face for publicity, the one where I'm wearing the fedora.'

'Ah yes . . .' Sammy looked uncomfortable. 'I wanted to have a word with you about those . . .' He looked down at his hands, one podgily intact, the other a partial, rosy stump. 'I was thinking that a little change of tactic might be in order . . .'

'What d'you mean, "tactic"? I thought they were jolly good.'

'Yes, but I'm not sure that making you look so very . . .' He searched for a word, his expression pained. '. . . so very *callow* is quite the direction that . . .'

Ambrose found himself temporarily bereft of speech. Sammy floundered on: 'I think it might be more fruitful in terms of casting to embrace your . . . your . . . your . . . your . . . your . . .

exshperience – yes, your impressive exshperience. More fruitful. In terms of casting. In terms of being in line for the role of . . . of senior ranks in service movies, for instance, there's going to be a lot of call for that, I'd imagine, rather than for the . . . the . . .' He looked desperately around the room. 'I say, they're an awful time with the order, aren't they?'

'Clive Brook,' said Ambrose, his voice a sliver of steel. 'Clive Brook is *older* than I am and he is still playing leading men. Are you going around telling Clive Brook that he should start playing *senior* roles?'

'Not my client,' said Sammy, in a tiny voice, pleating the tablecloth between his fingers.

'Leslie Banks – again, *older* than me. Are you telling Leslie Banks that he—'

'Ambrose . . .'

'. . . that he should be playing Polonius instead of Hamlet?'

'Ambrose, my job is to find you work.'

'Well, why don't you *do* your blasted job, then?'

'Because I can only do it with your cooperation. You may remember that you turned down a perfectly decent film offer last month.'

'Playing Audrey Cane's uncle? Fifteen lines, shuffling round in a smoking-jacket, while Leslie Banks – *older* than me – gets to do an entire mad-act as her unstable lover?'

'You turned down *The Merchant* at Wyndham's.'

'Playing *Old Gobbo*?'

Sammy shrugged, his little currant eyes blinking unhappily. 'Character roles,' he said, softly, 'are not to be shneered at.'

'Christ, Sammy, have you seen the "Character Actors" section of *Spotlight*? You can't honestly think that I . . . ?' Ambrose lifted his spoon and peered at the convex side; he saw a giant nose, a slit-trench mouth, eyebrows like twin hedges. His eyes, though, even through the distorting murk, were still as green as Venetian glass. Reassured, he dropped the spoon. 'I can't bear all this labelling,' he said. 'It's meaningless. An actor *acts*. You may as well ask a river what it thinks of its name – Thames or Tiber, Rhine or Styx, it makes no damned difference – it simply goes on being a river.'

'Oh now, don't tell me,' said Sammy, fluttering his fingers. 'That's from *Inshpector Charnforth and the . . . the Red Rose Mystery*.'

'*Blue Sapphire Mystery*, actually. My point, Sammy, is that—'

He saw the object out of the corner of his eye and ducked; the noise and explosion of glass seemed simultaneous and a half-brick crossed the room and shied a bottle from the table beyond theirs. A woman screamed.

'Filthy Eyeties!' shouted a figure in the street, already running. 'Good God,' said Ambrose, shaking a splinter from his hand. The table was heaped with glass, the gin tumbler crammed with lethal fragments. A waiter burst out from the kitchen, took a fleeting look at the damage and ran back in again. Ambrose pushed his chair away from the table.

'Don't move,' said Sammy. He reached his good hand towards Ambrose's face, and plucked gently at something. There was a tiny prick of pain beneath one eye, and Sammy was holding a wicked shard between his fingers, two inches long, a needle's-breadth wide. One end was tipped with a dot of blood.

'Tell me, I've not—' said Ambrose, heart stopping.

'No scar,' said Sammy. 'Nothing that can't be fixed with a dab of greasepaint. *So*—' He looked around the restaurant, at the other diners squawking and flapping, at the kitchen door, now firmly shut. 'I wonder . . .' The door opened suddenly, revealing the head waiter, his face grey.

'I regret to announce to our valued customers that we're closed,' he said, 'until further notice. The staff of La Venezia wish to point out that we are in full support of the Allied cause. God save Mr Churchill. Fuck Hitler.' The door closed again.

Sammy gave a little whistle. 'Italy's in the war, then.'

'Looks rather like it.' Ambrose touched the little wound beneath his eye, and examined his fingertip for blood; there was none. He rose slowly and shook his jacket above the litter of glass on the floor. 'Apropos of your earlier comments,' he said, checking behind the lapels. 'I'm prepared to be pragmatic. I am not an unreasonable man. I will, if nothing better turns up, take the occasional character part.'

'Oh!' Sammy looked suddenly hopeful.

'Provided that it is an *extensive* role. I will not play Old Gobbo but I might consider, for instance, playing Falstaff.'

'Oh,' said Sammy again, less hopeful this time.

'What you don't seem to understand is that I've never been interested in cameos. What is paramount for me is the chance to build up a character over a number of scenes, whereas—'

Like Banquo's ghost, Chick appeared suddenly in the gap where the window had been. 'They want yer,' he said.

'Relentless,' muttered Ambrose, putting on his jacket and hat. 'I've not eaten, of course, and there's no catering at that damned little studio, not even a cup of tea. It's "Mr Hilliard", incidentally,' he added, in Chick's direction. 'Not a hard name to remember, I would have thought.' He followed Sammy through the door. 'Until next week, then.'

'Next week *where*, is the question,' said Sammy. 'Perhaps we had better postpone.'

'No . . . no, I don't think so.' The idea made Ambrose strangely uneasy. 'No, we could try Veeraswamy's. The Indians are, at least, on our side.'

'I'll book,' said Sammy. He hefted his sheep's head and waggled his fingers in his usual girlish farewell. 'Au revoir.'

Walking beside Chick, Ambrose felt like a prisoner under escort. He lengthened his stride and tried to pretend that he was walking back to the studio on his own. He had, he calculated, seven lines in the next scenario, two of which were 'Yes, dear' and one of which was the syllable 'Ugh'. First eskimo, now caveman; it really was enough to make one weep.

SUPPORTING FEATURE

August 1940

Late on Thursday afternoon, Dolly Clifford, who was celebrating her fortieth birthday for the third year in succession, handed a box of chocolates around the sewing-room and Edith ate a violet fondant, just to be polite. The next morning, when she woke at 3 a.m. with the impression that her head was being split in half with a blunt axe, she knew that she had discovered yet another addition to the list of foods that set off her migraines.

'Ooh, we all get headaches,' Dolly had once said, dismissively, but there was no similarity between what Edith thought of as her 'usual' bad heads – that dull grey band across the brows, concomitant with Sunday afternoons – and this terrible, cleaving, Technicolor pain. She groped for the handkerchief under her pillow, wet it in the glass of water on the bedside table, and laid it over her eyes.

She awoke again much later, her head stuffy, the pain diminished and distant, as if telegraphed from another room. The daylight was hidden by the blackout curtains, but she knew from the noise of the plumbing that it was well after her normal waking hour of six thirty. By now, she should be walking to Wimbledon station, or standing on the platform with a thousand others, waiting for a District Line train to Edgware, via Paddington. She could not, at this moment, imagine even trying to stand upright.

There was a gentle knock at her door. 'Are you awake, Edith?'

'Yes, I am.' Her voice, to her own ears, sounded limp and pasty.

'I think you've slept in, dear. I'm afraid you may be rather late.'

'I have a headache, Mrs Sumpter.'

'Oh I'm so sorry. Can I get you some tea? Or an aspirin?'

'No thank you, Mrs Sumpter. I'll just lie here for a while.'

'As you wish, dear.' She heard Mrs Sumpter's poor swollen feet limp back down the corridor to her room.

The next knock was more peremptory.

'Are you requiring breakfast, Miss Beadmore?'

Edith winced at the thought. 'No thank you, Mrs Bailey.'

'Then I have wasted your egg.'

'Perhaps Pam can have it.'

'Pardon?'

It hurt her head to speak loudly. 'Give it to Pamela,' she said, with an effort.

'If you're sure.'

'Yes I am. Mrs Bailey . . .'

'Yes?'

'May I use the telephone later?'

There was silence.

'To ring work, Mrs Bailey? To tell them I'm not feeling at all well?'

'I use the telephone myself on Friday mornings.'

For heaven's sake, thought Edith. 'It would only be a very short call, Mrs Bailey. To tell them that I can't come in.'

'If you're at home all day I have nothing in the house for your luncheon, Miss Beadmore.'

'I won't be wanting anything to eat, Mrs Bailey. I would simply like to make a phone call.'

There was a long pause.

'Very well, then.'

Edith sank back into the pillow. Conversations with Mrs Bailey were always like this – a verbal variation of 'scissors-paper-stone' in which each exchange was a phase of combat, with firm rules and a definite winner. It required a clear head and good reflexes on the part of the other participant, and Edith felt exhausted by her marginal victory. She was still recovering when there was a third knock, this time simultaneous with the door actually opening.

'If you're ill are you going to use the bathroom?' Pamela's silhouette was visible in the light from the hall, her dressing-gown pulled tightly around her. She had, as yet, little in the way of bust or hips but posed as though she had lashings of both. '*Are* you?' she repeated, impatiently.

'Not for a while,' said Edith. 'And please don't open the door until I say you may. It's very rude.'

'Sorree, I'm sure. Shall I take down the blackouts for you?'

'No.'

Pamela opened the door a little wider so that light from the hall spilled across the room. Edith could see her face now, preternaturally mature, her eyes judgemental. 'Your room is very, very neat,' she said, in a tone that implied that neatness was a solecism. 'Do you always line up your shoes like that?'

'Close the door, please.'

'In a moment.' Looking exhilarated by her own daring, she pushed it open still further. 'Why do you arrange your dressing-table in that way? It's like something in an exhibit.'

'Pamela, close the door.'

'And why do you wear gloves in bed? It looks awfully stupid.'

Sitting up suddenly made Edith feel quite dreadful, but it had the desired effect. Pamela fled, leaving the door open, and after a minute or two Edith was able to walk across and shut it. She switched on the light, and sat down at the dressing table and rested her head on her gloved hands. The gloves were cotton, and she wore them to prevent the almond oil, with which she massaged her hands at night, from marking the sheets. She had seven pairs of gloves and she washed a pair nightly, drying them on glove stretchers to prevent shrinkage. Her six pairs of shoes were lined up according to colour, from black lace-ups at one end, to pale beige pumps at the other, the latter so beautiful and so vulnerable to dirt that she had barely worn them. Her clothes in the wardrobe were arranged by category (skirts, dresses, blouses, jackets, coats), and by colour within each category. The drawers of the tallboy contained sachets of lavender, and stockings and underclothes folded into beautiful, parallel rows. On the dressing-table (damp-dusted daily) her mother's rosewood-backed mirror and twin brushes were arranged in an elegant fan. Edith's night cream, day cream, powder and lipstick were kept in the top drawer, so as not to detract from the symmetry. She had sewn the curtains herself, and had made a matching coverlet for the bed, all in a heavy ivory slub. She had also made the ivory wool rug with brown geometric pattern that lay in the centre of the floor. Her laundry was hidden in a pale woven-fibre chest that doubled as a stool. The empty fireplace was concealed by a matchwood screen (also her mother's). Pamela was right: the room was very, very neat and Edith was perversely pleased by the observation, although she knew that the phrase had not been used kindly.

There had been a time when Pamela had called her 'auntie', and had played quietly in her room, sorting through the button drawer, building cotton reels into towers and stockades, learning to crochet long, helical scarves for her dollies. She had been five when Edith had answered the advertisement ('good-sized room available in comfortable family home, would suit quiet business lady'), and Mrs Sumpter, Pamela's grandmother, who owned the house, had been in her late sixties. She had been a vigorous, kindly woman who had managed to combine the role of landlady with that of hostess, and she had made it a welcoming place to live. The change in her had been gradual – a slowing, a tiredness, an occasional wheeze that had become, imperceptibly, constant. It was her heart that had grown large and dragged her down, she said, and the small blue pills from the doctor only gave her a dry mouth and did nothing for her chest. And then Poland had fallen and Mrs Sumpter, who had lost her husband at Ypres, had sagged overnight, had lost all of her remaining vim as if the advent of another war had somehow filleted her, and Mrs Bailey, her daughter, who had discarded her own husband at some (never-to-be-discussed-or-even-mentioned) point, had snapped to attention and started to impose her own regime on the house, cutting the comfortable corners and snipping at the more decorative trimmings of life at Number 40. And Pamela, who had been pudgy and sweet, had all of a sudden become pretty.

It was a self-conscious prettiness, reaffirmed in every mirror that she passed (and in every window and polished surface), and boys had started to walk her home from school, and even ask her out to the cinema, although she had not been allowed to go. And now that this prettiness had placed her in a new world, she had begun to notice, with apparent pleasure, that not everyone was as pretty, or as popular with the boys, as she was.

She had started to walk home from school with little Margaret Raleigh from three doors down, who wore spectacles and had curves in all the wrong places and who, it was evident from Pamela's demeanour, provided an especially flattering contrast to her own appearance. At home, she had begun to watch Edith, sometimes covertly, sometimes openly, with the expression of a zoologist viewing a new, inferior and slightly amusing species. Edith, mid-breakfast, would suddenly realize that Pamela was staring at her nose, or her hair, or her hands, her nails, her mouth; a hard, assessing stare that would make her self-conscious so that she rattled her cutlery, or clinked her teeth, in a clumsy way, against the water glass. Only once had Edith protested. She had said: '*Please* don't stare at me when I'm eating, Pamela' and Pamela had looked amazed.

'I wasn't staring,' she'd said, in a wounded voice, 'I was

admiring your necklace' and Edith had been left in the position of having to apologize to a thirteen-year-old. Afterwards, meeting on the stairs, Pamela had given her a triumphant look.

It was ridiculous, of course – ridiculous for an independent woman of thirty-six to be intimidated by a child, but Edith had found herself beginning to glance around furtively as she scurried through the communal areas of the house, to cut short her little walks in the garden with Mrs Sumpter (a garden that was overlooked by Pamela's bedroom), to retreat to her own room more and more. There, in the pleasant place that she'd made for herself, she could cut out a pattern, or read, or listen to the wireless, or write letters, without worrying about whether her chin was particularly shiny, or her hair in need of a wash. Because, although she had always tried to do her best with what God had given her, what He had given her was straight hair, a beaky nose, a small mouth and a permanent shadow under each eye, the whole packaged into an expression of perpetual anxiety, unchanging even when she was feeling particularly merry or at ease. It was true that He had also given her a pair of useful (if large) hands, a discriminating eye for line and colour, a near-perfect memory and a neat figure, but she knew that those were not items that had ever really counted. Pamela was only doing what Edith had done to herself at the same age – dissecting her appearance feature by feature and finding each one wanting.

At the dressing-table, Edith took off her gloves and massaged her forehead. Lavender oil, she had heard, was good for headaches. Perhaps it was Mrs Sumpter who had told her; she felt too muzzy to remember. There was an unused phial in the drawer, a birthday present from her cousin in Norfolk, and she extracted the tiny cork and dabbed a little of the essence on her temples. The astringency seemed to cut through the fog behind her eyes and she held the cork under her nose and took a longer sniff. It was a purple smell, shot through with silver – a tiny, clean bolt of lightning that zipped through her skull. She smiled for the first time that day, recorked the bottle, switched off the light and lay down on the bed again.

She dreamed of Red Indians. They were dancing in a circle on the lawn, chanting menacingly and waving their tomahawks, while Pamela sat on the back wall and swung her legs in a provocative manner. Edith herself was carrying a tray of cups, and wondering how to explain to the visitors that Mrs Bailey had imposed a household limit of no more than two spoonfuls of tea per pot, regardless of the number of takers. And then she was awake, and the war-chant was still audible, a low-pitched chorus, sinister and uneven, emanating not from the garden but from the sky above. The siren came late, as if triggered by her own fumbling realization, and in its wake came Mrs Bailey, rushing up the stairs and throwing open the door.

'They're coming, they're coming,' she shouted, 'I've switched off the gas' and then she was gone again and Edith was groping for her slippers, and all the time the swoop of the siren continued, and beneath it the stammering throb of the engines. And she couldn't believe (her mind still bleared with sleep), she simply couldn't believe that after a year of waiting, of endless false alerts, of lectures and leaflets and fortnightly air-raid drills at work, of month after month of dreary preparation and dire warnings during which the frightening and the immediate had gradually flattened into the mundane, that now, today, really, actually *now*, the bombers were here. She sat up and smoothed her hair. She put on her dressing-gown, and tied the belt into a bow, and then re-tied it so that the tasselled ends were exactly the same length. She straightened the bedclothes and took a further second or two to remove a loose thread from the rug, and yet another to tip the dressing-table mirror forward so that the frame wasn't touching the wall; and then a great whistling roar outside drowned even the siren, and the stomach-shaking crash that followed was a starting-gun that propelled her through the door. And what if I die, she thought, running down the stairs, across the hall, through the kitchen, what if today is my last day on earth? What if I have only a minute left to live, half a minute, ten seconds? For a moment she seemed to see the pilot's viewpoint, a vast patchwork of lawn and tile and tarmacadam, splashed with the pink and blue of hydrangeas, the flapping white of drying sheets and the scarlet of her own dressing-gown as she ran out of the back door and across the grass towards the shelter, newly built, its roof a curl of shining metal. And then there was a tearing noise, as if the sky had been ripped in two and the air seemed to slide sideways and drop away like a cut necklace and she was lying on her face in the flowerbed, clinging to the ground as the wind dragged at her, while behind her a giant sledgehammer laid waste to a wall.

And then the buffeting eased and stopped, and she released her grip.

Her hands were full of broken stems, the palms lightly scored with cuts. Her mouth was stuffed with earth, and, kneeling, she hawked and spat on the lawn, and wiped mud from her lips. The sky above was empty, faintly traced with vapour, but from the Raleighs' garden, three doors down, a plume of dust was rising, and there was no roof on their house, and no wall on the first floor so that the Raleighs' bathroom was shamelessly displayed, a used towel abandoned on the lino, the wallpaper blotched with damp, while in the next room a pink-quilted double bed protruded over the broken floorboards like a vulgar tongue. The house beside it was windowless and oddly bowed, as if sagging at the knees, and the next along had coughed its back door clear across the garden, while a severed pipe burped water through the gap. Edith wiped her mouth again and looked at Mrs Sumpter's house. For a moment she thought it untouched, and then she registered the slight shift in angle of the guttering, the hunched look of the roof gable, the strange clarity of rooms seen through empty frames. There was silence, utter silence inside her head, and then, one by one the sounds slid back – a tile skittering down the roof, the splatter of water from next door, dogs barking, a man shouting hysterically, a fire-engine bell, the bombers – the bombers still somewhere overhead, and then her own name being called, over and over again. Quite calmly, she stood up and walked round to the entrance to the Anderson shelter.

They sat, knee to knee, in the near-darkness, a crack of light framing the ill-fitting door, and there were four more explosions, each further away than the last, and the gradual diminution of engine noise, and a long, inexplicable wait before the sounding of 'Raiders Passed'. And, by then the conversation had become a sealed loop, rotating endlessly.

'Dear God,' Mrs Sumpter would say. 'Who'd have thought the Zeppelins would come again in my lifetime? Who'd have thought it?'

Then Pamela – 'They're not Zeppelins, they're aeroplanes' – at which point Mrs Bailey would let out a low moan and take Pamela's hand. 'I shouldn't have listened to you, I shouldn't have let you come back home, I should have left you with the Collins sisters in Leighton Buzzard where you were safe,' and Pamela would wrench her hand away and mutter, 'I wasn't staying with those old witches for anything, I'd rather stay in London and die. Anyway, it smelled of cat's piddle.'

'You're going back.'

'I'm not.'

'Is the house much damaged, dear?' – Mrs Sumpter to Edith.

'No.'

Mrs Bailey: 'It must be. She's shocked, you can see she's not all there, she doesn't know what she's saying. It'll be flattened, I know it will.'

'Dear God,' (Mrs Sumpter). 'Who'd have thought the Zeppelins would come again in my lifetime . . .'

Round and round – aeroplanes, Leighton Buzzard, witches, cats, shock, Zeppelins, no *not* Zeppelins. And Edith sitting on a plank raised on loose blocks, because the shelter was too new to take any drilling, her hand-sewn felt slippers drinking up the damp from the earth floor. And inside her head, exhilaration, the most extraordinary exhilaration, her skull awash with light, her thoughts exultant, flying, singing with triumph. A bomb had lifted her up and cast her down and here she was without a scratch and nothing now could touch her. She was shaking with the thrill of it, she was skimming the ground with such speed that she might leave a trail of stars, and the climbing note of the All-Clear lifted her still higher, so that once again she was looking down at the gardens and roofs of west Wimbledon and watching as three women and a girl emerged into the white light of a cloudy August day.

Mrs Sumpter staggered, and Mrs Bailey took her arm and screamed at Pamela who had run ahead to the back door, so that in the end it was Edith who entered through the crooked frame, and picked her way across a floor covered with glass and smashed plates – Edith who was still hovering, still somewhere beyond herself, able to watch dispassionately as the figure in the dressing-gown crossed the hall and passed the front door with its empty oval where, instead of a red glass ship on a blue glass ocean, a stretch of pavement was visible, and a gaggle of sight-starers, gaping at the damage. Then up the stairs, the ruined slippers leaving a trail of imprints in the dust, and under the section of plaster that swung from the ceiling like a flag, and over to the door that looked intact but which wouldn't open, twist the handle as she might. It was the shove that did it, the unladylike shoulder heave that forced it open a few inches, gouging a groove in the floorboards and flinging Edith back into herself so that when she edged around the door and saw what had happened to her room, there was no comforting distance between herself and the pyramid of plaster and lath and viscous black attic dust from the fallen ceiling, or the smashed wigwam of her wardrobe, from which a shredded organdie sleeve semaphored for rescue. Nothing ivory was visible, nothing beige, nothing smooth, nothing cherished. And she was no longer shaking with the thrill of it, only with the disgust, and from the garden she could hear Mrs Bailey screaming, calling her mother's name.

★

Dear Edith,

Well the news from London is very bad I must say, and I'm very sorry to hear about your landlady, her heart giving out though I can't say I'm surprised, it must be terrible with those Bombs falling. We said a special prayer in chapel this Sunday for people in London and Reverend Stead the visiting preacher said that if more people in London were Observant then God might fling his shield of righteousness over the city but things being as they are then the good must perish with the evil, sustained only by the sure and certain hope of their salvation. I don't say that I agree with this Edith, but Reverend Stead lived in Croydon for many years and he says that the taint of sinfulness is everywhere to be seen there. Of course it may be different in Wimbledon.

We are all as well as can be expected. Myrtle has started at the grammar school and received a Highly Commended for her first composition, the title was 'My Happiest Memory' and she wrote about going to London on the train on her own and seeing Buckingham Palace and Trafalgar Square and Betty Grable walking past in an evening gown all imaginary of course, but the teacher didn't know that and said it showed wonderful Powers of observation so of course I had to write a note explaining that none of it was true.

I am more busy than ever, everyone is worried that there will be clothes rationing and I am Snowed Under with orders in the shop, two overcoats this week in Astrachan fabric one with an Indian lamb collar the other with Chinchilla Plush. I had Elsie Breen working for me but she's gone into munitions. In fact Edith, I wanted to say that you are always welcome to stay here with us in Badgeham while London is bad, not that the war isn't here too there's all sorts of wire and tank traps and a minefield on the beach and a gunnery school in the wood behind the dunes, so we are full of soldiers and you need a permitt to come further than Ipswich on the train, though you being family it shouldn't be a problem.

God bless you.

If you gave me a Hand I could pay you what I gave Elsie, minus your keep.

Your loving cousin, Verna

No, thought Edith, re-reading the letter. Things were bad in London and worse in Wimbledon, but it hadn't yet come to working for Elsie Breen's wages minus keep. Though if she closed her eyes she could see the long empty curve of sand along Badgeham Bay and almost feel the cold, clean wind. She'd spent every holiday there as a child. She could still remember the sense of boundless space.

In Number 40, there was no space at all. Three and a half ceilings had come down and until Mrs Bailey could find a carpenter, a plasterer, a tiler and a general labourer to cart away the debris, the remaining occupants were confined to two bedrooms, one containing Mrs Bailey, and the other Pamela and Edith. 'This is *my* part of the room,' Pamela had declared, indicating an area which included bed, wardrobe, chest of drawers and access to the door.

'Don't be silly,' had been Edith's feeble reply, but she'd *felt* feeble, her salvagable possessions in a sad little pile on a chair, her hip bones aching from the row of cushions she was using as a makeshift mattress. The whole house felt coated in dust and jammed with clutter, no surface free, no square of carpet that she could keep clear and call her own. It reminded her of the lodgings she'd lived in during her first years in London – sticky landings, shared kitchens, stains on the ceiling, tiny oddly-shaped rooms with six corners and two doors, horrid furniture, the upholstery whiskery with horsehair, the crevices stuffed with stubs of pencil and boiled sweets and ancient farthings.

Mrs Sumpter's advertisement had saved her from all that, and now poor Mrs Sumpter was lying beneath a bunch of carnations in the ochre clay of Wimbledon Municipal Cemetery, and Mrs Bailey was busily assauging her grief by putting up the rent.

'There's repairs to pay for,' she'd pointed out, reprovingly, as if Edith had been caught axing the roof-tree and punching out the windows. In the frowsy atmosphere of the shared bedroom, with the blackouts trapping in the last heat of the summer, Edith would lie awake and listen as Pamela talked in her sleep, her cool clear voice ordering some little minion to buy her sweets and magazines and packets of hair grips, or complaining about the meanness of the teachers. Once Edith heard her own name mentioned: 'There's old birdy Beady coming . . . old greedy Beady.'

'*Greedy?*' she'd thought. 'But I've never been greedy.'

Sometimes she felt breathless, hemmed in, and her mind would sketch a large and empty room with lime-washed walls and a wooden floor that echoed as she walked across the boards.

At work she'd had interest and sympathy, oceans of it, far exceeding the little trickle that normally accompanied a colleague's misfortune or illness. 'Edith has *been bombed*,' had been the awed whisper the Monday after Wimbledon had caught it, and there'd been a stream of visitors to the wardrobe room, each wanting her to recount her story. And she hadn't minded at all; it had been rather exciting to have the normally aloof Head of Moulds shaking his head in wonder as she told of her dive into the snapdragons. Dolly Clifford, in particular, had been awfully solicitous, plying Edith with cups of sweet tea and putting out a steadying hand whenever she stood up or turned around sharply.

'I feel quite well,' Edith had been moved to say at one point.

'I once heard of a man—' Dolly paused dramatically, and then put a hand to her lips and turned away. 'I shouldn't,' she added, over her shoulder.

'Shouldn't what?' asked Edith.

'Shouldn't tell you.'

'Well, you needn't.'

'But I think, perhaps . . . you should *know*.'

Edith had been reattaching paste pearls to Ann Boleyn's stomacher – children *would* keep ducking under the ropes and pulling them off – but she paused, needle in hand, and looked at her colleague warily; most of Dolly's stories began, 'I once heard of a man', and none of them had happy endings.

'He was in his bathroom when the gas geyser exploded,' said Dolly, her voice charged with doom. 'And he was thrown twenty yards through an open window and landed in a hedge. Not a scratch on him. He said he'd never felt better. The next day someone asked him if he wanted milk in his tea, and he gave a nod and dropped dead. When they cut him open they found that the blast had sent a razor blade straight into his neck, and when he'd nodded, the razor had moved and cut his spinal column right in half, all the way through.'

In the momentary silence that followed she swung the hinged ironing board down from the wall and kicked the legs into place.

'Did his head fall off, then?' It was Nora, one of the juniors, who asked the question, though it had crossed Edith's mind as well.

'Don't be silly,' said Dolly, huffily, hefting her iron and dabbing it with a wetted finger. The hiss and crack were satisfactory and she stretched George Washington's lace jabot across the board, covered it with a damp cloth, and applied the iron.

'I feel quite well,' said Edith again, more to reassure herself than anything, though her hands were not as steady as usual and she kept dropping the pearls and having to pounce on them before they rolled off the table. 'I'm just awfully sad about Mrs Sumpter. And then there's all the horrible mess – you should see it . . .'

'There's one thing I *do* know about bombs,' said Dolly, through a veil of steam, 'and that's that they never fall in the same place twice, so you'd be wise to stay put, however much of a trial it might be. Now who's that?' she added, at yet another knock on the door.

'Just me,' said Miss McNally, Head Coiffeuse and Chief Thorn in the Side of Wardrobe, a woman who thought that people came to Madame Tussauds in order to see the wigs. She was smiling, not an activity that came naturally to her. 'I've come to talk to Miss Beadmore about her terrible ordeal – that is, if it won't upset her too much . . .'

The interest dwindled rather quickly. Perhaps it was because she didn't tell the story well enough, didn't add the gruesome flourishes that Dolly would have managed so well. Perhaps it was because she couldn't banish the disbelief in her own voice as she spoke of an incident so dramatic that, surely, it must have happened to someone else. In any case, alerts were coming more frequently now and other people were beginning to acquire stories of their own: Mr Clay, the curator of the Chamber of Horrors, had been third on the scene when a Spitfire had downed a German fighter in a field outside Harrow, and had seen the incinerated corpse of the pilot; Dolly's neighbour's niece in Liverpool had injured her back in a raid and would never walk again; Miss McNally's elderly cat lay panting with fear under the stove every time the wobbler sounded, and had to be put down. Every day, Edith's own little tale was shuffled further down the pack. In the evenings, if the sky was silent, she sat in the lounge with Pamela and Mrs Bailey, trying to read while mother and daughter snippily discussed the merits of the latter's return to Leighton Buzzard, and if one or the other happened to look at Edith during those hours it seemed it was only by chance, in passing, in the same way that they might glance at the mantelpiece, or at the framed picture of the jaunty dog smoking a pipe, or at Mrs Sumpter's empty chair.

★

September 1940

The two juniors, Pearl and Nora, looked so much alike that they might be mistaken for sisters. Both were sixteen, toothpick-thin, with washed-out complexions and pale blue eyes. Both looked as if they scarcely possessed the energy to lift a pin, but presumably shared some powerful hidden dynamo, since they worked like billy-o, talked all day, and went dancing every single evening, apparently popping home only for the purpose of having an argument with their respective parents about the impropriety of staying out until all hours.

They talked about lipstick and hairstyles and shoes and royalty, and whether John Clements was better-looking than Leslie Howard, and how many times they'd been to see *Gone with the Wind*, and who they'd seen it with. They talked about current boyfriends and ex-boyfriends and prospective boyfriends and boys with whom they couldn't possibly bring themselves to dance (no never, honestly, I *couldn't*, never mind how many times he asked me). They talked about what Ronnie said to Audrey and to Audrey's friend Freda just before Audrey slapped Ronnie and went off with Freda's ex-boyfriend Alan. They talked about the hilarious time when they'd walked the wrong way in the blackout and ended up nearly falling in the river, and about how that queer man had approached them behind the Palais and they'd thought he was going to try some funny business before he opened his coat and tried to sell them a slab of Bourneville so old that the chocolate had gone white.

What they never talked about was the actual war. 'We don't need to know anything,' Pearl had said, 'it's nothing to do with us,' and she had been utterly unembarrassed by the incident in May, when the waxwork of Chamberlain had been hauled off to the History of British Politics gallery while that of Churchill had taken his place in the Tableau of the Allies just in front of De Gaulle and General Sikorski. Pearl had stared at the pugnacious red face for a good five seconds and then said, 'I know him. Isn't he the one in *My Little Chickadee*?'

Nora had shrieked with laughter at this, but since she herself had once identified the undressed dummy of Herman Goering as, 'The fat one in the Three Stooges', she had little grounds on which to sneer. But it was Goering who came for Nora in Bermondsey on Saturday the seventh, sending a skyful of bombers to the docks in broad daylight, and it was Nora who had the story to beat all stories when she came into Tussaud's, only a few minutes late, on the Monday morning.

She sat on the very edge of the chair, her eyes bright, her face even paler than usual, and she counted on her fingers: 'My gran's house is gone, my nan's house is gone, my auntie Kate's house is gone, my friend Sadie's house is gone, my old school is gone, the house on the corner of our street is gone, and the two old ladies who live there are still underneath it, and there was a dead body on the pavement just outside our front door that was blown from two roads away!' And then someone new would come into the sewing-room and Nora would uncurl her fingers and count again: 'My gran's house is gone, my nan's house is gone . . .'

Even from as far away as Wimbledon, it had been possible to see the russet light in the sky to the east as the docks burned, and it had been there again the night afterwards, a Looking-Glass sunset that began after dark and lasted till dawn. Edith had spent both nights with the Baileys in the dank back-garden shelter, wrapped in an eiderdown, sleeping in snatches, taking tiny comfort from the fact that the war seemed to have moved on, that Wimbledon had been nudged by the toe of history, and then abandoned for mightier targets. Such as seven-stone Nora, she thought now, with a spasm of guilt, as the girl told her story again.

'My gran's house is gone, my nan's house is gone . . .' She'd refused the unprecedented managerial offer of an afternoon off ('My mum says I'll be safer in town than what I am at home') but as the day passed and the repetitions multiplied, she seemed to sit ever more upright, her voice tighter and faster, one hand tugging at the fingers of the other.

'Nora,' said Edith at last, driven to decision, 'could you give me a hand with the A and R?'

'Oh no,' said Dolly. 'I don't think we need to bother Nora with work today, do we? Pearl can do it.'

'I'd prefer to have Nora,' said Edith, which was no more than the truth, since Nora was better than Pearl at spotting the tiny loose threads and crumpled corners and spots of grease from inquisitive fingers that, cumulatively, unless Assessed and Rectified on a regular basis, would spoil the splendour of the costumes.

'I'll do it, Miss Beadmore,' said Pearl.

'No, really, I'd like Nora to come with me.'

Nora stood up like a little wooden puppet, picked up her work basket and followed Edith.

Dolly pursed her lips in disapproval and mouthed the word 'Shock' at Pearl. 'I once heard of a girl . . .' she began, as Edith closed the door.

There were certain items that the general public simply would not leave alone: Hitler's moustache, Nelson's eyepatch, Gandhi's spectacles – all were picked at, adjusted, dropped, swapped and occasionally stolen. Marlene Dietrich's top hat had been replaced, serially, by a boater, a policeman's helmet and a knotted handkerchief, while the husky that accompanied Amundsen to the Pole had gone missing twice, on the second occasion turning up outside Battersea Dogs' Home with a note tied to its harness. Other damage was less deliberate and more insidious – satin gowns were stroked, medals fingered, bald heads patted, and skirts lifted and peered under by filthy-minded small boys. Poor Mary, Queen of Scots, lying on the ground in clinging black velvet, her head resting on the block, was particularly vulnerable to unauthorized clothing adjustment, not to mention dust, and, at Edith's request, Nora knelt beside her and spent a calming ten minutes picking lint off the dress and rearranging the heavy folds.

Edith worked her way along the row of Henry the Eighth's wives, feeling, as she always did during this procedure, like a sergeant major inspecting his favourite platoon: kirtles and partlets all present and correct, coifs, cornets and bumrolls to the ready. Such gorgeous, heavy fabrics, such a rich and strange nomenclature . . .

She had thought, when she had started working at Madame Tussaud's in 1931, that she might one day aspire to designing such costumes, that her evening studies and her year at art school (dreamed-of for a decade, gone in a blink) might mark her out as someone with potential. She'd been wrong, of course: designers, she found, came from another world. They swept into Tussaud's with a bundle of sketches and then swept out again, they were vivid and glossy and memorable, and Edith had stayed in the workroom and inched her way from the title of under-seamstress to that of seamstress. 'Miss Beadmore,' as the manager of the museum had once said, in a phrase that had lodged uneasily in her memory, 'is our backbone.' She would remind herself, if feeling a little low, that in many ways the costumes were more truly hers than the designers', and that there was really nothing finer than her daily privilege of walking through the galleries before opening hours when the displays were all pristine, radiant, unsullied by punters. There was order here, too, and space and neatness, all the qualities so dreadfully lacking in her current home life.

'I've done that, Miss Beadmore,' said Nora, standing up and dusting off her skirt. 'What shall I do next?'

'You could come along with me to Heroes and Heroines –

I want to check on the new figure. If you feel up to it, that is.'

'I'm fine now, Miss Beadmore.' Nora trotted along, willingly enough. Separated from Pearl she was always quiet and respectful, and it was hard to tell whether her current silence was in any way abnormal, or simply indicative of her boredom in adult company.

Edith had no knack for talking to the youngsters, no instinct for what might catch their interest, but perhaps it was better not to try at all than to attempt, like Dolly, to use slang, or to claim to have a 'pash' on the same film stars that the girls shrieked over. Edith could blush, sometimes, for the conversations that took place in the sewing-room, though she tried not to show her embarrassment; it would only encourage their silliness, to think her a prude. She would rather be labelled reserved, or over-serious.

'So have you seen it?' she asked Nora, as they took the short-cut through the almost deserted foyer, where a single Canadian airman stood with a guidebook.

'Seen what, Miss Beadmore?'

'The new figure in the Heroes of War tableau.'

'No I haven't, Miss Beadmore. Is it a soldier?'

'Yes, he's called Captain Warburton-Lee.'

'Oh.'

'He won the Victoria Cross for gallantry at Narvik.'

'Oh.'

'That's in Norway.'

'Oh.'

'And they're almost finished in the moulds room with another one – a hero of Dunkirk.'

Nora glanced up at her, suddenly interested. 'Is it the twins?'

'No, it's a Lance Corporal Nicholls. Who are the twins?'

'The *Starling* twins,' said Nora, apparently amazed by Edith's ignorance. 'They were in *Tit-Bits* two weeks running. With illustrations. They went all the way to France in their boat and they picked up soldiers from the water, and then they brought them all the way back again, and there was explosions and torpedoes and all that, and it was ever so brave of them.'

'I see.' Edith thought of the countless similar stories she had read in the press, and wondered what it was that had marked the twins as especially memorable. 'Were they very handsome?' she asked.

'They were *girls*,' said Nora, triumphantly, her war knowledge having topped Edith's at last. 'It said someone named a rose after them, and they got a letter from the Queen and from the princesses, and they—' From somewhere outside, the unmistakable slow howl of the siren began and Nora's lips bunched inward as though she had bitten on a rotten tooth.

'They won't come here, will they?' she asked.

'I hope not.'

But there was another note behind the siren, a low, uneven growl, and they both heard it, tilting their heads like pointers. They found me in Wimbledon, thought Edith, and now they're looking for me again – though she knew that the thought was nonsensical, that those boys in the cockpits saw nothing, really, except the flames of their own making, and the glint of the river.

'Shall we go to the basement?' she asked, and Nora nodded, and, after a moment, took her hand.

It wasn't until the evening that the bomb fell. Sirens came and went all afternoon until no one could remember whether the last one had been the alert or the all-clear, and no one knew whether to make the dash for the underground, or to stick it out in the dusty basement. The noise, when it came, was colossal, the darkness instantaneous, but Edith, with the ceiling dropping around her, felt none of the terror and euphoria of her first bomb; her heart gasped once and then raced steadily onwards, and she knew that she was alive, and likely to stay that way. So when she took her torch and climbed the stairs into the rubble and chaos of the museum, and – under the broken roof, with the searchlights tilting overhead – began her second

Assessment and Rectification round of the day, she couldn't (as Dolly afterwards tried to) ascribe her actions to shock. It was more of a terrible curiosity – the same emotion that had driven her up the stairs at Wimbledon. And just as at Wimbledon, where Pamela's prissy little room, and the dank scullery and the lounge that Edith didn't give a fig for had survived intact, so the mannequins in the Enemies of Great Britain display needed little more than a brush down and the Hall of Sporting Champions had suffered nothing worse than a toppled footballer or two, while her favourite room, her own room, the central gallery where the kings and queens of England posed in finest silk and stiff brocade, in ermine and velvet and Bruges lace, in gowns of deepest crimson, of ivory and of midnight blue, was devastated. The soft smudge of torchlight swept across a royal massacre, a waxen Ekaterinburg.

There was Mary, Queen of Scots blown into the ranks of the Plantagenets, there was George IV pinned under a roof beam, and poor, plain, unlauded Queen Anne half-stripped and decapitated. And in a line across the centre of the room, each lying on the legs of the next like a coxless six, lay Henry's wives. Here and there, through the layer of filth and plaster that covered them, a tiny spot of colour showed – the green lining of Anne Boleyn's sleeve, a hint of crimson at Catherine Howard's breast. A tiny pattering noise began, like weak applause, and, unthinkingly, Edith raised her torch towards the roof. A fine rain slanted across the beam.

There was a shout, and the crunch of running footsteps. '*Off.* Turn that bloody torch off.'

'Sorry.'

'I should bloody well hope you are. Anyone hurt in here?'

'I don't think so. We were all in the basement.'

'I'll go and check, then.'

She stood in darkness as the warden walked away and she listened to the rain falling, to the dust turning to mud and the plaster to glue.

NEWSREEL

November 1940

There were two viewing rooms at the Ministry of Information: the superior, with padded seats and a ventilation fan, for official screenings, and the intra-departmental, with sticky wooden benches and a pervasive smell of sweat. Catrin, in the latter, remained standing and breathed through her mouth while watching the scrap of film, stopwatch and script in hand.

INTERIOR OFFICE

Two women sit either side of an interview table.

Woman 1

Are you good with your hands? *3 seconds*

Woman 2

Yes

Woman 1

Have you ever used an electric sewing machine either at home or in a factory or workshop?

6 seconds

Woman 2

No.

Woman 1

Do you think you could learn? *2 seconds*

Woman 2

Yes.

Woman 1

Good. Because our soldiers need parachutes, and we need women who can make them.

5 seconds

Woman 2:

(Smiles.)

The scene was a two-shot, filmed over the shoulder of Woman 1, so that whereas Woman 2's face was fully visible, only part of the back of Woman 1's head was in view. This was known in the films division, Catrin had discovered, as a 'salvage shot', since Woman 1, her lips invisible, could be redubbed to say anything that would fit in the gaps between Woman 2's replies, thus saving on the cost of shooting new footage.

Back at her desk, Catrin underlined the words 'Food Flash' at the top of a piece of scrap paper, re-read the Ministry of Food guidelines she'd been sent, took out the stopwatch again and set to work on a draft.

INTERIOR OFFICE

Two women sit either side of an interview table.

Woman 1

Do your family often eat carrots?

Woman 2

Yes.

Woman 1

Did you know that the Vitamin A in carrots can improve night vision by 50 per cent?

Woman 2

No.

Woman 1

Will you eat even more of them now?

Woman 2

Yes.

Woman 1

Splendid. Because if they're good enough for our night fighters then they're good enough for our children.

Woman 2

(Smiles.)

STOCK SHOT OF BUNCH OF CARROTS.

V/O

Raw or cooked, they're healthy, nutritious and economical.

She missed Ivy and Lynn. The So-Bee-Fee campaign was still extant – she had spotted the latest instalment in *Woman's View* – but someone else was writing the captions now, and the characters' dialogue, which she'd tried so carefully to differentiate, had become interchangeable. Bert had also become interchangeable, carelessly appearing as Lynn's husband one month, Ivy's the next, while the illustrations were once again spiralling away from reality: in the last one she'd seen, Ivy had been frying sausages while wearing an evening stole.

Catrin read the Ministry of Food memorandum again. *Also swedes*, it said at the bottom.

FOOD FLASH #2

INTERIOR OFFICE

Two women sit either side of an interview table.

```
Woman 1
  Would your family like to try something new?

Woman 2
  Yes.

Woman 1
  Can you think of a vegetable that's not only gaily
  coloured and British-grown but which won't break
  the bank?
```

The office door opened and one of the script-editors stuck his head in.

'Call for you in scenarios,' he said, disappearing again.

There was a telephone on her own desk, but it wasn't connected to anything. The words 'her own desk' were similarly redundant since she shared it with one of the office messengers, a man in his sixties who had generously come out of retirement in order to contribute to the war effort. Personnel had decided to utilize his forty years in industry by giving him the job of occasionally taking pieces of paper from one floor to another, and he spent most of his time sleeping with his head next to Catrin's typewriter. He opened an eye as she stood up. 'Any jobs?' he asked, plaintively.

'Sorry, Clive. Bad night?'

'Incendiaries,' he said. 'Don't mind incendiaries, you can do something about them. Feel useful.' He closed his eyes again, and Catrin took her notepad and left the office. There had been incendiaries in her own street, too, a clatter at midnight like a shower of tin cans, and she'd pulled on a coat and grabbed the bucket of sand, and hurried up the steps from the basement to find that one of the silver cylinders had lodged in the guttering above the porch and was burning fiercely. The boy from the first-floor flat had leaned out of the window with a mop handle and flipped the canister on to the pavement, and Catrin had doused the flame with the sand, and in the sudden darkness she had seen a dozen other hurrying silhouettes, a dozen other small, bright fires.

There had been, in addition, the usual disturbances of what she was coming to regard as an average night: the near-continuous drone of the raiders, the distant crumps that would suddenly move nearer, as if a Titan were striding across London, and the thunderous, reassuring noise of the guns firing from the park half a mile away, each rolling discharge followed by the crack of the shell-burst, the plink of shrapnel on pavement and road. The all-clear had sounded at a quarter to four and Catrin had slept after that, but Ellis had snored through the lot, curled like a comma on their mattress under the stairs. He was spending three nights a week now on duty at the ARP post beside Baker Street, and another two sharing a fire-watching rota on the roof of the Paddington studio, and on the evenings that he spent at home he ate hugely, and fell asleep at the table.

Catrin had made him a cup of tea before she left for work, and had kissed him between the eyebrows, the only area of skin visible above the quilt. Outside the flat, she'd paused, yawning, to watch an auxiliary fireman collecting the spent incendiaries in a sack, and the fireman had yawned too, and almost everyone on the bus had been dozing. Sleep, in London, was no longer a nightly staple but a sporadic snack, to be snatched at and savoured during any spare moment.

In the scenario office, the boys were swarming around a desk at one end; at the other, a telephone receiver lay on top of a pile of scripts.

'Is this for me?' called Catrin. One of the heads looked around and nodded impatiently. She lifted the phone and heard nothing but a low roaring sound, like a distant sea. 'Catrin Cole,' she said. 'Hello?' There was no answer. After a moment or two she replaced the receiver on the cradle.

'Who was it from?' she asked, wandering over to the group. Greville, a boy of twenty with spectacles and an unpleasantly vigorous moustache, looked round at her and shook his head.

'Haven't the foggiest. Gone dead, has it?'

'Yes.'

'There was a landmine on Tottenham Court Road last night, hole the size of a bus outside Heal's. Probably nixed half the cables in the area.' He was already turning back to the object of general interest (not to mention hilarity): a small sheet of paper with a block of typing on it.

'What are you looking at?' asked Catrin, hovering behind them. 'May I see?' For a few seconds the wall of shoulders seemed deliberately to exclude her, and then there was a grudging shift, and a narrow gap opened up.

'It's just a memo,' said one of the sets of shoulders, tetchily.

12 November 1940

I wish to pass on the results of several recent meetings with representatives of American distribution companies. These representatives are somewhat disturbed by what they invariably describe as the 'lack of oomph' in the films with overseas potential produced under the aegis, or with the guidance, of this department. This is, in part, a reflection of the difficulties the American public have with the British tradition of understatement, and the laconic way in which much bravery is habitually reported and portrayed. There is also the perennial American problem with the British accent, usually defined as 'plummy and muffled', but underlying everything is the key question of how <u>entertaining</u> these films are – and by 'films' I refer to both documentary shorts and theatrical productions. The need to maintain and accentuate pro-British feeling in the USA cannot be overstated, and it is imperative to remind ourselves – every day, if necessary – that <u>for a film to be good propaganda it must also be good entertainment</u>.

While the following list of suggestions by a prominent American distributor may not be seen as possible, practical, or even desirable, I would ask you to read and absorb it without derision, as a useful reflection of the minds of our American cousins, whose continued goodwill towards us is vital. Remember that the Nazis have never underestimated the propaganda power of the moving image; it would be stupidity itself for us to do so.

S Bernstein
Special Advisor, film division.

Mr Goldfarb's suggestions:

i) Plenty of oomph factory girls at work and play.
ii) Plenty of oomph army/navy/flyer girls at work and play.
iii) A reel with commentary by the Queen, dealing with a non-military subject: women and children, brides in wartime etc.
iv) Bangs, crashes, walls falling over, men shouting, ambulances careening (skidding) round corners are all good, but can you make the bangs really loud. American viewers want to be knocked off their feet.
v) Something with George Bernard Shaw in it. Just a reel, though, I don't think our audience could take anything longer.

By the time that Catrin had finished reading the memo, she was standing entirely on her own, the others having reassembled at the far end of the office, where the tea-trolley had made an appearance. She would have liked to ask someone why it was that cinematic bangs and crashes were, indeed, never as loud as the real thing. She would have liked to speculate on what the desired 'something with George Bernard Shaw in it' might be. (A best beard contest? A display of Irish dancing?) She would have liked to discuss the air of strained urgency that the memo seemed to exude, and the intense seriousness of what was, at least nominally, a note about entertainment. Instead, she was left doing her usual impression of The Last Kipper in the Shop.

It had been like this since she had first started at the Ministry.

Once it had been established that she was not the extra stenographer that scenarios had been hoping for (and some of the boys had asked her several times, as if she might have banged her head on the way in and be suffering from temporary amnesia), then the welcoming smiles, the appreciatively raised eyebrows, the race to take her coat and to find her a chair had all stopped. It was universally viewed as unfair, as *insulting*, she gathered, that a woman had been brought in especially to write women's dialogue. 'If there's a dog in the script then we don't employ a Jack Russell to come up with "woof woof", do we?', as one of her colleagues had put it, and she'd been allocated an office two hundred yards from everyone else, and largely ignored, her assignments arriving by messenger and being dispatched the same way. At story meetings from which she couldn't be excluded she was invariably the note-taker ('I'm sure Catrin will type that up for us'), while at lunchtimes her colleagues disappeared to the pub, failing to invite her on every occasion. Sometimes, at the end of a day on which Clive, her desk companion, had been particularly busy or determinedly unconscious, Catrin's throat would ache with the pressure of unuttered speech.

At the tea-trolley, Greville was discussing North Africa with the authority of someone who had both the ear of Winston Churchill and access to the complete military plans of both sides. There were no biscuits left. Unacknowledged, Catrin slid away, and was halfway down the corridor when someone shouted her name. Another phone call. She trudged back and picked up the receiver.

'Buckley,' said the voice, dry as chaff. 'I'm heading in on one of my special advisory visits. Unpaid of course. Where are you having lunch?'

⋆

Gravy soup v
Irish Stew
Curried vegetables and rice v
Mock-chocolate pudding v
Marmalade tart

'What's the 'V' stand for?' asked Buckley.

'Victory,' said Catrin, picking up a tray. 'We're supposed to have at least one item off the victory menu every day. They're made from ingredients that don't have to be imported.'

'Yes, I'd heard talk of the Kentish mock-chocolate harvest.' He looked around the Ministry canteen and shook his head. 'Put that back,' he said, indicating the tray. 'We're going elsewhere.'

'I'm sorry, but I can't afford to go to a restaurant.'

'Elsewhere's not a restaurant.'

Elsewhere was a pub, very dark and somewhere near Charlotte Street. Catrin, ravenous, sipped a gin and orange and felt instantly drunk.

'I'm working for Baker's at the moment,' said Buckley.

Catrin nodded.

'You don't know what that is, do you?'

'No,' she said, blushing.

'They make variety films, and comedies – did you see *The Beaux and the Belles?*'

'No.'

'*Mr Harper's Hat?*'

'No.'

'*Just Around the Corner?*'

'No.'

'I bet you watch French films, don't you?'

'I don't,' she found herself saying, defensively, as if accused of an impropriety. 'Well yes, sometimes. Did you see *La Grande Illusion*?'

'No.'

There was a pause, while Buckley drank the whole of his pint and a brandy chaser. 'They've got quite a bit of clout,

Baker's,' he said, carrying on as if he'd only taken a breath since his last sentence. 'You might not know who they are, but they make a lot of money, pay a lot of taxes to the Treasury. Entertainment for the masses. Know any?'

'Any what?'

'Any of the masses.'

'What do you mean?'

'Just wondering.'

'Do you—' Infuriatingly, she could feel herself beginning to blush again. 'Do you think I'm a . . . a nob or something?'

'I don't know. Are you?'

'*No*. I'm Welsh.'

'Plenty of Welsh nobs.'

'Not in Ebbw Vale. My father's a joiner.'

'And what about your husband?'

'He's an artist.'

'Plenty of swanky artists.'

'He's not swanky, he's part of the Paddington Group. It's a collective.'

'What does that mean?'

'It's a group of artists who share the same aims and principles. They don't work for the commercial sector.'

'How do they eat, then?'

'They undertake commissions for organizations with sympathetic beliefs.'

'Can't be too many of those.'

'And they hold exhibitions.'

'Oh, they're allowed to sell their paintings?'

'Of course they are.'

'But not to capitalists, presumably. So this set of painters, The Battersea Bunch—'

'The Paddington Group.'

'Are they all starving for art or do some of them come from money?'

'I think one or two of them have a private income.'

'Does your husband?'

'No, he doesn't. He was an apprentice engineer before he went to art college.'

'So does he have *any* income?'

'He used to—'

'Beside yours, I mean.'

'. . . he used to teach,' she continued, determinedly. 'And he's curated exhibitions, and written catalogues. And he works all the time. He hardly ever stops.'

'And does he paint proper pictures or is he a member of the upside-down brigade?'

'He's . . .' But she couldn't do it, she couldn't offer the phrase, 'the perceived domination of man by the artefactual landscape', to that coarse, sarcastic face, it would be like handing a trembling faun to a man with a club. 'If you saw his pictures, you'd know they were good,' she said, simply.

He nodded and picked up his beer glass. 'Another drink?'

'No, thank you. Can I ask what this is all about? Only, I should really get back to work.'

'This is work.'

She waited while he bought another pint and another chaser. 'Baker's,' he said, sitting down again, 'was founded by Edwin Baker who was actually a butcher, in Hornchurch, who wanted to make films. And he did, just after the Great War, he bought a camera and hired some actors and made one about Vikings in a wood by his house. And then he made another one, about cave-men, and then he stopped making films himself and just ran the company. He's still running it. Him and his brother.' Buckley took a long swallow and eyed the ceiling for a moment or two. 'I write for them sometimes. Usually with a man called Parfitt. Usually comedies. I do structure, Parfitt does jokes. *The Ladder Gang* was the last one, about firemen. Graham Moffatt was in it, made a packet. You won't have seen it, of course.'

Catrin folded her arms.

'Sure you won't have another drink?' asked Buckley.

'No, thank you.'

'So what's happened now is that Edwin Baker, being a patriotic sort of chap, three grandsons in the army, wants to break the Baker's mould and make a war film, the whole she-bang, main feature, bombs and bullets and so on, not a good idea, in my opinion—'

'Why not?'

'Because people want to go to the cinema to get away from all that, but never mind. So Baker's very wisely got me and Parfitt on board, since we've spent four months throwing ideas at the Film Division trying to get one to stick. You know their criteria?'

'No,' she said, with sudden irritation. 'I don't know anything.'

He smiled, apparently pleased at having goaded her. 'They want films about what we're fighting for – the British way of life and civilian endeavour and all that sort of thing. And they want it optimistic but they also want it realistic, because half of us have been bombed, and all of us know someone in the forces.'

'And have you got an idea to stick?'

'Very nearly.' He leaned back and linked his hands across his stomach. 'They've latched on to the idea of dramatizing true stories – John Citizen fights back, hurrah for the little man and so forth – and Parfitt spotted a likely one in a newspaper. We've mentioned it to the bigwigs and they've given us some preliminary encouragement, but they're tiresomely keen on authenticity. *Tiresomely* keen . . .'

⋆

South of Regent's Park there were no straightforward journeys any more. Every third street had a yellow diversion sign and a rope slung between the pavements, from which fluttered a collection of handwritten notices: '*For Wallace & Sons, please enquire at . . .*' '*Bettafitt Shoes relocated in . . .*' Beyond the rope there might be devastation or there might be an eerie intactness, the latter supplemented by a notice reading 'UNEXPLODED BOMB' and a bored policeman. Every morning brought a fresh rewrite of the bus routes – or, rather, not a rewrite but a wild, free-form extemporization of how to get from A to B via Q, H and Z.

There were side streets that had never seen a bus before, where the pavements were so narrow that pedestrians had to flatten themselves into doorways, and passengers found themselves face to face with a tortoiseshell cat in a window, or an old lady rinsing her teeth. There were buses that had never been to London before, buses sent from the north and the west to replace the damaged fleet: brown buses, fawn buses, buses with a destination board that read 'All Stops to Harrogate', and which might be the 279, or the 24 or the 73, depending on the day, the hour and the whims of the Luftwaffe. Catrin, travelling east, waved down a maroon single-decker ('Corporation of Weston-Super-Mare') that seemed to be heading roughly in the right direction.

Her thoughts were still sticky with sleep, and she found herself staring out of the window, listening to the conversation of the two girls in the seat behind.

'I said, "I'm not staying in every evening." I said, "You've got to be flipping well joking." '

'What did she say?'

'She said, "You're coming to the shelter with us whether you like it or not." '

'That's not fair, is it?'

'No, it's not.'

'What sort of life is that, going straight from work to the shelter?'

'I know. And Alan had got the tickets already, for me and Shirley and Ivor, and she just wanted me to waste them.'

'So what did you say?'

'I said, "It's not fair, you've had *your* time, haven't you, but you don't want us to have ours." I said, "I'm going to ask my dad." '

'And what did he say?'

'Oh, I got round him all right . . .'

The bus passed a succession of newly pulverized buildings, smoke still rising from some, fire hoses snaking across the broken bricks, rescue workers standing caked in red dust, the whole enveloped in the same filthy, pervasive smell of rubble and household gas and spent explosive that lingered on Ellis's ARP clothes when he came home. His eyes were permanently bloodshot from the dust. On most mornings he went straight from the wardens' pillbox to the studio.

'Have you got the list?' said one of the girls in the seat behind.

'You picked it up.'

'Yes, but then Miss Clifford took it back again, didn't she, and added the muslin and pins? And then she gave it to you.'

'She didn't.'

'She did. She gave me the coupons and the map and she gave you the list.'

'She *didn't*.'

'She did, Nora. Look in your bag.'

The sounds of frantic searching ensued.

'Well, it doesn't matter, I can remember most of it. Six yards of butter muslin, thirty packets of pins . . .'

'She said even *one* packet would be a blessing.'

'Number 3 Singer sewing machine needles, to send to Miss Beadmore.'

'Ooh yes. Did you see that picture postcard she sent?'

'I did. I said to Miss Clifford that I thought it looked a dump.'

'I know, that's just what I said, I thought it looked a terrible dump.'

'No shops. No parade. No pier.'

'Grass going right up to the beach.'

'A real hole.'

'I'd go mad if *I* lived there . . .'

The bus juddered over a series of metal plates that formed

a temporary bridge across a chasm in the tarmac, and then halted. In the road ahead, a man was sweeping glass into the gutter. That noise – rhythmic, almost musical – was to be heard everywhere now, the signature-tune of daytime London. A second broom joined the first, syncopating the beat, and the bus driver switched off his engine. A church bell became audible, ringing the three-quarters. Catrin craned her neck to view the road ahead and then caught the conductress's eye.

'Where are you off to?' asked the woman.

'Liverpool Street Station.'

'If I was you,' she said, 'I'd get a taxi.'

The novelty of taking an authorized trip to the seaside wore off very quickly. Even though Catrin arrived on the platform just after seven thirty, the 8.05 to Southend was already full – and not 'full' in the pre-war sense of there being no seats left, but 'full' as in the dictionary definition; the windows were a flattened collage of coats and duffle bags and the odd whitened palm.

'Want a seat?' asked a private, as Catrin passed his carriage. He was wedged diagonally across one of the open doors, acting as a human brace against the press of people behind him. 'Come on, gorgeous, I'll get you a seat.'

'There aren't any seats,' said Catrin.

'Yes, there are. Give us a kiss and I'll get you a seat.'

'Give me a kiss, too,' shouted another face, appearing under the private's armpit.

'Honestly,' said the private. 'I can get you a seat. A kiss would be nice but it's not compulsory.'

'Where's there a seat?'

'I'll show you. They're keeping it warm for you – they told me to look out for a peach.'

He stuck out a hand, and after a moment's hesitation, Catrin took it and found herself being hauled through the crush, ducking under elbows, stumbling over cases, edging past vertical card schools and children sleeping in luggage racks. 'Here you are,' said the soldier, stopping suddenly and moving to one side to reveal a narrow doorway billowing with cigarette smoke. 'Your barouche awaits.' It was the train lavatory – a lavatory, moreover, already occupied by three Anzacs, one of whom was sitting down.

'Please,' said the latter, getting hastily to his feet. 'Be our guest. There's no lid, but when your bum's covering the hole the stink's not nearly so bad.'

At ten to ten, the 8.05 crept from under the blacked-out glass roof of the station and into the sunlight, and Catrin took a batch of mimeographed press cuttings out of her handbag. They had arrived in an envelope the day before, with a note from Buckley that read, '*You may as well have a look at these*', and she had saved them for the journey. The briefest was from *The Times*, though it formed part of a full-page article describing civilian endeavours at Dunkirk.

> *. . . among the crew of the Leigh-on-Sea cockle fleet, seven of whose vessels made the cross-Channel journey, and six of which returned, were a boy of fourteen, a man of seventy-five, and twin sisters who piloted their father's boat, returning safely with over fifty evacuated soldiers on board . . .*

The *Daily Express* was a little more expansive, giving the sisters' names (Rose and Lily Starling) and the precise number of rescued soldiers on board their vessel. (Fifty-four, twenty-two of them French.) The *News Chronicle* had discovered that the twins' father, whose boat it was, had been bedridden, and that they had set out without his knowledge or permission. They cited the sisters as 'modest' and quoted Rose Starling as saying: 'We'd rather not talk about it, we were only trying to help.' The *Daily Mail* had decided that the name of their boat, the *Redoubtable*, summarized all that was great about the British people in their time of trial: 'A time in which even the fragrant English rose has discovered its thorns.' All three newspapers had compared the twins to Grace Darling, while the *Daily Mirror* had gone one better and dubbed them 'Britannia's Daughters'. *Tit-Bits* had pulled out all the stops and given the sisters a double-page spread in their 'true-life story' section, with an illustration showing the *Redoubtable* ploughing through mountainous seas, piloted by two wasp-waisted blondes, both apparently oblivious of a Stuka heading directly for the wheelhouse.

> *. . . Lily's gaze met that of her sister. 'Is it very wrong of me to be afraid, Rose?' she asked.*
>
> *'No, of course not,' her twin replied. 'My heart's pounding like a drum, but there are Tommies waiting for us, needing our help, and at last we have the chance to fight a little bit of this blasted war ourselves. Let's grit our teeth, Lily, and try and get there as fast as we can.' As she spoke there came the deadly roar of a fighter, and the ratta-tat-tat of bullets along the wooden hull of the little ship [see illus]. 'Missed,' shouted Lily, shaking her fist as the 'plane roared away. 'Attagirl,' said Rose, laughing, 'and look!' she added, pointing ahead.*
>
> *Lily gasped. 'Dunkirk,' she said, in an awed whisper.*

After picking up a boat-load of soldiers ('*Lumme, Sarge, they're girls!*') and dodging torpedoes on the way back ('*They may be girls, but they're as good as any navy man*'), they returned home to their crosspatch father, who first told them off and then toasted them, gruffly, with his last nip of pre-war whisky. Buckley had written: 'GOOD ENDING' beside the final paragraph, and a sarcastic 'PITY GRABLE AND STANWYCK AREN'T AVAILABLE' across the drawing.

'What's that bit about Grable?' asked one of the Anzacs, squinting over Catrin's shoulder. She passed him the article and he looked at it, frowning. 'Not available for what?'

'For the film of this story.'

'Grable and Stanwyck, playing *twins*? No, I don't see that.'

'I think—' began Catrin.

'Betty Grable?' said the youngest of them, a blonde boy with gentle, sleepy eyes. 'She's my favourite, she's . . . she's . . .' Words failed him.

'Grable's what you'd call *cute*, but Stanwyck's more of a . . . a *broad* if you get my meaning. Of course, it depends if these girls who went to Dunkirk are identical or not. Are they?'

'I don't know,' said Catrin.

'So when's this film out?'

'Oh, not for ages. It hasn't even been written yet.'

'But you know about it?'

'Yes.'

'How do you know about it?'

'Because . . .'

'Because you're an *actress*?' asked the blonde boy.

She snorted. 'No. Because I'm working for one of the writers, and he needs a first-hand account of the story.'

'You mean you're going to talk to these sisters?'

'Yes.'

'When?'

'Oh . . .' She checked her watch. 'In about an hour.'

It was three hours, as it transpired. There was a long delay just outside Southend while the local police checked passengers' travel permits, and then the coastal line turned out to have been closed by a time-bomb, and there were no taxis to be found. In the end, she hitched a lift, and arrived at Leigh-on-Sea by coal lorry.

Number 15, Whiting Walk was not the picturesque fisherman's cottage that she had envisaged, but an end-of-terrace with a cracked gutter, from which a long smear of green stained the brickwork. The glass in the front door was missing, and the gap had been plugged by a piece of tea chest, across which the letters INEST CEYL were still legible. Catrin waited a good minute after knocking, and was reaching for the brass anchor again when a noise from the interior stayed her hand. There was whispering, and then the sound of a woman nervously clearing her throat. After a moment, the door opened just an inch or two. Catrin could see nothing but a section of wallpaper, and an elbow, clad in grey wool.

'Is that Miss Starling?' she asked. 'One of the Miss Starlings?'

'Yes it is.' It was a chirrup of a voice, the sort of voice that a child would invent for a doll.

'My name's Catrin Cole. Did you receive my letter?'

'Yes.'

'So you understand that I was hoping for a chat with you – with both of you? About your story?'

'Yes.'

The door remained almost closed. There was another whispered conversation from within and then the resumption of the chirrup.

'Dad said we wasn't to talk to the newspapers.'

'But I'm not from a newspaper.'

'We know. You're from the pictures, aren't you?'

'Yes . . .' said Catrin, uncertainly.

There was a final burst of whispering ('*It's all right, Lily*'), and then the door opened suddenly. The tiny voice belonged to a woman at least six inches taller than Catrin, with a round, pale face, fine hair pulled back into a bun, and large, red hands, one of which took Catrin's wrist and drew her into the unlit passage. The door shut firmly behind her.

'We're not supposed to let no one in,' said the woman, and then giggled, suddenly, hand over her mouth. The giggle was echoed by her sister, standing just behind her. They were identical, dressed in matching grey cardigans and rose-print house-dresses. 'If Dad comes back,' said the first, 'we'll have to let you out the yard. There's a gate into the lane.'

'Are you expecting him?' asked Catrin.

'No. He's shrimping.'

'Shrimping,' said her sister, in a tiny voice.

'He shouldn't be here till dark.' Though it was already dark in the hall, the only source of illumination an open door into a back room, through which an oblong of daylight extended.

'So can we have a chat?' asked Catrin, tentatively.

The sisters looked at each other. 'All right,' said the first, with sudden daring.

'And can I ask – who's who?'

'She's Lily,' said the first, 'and I'm Rose.'

They chose the front parlour to sit in, and Catrin, ushered to an upright armchair upholstered in slippery chintz, knew that she should feel honoured. It was, clearly, a room used only for special occasions – for funerals, at a guess, and for Christmas Day, judging by the pair of faded paper stars on the mantelpiece. The grate was empty, and spotless, the room frigid. The sisters sat together on a tiny sofa facing the window, the light on their faces revealing that they were much younger than she'd taken them for – those awful clothes, the old-fashioned hairstyles, had deceived her, they were barely in their thirties. And they weren't identical: Lily's nose had a deep horizontal groove above the tip, like a thumbnail-print scored in clay. They were strapping girls, wide-shouldered, clearly strong. For the first time since seeing them, since hearing those baby voices, Catrin could imagine the sisters handling a boat, setting out across the Channel towards a pall of smoke.

'So,' she said, realizing from the deepening silence that she should speak first. 'You went to Dunkirk.'

Rose glanced at Lily and then back at Catrin. 'No,' she said.

For one wild moment, Catrin thought she'd come to the wrong house: perhaps the Starling sisters, loquacious and cinematic, were next door. 'You *didn't* go?'

'No. We meant to go but the engine stopped five miles out and it was a broken bearing, so we couldn't do nothing about it, and we was drifting because there wasn't no wind. And then this steam tug out of Sheerness was coming back from France full of soldiers, so they give us a tow to Dover, and we took some of their soldiers because there was so many on board they was spilling over the rails.' Her sister nodded in mute confirmation. 'And someone must have seen us get back there,' continued Rose, 'and thought we'd gone all the way to France, but Dad said we wasn't to talk to no newspapers so we couldn't tell them they was wrong.'

Catrin looked at the blank page of her notepad. She had travelled for five and a half hours for this. 'Flesh out the newspaper story,' Buckley had said. 'We're looking for a bit of colour, a few scraps of authenticity to wave at the men from the ministry.'

Scrapless, she groped for another question. 'What sort of boat was it?'

'Flat-bottomed thirty-six-foot gaff-cutter Bawley with a Kelvin petrol engine.'

Catrin watched her pen obediently write '*36 foot*' and '*petrol engine*'. Her brain seemed to have entirely stopped working.

'And did . . . did anything else happen on the journey?'

'Well . . .' Rose gave a sudden hiccough of laughter. 'When we got to Dover, and they was all disembarking, one of the soldiers had a kit bag with him and suddenly it woofed and it give us such a fright, and it turned out there was a dog in it he was trying to smuggle in. And then one of the Frenchies give Lily a kiss.' Her sister smiled shyly, and then whispered something to Rose.

'Lily wants to know, if you're in films have you met Robert Donat?'

'No,' said Catrin, 'I'm afraid not.'

'Or John Clements?'

'No.'

'Lily's favourite's Robert Donat and mine's John Clements, and Lily likes Errol Flynn as well. We always go to the Corona on Tuesdays and Thursdays when Dad goes to Oddfellows, and sometimes we go on Sundays.'

Catrin smiled and nodded. If I leave now, she thought, and I'm lucky with a lift to Southend, I might still get back to London before the evening siren. She closed her notepad; Rose's eyes followed the movement.

'Will it be a film?' she asked, and there was such raw hope in her voice that Catrin almost flinched. She opened her mouth to attempt an answer.

'Because they change things in films, don't they?' said Rose. 'And they—' she broke off and both sisters turned their heads in synchrony. There was a tiny noise from the street, a scuff of feet on the doorstep.

'*Dad*,' said Lily, and she was on her feet and pushing Catrin towards the parlour door and along the passageway to the kitchen, and Catrin, infected by the panic that imbued the air like gas, had run halfway across the yard, and was struggling to find a gap in the vast damp barrier of pegged sheets, when there was a call from the house.

'It's not. It's not him.'

She looked back, and saw Lily and Rose holding hands in the kitchen doorway.

'It's not him,' said Rose. She was still a little breathless. 'It was the Street Savings Committee woman, Mrs Gerraghty. She usually comes tomorrow.'

'Oh . . .' Catrin, feeling idiotic, let drop a section of sheet.

'She's collecting for a Spitfire.'

'I thought it was Dad,' said Lily. Red circles stood out on her cheeks, like stage make-up.

'It's all right, Lily,' said Rose. 'It's all right.'

Catrin looked from one to the other. 'What's the matter? What would happen if he found me here?'

It was Lily who answered with an unconscious gesture, her hand lifting towards her damaged nose. Catrin found herself echoing the movement, and clamped her fingers together.

'When did he do that? Was that when you got back from Dover?'

Lily shook her head. 'No, it was last year.'

'But—'

'We shouldn't stay out here,' said Rose. 'The neighbours might see you.'

In the kitchen, beside the unlit range, they formed a little huddle, Lily a step away from the others, keeping one ear cocked for the front door.

'He won't be back until dark,' Rose repeated, but there was a pervasive feeling of urgency, as if the sisters were correspondents under fire, relaying news between shell-bursts. Catrin looked at Rose's face, a foot from her own, at the mild grey eyes, at the white line, like a diagonal parting, that ran through one of her eyebrows.

'Why does he do it?' asked Catrin.

'Well, he's got a temper on him,' said Rose, in the same tone with which she might have complained of smelly feet, or a tendency to snore. 'If he gets angry then you have to watch out.'

'What makes him angry?'

'Burnt bits in food,' said Lily, pulling at a button on her cardigan.

'And singers on the wireless,' said Rose. 'And talking at table. And he won't have strangers in the house.'

'But you let me in,' said Catrin.

'We oughtn't to have, really.'

Lily let out a little sigh, like a kettle taken off the hob. 'But you're in the pictures,' she said.

'I'm only . . .' Catrin looked at Lily's expression and couldn't bring herself to admit the tenuousness of her connection.

'And whistling indoors,' added Rose. 'And feeding crumbs to birds because that's like throwing food away. And opening the windows at night.'

'Hair curlers,' said her sister, in a voice barely audible.

'Hair curlers, that's right. And he won't take the smell of cabbage cooking, and we can't have . . .'

Item after item, suffocatingly, the list uncoiled; Catrin felt her throat constrict. 'But however in the world did you come to take the boat?' she asked. It was a feat that suddenly seemed to her more courageous than a dash through gunfire.

'Oh . . . well, the navy at Southend told all the cocklers they wanted boats with crews that could work the beaches, and our dad said he couldn't go to France because the engine wouldn't take it, and the other cocklers give him a bit of stick for that, so he went off and got a bottle.'

'He got tight?'

'Yes, and we knew he'd be asleep for most of the day, so we thought we could get there and back before he woke, but we was sure they wouldn't want women to go, so we went separate from the other cocklers. We thought we'd follow them from a mile back, but then dad was right, he wasn't just saying that about the engine, because we broke down, didn't we?'

'And what happened when you got back?'

'Dad chucked a boot at me, but it missed and went through the front door. And then he chucked the other boot.' She hesitated before touching her eyebrow, lightly.

'But . . .' There was, she realized, a part of the story still missing. '. . . what made you actually decide to go to France? You must have known that it would be terribly dangerous – in all sorts of ways.'

The sisters exchanged the look that Catrin had come to recognize as a simultaneous asking and granting of consent. As usual, it was Rose who answered.

'Eric Lumb, what used to be Dad's first mate, is over there.'

'In France? With the BEF?'

Rose nodded.

'And he's a friend of yours?'

A pause and then another nod.

'And did he get back safely?'

A smile, this time. 'His nan got a postcard. From in Scotland somewhere.'

Lily leaned across and whispered something in her sister's ear.

'Go on, then,' said Rose. 'You get it.' They both watched her disappear into the gloom of the hall.

In the silence, Catrin met Rose's eyes. She didn't ask the question aloud, but Rose answered. 'We promised Mum, see, that we'd look after Dad.'

'But . . .'

'And he don't lay a finger on Lily no more.'

'Why not?'

'Because after she burned that chop I told him it wasn't fair, because she's not as quick as other people. And I said if he did ever chuck a plate at her again I'd push him over the rail next time we was out. He can't swim,' she added.

It took a couple of attempts before Catrin could speak. 'What did he say, then?'

'He didn't say nothing,' said Rose in that little Toytown voice. It was, almost, an admission of triumph.

Lily came back down the stairs with an envelope in her hand. She gave it to Catrin, and watched her face as Catrin extracted two tissue-wrapped publicity photographs.

'Eric got them us for our birthday before he went to France,' said Rose. 'That's Robert Donat in *The Citadel* and that's John Clements in *The Four Feathers*. John Clements's is signed.'

'*Signed*,' repeated Lily, her voice a sigh.

Catrin exclaimed, and admired, and exclaimed again, and held the photographs between her fingertips, as if they were beyond price.

*

In his room on the third floor at Baker Productions, Buckley read her report in silence, holding the paper in his left hand, and scraping his teeth with the nail on the little finger of the right, an activity that seemed to help him to concentrate. Catrin stood with her hands clasped, her shoulders taut with nerves.

She had sweated over the account, aiming for utter verisimilitude, taking as much of the sisters' actual story as was fair and tactful, recounting something of the narrowness of their lives, of their parental burden, keeping their diffidence and their reason for going to Dunkirk, and then filling the thirty-mile gap between engine failure and the French coast with a few understated and plausible phrases, adapted from newspaper reports *('the beach was covered with soldiers and long queues led into the sea . . . As the troops climbed on board the* Redoubtable, *they came under fire from a German plane . . . After ferrying soldiers several times from the beach to one of the larger ships, the sisters were told to pick up a final load and head for home . . . Five miles from the British coast, the boat developed engine problems, and was towed to Dover by a passing steam tug . . .')*. All she had done was to give an account of what *should* have happened, of the story that Rose and Lily deserved.

Buckley reached the end, and gave his incisors a valedictory wipe. 'You haven't described what they look like,' he said.

'Oh . . . they're tall. Light brown hair. Identical. Well, almost identical.'

'Almost?'

'One has a scar on her nose.'

'Can't have that . . . And they're shy?'

'Yes. One's shyer than the other.'

'One shy, one chatty.'

'No, they're both shy.'

'If they're both shy, there's no dialogue. Did you meet the father?'

'No.'

'Sounds a bit of a sod.'

'Yes.'

'What about the boat? Did you see the boat?'

'No.'

'Pity. Still, there's a few useable nuggets to bounce off the MoI.

Have a look at this, Parfitt.' He reached across and slid the paper in front of his co-writer, a man with sparse grey hair and a marbled complexion the colour of brawn. Apart from a monosyllabic greeting when Catrin entered the room, he had neither spoken to nor looked at her, but had sat twirling an unlit cigarette between his fingers and staring out at Soho Square, where a platoon of shirt-sleeved firemen was digging allotments beneath the leafless trees. Now he obediently turned his attention to the report, scanning it rapidly and jabbing a pencil at the odd line.

'Yep,' he said, cryptically, handing it back.

'We can use the smuggled dog,' said Buckley.

'Yep.'

'And the search for the boyfriend. Make him a fiancé.'

'Yep.'

'They'll have to actually find him, of course.'

'Yep.'

'Injured?'

'Yep.'

'Bit of slop.'

'Yep.'

'Father?'

'Don't like him.'

'Nor me, leaves a nasty taste. The drunken sailor aspect's a nice touch, though.'

There was a moment of brooding silence.

'Make him an uncle?' suggested Parfitt.

'That's good, and less chance of the old bastard finding a lawyer. And maybe unc should be on the boat with the girls. Soused. Wakes up with a hangover at Dunkirk.'

'Yep.'

'Tells them to turn down the noise.'

'Yep.'

'Double-take when he sees the Stukas. See your way to a gag or two?'

'Maybe.'

'The stuff on the beaches is fine, needs a story for the way home. Getting a tow's no good.'

'Uncle mends the engine?'

'Miserable sod comes good under fire?'

'Yep.'

'Takes a bullet, maybe. Honourable death, tears all round.' Buckley turned to Catrin. 'All right, we'll work on it.'

'But . . .' She couldn't quite believe the speed with which her carefully constructed story had been first accepted in its entirety, and then torn down and carelessly rebuilt. 'But they did it all by themselves,' she said.

'What?'

'There was no one on board with them. You're giving credit to someone who doesn't even exist.'

Buckley examined his fingertips. 'It's a film.'

'But it's supposed to be based on a true story.'

'All right, let's take a look at this true story.' He picked up the sheet and pretended to re-read it. 'Two spinsters who hardly talk. They go to Dunkirk. They come back. Nothing else happens.' He glanced at Parfitt. 'I told you she was keen on those French films.'

Parfitt made a revving sound which might have been a laugh.

'But . . .' She opened her mouth and then closed it again. *But your version isn't real; but you've made things up; but it won't be the actual truth*. She could say none of these things, she realized. She had momentarily forgotten, in her partisanship, that she herself had invented far more than either of these two men.

'But what?' asked Buckley, bluntly.

She groped for the nub of her argument. 'But I wanted to show how awfully brave they were.'

'Oh, I see.' His tone implied that she might, at last, have said something reasonable. 'We'll be doing that, all right. That's the whole point of it. Was that all?'

'Yes. No. What did you mean by "bit of slop"?'

'"Bit of slop?" It's lovey-dovey stuff, isn't it?'

'Girl talk,' said Parfitt.

'Oh Ian, I thought you were dead,' said Buckley, linking his hands behind his head and addressing the light bulb. 'Oh Jacintha, I couldn't die without seeing the cornflower blue of your eyes a final time.'

'You're not going to write it like that are you?' asked Catrin, horrified.

'Why? How would you write it?'

'Plainer, I suppose. Less flowery. The way that people actually talk.'

'Oh would you, now?' He caught Parfitt's eye for a second and then resumed his wooing of the light bulb. 'Oh Ian, with your strong arms around me, I could travel to the ends of the earth and beyond.'

'I'd better get back.' At the office door, she hesitated. 'So will it be a film?' she asked.

'Depends on the Ministry,' said Buckley.

She thought of Rose and Lily, queuing at the Corona. 'I do hope it happens.'

'And after that the War Office has to pass the storyline. And the army and the navy and Uncle Tom Cobley and all. But if it does go ahead . . .' There was a long, deliberate pause. '. . . we might need someone who can write us a bit of slop.'

It was a moment before she understood him. 'Me, you mean?'

'We tend to use a female for the slop side of things. Parfitt, what was the name of the Scotch one we used last year?'

'Jeannie.'

'Jeannie. Wrote wireless plays before the war. She wasn't too bad. Just getting the hang of things when Baker's had to let her go.'

'Why?' asked Catrin.

'Bun in the oven.' His eyes drifted across to Catrin's. 'Wouldn't want that to happen again.'

She blushed on cue and Buckley grinned, apparently gratified. 'You'd like to work on this film, then?'

'Yes. Very much.'

'You wouldn't get a screen credit.'

'I don't mind.'

'Temporary secondment to this office.'

She nodded.

'Ministry pay.'

'That's all right.'

'Fire-watching rota.'

'Fine.'

'Toilet-cleaning duties.'

'*What?*'

Buckley smiled carnivorously. 'She has her limits, Parfitt.'

Parfitt made the revving sound again. 'We'll test 'em,' he said.

Ellis's studio was flooded with winter sunlight, and full of tiny, early-morning noises: rustles and chirrups from sparrows in the rafters, a pan of size bubbling softly on the gas burner, the scrape of Ellis's spoon as he devoured the cold macaroni cheese that Catrin had brought him in a biscuit tin from home.

'And I've made you some sandwiches,' said Catrin, setting the packet on the table. 'Only meat paste, I'm afraid.'

He nodded, ate the last mouthful and set the tin down. He looked exhausted. There was soot in the lines around his eyes.

'Bad night?' asked Catrin.

'Mmm.' He never told her anything – kept it, she supposed, for the paintings.

'Oh, and I've brought you an apple.' She took it out of her bag and polished it carefully on her skirt.

At the far end of the garage, Perry folded back the doors of the pit, and hopped inside, emerging a few seconds later with a canvas. There was no one else about. Call-up had almost emptied the studio.

'Is there anything else you need? I can come back this evening.'

Ellis shook his head, ran a hand through his hair and shut his eyes for a moment or two, blinking as he re-emerged.

'I'm tired,' he said.

'I know.'

'I'll be better after a coffee.' He brushed her cheek with a finger. 'You're all right?'

'Yes, I'm fine.'

'Anything worrying you?'

'The new job, a bit. I keep thinking that Rose and Lily must have—'

He shook his head. 'Anything serious, I meant.'

'Oh. No.'

'And you always sleep under the stairs even when I'm not there?'

'Yes.'

'Good. Damn sight safer than that public death-trap they've flung up at the end of the road. One skin of bricks and a cement roof . . .' He was turning from her as he spoke, swinging round towards the canvas he'd been working on when she arrived.

The composition was very nearly symmetrical, as if he'd set his easel in the middle of the cobbles. Ahead stretched a terraced street, empty but for a single, distant figure, the perspective forced so that the end of the road was a lurid dot in the middle distance. The long brick facade on either side was intact, but there was no roof above, and nothing behind the front doors but ochre rubble and a low black sky. It was like a vision from a nightmare, the colours heightened, the proportions distorted, and yet it was also, in another way, utterly real. Catrin dabbed at the thought, as if with a fingertip, and then shied away; she had been present at too many heated discussions on the nature of truth in art to feel confident about her own thoughts on the subject.

The word 'serious', though, was another matter. In a way Ellis was right: her current fretting about the script couldn't really be defined as 'serious', and yet, in this strange new existence, the word seemed to have acquired a host of meanings. Every night was serious: you crouched in the dark and the engines stuttered overhead, and then along came morning, and you were still alive, and once you'd got over that surprise you prepared the breakfast and accidentally dropped the only egg on the floor, and for a moment or two *that* was serious, or you discovered that the gas was off when all you had in the house was sausages, or you were halfway to work when your heel broke, and even though you were passing a bomb-site at the time, even though there were ambulances standing by and Heavy Rescue men lying listening for noises in the rubble, it still felt quite serious that you were standing on one leg, half a mile from the Ministry, with the roads all strewn with glass and not a spare minute in the day ahead with which to find a cobbler. It was as if the load were too heavy, the horror too horrible to keep in the head for long, so that the mind kept bobbing back to more manageable degrees of misery, to the Plimsoll line of the ordinary.

And perhaps it was different for Ellis – perhaps that was what people meant by artistic sensibility. Perhaps because eggs and heels and queues and dust and dropped half-crowns meant nothing to him, he could retain that feeling of horror and transmit it on to canvas, but that didn't stop eggs and heels and queues and dust and dropped half-crowns being awfully important in their own way.

'I should get to work,' she said.

She dozed off on the tube, and dropped the biscuit tin, and woke with a start, reaching for the handle of an imaginary bucket.

FOOD FLASH

December 1940

Next door's char, a woman who spent more time arranging things in attractive patterns than actually cleaning them, had lined up the Christmas cards on the mantelpiece in order of size, starting at the austerity end with a two by three inch festive greeting from Ambrose's tailor, and ending at the other with a vast fake-snow-and-glitter affair from 'Cecy and Tommy', which on closer examination turned out to be the front of an old card glued on to a fresh backing. Under her signature, Cecy had written, '*Am treading the boards again – season at the Ipswich Grand, starting with small but delicious part in* The Wild Duck. *Do drop by!!*' Ambrose had amused himself for a moment or two by trying to imagine a less enticing prospect than travelling nearly two hundred miles in order to see Cecy Clyde-Cameron clamp her chops around a morsel of Ibsen: the only rival he could think of was the prospective 'Yule-Tide entertainment' in the basement of Selfridges, the highlight of which – according to the solitary poster he had seen – was to be a demonstration by Camden boy scouts of how to disable a German parachutist.

The only card that had filled Ambrose with an approximation of Christmas cheer was the one at the centre of the mantelpiece. The picture, of course, was execrable: his ex-wife had always favoured the 'Dignity and Impudence' school of sentiment, and the card bore an illustration of a wide-eyed kitten nestling in a warden's helmet. The true seasonal jollity was all on the inside:

Anthea and Harris Pym invite you to see in the New Year with as much good spirit (and good spirits!) as can be mustered. In the event of unwelcome visitations, we shall reconvene in the basement . . .

Beneath these lines, the powerful diagonals of Anthea's signature leaned menacingly over Harris's little scrawl. So with the signature, thus with her marriage. If only as an annual reminder of the joys of divorce, Ambrose welcomed the Pym party – but there were reasons beyond this, reasons that sustained him through an otherwise austere Christmas.

It had been blessedly quiet, of course – at least, until the night of the 29th when the City had caught it – but also unrelievedly dull. There had been none of the usual West End after-show parties or studio thrashes, only a tiny get-together at Sammy's cramped offices on St Martin's Lane, to which not only all the clients had been invited, but also the administrative staff. Ambrose, attending purely as a matter of business, had found himself jammed into a corner with a pimply tea-boy and a middle-aged stenographer whose gigantic bust had pummelled him every time she'd reached past his shoulder for a mince pie. 'The filling's made with *grated parsnip*,' she'd kept saying, as if that were in some way a recommendation. Sammy had made a speech, boasting what an unexpectedly busy year it had been for the agency, and Ambrose had forbore to heckle, although 'unexpectedly busy' seemed a bizarre definition of his own experience: eight short propaganda films, one feature and an offer of rep at Colchester (declined). The feature had promised well – *A Bad Business for the Duke* with Ambrose as the eponymous duke – until he had read the script and found that after three pages his character was found on the floor of the library with a halberd in the back of his skull. It had taken two hours to shoot his dialogue – '*Bring me a whisky, Berners.*' '*A small one, sir?*' '*A large one, damn you, and make it quick*' – and an entire half day lying face-down on a moulting carpet to nail the reveal shot. He had sneezed for hours afterwards.

'Unexpectedly busy?' he said acidly to Sammy after the speech.

'Ah, now . . .' Sammy, sozzled on three-quarters of a pink gin, wagged a finger. 'I was waiting to see you, Ambrose, things are starting to happen.'

'What things?'

'Shtudios re-opening. The industry re-awakening after its long shleep. I've just this week put you forward for a good little role which . . .'

'*Little?*'

'*Good*. A good role. By 'little' I meant, you know . . .' He waved his stump, vaguely.

'Large?' suggested Ambrose.

'Supporting. But *good* supporting.'

'Senior?'

'Your own age.'

'Character role?'

'In a manner of shpeaking, but—'

'Still alive at the end of the film?'

There was a nasty pause.

'For God's sake,' said Ambrose. 'Not another corpse role.'

'No, no, no. It's a very good part. Memorable. You'd be excellent in it, trust me.'

'What is it?'

'No, we'll talk all about it over lunch. You're coming for New Year's Day, of course, with Sophie and me?'

'What *is* it?'

'No,' said Sammy, imbuing the word with an awful arch primness. 'We'll talk about it in 1941. But you should trust me on this, you know, Ambrose, because I'm a very good agent.' He placed a moist palm on Ambrose's shoulder. 'You should take my advice because I always have your very, very best interests at heart.'

Ten per cent of them, thought Ambrose, taking a step backwards. Something collapsed softly beneath his heel and he looked down to see the remains of a mince pie.

'Ooh,' said Sammy, 'give it to me, give it to me! I know a little doggie who'll just *shnap* that up.'

The parsnip mince pies, as it turned out, had been just the start of a thoroughly ersatz Christmas. Next door's char (clearly angling for a tip) had brought him a slice of her home-made plum-cake, and had watched him actually bite into it before informing him that the icing was made from dehydrated potato flavoured with vanilla essence, while Gaston's, the tiny, failing restaurant at the end of the road, where Ambrose ate the occasional meal, had come up with a Christmas lunch of mock foie gras (ingredients unvouchsafed), and a wedge of leather masquerading as 'chateaubriand'. An attempt at decoration had been made – strips of newspaper cut into fringes and patterned in purple ink – but the overall effect had been grim. Ambrose had refused a pirate hat, drunk a bottle of indifferent red, and spent the afternoon asleep in front of the wireless.

Throughout this, he had been succoured by thoughts of New Year's Eve, of the largesse which that awful little spiv Harris Pym, with his so-called 'industrial connections', always managed to provide, and which Ambrose had sorely missed the previous year when 'owing to the international situation' (and how he wished he had a pound for every time he'd heard *that* phrase) there'd been no party. The food! Oh God, the food! There'd been a ham three years ago whose treacle rind and melting coral flesh he could still taste in dreams. There'd been pheasant sandwiches and raised pies, and in 1938 there'd been a vast pink salmon which had lain across the table like a naked naiad. And then there was the wine. And the brandy. And the liqueurs. And the glorious trifles that were always the centre-piece of the buffet, and the rum jellies, and the delicate little langue de chat biscuits that crunched prettily in the mouth. Of course, one had to put up with Anthea's braying friends and their banal conversation, and the terrible swank of the house, and the three brainless Pym boys who looked like replicas of their pop-eyed, slope-shouldered father, and *their* friends (galumphing girls covered in yards of chiffon), and Anthea's mother (pure poison) who always fixed him with eyes like twin bayonets and said, 'How extraordinary! Why on earth did Anthea invite *you*?' To which the correct answer was, undoubtedly, to demonstrate to Ambrose the fabulous and vulgar wealth into which she'd re-married. In some ways he saw his attendance at the party as a favour to Anthea: ostentation needs witnesses, and if he received a little alimentary reward for his kindness, then so much the better.

It was, perhaps, the prospect of a well-filled evening that made the earlier part of New Year's Eve hang rather heavily. It rained all morning, and by lunchtime Ambrose had traced an indefinable ticking sound to the box-room, where a long crack in the ceiling, legacy of a thousand-pounder five streets away, was oozing a bead of water every couple of seconds. He stared glumly at the dark circle on the rug. More bloody expense. He'd already had to replace all the windows, and now it looked as if the builder (a shifty-eyed profiteer straight out of Central Casting) had been right, and the roof actually *did* need looking at. And now it was too late because the entire bloody world needed a new roof, and he was going to have to spend the rest of the war with a zinc bucket in his spare room, and the smell of sodden plaster permeating the house. He put on his coat and hat and went out into the mews. Crossing to Number 8, opposite his own front door, he turned and looked up, and saw a gap in the profile of the gable where a line of ridge tiles had been blown away, the specific moment unnoticed amidst the usual night-time cacophony. The entire front of the house looked assaulted: the new window frames drear with grey undercoat, three panes cracked already, a deep pock-mark above the front door where a chunk of brick had been scooped out by shrapnel. It was not alone in its shame; the previous paintbox prettiness of the mews had gone completely, and shabbiness abounded. Half the houses were actually boarded up, the owners having fled to funk-holes in the country, there presumably to play bridge and leaf through old copies of the *Tatler* until the final All-Clear.

'And are you not leaving London, Mr Hilliard?' his elderly neighbour had asked him, inserting her pugs into a taxi early in the summer.

The idea had barely occurred to him. An actor had to remain visible – if he left London then who would look after his interests? Technically, of course, that was Sammy's job, but Sammy had other clients to deflect him from his duty – and his duty was to remind people (continually, eloquently, forcefully) of Ambrose's existence, because God knows there was no loyalty in the industry any longer. Directors, casting directors, heads of studio; none had the memory of a goldfish, none had a thought beyond 'That actor fellow I saw in that movie yesterday – yes, he'll do, I'm sure he'd be perfect as the lead' and never mind that 'that actor fellow' possessed hands with all the expressivity of a bunch of bananas and a voice like a piccolo, if he were this month's pin-up (or, for that matter, the nephew of the producer) then the job would go to him. Depth, versatility, experience, all counted for nothing. And now, to make matters even worse, those clowns in interest films (or 'documentaries' as one was supposed to call them) had started giving roles to non-actors – actually giving lines of dialogue to people who had been dragged away from their usual jobs in order to re-enact their usual jobs, people who moved like library ladders, spoke like somnambulists and had to be reminded not to stare with cretinous fascination at the camera. Of course, the end result was awful, unbearable, but the party line in the critical press was that it was marvellous, fresh, thrilling etc., and, presumably, if this continued, airmen and firemen and wardens would be spending all their time making films, and actors would be forced to step into the breach and actually fly aircraft and put out fires. It was a vision of anarchy. He had said as much to Sammy at their most recent luncheon at Veeraswamy's and Sammy had agreed, albeit while covertly stuffing an entire

Indian bread into a bag for his dog, and simultaneously trying to catch the eye of a producer on the next table, who was rumoured to be casting a film about the WAAFs with a lead role that was apparently perfect for some little tart on Sammy's books. That was the root cause of Sammy's problem, of course – too many distractions, too many other clients.

New Year's Eve dawdled onward, the rain continuing, and at three o'clock, maddened by the hypnotic 'plink . . . plink . . .' emanating from the box-room, Ambrose took his umbrella and set out along Wigmore Street with no aim in mind other than escape. From Portland Mews to the Serpentine was a vigorous forty-minute walk, and one that he often used when trying to fix dialogue in his memory. Certain, cherished lines had become immoveably attached to particular localities. Cavendish Square, for instance, was a tongue-twisting speech from *The Mysterious Maharajah* (a nice little supernatural thriller, badly photographed, in which he'd played a counterfeit fakir), beginning '*From all the seven seas and the sunsets beyond the seas, and the sirens who serenade in the sands beyond the strand* . . .', while the quarter mile from the back of Bourne & Hollingsworth to Marylebone High Road was the marvellous scene from *The Two Doctors* (1931), in which Dr McFarlane had comforted his dying mentor, Dr Frome: '*My dearest friend, you've taught me not only wisdom, but compassion, not only skill but kindness, you've taught me to use more than my brain – you've taught me to use my heart* . . .' Ambrose had played McFarlane as a Scot, each 'r' rolled to perfection; he'd always had a gift for accents.

It was the Inspector Charnforth Mysteries, however, that had fastened themselves to the final long Hyde Park section of the walk – those complex speeches in which Ambrose's character, Professor Gough, had ruminated upon the case in question, gradually teasing the truth from the web of deceit and presenting it, like a specimen on a plate, to that rough-hewn man of action, Inspector Charnforth. '*Let me see* . . .' the speeches had always begun. '*Let me see if I understand this correctly . . .*' And then, after a series of observations, startling in their perspicacity, the inevitable line, '*But perhaps I should explain . . .*' The director had decided that all academics were strangers to the hairbrush, so Ambrose had been landed with a hideous Einsteinian sunburst of a wig, unflattering in the extreme, but the role itself had been a joy, making up in importance for what it lacked in screen time, each revelatory speech providing the very core of the story.

There had been four films, four nice little box-office successes, and then that rough-hewn man of action Reeve Callaghan, the actor playing the Inspector, had been caught with his arm down a chorus boy's trousers, and the fifth of the series (*Inspector Charnforth and the Mystery of the Yellow Topaz*) had been shelved two weeks into shooting. Reeve had fled to Tangiers, and Ambrose had suggested a series entitled 'The Professor Gough Mysteries', but there had been the usual failure of imagination on the part of the studios, and one of the best roles of his career had been mothballed. And people like Sammy told him that he shouldn't be bitter!

He could still remember the unfilmed speech: '*. . . but perhaps I should explain, for there are as many angles to this mystery as there are facets on the tawny stone at its centre. Each one, in turn, can capture the light and guide it towards our eyes . . .*' It was supposed to have been uttered in the Fellows garden at an unnamed Cambridge College, and by the time the picture was cancelled, the set had already been built in a corner of Stage 4 at Pinewood, a painted Eden of greensward and roses, hollyhocks and lilies. '*. . . for imagine how simple it was for Philip Jeffrye-Hale, every inch the lord, to hide himself in the company of other aristocrats – as if, in this lawn on which we stroll, one had concealed a single blade of grass amidst other blades of grass.*' It would have been a bloody sight harder for him to conceal himself in Hyde Park, thought Ambrose, skirting the row of trench shelters that had been gouged into the turf. The Serpentine was half-drained, a puddle in a collar of mud, and beyond the lake, beside Rotten Row, stretched a towering ridge of rubble, several hundred yards long – a lorry was at one end, tipping last week's broken buildings on to the pile. The noise filtered through the hiss of the rain like distant thunder.

Well, that was the walk. The rest of the afternoon, and the early part of the evening, stretched ahead of him like a length of grey linoleum. He lit a cigarette and watched a boy try to rescue the remains of a sunken toy boat, marooned in the mud.

He'd never thought of boredom as a permanent state before; it had been an occasional visitor, like a head cold, or a bee trapped in the house. Now, it seemed, the only time that he wasn't bored was when he was lying in bed waiting to see whether one of the droning bastards overhead was going to drop a bomb on him. What on earth had he done on winter afternoons before the war? Taken the motor for a spin? Started early on the whisky? Dozed in a deep and scalding bath? Well he'd *had* those. He looked savagely at the tasteless cigarette and tossed it into the mud. Half a dozen ducks, alerted by the gesture, flew across and fought noisily over the butt – it was reminiscent of the type of supposedly symbolic scene that appeared in 'significant' foreign films, usually intercut with a rioting bread-queue and bearing portentous subtitles: 'Like Animals They Struggled, and for What? Nothing.' The victorious duck, by contrast, swallowed the fag-end with evident satisfaction and then went off to harass a woman who was waving around a delicious-looking lipstick. Ambrose turned back along the path towards Marble Arch. There had to be *somewhere* where he could spend the afternoon.

He almost missed the sign. On the sole poster displayed outside the Granada in Oxford Street, *Night Train to Munich* was spelled out in letters eight inches high, while the title of the supporting feature was barely visible, half-concealed by the oblique banner that read 'Continuous Programme', and he had walked three paces past the entrance before the significance of '*Inspec . . . ed Rose Mystery*' struck him like a sandbag. He stopped so suddenly that a Polish airman cannoned into him, but not even an elbow in the ribs could dent the pleasure of the moment, a moment akin to an unexpected glimpse of a much-loved and extremely generous old friend.

The only seats still available were the most expensive. Peering down from the front row of the balcony, Ambrose wondered briefly who might be left actually fighting this war, since the entire British army seemed to be jammed into the stalls, together with a fair sprinkling from the other services, each with a girl by his side, none of them watching the screen, the newsreel having been succeeded by a series of badly-scratched advertising slides.

'Soap Will Go Twice As Far with
MAZO Soap Energizing Tablets.'

The organist was playing 'Wish Me Luck', and Ambrose found himself tapping an accompaniment on the balcony rail; how delightfully things could change in a single moment. There really was nothing to compare with seeing one's face projected across a gigantic screen in front of a packed and eager audience – and this was not vanity speaking, but professional necessity. In other trades it might be possible to judge almost immediately the effects of one's skills – the patient is cured, the pupil learns to read – but for the film actor such rewards were distant, speculative. One sent one's performance off on a journey, packed its sandwiches (so to speak), straightened its collar and waved it goodbye, hoping that it would be greeted appreciatively. Months would go by. A letter, in the form of a review, might land on the mat; a friend or acquaintance might report back with a sighting ('Awfully good, old man'); but ultimately, one had to make the journey oneself, one had to sit in a darkened auditorium with a host of strangers and gauge, with them, all the strength of that performance, all the subtlety, all the ability of the character to toy with the audience as a zephyr with a leaf, to steer the emotions with the skill and elegance of a gondolier.

'Sanatogen: How to Win *Your* War of Nerves.'

Of course that sometimes meant having first to sit through hours of torture. Cinema programmes had stretched to quite ridiculous lengths these days, and there was no respect given to the content – patrons wandered in and out, seats banged during key moments of dialogue, people shouted profanities during the newsreel, managers clambered on stage and announced in stentorian tones what should be done in the event of an alert (as if, for God's sake, Londoners hadn't caught on by now), matches flared during night scenes, fish-paste sandwiches added their mephitic stench, and over everything sounded the turbid ebb and flow of bronchial clearance.

'Shelters Protect You from the Germans – Let Vicks Protect You from Germs!'

The woman behind Ambrose greeted the new slide with an explosion of coughs, and the organist began to draw 'Wish Me Luck' to an absurdly elaborate conclusion – great swags of arpeggios, and a trill that seemed designed to leave the eardrums bleeding. The screen went blank, the curtains closed briefly, and then re-opened to the sound of a cymbal clash. An animated squiggle was succeeded by the caption 'Food Flash'. The audience groaned and a fresh wave of coughing began, but Ambrose leaned forward, his attention caught. The words were replaced by the title card:

'Alterations to Your Ration Book.'

He leaned back again; not one of his.

'Get comfortable, will you?' said the soldier next to him, a sharp-faced sliver of a man with his arm round a charmless blonde. Ambrose gave him a look and then turned back to the screen. And saw his own face.

'*That's right*,' his own face was saying, while his own hands fiddled with an unlit pipe. In the foreground was the back of a woman's head – Cecy's, it was obviously Cecy's head, he recognized the bun – but the female voice issuing from the back of Cecy's head was not Cecy's. The strange woman's voice was remarking that she'd had to fill in the address on page 4 of her ration book in accordance with instructions from the Ministry of Food, and then Ambrose's own voice, issuing from the image of Ambrose on the screen, uttered the syllables, '*Uh huh*.' The voice that wasn't Cecy's spoke again, the celluloid Ambrose replied, the extraordinary conversation continued, and the real Ambrose, sitting in the audience, struggled to assimilate what he was watching.

'Here,' said the sharp-faced soldier in the next seat. 'That's him.' He gave Ambrose a nudge. 'That's you, isn't it?'

Ambrose nodded, trying to keep one eye on the screen. The picture jumped suddenly to a front view of Cecy, and in the foreground was the back of his own head. A man's voice – a nasty, thin, reedy, expressionless voice that was *nothing* like his own, and yet was clearly supposed to be issuing from his character – said, '*Is there anything else we have to do?*' And Cecy shook her head and picked up her knitting before the picture faded to black. The curtains closed again.

Ambrose sat as if concussed.

'Are you an actor, then?' asked the soldier's girl, incredulously.

It was a moment before he could respond, and then he groped for his hat and stood up so suddenly that she recoiled. 'I thought I was an actor,' he said, and sensed, rather than saw, the rows of heads turning towards him all across the balcony. 'I thought I was an actor,' he repeated, more trenchantly, 'but now I've realized that I'm simply a *whore*.' He put on his hat, tipped the brim, edged past the soldier and his girl, and strode up the steps towards the back of the auditorium. And although he was feeling soiled, humiliated, *raped*, there was still a little part of him that wondered if he'd ever made a finer exit.

'Canonbury 4541.'

'Sophie, it's Ambrose Hilliard. I have to speak to Sammy.'

'Hello, Mr Hilliard.' She was softly spoken, her speech more heavily accented than Sammy's, her tone altogether less buoyant. 'My brother is walking his dog. Can he return your call?'

'No, I'm in a telephone box on South Molton Street.'

'I see.'

There was a pause; Sophie, he'd noticed in the past, never filled in conversational lacunae – that, presumably, was Sammy's role in the household. In the lengthening silence, Ambrose could feel his dudgeon beginning to slip.

'Is there anything else?' asked Sophie.

'Yes.' He thought again of the humiliation that he had just sat through and felt a surge of fresh anger. 'Yes, there is. You can tell that brother of yours—' Distantly, at the other end of the line, a door slammed.

'Wait one moment,' said Sophie, and there was a clunk as the receiver was laid on to a hard surface. Her footsteps receded. For a few seconds nothing was audible and then Ambrose became aware of a clicking sound, a gentle 'tickety-tackety tickety-tackety', as if Sophie had slipped on a pair of tap shoes and was tiptoeing back across the hall to the telephone table.

'Hello?' he called, warily. 'Hello?'

The clicking stopped, there was a delicate snuffle at the earpiece and then a noise like a twelve-inch mortar.

'For Christ's *sake*,' shouted Ambrose, dropping the phone.

From the dangling ear-piece he could hear a repetition of the noise and then the tinny yap of his agent's voice, calling his own name. Cautiously, he lifted the receiver.

'Sammy?'

'Oh there you are, Ambrose! Did you hear Cerberus wishing you a shplendid New Year?'

'Hang Cerberus.'

'Victory in nineteen forty-woof, he was saying.'

'Never mind the dog.'

'Join the WOOFS and win the war!'

'Sammy, *listen* to me. I've just seen a short film that I did for the MoI chopped to buggery, re-voiced by someone else, and plastered all over the screen. Did you agree to that?'

'Did I agree to what?'

'Re-using the footage. Allowing them to show me reacting to a speech that I never heard in the first place. Getting some twerp of an office boy to splutter lines of dialogue over a shot of the back of my head.'

'I don't think they asked me shpecifically.'

'Well they certainly didn't bloody ask *me*.'

'You seem very upset.'

'Of course I'm upset.'

'Was it done badly?'

'It was *done*, Sammy. Can you not see the insult implicit in that? They're saying, "We don't really need an actor for that, let's get Watkins in accounts, he'll do a perfectly good job and we don't have to pay him, either." '

'Ah yes. The trouble is, Ambrose, that these Ministry film roles are on a buy-out. The budget's so tight that—'

'I don't need to know about the budget, Sammy.'

'But there's a clause in the contract that—'

'I don't need to know about clauses. Anything to do with the word "clause" is your bag, not mine. My job is to go out there and act, yours is to make sure that I'm offered decent jobs, that I'm paid adequately and that my skills are neither exploited nor abused, and it increasingly seems to me that you're doing none of those things.'

'Ambrose, old fellow—'

'If I were a painter, I suppose you'd be happy for my canvasses to be cut up with a pair of pinking shears and stuck on greeting cards?'

'Ambrose, please—'

'Or perhaps you'd give me a bucket of whitewash and point me towards the nearest wall?'

'Please be calm, Ambrose.'

'I am calm.'

'No, you're angry.'

'It's a controlled anger, Sammy, tempered with an icy detachment. It's one of the many subtle emotions of which a good actor is capable.'

'Let's talk about this tomorrow.'

'Why tomorrow? I want to discuss it now. You don't realize quite what a—'

'Tomorrow when you come for luncheon. You haven't forgotten you're coming here?'

'Of course I haven't.' Of course he had.

'Two o'clock. We'll have a lovely meal – lokshen, you know – and we'll take Cerberus for a turn around the Shquare, and then I'll tell you all about the new Baker's feature with that nice little role I was mentioning at the . . .'

'For Christ's sake, Sammy, how many times do I have to say it?'

'Say what?'

'That I don't want *nice, little* roles.'

'But that's just—'

'I don't want them.'

'That's just a shlang phrase, it's a—'

'If you can only get me *nice, little* roles then I can see very little point in continuing our association.'

'But if you could just read the treatment—'

'In fact, I can see no point at all.'

'I'll fetch it for—'

'Goodbye, Sammy.'

Ambrose downed the receiver and took a long, gratified breath. It was more than a year since he'd concluded a Sammy conversation in this precise way, with the slam of a telephone, and he'd forgotten the deep satisfactions of the gesture. *Nice, little.* How ironic that Sammy had swallowed whole the mealy-mouthed parsimony of the English language, where every word was qualified and diminished, where all was *nicely* and *fairly* and *slightly* and *quite*, when what an agent really needed was a hefty slug of Teutonic ambition and the ability to bark orders. It was a pity about tomorrow's meal – Sophie was a superb cook, as her brother's figure testified – but accepting Sammy's hospitality so soon after an argument smacked of capitulation. A few days of deliberate silence was needed, a chance for Sammy to reflect on his client's needs, to pledge a better class of service in the future. Besides, tonight's beano would counterbalance any deficiency on the morrow. He could smell that ham. He could almost taste it.

He checked his watch. It occurred to him that there was still time to go back into the cinema and see *Inspector Charnforth and the Red Rose Mystery*. Of course, he'd have to see if a vacancy had arisen in the stalls – he couldn't return to his balcony seat; an exit was an exit, after all, a reappearance could only be bathetic.

The light was already dropping from the sky. He joined the short queue at the box-office, and thought how strangely cheerful, all of a sudden, Oxford Street was looking. In the brief spell of twilight, before blackout hour arrived and the shutters were dragged across, the lights in the shops could twinkle just as they had before the war. The vacant lots and burnt-out husks of buildings became invisible, and all was bustle and shine.

'How kin I help yew?' asked the girl in the booth, her accent a muddy emulsion of East End and elocution lessons.

'One for the stalls. Ah—'

He could hear, seeping through the foyer, the looping, rather sinister clarinet theme that accompanied the Charnforth films. It drew him, like a snake-charmer's melody. He paid his money and took the ticket and walked through the dark tunnel that led to the stalls.

The skies above St John's Wood were quiet, but over to the east there were searchlights prodding the cloud cover, and the flicker of shells. The occasional aircraft engine sounded above the gunfire, and as Ambrose followed the feeble light of his torch along the pavement, he heard the unmistakable sound of a power-dive. It was impossible not to duck, and he found himself cringing beside the overhang of a neglected hedge, his hand shading the beam of the torch as if the Hun might spot its glow-worm dribble and send a stream of bullets straight through the bulb. He waited for the dive to flatten out, and then straightened and continued his walk; the houses that lined the route were vast, five storeys of ostentation, their detail lost in shadow.

People spoke of 'Jerry' now, of course, and not the Hun – he knew that, just as he knew not to talk of Blighty, or of Tommy Atkins; one had to move with the times, to keep abreast, especially in the acting profession, where at the slightest opportunity one might be pigeon-holed, filed and forgotten. It was only the sounds of war – the changeless thump of the batteries, the whizz of shells, that immeasurable beat of silence before the explosion – that sometimes catapulted him back to the old words; even the bray of a donkey, heard as he'd stepped off the bus beside the zoo, had made him think instantly of mules, protesting drearily as they'd hauled the guns through belly-high mud.

His torch started to fail as he turned the corner into Anthea's street, the beam imploding into a lemony wash, too diffuse for picking out the numbers on the doors. Walking slowly, he traced a hand along the stucco garden walls, counting the front gates, and stopped when his fingers caught on a series of soft spikes protruding over the brickwork; he plucked at one of them and the air filled with the astringent odour of rosemary. The Pyms' house. He pushed open the gate and climbed the steps.

Behind the glass of their front door (still miraculously intact) someone had cut a stencil of the word 'welcome' into the blackout material and filled the gap with violet gauze. The result was friendly, pubbish. Ambrose straightened his coat, tilted his hat and gave the bell-pull a yank.

Anthea had lost weight. She had always possessed a fine figure, firm yet curved, like a ship's figurehead, but now she'd acquired corners and edges. Above the neckline of the slate-grey dress, her collarbones protruded like chisel blades.

'Ambrose,' she said, spotting him beside the supper-table. 'I thought I might find you here. Do help yourself.'

'Very funny. Whose idea was this?'

'Mine, actually. I thought there was something rather dreadful about a houseful of guzzlers when the whole future of our country is in jeopardy, and of course I run the local Savings Group and we're on a Weapons Drive so I came up with a novelty idea. I call it the Battle Buffet.' She glanced towards the array of dishes, each containing a scattering of coins rather than food, and sporting a hand-written flag on a spike. 'We're doing quite nicely, I see. Have you contributed?'

'Yes.'

'Towards the . . . ?'

'Spitfire.'

'Half a crown – very generous. Still, this chap here looks awfully empty, doesn't he . . . ?' She nudged the salver labelled 'Wellington bomber: 5/-' towards Ambrose and, after a bitter pause, he reached for his wallet. As he did so, Anthea caught sight of someone on the other side of the room, exclaimed

'Binnie!' at a volume that would have reached the length of a hockey pitch and hurried away, and Ambrose relaxed his grip on a florin and instead took out two threepenny bits and dropped them into the 'Hand-grenade: 6d' tureen. He looked up to see that Anthea's mother had silently arrived at the other end of the table and was watching him with the intensity of a Russian border guard.

'Oh,' he said, both displeased and startled. 'Hello, Mrs Whartley.'

Without replying, she dropped her gaze to his wallet and he found himself, as if hexed, once again raking through the change purse, this time extracting five shillings. The money tinkled into the dish and he reflected that so far this evening he had expended the price of a half-decent restaurant meal without actually eating a single thing. Glumly, he finished his glass of insipid punch (the only drink on offer) and saw that the old bitch was still staring at him. She looked much the same as ever – four foot ten of gristle and malevolence. 'So how are you?' he asked, not even attempting to inject a note of interest into his voice.

She looked at him with sharpened interest. 'Gerard?'

'No, I—' He actually glanced over his shoulder in case she was addressing someone else, but there was no one behind him apart from a group of girls. He turned back. 'I'm not Ge—'

'Gerard!' She scuttled the length of the table and fastened herself to one of his arms, her face upturned to his with an expression of girlish delight, hideously at odds with her appearance. 'Gerard,' she repeated with a happy exhalation, her teeth slipping.

'No, I . . .'

'Gerard.'

'I'm *Ambrose*,' he said, desperately. 'Your ex-son-in-law. The one you hate.'

'Mother—' It was Anthea again, returning. She gently detached the old lady from his arm. 'You're looking rather stunned,' she said. 'Did mother just call you Gerard?'

'Yes, she did, actually. Who is Gerard?'

'A cousin of hers, I think. My mother no longer recognizes people that she doesn't see regularly. It happened rather quickly, the doctor says it was probably a type of brain seizure. This isn't Gerard, mother, it's Ambrose.'

Her mother smiled again, took one of Ambrose's hands, raised it to her mouth and kissed the knuckles.

'She's pleased to see everyone now,' said Anthea. 'Extraordinary, isn't it? When you remember what she used to be like.'

'Indeed.'

'So how are you, Ambrose?'

'Oh . . .' He shrugged. 'I had an appalling experience this afternoon.'

'Oh yes?'

'I went to the cinema—'

'I didn't think you had a picture out at the moment.'

'It was a re-issue.'

'Oh I see.'

'And I was watching an informational short that came earlier in the programme when I suddenly realized that it was a re-edited version of a piece that I'd shot last June. Someone had taken the film, disassembled it and . . . Anthea?' She'd been standing with her head cocked, her attention clearly elsewhere.

'Sorry, thought I heard the start of the wobbler. Imagining it. You were saying about the appalling thing that happened.'

'Yes. Someone had re-voiced one of my shots and re-used it in a completely different context. Actually re-voiced it!'

She nodded, but absently, having clearly missed the import of the story. In the momentary silence his stomach gave an audible moan. 'Is there really nothing to eat?'

'I'm afraid not. There's plenty of punch.'

'I've had some.'

'Food's the last thing on my mind these days.'

'You're thinner, certainly.'

'It's all the worry.' She smiled, bleakly. 'Still, we all have worries.'

'Of course.' He wondered which of his own troubles he could usefully lay before her. 'I spotted today that half my bloody roof's been blown off.'

'Snap.'

'And I can't get a man to come and mend it.'

'Double snap. I had to send Harris up there last week with a tarpaulin.'

'Oh.' That was no good, then; he pondered for a moment. 'I'm stuck for a domestic as well. I don't suppose your housemaid could stretch to a . . . ?'

'She's off making shells.' There was a pause, which Anthea seemed disinclined to fill. Ambrose glanced around the enormous drawing-room, at the heavy curtains, almost theatrical in their dimensions. 'God, those windows must be the most appalling worry. I can't see why you and Harris don't board this place up and get out of London. I couldn't go, of course, it's simply impossible in my line of business, I need to be on the spot to . . .'

'For heaven's *sake*, Ambrose.' She said the words with such vehemence that her mother started and one or two people looked round, curiously. She lowered her voice. 'Do you honestly think that I'm worrying myself to a shred about windows? Or roof tiles? Do you think it's the *servant problem* that's running through my mind, day in, day out, every second that I'm awake, and most of the time that I'm asleep?'

She had always been mistress of the flung question; if one waited, then the answer would follow. Ambrose raised his eyebrows expectantly. Seconds passed. He lifted his punch glass, forgetting that it was empty, and Anthea removed it from his hand and placed it on the table.

'The reason I'm worried, Ambrose,' she said, leaning towards him and speaking slowly, 'is because I have three stepsons whom

I adore, one of whom is at sea, one of whom is God knows where or in which continent, and one of whom is probably somewhere over Europe as we speak.'

'Oh yes . . . the Pym boys.'

'They're my boys, too. I've been their mother for nearly nine years.'

'Of course.' He still thought of them as schoolboys, barely out of short trousers. 'Philip, isn't it? And Jeffrey, and er . . . Hale . . .'

'Alec, Simeon and Lesley,' she said, coldly. 'You're not even close.'

And yet the names Philip and Jeffrey (and Hale) seemed strangely familiar to him; he dug around in his memory. 'Good Lord,' he said, unearthing them, 'this'll amuse you. I know where I got those names from, they're from a character in one of the Inspector Charnforth Mysteries, Philip Jeffrey-Hale. I was thinking about him earlier. He's a traitor and jewel thief who's eventually shot after selling . . .' Anthea was shaking her head. '. . . after selling military secrets to the . . .' She was still shaking her head. '. . . to the Russians via the House of Lords. What on earth's the matter?'

She looked at him queerly. 'I've had enough, Ambrose.'

'Enough of what?'

'Of you. The joke's lost its savour.'

'What joke?'

'The joke of . . . of . . .' Uncharacteristically, she broke eye-contact and started fiddling with the platefuls of coins. '. . . having a little bit of glamour in my history. Having an ex-film-star ex-husband who comes along to my parties and talks about his pictures as if he's Clark Gable and Errol Flynn rolled into one, as if there's nothing that's more important in the entire world than the tiniest, most fiddling detail of his own career, or what's left of it. I used to think it was funny that there was no topic that didn't somehow lead back to one of your films, that someone could mention anything at all – could mention, I don't know . . . the word *spoon* – and we'd find ourselves listening to how Louise Brooks stirred your tea on the back lot at Denham when you were rehearsing *Just Another Springtime* in 1925, and I'd laugh about it with my friends, and now I don't find it funny any more. I don't. There truly are more important things going on, Ambrose, awful things, terrifying things, and no one gives a fig about whether one of your silly little films has been played upside down or at the wrong speed or whatever it was—'

'*Re-voiced*. It was re-voiced.'

'I don't care, Ambrose. No one cares. Why on earth should they care when you don't show the slightest reciprocal interest? I used to think that it was a case of pure selfishness but since mother's little do I'm beginning to wonder if there isn't a tiny bit of your brain missing. You've read that Mr Forster book – you know, "only connect" – well, I think there must be a bundle of wires somewhere in your head that's . . . oh *blast*.' There was no mistaking it this time, the dreary swoop of the siren slicing through the chatter. 'Into the basement!' called Anthea. 'Everyone into the basement! Someone help me with the buffet, please, we can't leave all this lovely money lying here. Ambrose, please take mother. Into the basement, come along now!'

A bottleneck formed at the door. Beyond the mêlée, Ambrose caught a glimpse of Harris Pym clapping on a white warden's helmet. It had been at another party – a film industry party, as a matter of fact, held at the Rock Studios in Elstree in 1930, to celebrate the release of *Forever Gay* (Ambrose had played Ivor Novello's suicidal brother: 'Ambrose Hilliard gives a performance of great intensity' *Daily Mail*) – that Harris and Anthea had first met. 'Harris Pym, Pym's Cooked Meats,' the little man had said, shaking hands with Ambrose. 'We've just won the supply contract for the new refectories.' He'd been an ugly little bugger then, too.

'Come on, everybody,' called Anthea, from the doorway.

Ambrose looked around for his ex-mother-in-law, and found her standing directly behind him.

'Mrs Whartley?'

She looked up at him with a start of pleasure. '*Dear* man,' she said.

He felt an odd internal dislocation, a spasm of recollection that seemed to heave within him, momentarily, like a mole beneath a lawn. When was it that he'd last seen precisely that expression? He tried, and failed, to pinpoint the memory.

'Dear, dear man,' she repeated.

The siren wound down, and in the sudden quiet he could hear the insistent, broken beat of the Heinkel engines approaching; he took the old besom's arm and hurried her towards the stairs.

That night he dreamed of food – of bortsch, piquant and ruby-red, of leg of lamb, of potato cakes with a sweet onion sauce, of noodle pudding, cinnamon-scented and studded with raisins. 'Eat, please, eat,' urged Sophie, piling a second helping of lokshen into his bowl, but as he reached for his spoon he heard a great gurgling roar that dragged him away from the table and flung him into the darkness of his bedroom. He lay where he'd landed, listening to the yodel of his empty stomach, watching, through half-closed eyes, the progress of a thin band of light that poked from behind the shutters and crept gradually along the wall like an extendable ruler.

He'd reached home by half-past midnight. The raid had been a short one, but he'd felt disinclined to stay at the party after the all-clear. He'd seen in the New Year at the bus stop, where a group of sailors had slurred their way through an obscenity-laden version of 'Auld Lang Syne', the opening lyric, 'Fuck Auld Acquaintance up the Arse', striking Ambrose as a distinctly apposite comment on the whole evening.

Strain was a peculiar thing, of course – it could sharpen the mind but it could also blunt it, it could turn ants into lions, and lions into kittens, and, in Anthea's case, it had clearly sent her round the bend. It was fortunate, really, that a lifetime in the industry had inured him to such petty personal attack. Thus when the missiles of bile and jealousy were hurtling across the set, he could quietly don the breastplate of professionalism and the shield of feigned deafness and continue unscathed. As a result, he bore neither scars nor grudges. Speaking of which, he could really see no reason not to take up Sammy's offer of lunch; it was a crime to waste food, and, after all, one had to placate as well as chastise . . .

A foreign-looking woman in a headscarf answered the door of Sammy's flat. She stared at the bunch of anemones he was holding, and then glanced sharply at his gardenia buttonhole.

'Miss Smith don't want to see nobody,' she said.

'I've been invited for luncheon.'

'No.'

'Sammy has invited me for New Year's Day luncheon.'

The woman moved her jaw very slightly, as if chewing on his statement.

'He ask you?'

'Yes.'

'Wait.' She closed the door, leaving him alone in the communal hallway. It smelled of beeswax. There was no aroma of roasting meat issuing from the flat, no rattle of pans. Disconcerted, he lit a cigarette. He had smoked half of it by the time the door opened again.

'Mr Hillier, you are?' said the woman.

'Hilliard. Yes.'

'Miss Smith say to tell you that Mr Smith dead in bomb.'

'What? Nonsense . . .' Stupid woman. 'I spoke to him yesterday afternoon.'

She looked at him silently. The whites of her eyes were very red.

'What bomb?' he asked. 'Where was there a bomb?'

'His office.'

'He wasn't in the office, I spoke to him here. It was New Year's Eve, why would he go to his office?'

Behind the woman, somewhere off the dark corridor that ran the length of the flat, a door smacked against the wall. There was a bursting rush along the parquet, and Sammy's brindled dog hurtled past the coat rack and came to a scrabbling halt between the door frame and the foreign woman's legs. It looked up at Ambrose, panting, and then looked past him, into the empty hallway. The thumping tail slowed a little.

'He went into his office especially, Mr Hilliard. To collect something for you.' It was Sophie's voice, issuing from the doorway of an unlit room. Ambrose could see nothing of her but a shoulder, the crook of an elbow.

'For me? What do you mean, "for me"?'

'He wanted to fetch a film treatment for you to read. He expected that you'd turn up for lunch today. Even though you were so rude to him.'

The cigarette was burning his fingers. He dropped it hastily. 'Are you sure that he's . . . ? I mean, how do you know that he's . . . ?'

'They sent a policeman to tell me.'

The dog yawned, a noise like the squeal of an unoiled hinge. It seemed to Ambrose that time had passed and yet the scene remained static – the visitor at the door, the foreign woman with the accusatory stare, the voice from the shadows. It was as if one of the characters had dried on their next line; he searched through his own script. 'Dreadful,' he said. 'That's dreadful news. Of course, if there's anything I can do . . .'

There was another gap without dialogue. Cerberus sighed gustily and ambled back into the flat, toenails clicking.

'Yes,' said Sophie. 'They've asked for someone to go and identify him. Will you do that for me, please?'

*

He had done it before. In *Looking-Glass* (1928) he had been shown the body of his young wife, killed when her circus act was sabotaged by a jealous knife-thrower. The script had said, '*Langley Austen, his face a mask of anguish, embraces Thecla's lifeless form and swears to the gods that he will be avenged*' but Ambrose had argued, successfully, for a less exaggerated approach – the bereaved man's head drooping brokenly, his shoulders hunched with pain, one hand reaching out hopelessly towards the lifeless form and then withdrawing, like a wounded animal, and then a slow, almost imperceptible forging of the inner will, a whitening of the knuckles, the gradual lifting of the face to show eyes that glowed with determination and burned with molten hatred. In the event, the first thirty seconds of subtle emotional play had been hacked off in the cutting room, leaving a brief glimpse of his character looking utterly demented, followed by the caption, 'I Will Have my Revenge on that Beast from Hell!', a fine example of the crass technique of those who claimed to have artistic control of the kinematic industry. He'd also had occasion to enter a mortuary in the role of Professor Gough (*Inspector Charnforth and the China Clay Mystery*), although the camera in that case had remained tastefully on the threshold, panning from the closing door to the sign on the exterior wall.

There was no sign on the wall of the temporary mortuary in the warehouse on Floral Street, and no door either. A piece of sacking hung from the frame, and as Ambrose paid the taxi-cab driver, the hessian was pushed aside by two ambulance-women carrying an empty stretcher between them. They paused to light cigarettes, and the taller of the two girls flicked the spent match in his direction. She had a round face, as plain and unadorned as a turnip.

'You here for an identification?' she asked.

'Yes.'

She shook her head. 'Not this entrance. You reely don't want this entrance.'

Her companion emitted a little squeak of agreement.

'Where, then?' asked Ambrose.

'Through the alley and round to the right.' She stood casually, booted feet at ease; her overalls were bunched around her torso, unsexing her. She reminded Ambrose of a stage hand, brawny and unbiddable. He walked past her, not letting his eyes stray towards the sodden canvas of the stretcher.

It seemed sunnier at the front of the building. The other entrance had a red cross painted on the wall beside it, and a pretty little nurse so crisp and clean in her uniform, so delicate in her enquiries, that he felt like congratulating the casting director.

'In here,' she said, and, 'Please wait', and 'Do you need a chair?' And then she hurried away and returned after a short time, and led him along a corridor and into a starkly-lit room where sheeted bodies lay on tables, and bowed figures stood in tableaux beside them.

'I need to warn you,' she said, 'that Mr Smith may not look quite as you remember . . .'

The sheet that covered Sammy was not a bed-sheet, but a length of unbleached cotton, like the material of a flour sack. Pure white was supposed to be difficult to light, of course – cameramen were always complaining about the brightness of white shirts, and requiring that white walls were 'dirtied down'. If he had earned a guinea for every time that he'd been forced to wait in full make-up under baking lights while some junior member of the art department idly daubed a wall with—

'Really – if you don't feel that you can do this, Mr Hiller . . .'

'Hill*iard*. Of course I can do it. Take the sheet away.'

Carefully, she folded back the top section. Something quite fundamental had happened to Sammy's face. The convexity had been lost, the nose split from bridge to nostrils, a dark pulp filling the fissure, and though an effort had been made to wash him, the remaining features were outlined in black, as if with a grease pen. Shake a London building and there was filth, centuries of it. The neck was webbed in grime; even the fingertips, just visible under the edge of sheet, looked like those of a navvy, dirt rammed beneath the nails.

The nurse touched Ambrose lightly on the sleeve. 'Mr Hillyer?'

'Hill*iard*.' Dirt rammed beneath the nails . . .

Dirt rammed beneath the nails . . .

It was the cryptic sign that hung in plain sight, the clue too obvious to be deemed a clue, except in the oblique vision of an academic seen by some as eccentric but by others as a focused beam of pure thought. Professor Gough smiled at the nurse.

'I'm sorry,' she said, looking confused, 'but can you confirm that this is Mr Smith?'

'I'm afraid I cannot.'

'Oh. You mean—'

'I mean, my dear,' he spoke gently, almost absent-mindedly, 'that this is not Mr Smith. Someone has obviously made a mistake – a very, very simple mistake, but one that might possibly fool the less vigilant. But perhaps I should explain . . .'

He held the look – wry, a little melancholy – and waited for the cut. They'd possibly need another take for sound; one of the background extras had sniffed loudly during the last speech.

'Mr Hilliard . . . ?'

The nurse was looking at her watch. The world dropped back around him: the cold light, the metallic scent of blood. The extra was weeping, not sniffing.

'I apologize. I was somewhere else entirely.'

'You were saying that this isn't Mr Smith.'

'That's correct. Sammy Smith is missing three fingers from his left hand, he lost them in an accident in a timber yard when he was a young man. This fellow's left hand is intact . . . poor soul.' He looked soberly at the figure on the table. 'I can perhaps see how the mistake was made; the face isn't dissimilar.' It occurred to him that Sammy might be wandering around in a daze, he might be in a hospital bed, or at a rest centre, queueing for the use of a telephone, fretting about whether or not Cerberus was being served his correct daily ration of finest sweetbreads simmered in sherry consommé. 'Should I call at a police station, do you think, or—'

There was a tiny noise, a batsqueak of distress, and when he looked at the nurse she was crying.

'I'm so sorry,' she said. 'We try so hard to make people look the way that their relatives remember. We didn't . . .' She plucked at the edge of the sheet, drawing it down so that it covered the exposed fingers. 'We couldn't have known, you see.'

He stared at her, uncomprehending, and she wiped her eyes, quickly, with both hands. 'You have to understand, Mr Hilliard, that the rescue services don't always . . . find everything. Sometimes the injuries are just – sometimes we don't know what belongs to whom and – we do our best. We try to make a whole person, but that hand . . . that arm must be from someone . . . It's awful. It's an awful thing to have happened. I'm so sorry.'

He could think of nothing to say. He looked back at the table, at the smooth contour of the sheet that covered a bloody jumble.

'So do you think that that's your friend?' asked the nurse, tentatively.

'My agent,' he corrected. He looked again at the face. 'Yes. That's him.'

INTERMISSION

January 1941

The guards from the gunnery knew Edith by now. Every day except Sunday she arrived at the gap in the barbed wire at half past seven in the morning, and was waved along the path that uncoiled through the dunes. For the first hundred yards there would be near-silence – the hiss of air through the long grass, the muffled footsteps that seemed to come from yards away, rather than from the end of her own legs. The air was icy but still, the sand so cold that she could feel it through the soles of her shoes. Then gradually, a low roar would become discernible, increasing in volume with every turn of the path until the final dune was reached, and then Edith would brace herself and turn the corner and stagger a little as a wind that had skimmed the Urals came screaming at her from the length of Badgeham Beach. Away from the dunes the sand was packed as hard as brick, a single, sugared surface that sloped almost imperceptibly towards the sea, the pale sweep broken only by what looked like a series of giant hairpins stuck in the sand. A quarter of a mile away, a hedge of wire marked both the edge of the minefield that guarded the battery position and the limit of Edith's morning walk; the journey back, with the wind behind her, made her feel like a gull.

There was so much time here. After years of waking at six thirty, she was incapable of sleeping for longer, and after she'd washed and dressed, and had breakfast, there was still an hour and a quarter before the shop opened. On most days she had the entire beach to herself. Sometimes she found herself singing, the wind snatching the words away as soon as they left her mouth. She had a thin but true voice, and the songs were ones she'd learned at school, sea shanties that had always reminded her of holidays with her auntie and uncle and cousins on the coast: 'Blow the Wind Southerly' and 'Johnny Todd', 'Fire Down Below' and 'Heart of Oak':

They swear they'll invade us, these terrible foes
They frighten our women, our children and beaus,
But should their flat bottoms in darkness get o'er
Still Britons they'll find to receive them on shore.
Heart of oak are our ships,
Heart of oak are our men;
We always are ready,
Steady, boys, steady!
We'll fight and we'll conquer again and again.

At school, of course, she'd tittered with the others over the 'flat bottoms' line, but now the verse had a dreadfully chilling edge. The new and terrible foes were just beyond the horizon, and the east coast was spiked with guns and encrusted with khaki. There were no trippers allowed here any more, no buckets and spades for sale in the shops by the harbour, no green glass floats.

Her own visit, of course, could scarcely be classified as a holiday (cousin Verna, for all her lavender cardigans and chapel talk, ran her sewing-room like an East End sweat-shop), but nevertheless there was still an air of respite about it. Edith had arrived at Badgeham-next-the-Sea like a gypsy, London's dirt in her hair, its smell lingering in her clothes, a rabbity nervousness to her gestures, and Badgeham had scoured and sand-blasted her, and bleached her in its white light. Her Sunday afternoon headaches had gone and she felt altogether more like herself than she had in a very long time, although 'herself', of course, was still only Edith Beadmore. She felt, obscurely, that two near misses in as many months should have effected some visible alteration, but there was no change in the pale beaky face that peered out from the mirror, no hint that its owner might have experienced anything more traumatic than a crowded journey on the north-bound District Line.

On the morning that she saw the men, she had just turned back from the minefield and was singing 'The Keel Row'. A long way ahead of her, a figure stood at the edge of the surf, while another walked into the sea. He was five yards out before the water reached his knees, ten before he halted; Edith was near enough by now to see that he had left his trousers on the beach, and that the sea was still a half-inch or so below the hem of his short underwear. After a shouted exchange with his companion, he walked back towards the sand and Edith averted her eyes and altered her course slightly, so as not to embarrass him. In fact, he was still buttoning his fly when his companion hailed Edith, and she was apparently the only one of the three to find the situation at all awkward.

'Do you know if the whole beach is like this?' asked the one who'd called over to her.

'Like what?'

'On such a shallow rake?'

'I don't know,' she said. 'I've certainly never seen a boat come up here, they all go to Badgeham Bay just round the headland.'

The two men looked at each other. 'Well, that's all right,' said the fly-buttoner. 'Best we've seen, anyway.' He was in his fifties and dressed, like his companion, in flannel trousers and a shabby tweed jacket, the pockets stretched and sagging.

'You're not from round here,' he said to Edith, a statement rather than a question.

'No.'

'D'you know anything about boarding houses in the area? Or hotels?'

'Not much, I'm afraid. There's the Crown and Anchor behind the green in Badgeham, and I think that quite a few other people take in boarders for the summer. Cromer's the place where most people stay, though – it's about twenty miles east of here.'

He nodded, and took a camera from his canvas haversack, and Edith felt dismissed, her usefulness over. She left the men taking photographs of the beach, and it wasn't until she was walking back to Badgeham along the twisting path between the dunes that it suddenly occurred to her that she had merrily volunteered information of potential vital military importance to two complete strangers. They had asked her and she had told them, without thought or scruple, and the whole incident was horribly reminiscent of a short film that she'd seen during a recent matinee in Holt, in which a naïve spinster called Miss Moss had handed over a set of local maps to a party of 'lost' walkers, one of whom had then given away his origins by complimenting his benefactor on her garden full of 'vallflowers'. *Miss Moss Shows the Way* had been the title, and at the time Edith had thought it rather silly. Now, she felt the back of her neck turn cold. *Miss Beadmore Informs the Invaders. Miss Beadmore and the Beach Landing.* She hurried towards the guard post, a wretched little shack on which the words 'Teas & Ices' were still visible under a coat of grey paint.

'Excuse me.'

A boy of about nineteen, with dark red hair and a nose to match, looked out warily.

'I think I've been rather stupid,' said Edith.

'Oh yes.' He looked unsurprised.

'There were two men on the beach. I've never seen them before and they were asking questions about sea levels and local towns, and I'm afraid that I told them about—'

'S'all right,' said the boy. He blew on his hands and rubbed the knuckles.

'Is it?'

'They're official.'

'Really?'

'They've got passes. It's ministry business,' he added.

'Which ministry?'

'That's er – whatjermacallit – classified,' he said, vaguely, retreating into the shelter of the doorway.

Edith saw the men again, later that day. They were standing on the harbour wall watching the fishing boats through binoculars. The younger one was making notes.

★

The summons to the Ministry of Information came at eleven o'clock on a Tuesday morning, just as Buckley had started *The Times* crossword.

'For God's *sake,*' he said, throwing down the newspaper. 'I thought we'd finished with all that. What do they want now?'

'They didn't tell me,' repeated Edwin Baker's secretary, patiently. 'They just said that they would like to see you and Mr Baker and Mr Parfitt at Malet Street at midday on an urgent matter. I'm just about to find a taxi for you.' She closed the door quickly.

Parfitt put his head down on the desk and groaned.

'Can I do anything while you're gone?' asked Catrin.

'Yes,' said Buckley. 'Protect the contents of this office from that ginger bitch downstairs. If she gets hold of a single page without my say-so, then you're sacked.'

'Anything else?'

'You can do a bit of tidying.'

'Title,' said Parfitt, his lips still squashed against the desk.

'Oh yes,' said Buckley. 'Draw up a shortlist of titles. That ass Shipton's on our tail about it, as if it's anything to do with him. Bloody accountants.'

'Tidying the office' was a relative term, since apart from the ashtrays and the crusted cups Catrin was not allowed to touch anything on either man's desk, nor was she allowed to move any pieces of paper that were lying on the floor, since it had been impressed upon her that it was not so much a floor as a two-dimensional filing cabinet. She was not allowed to open the window to release the smoke of a million cigarettes in case a draught disorganized the exquisite arrangement on the floor. She was not even allowed to empty the waste bin, because the waste bin was merely a holding bay for pieces of paper that weren't needed at the moment but which might, at some future point, be frantically searched for, pounced upon with a cry of triumph, smoothed out and declared to be a far, far better version of Scene 27 than the rewrite that they had been slaving over for three days.

What 'tidying' actually boiled down to was the removal of crumpled cigarette packets and biscuit crumbs, and the revolting ritual of wiping Buckley's typewriter, key by key, in order to remove the daily build-up of brilliantine accumulated from the running of worried fingers through rarely-washed hair.

Her final housewifely task was to renew the spirit gum that attached the various notices to the wall. These ranged from the rules of the room (*1. No bomb stories, 2. No public transport stories, 3. No ITMA catchphrases*) to a selection of articles and cuttings that had caught Buckley's sarcastic fancy, including a lightly charred government leaflet that detailed how to construct a home-made heater for an Anderson shelter out of two large flower pots and a candle.

The longest wall, however, was entirely taken up with row upon row of small cards. On each was written a brief scene description, and if read sequentially they built into the entire storyline of what was still known, for administrative purposes, as *Dunkirk Film*. Three months ago, Catrin had watched its slow construction. 'Right,' Buckley had said, standing in front of the blank wall, 'we know what comes in the middle.' He wrote '*Boat arrives at French coast*' on a card and stuck it at the centre of the wall. 'We know what comes towards the end.' '*Engine fails. Uncle mends it while under fire*' took its place a foot or so above the skirting board. 'And we know what happens about half an hour in.' '*Boat sets out from England*' joined the other cards. 'And if' said Buckley, nodding towards the bottom of the wall, 'the engine packs up there, then we need to prefigure it, don't we?'

He placed '*Uncle tells friend in pub that boat has engine problems*' close to the top, and '*Engine stutters but the twins are too busy to notice*' on a card halfway down.

'What's the very first scene?' he asked, turning to Catrin. 'Come on.'

'The twins listening to the wireless – learning about the evacuation?'

'Hear that noise?' asked Buckley, cocking his head. 'It's your audience muttering that they thought they'd paid to see a war film and instead they're looking at two tarts in armchairs. Parfitt?'

'France.'

'France. Set the scene. Who's in France?' he asked Catrin.

'The fiancé.'

'Give him a name.'

'Eric.'

'Hear that noise? It's your audience sniggering at a hero called Eric. Try something more manly.'

'John.'

'Dull.'

'Johnnie?'

'Better. Who else do we meet in France?'

'The dog,' said Parfitt.

'That's right. Because audiences love dogs more than they love people. So . . .' He thought for a moment and then wrote something on a card, and stuck it at the very top of the wall.

'*British army unit pinned down in France. Stray dog hanging around.*'

'What else do we need to do in France?' he asked, looking at Catrin.

She shook her head.

'Well, who else is in this film?'

'Rose and Lily.'

'So we need to set up Rose and Lily, don't we? How can we do that?'

'Set them up?'

'Yes.'

'You mean find out about them before we see them?'

'Yes.'

There was a long pause. 'I'm not sure,' said Catrin, blushing.

'God help us.' Buckley rolled his eyes. 'Bring back Jeannie, all is forgiven. Parfitt?'

'Johnnie talks about them.'

Buckley leaned forward and added the words *'Johnnie talks to fellow soldier about fiancée and her sister'* to the first scene.

'Right,' he said, taking another card, 'what's next?'

Over a week, over two weeks, the scenes had gradually accumulated – had been shuffled, swapped, combined – had acquired detail, and had finally coalesced into a single story. A few more days of tweaks, of meetings with the producer, of transposed cards and scribbled amendments, and then Buckley had sat down, and typed the words

Treatment for
DUNKIRK FILM

and had begun to write, at immense speed and with an intensity that had rendered him deaf to alerts, a thirty-page prose version of the film that read like a racy novelette. 'That'll do it,' he'd said, exuding sweat and satisfaction, as he ripped the final page from the machine.

From Baker Productions, the treatment had been forwarded to the Ministry of Information for approval. There had been a meeting and Buckley and Parfitt had stamped back into the office in Soho Square and started snatching cards off the wall.

‘We’re not entirely convinced that the portrayal of the rescue efforts present the national case in a sufficiently uplifting way,’ said Buckley, doing an impression of someone with an effeminate voice and no chin.

The second draft of the treatment had stalled at the War Office (‘We are concerned that the controlled evacuation of the British Expeditionary Force may be represented as a retreat in disarray’) and just after the third version had been grudgingly given the nod by both parties, with the proviso that a special advisor in military matters would be present at every stage of the filming, the Admiralty had taken a gander, reeled back in horror at what it read and dispatched a hysterical memo to the MoI concerning two minor inaccuracies in maritime terminology.

By the time that Buckley and Parfitt actually started to write the script, the cards on the wall had been altered, moved, scrapped and reinstated so many times that they were covered in thumbprints and almost illegible. In her spare moments, Catrin touched-up the fainter words with a black crayon.

Now that the story was locked, the office had acquired a different atmosphere. The vigour of the plotting process had given way to the slow grind of scripting, and Buckley had lost some of his spark and bite and spent the days leaning glumly over the typewriter, pecking out lines of dialogue in a steady rhythm that smacked of the production line. He was not, Catrin was beginning to think, terribly interested in the characters; the dialogue that he wrote was functional, the glue that held the story together and nothing more, and he would invariably pass the first draft of each scene on to Parfitt with a request to ‘add a bit of fizz’.

Parfitt’s fizz-addition was selective. If the scene was complex – a three- or four-hander involving action or argument – or if it contained potentially jokey banter or a bit of knockabout humour, he would crunch himself up in his chair, grip the edge of the desk with both hands and fix his eyes on the script with the look of a man planning a particularly grisly murder. Time would pass and he'd mumble occasionally, sway a little.

'We should rope him off,' Buckley would say, tiptoeing past. 'Danger UXB.'

Elsewhere in the room, tea would be made and drunk, newspapers read, sandwiches eaten. And then Parfitt would awake suddenly, exhaling like a diver, and would grab a pencil and make his amendments with rapid fluency, not inventing but merely transcribing the lines that were already written inside his head.

If, however, there was nothing in the scene that caught his fancy, then he'd spend twenty minutes sighing and shifting around in his chair before scribbling a few perfunctory changes and then slamming the pencil back on the desk. Catrin came to know her cue.

'Mine?' she'd ask, keenly, reaching for the pages.

'Yours.'

In some of the scenes that were passed to her it was simply a matter of changing the odd word or phrase, so that Rose and Lily might sound like two young women as opposed to two middle-aged men. In others, Buckley and Parfitt's imaginations had failed them entirely and a blank had been left in the dialogue, together with a descriptive note. (*'Twins chatter while preparing an evening meal for their uncle, then Rose turns on the wireless'. 'The twins discuss what to wear on the boat, and decide to dress as men.'*) She couldn't, she knew, write the true Lily and Rose, but she could make Rose the bolder of the two, she could make Lily sweet and shy and film-mad. She could make them both brave.

LILY

There'll be guns going off, I suppose.

ROSE

I expect so. We'll probably hear them long before we get to Dunkirk.

LILY

And will there be explosions?

ROSE

There might be, it depends if the Germans have sent any planes. It'll be awfully noisy, anyhow. Do you still want to go, Lil?

LILY

Oh yes. I don't mind a bit of noise.

ROSE

Don't you, Lil? Won't you be frightened?

LILY

(tucking her hair into a man's hat) No. I'll just pretend that I'm Errol Flynn. Nothing frightens him.

'Flabby', Buckley had said, after she'd sweated over the Errol Flynn page for three and a half hours, mouthing the lines to herself over and over again, first as wide-eyed Lily, then as sensible Rose. 'Look at it, every line's twice as long as it needs to be, your audience'll be dropping off, they'll start gossiping about last night's bomb. You only need to say everything once, you know, it's not a novel. Here—' He'd licked the end of a pencil, crossed out half the scene and added a word. '*Now* it's just about useable.'

LILY

There'll be guns going off, I suppose.

ROSE

I expect so. ~~We'll probably hear them long before we get to Dunkirk~~.

LILY

And ~~will there be~~ explosions?

ROSE *Perhaps.*

~~There might be, it depends if the Germans have sent any planes~~. It'll be awfully noisy, anyhow. ~~Do you still want to go, Lil?~~

LILY

~~Oh yes~~. I don't mind ~~a bit of noise~~.

ROSE

Don't you, Lil? ~~Won't you be frightened?~~

LILY

(tucking her hair into a man's hat) No. I'll just pretend that I'm Errol Flynn. Nothing frightens him.

'And look—' he'd jabbed a finger at the text. 'There's a possible title there as well.'

'Which line?'

'*Nothing Frightens Them*. Stick it down.'

Dutifully, she'd added his suggestion to the annotated list that she kept at the back of a notebook. 'When we find the right one, it'll shout "Bingo",' Buckley had said, but the list now ran to two pages and no one had done any shouting yet.

The last ashtray emptied, the last smear of Brylcreem wiped from the shift key, and Catrin took a pencil and opened the notebook. She would go by impulse, she decided; anything that looked like the type of film that she might actually be tempted to go and see would be marked with an asterisk.

Channel Crossing (NB, Parfitt says already a film called this)
Channel Incident (ditto, last year, Denham & Pinewood)
Channel Firing
Channel Rescue
Channel Drama
Channel Danger
Two for Dunkirk

Three for Dunkirk
To Dunkirk
Back from Dunkirk
To Dunkirk and Back Again
*Dunkirk**
Buckley's Water Frolics
Nothing Frightens Them
They Were Brave
*Into Danger**
*Dangerous Crossing (*NB RKO already in production with *Dangerous Moonlight)*
On the Beaches
Across the Waves
Towards the Enemy
Through Shot and Shell
Twin Danger
Double Danger
Twin Crossing
Double Crossing (ha ha!)
Flowers of the Sea
The Little Barge
*The Little Ship**
The Little Boat
Cockles and Mussels
A Pair of Fishwives
Girls at Sea
Women of the Waves (Raymond Parfitt award for worst title of the twentieth century)
Just One Story
A True Story
It Happened Like This . . .

Her pen hovered beside the last suggestion, but she couldn't, in all conscience, place a mark by it. Nothing, *nothing*, in the script so far bore the slightest resemblance to the actual events of Sunday, 2nd June. A thought suddenly occurred to her, and she added another suggestion to the list.

'Got anything for me?'

It was Phyl, the continuity girl from the production office downstairs, peering around the half-open door; Catrin put down her pen. 'Yes, come on in – only tell me, do you think you'd go and see a film called *It Happened on Sunday*?

'Only if it starred Rita Hayworth.' Phyl picked her way across to Buckley's desk and lifted the piece of paper drooping from the typewriter. 'Is he *still* on that page?'

'Yes, but Parfitt's just finished the whole of the section where the engine breaks down. That's er . . .' Catrin scanned the floor. '. . . here.' She marked the spot with a scrap of newspaper, and handed the typed pages to Phyl. 'That's three-and-a-half scenes,' she added, placatingly. 'You will do it quickly, won't you, so I can replace it before they come back?'

Phyl nodded and glanced around the office; she was at least forty, but she stood like a fashion mannequin, her weight all on one hip, one hand elegantly adjusting the knot of sandy hair at the nape of her neck. 'This morning,' she said, 'the location manager wired me from somewhere near Cromer, I've had two calls from the casting office, two from the scenic department and one from someone who I think must be the director, although if I'm right then God help me since he's clearly one of the non-speaking variety. It goes without saying that the script secretary's in tears, and I've also had a rather menacing visit from the third AD, he's the same one we had on the *Careless Talk* shoot, the one with the dog – which reminds me, actually, I must speak to the casting director – and that pathetic little accountant Shipton has practically put up a tent in my office. Can you imagine what they're all begging for?'

'A complete first draft,' said Catrin.

'That's right. Not for putting in front of the camera, not for mass publication, just for issuing to all the poor so-and-sos who are trying to draw up preliminary lists, and book studios and build flattage and basically get the damn thing made. You realize that we're supposed to be filming the location scenes in March.'

'I know, and I do try and nag them, Phyl, honestly, but . . .'

'No, it's not your fault – it's just Buckley enjoying his little bit of power, he uses perfectionism as an excuse for brute laziness. I'm only grateful that there's someone in here who's on my side.' She gave a brisk smile and then raised her head sharply, like a pointer. 'You know,' she said, 'I can actually smell him. There's a Buckley-shaped scent hovering just above this chair – three parts ego to one part hair-oil. Tell me, does he ever try it on with you?'

Catrin hesitated. 'You mean . . . ?'

'Chase you around the desk? Pinch your behind?'

'No. Not as such.'

'Is that so?' Phyl gave her a long look, part-warning, part-disbelief. 'Only he has a frightful reputation with pretty girls. Don't say I didn't tell you.'

She left with the pages of script, and Catrin sat for a while, twirling the pencil between her fingers. It was quite true that Buckley had never pinched her behind or chased her around the desk. He had, however, on her very first day in the office, tactfully choosing a moment when Parfitt had gone to the Gents, informed her that she was a very attractive young woman, that she must be awfully lonely during the many evenings when her husband was on duty, and that it was only the fact that Ellis was (in effect) serving his country that prevented him (Buckley) from Doing Something About It. 'I'm shackled by conscience,' he'd said, managing, nevertheless, to imply that those shackles were on the flimsy side and might drop off altogether were Catrin to apply even the slightest pressure. At this point Parfitt had returned, and Buckley had snapped back, without any apparent embarrassment, to his usual persona, that of Escoffier instructing a trainee kitchen maid. It was a role with which Catrin was far more comfortable, and she was beginning, she liked to think – she was just beginning – to understand the basic elements, to learn which knife to use and when to use it. She hardly blushed at all, these days.

Mercifully, Buckley hadn't mentioned the shackles again, but sometimes, when they were alone in the office, he would extend his linked wrists towards Catrin, and look martyred, and she would say, 'Don't, please', in as cold and collected a tone as she could manage. Far more tricky to cope with were his endless, nosy questions about Ellis.

'Is he older than you?'

'Yes.'

'Forty?'

'No.'

'Sixty?'

'*No.*'

'Want me to go on guessing?'

'He's thirty-four.'

'So why hasn't he been called-up yet?'

'He has a damaged eardrum.'

'Stuck a paintbrush in it?'

'Mortar-fire in Spain.'

'Oh, he's got principles, then. And were you his student?'

'*No.*'

'His model?'

'*No.* We met in a café . . .'

Silence on her part just provoked more questions; *answers* provoked more questions. Facetiousness, she had discovered, was the only way to shut him up.

'So what does he paint, then? Landscapes?'

'No. Industrial and urban subjects.'

'Oh, he's a house painter.'

'Yes, that's right.'

'Does he do guttering?'

'No, never.'

'Why not?'

'It's too specialized.'

'Who should I get for that, then?'

'Try Augustus John.'

Buckley had laughed at that – one bark, like a sea-lion spotting a fish.

Phyl returned the purloined scenes just a minute or two before the writers' tread was audible on the stairs.

'I hope,' said Buckley, entering the room, 'that we don't have a fifth-columnist in our midst. Only I could have sworn that that harridan downstairs gave me a smug look when we passed her office, and it struck me as the sort of look that might be worn by someone who's somehow got hold of a premature version of the script.'

'What happened at the meeting?' asked Catrin, brightly.

Buckley dropped into his chair and swung his feet on to the desk. 'Parfitt, tell her what happened at the meeting.'

Parfitt sat down more slowly, reached into his pocket and took out a hip-flask. 'All rot,' he muttered, unscrewing the top and taking a long pull. He wiped his mouth, and then took another. 'Bloody fools,' he added.

'*I'll* tell you,' said Buckley. 'We got there, and there were six other people in the room with fourteen jobs between them – under-secretary of this, advisor to the central committee of the military board of the propaganda arm of the civilian wing of that. Thanks—' he took the proffered flask, downed a mouthful and handed it back to Parfitt. 'Thanks,' he added, more hoarsely. 'So they sat us down and told us that we're doing a splendid job, but that they need our cooperation on a matter of extreme national importance about which they're getting a lot of ministerial stick. And Edwin Baker, being a fine and experienced producer, said that we would endeavour to help in any way possible provided that it was within our financial capabilities, and then some whinnying little civil servant cleared his throat and told us to put an American in it.'

Catrin stared at him. 'Put an American in what?'

'In the film.'

'In this film? In the Dunkirk film?'

'Yes.'

'Put an American in this film?'

'Is there an echo in here?'

'But an American doing what?'

'Do you know, that's exactly the question Parfitt asked. Wasn't it?'

Parfitt grunted.

'He asked, "An American doing what?" and the man from the ministry said, "Encouraging other Americans to watch the film and to support the Allied cause". It appears, you see, that American distributors aren't very keen on buying any of our recent films, mainly because they're full of British people with British accents being awf'ly British, and the Minister wants something done about it. The phrase used was, "We need to make a gesture". So . . .' Buckley glanced over his shoulder at the rows of scene cards, '. . . we have somehow to insert a token Yank.' He stood up abruptly and caught his chair just as it tipped over. He looked, Catrin thought, less outraged than he should have – he looked, in fact, strangely galvanized by the idea of once again re-shuffling the pack.

'But we can't,' she said. 'It doesn't fit the story.'

'Doesn't it? Oh well . . .' Buckley shrugged and reached for his hat. '. . . that's it, then. We'll just have to shut down the production. Come on Parfitt, get your coat, the expert from the Valleys has spoken.' Parfitt made the combustion-engine noise that indicated one of his rare laughs.

'But, really,' said Catrin, 'there weren't any Americans at Dunkirk, so how can there be one in the film?'

Buckley sighed and then made a lunge for a piece of paper that was lying on the edge of Catrin's table. He sat reading it, silently. 'Not bad,' he said, handing it back. 'Rose Starling dictated that to you, did she?'

'No.'

'You were eavesdropping on the platform, when she saw her fiancé on to the troop train?'

'No.'

'So how did you come to write those lines?'

'I just . . . I don't know, I simply imagined what they'd say.'

'And if this ever gets to the cinema, do you think that all the Mauds and Annies sitting in the one-and-nines blubbering into their hankies will believe that this is exactly what Rose Starling said to her Johnnie?'

Catrin stared at the scene. It had taken her three days to write, and she had barely slept for thinking of it, she had tested every word on her tongue, and yet now it looked to her as authentic as a posy of crêpe flowers. 'I don't suppose they will,' she said. 'No.'

'Baloney,' said Buckley, crisply. 'You're forgetting that we've *got* them, all the Mauds and Annies, they're *ours* – they're not members of the Kinematic Discussion Group, they're not in some lousy boulevard café debating the role of the artist, they're sitting in the dark and they're watching a story, and if that story's good enough – if it's well enough told – then for ninety minutes it'll seem real to them, and if it seems real to them, then they'll believe every word. Doesn't matter if it's not *true*. And in any case,' he added, taking up his old place in front of the wall of cards and bouncing on his toes a couple of times, like a PT instructor, 'in any case, the bastards in the MoI control the film stock, and if we don't give them what they ask for then the film doesn't get made. So if they demand a bloody elephant at Dunkirk then it's incumbent on us to come up with a convincing subplot incorporating Group Captain Jumbo of the Third Gloucesters and his adventures on the road to La Panne. Isn't that right, Parfitt?'

Parfitt turned his mottled face slowly towards his co-writer. 'So I've *heard*,' he said, with peculiar emphasis.

'Howdah you mean?' returned Buckley, pulling on a pair of imaginary braces.

'I mean, you're a hard tusk-master.'

Catrin ducked; a stampede of elephant-based puns was clearly on its way. She looked instead at the scene between Rose and Johnnie. It was a flashback, written to slot in between two shots of Rose at the tiller of the *Redoubtable* as she steered towards Dunkirk, her eyes on the horizon and her thoughts on her fiancé. Catrin knew the lines off by heart, and this time, as her eyes slid down the page, she tried to watch it rather than read it: John Clements as Johnnie, perhaps, Margaret Lockwood as Rose, their faces ten feet wide, a drift of blue smoke across the screen, the crunch of someone eating an apple in the row behind . . .

Rose is on the platform, Johnnie is on the train. He is leaning through the window and holding her hand.

JOHNNIE

You will write?

ROSE

Every single day.

JOHNNIE

You won't have enough news for every single day.

ROSE

I won't have any big news, but I'll tell you about the small things. I'll tell you about the shrimp catch, and the queue at the grocer's, and which film star Lily's fallen in love with this week. I'll tell you about the allotment, and how many eggs the hens have laid.

JOHNNIE

And will you tell me that you miss me?

She squeezes his hand.

ROSE

Every single day.

The whistle blows, the train starts to move. Rose walks along the platform, holding Johnnie's hand.

'Do you think,' asked Catrin, tentatively, 'that we might get Margaret Lockwood to play Rose?'

Buckley laughed. 'No actress who thinks she's famous and distinctive is going to want to play one half of a pair of identical twins.'

'Couldn't she play both? They do that, don't they, in—'

'In films that cost five times as much, yes.'

'Oh.'

'You have to use over-shoulder doubles and so on. It all takes far longer to shoot.' He folded his arms, and stared at the scene cards as if he could rearrange them through the sheer power of his eyeballs. 'Of course,' he said, 'another vital point that hasn't occurred to the assembled mandarins at the Ministry of Wanton Paper Shuffling is that all the American actors who were working in London before the war began suddenly found pressing engagements on the other side of the Atlantic once the bombs started dropping.'

'Couldn't they use an English actor – doing the accent, I mean?'

'Not unless we want the USA to side with Germany.'

'Oh.'

'They're allowed to inflict their lousy English accents on us, you see, but any Yanks who appear on screen have to be *orthennic*. So . . .' He stared at the cards for a few seconds longer, and then rounded on his writing partner.

'Parfitt, what's your opinion?'

Parfitt shrugged.

'Well *I* think,' said Buckley, as if Parfitt had advanced a closely-worded and passionate argument in favour of scrapping the entire plot and starting again, 'that we have to slide this Yank into the gaps – we don't want to tinker with the story too much, we've already got pretty girls and heroism and comedy and sacrifice and a dog.'

'All exits covered,' said Parfitt.

'Exactly. And if we add anything to location, Shipton in accounts will whip off that milksop mask and turn into a knife-wielding madman. Catrin, what would an American be doing at Dunkirk?'

'Er . . .'

'No, scrub that, what *wouldn't* an American be doing?'

'Fighting.'

'Good girl. So what would that make him?'

She thought hard. 'An observer.'

'Good girl again. Well done, Mrs Taff. Gives us a start, doesn't it – cynical, wise-cracking observer won over by the best of British pluck.' He smiled his wolfish smile and smacked his hands together. 'Gird your loins, Parfitt,' he said. 'Strap on your sword. There's work to do.'

*

Sophie wore an opaque veil at the funeral, and when offered condolences, merely inclined her head without speaking. She was surrounded for much of the time by an honour guard of tiny old ladies, their coats emitting a choking cloud of naphthalene, their ancient shoes cracked across the bunions and polished to mirror-brightness. Yiddish whispers, like an epidemic of throat clearance, rustled the air. At the graveside, Ambrose stood behind them and found himself gazing down at a sea of hat-crowns, the undulating black nap broken only by the occasional rakish feather or the wink of a jet clasp. From his viewpoint, Sammy's coffin was invisible. He was glad of that; it stopped him from having to think about how many people it might contain.

Sammy's other clients had congregated on the opposite side of the grave, beneath a charred yew tree. The half-melted canister of an incendiary lay wedged in a crook three yards from the ground, and above it the trunk had turned to charcoal.

Every gust of wind filled the air with filthy specks, and the respectful stance of the group was interrupted by discreet brushings and little shakes.

Philip Cadogan, chinless juvenile lead turned infantry lieutenant, was standing in the front row, as was Martin Brawley, all-purpose heavy, his wooden features bearing, in grief, much the same expression that they wore when called upon to portray joy, love or laughter. Next to him, weeping copiously, was Lalage Bunting (heading into her third decade as an ingénue), and beside her stood Christopher Allenby, the uniform of the Auxiliary Fire Service hanging from his matchstick physique like a banner from a pole.

Sammy, of course, had been loyal to the proverbial fault. His list had creaked with dead wood: promising saplings that had withered to nothing, fruit trees that had long since ceased to bear. During visits to the office, Ambrose had overheard him on the telephone, trying to persuade casting directors that Lalage still retained her girlish spring, that Philip exuded manly authority, that Martin could act. His enthusiasm had been unquestionable; what was suspect was his judgement. There was no doubt in Ambrose's mind that there had been occasions when a script entirely suitable for himself had been diverted to a client perceived by Sammy as being in greater need. 'Poor Chrishtopher,' Sammy might say, 'he's been having an awful time with his wife's teeth.' And then the next thing that one knew, Christopher would be paying his dentist's bill courtesy of a role that required patrician authority, a full head of hair and a height significantly greater than that of his leading lady.

'You see, I like to find my clients roles that will *shtrech* them,' had been Sammy's usual excuse, but the truth was that he had lacked the ruthlessness necessary for a good agent. His pruning hook had never left its sheath.

There was a sudden stillness in the graveyard; the long, unhurried Hebrew prayer had ended. The rabbi stepped aside, the undertaker's men moved forward and Lalage Bunting raised a lace-edged handkerchief to her eyes.

Above her, behind the branches of the yew tree, there was a flicker of movement. Ambrose glanced up and saw something amorphous – something grey and jowled that shuddered and disappeared once more behind the trunk. He heard the patter of loose earth as the coffin containing most of Sammy was lowered, and then the grey shape appeared behind the tree again, higher this time and swinging slowly in the wind, and it was obvious now that it was a barrage balloon, half a mile away. A barrage balloon, straining against its wire as it lifted into the sky, but for all that, it was extraordinarily, unmistakably Sammy-like: the absent waistline, the bulbous nose, the sheer inertia of its bulk. Someone fanciful, someone prone to religious whimsy might have found the sight symbolic – Sammy's soul floating into the ether, may flights of angels sing thee to thy rest and take thee onward to thy Saviour's breast – or whatever the Jewish equivalent might be. Abraham's bosom, perhaps. Moses's knee. Christ, he needed a drink.

There was no road to the cemetery gates, only a meandering path between the tombstones, wide enough for three to walk abreast. The groups on either side of the grave shuffled slowly into line, merging into a straggling crocodile with Sammy's clients forming the tail.

'Oh hell,' said Lalage, attempting to tuck her handkerchief up her sleeve and making heavy weather of it. 'I'm just a sodden *mess*.'

She tripped on the edge of a grave and dropped her handbag. Ambrose retrieved it and she took it from him without a word and stumbled onward.

'I need a drink,' said Martin Brawley. 'And we should raise a glass to Sammy, of course. Anyone know any decent pubs around here?'

'There's the Bull,' said Ambrose. 'It's just behind the station.'

'Wine,' said Lalage, over her shoulder. 'Sammy liked wine, we should toast him in wine, not bitter.'

'You're right, Lal,' said Brawley. 'We should try a restaurant.'

'I'm always right.' She dropped her handbag again and this time snatched it up before Ambrose could reach it. 'I hope you don't think *you're* coming,' she said, giving him a poisonous look. 'Fancy sending poor old Sammy into his office in the middle of a raid. You should be *prosecuted*, you beast. Poor old Sammy, he'd do anything for anybody, even a cold fish like—' She fell headlong, this time, into a hollow between two graves, and lay there snivelling until Brawley picked her up.

'Black coffee, I think,' said Ambrose. 'Otherwise she'll have the most frightful hangover.'

'Beast,' said Lalage again. She wrenched her arm from Brawley and wavered after the others.

Brawley glanced at Ambrose and shrugged. 'A bad business,' he muttered, 'a very bad business.'

'Indeed,' said Ambrose.

They walked a few yards in silence before Brawley cleared his throat. 'May I ask – have you thought what you'll be doing about future representation?'

Ambrose shook his head.

'Only I was wondering,' continued Brawley, 'what with Sammy having been something of a one-man-band . . .'

'I must say,' said Ambrose, stiffly, 'that I think it's a little early to be talking about such matters. The man's only been dead two days.'

'Of course. I didn't mean . . . it's just that our little troupe of players may present something of a drug on the market and in the current climate when things are so very . . .' Brawley cleared his throat uncomfortably. 'Of course you're absolutely right – it's much too early to start thinking about it. Dear old Sammy.'

It wasn't easy – offices had closed or moved, younger staff had been called up, phone lines were down, numbers had changed – nevertheless by the third day after the funeral, Ambrose had dispatched five letters and had managed to speak on the telephone or in person to seven different agents, or their assistants, and he was beginning to feel more than a touch of disquiet.

'We do try to have a nice range of experience on our books, Mr Hilliard, and I'm afraid that we already have more than one client of your calibre and playing age.'

'Is that two 'l's in Hilliard?'

'Could you just remind me of the last time we saw you on the cinema screen, Mr Hilliard?'

'Oh that's an unusual first name, isn't it, sir? Is that spelled the same way as the creamed rice?'

'Would you be willing to perform in pantomime, Mr Hilliard?'

He'd slammed the receiver down so hard after that one that he'd cracked the cradle, and now the damned thing buzzed all the time – another petty repair that wouldn't be fixed until after the Luftwaffe stopped visiting. Every upstairs ceiling leaked now, and since a landmine had descended on the Euston Road, none of the doors would close without a good kick. Still no housekeeper to be found, of course, and the drain in the area was blocked so that the bloody kitchen smelled like Calcutta. He could barely remember a time when coming through his own front door had been a pleasure.

After ten days he had received four postal replies. Two had misspelled his name and none were able to offer him representation. He threw them on to the fire. The fifth letter came back unopened, the address crossed out and the stark word 'GONE' written beneath it. Ambrose spent the next morning searching for his share certificates, and found them in a box at the back of the wardrobe. Felling's Superior Buttons, Caley's Chocolates, Dorita Iced Cream, Reissman & Moffatt, Gaiter and Whip Manufacturers to the Gentry, Corrie Fine Suet – duds the lot of them, the dividends minuscule. He should have shot his bloody broker, missing out on those *Daily Express* shares in 1931.

Another week passed. He bumped into Martin Brawley on The Strand and they talked in a guarded fashion.

'I've been dipping a toe in agency waters,' Brawley said, 'testing for nibbles. You?'

'Too busy, old chap.'

'Oh really? Anything meaty?'

Ambrose gave an enigmatic shrug. 'This and that,' he said.

Brawley was looking rather shabby, Ambrose thought, a stain on his hat-band, his coat frayed at the cuffs. Appearances were so very important.

Back at the house, Ambrose pondered his next move – perhaps a direct approach to studio casting, something casual: hello there, just passing through, had a long-standing lunch appointment with a fellow from head office, thought I'd drop by, awful thing about Sammy Smith, wasn't it? Yes, very sad. No, not busy at the moment, taking a bit of a break out of respect. Really? Well, if you think I'd be suitable . . .

Ealing might be a decent start – not too much of a journey and plenty going on there, by all accounts. He dressed, the next morning, with particular care, and emptied a whole packet of Kensitas into his silver cigarette case, the one presented to him by the management of ABPC at Elstree after *The Laird and the Lass* had been announced as the third most profitable British film of 1927. The inside of the lid was inscribed: 'May ye have a' the luck o'the Glens.' Outside, the wind was brisk and he wound a grey silk scarf around his neck before giving the front door its requisite heave.

It wasn't until he turned the corner into Portland Place, and saw the congregation exiting All Souls, that he realized that it was a Sunday.

He felt shocked – almost literally shocked, as if he had changed a bulb with wet hands. Timing, awareness of time, punctuality; they were more than professional virtues, they were the essence of the actor. He had thought it was a Friday, so where had the days gone? He groped back through the week. He had picked up his groceries on Tuesday. Or perhaps it had been on Wednesday. He had opened the garage door on Thursday and given the motor car a dusting, the poor old bottle-green Alvis, squatting on its bricks in the dark – or was it possible that he'd done that on the Friday? In which case, how had he occupied himself on Thursday? There'd been a brief but noisy raid one night; perhaps he'd slept through part of the morning. He'd taken a walk in the park one afternoon. He'd spoken to a neighbour about a broken chimney pot. Or had that been the week before?

He felt the days judder under his feet like a faulty escalator. Of course, he thought, reaching for a handhold – of course! The problem was that the one firm date had gone: Monday, lunch with Sammy. Over the years the venue had changed – Veeraswamy's, La Venezia, Pacani's, Josef, Maison Basque – but the day had remained constant, the arrangement only ever cancelled if Ambrose were filming, or Sammy taking his yearly holiday in Broadstairs. ('Not a shpectacular place, I know, but highly comfortable.') Monday had been a day for discussion; it had had a purpose and a shape, it had been the hook on which the rest of the week could be hung, and now that hook had been permanently unscrewed.

Ambrose walked back to the house, took off his coat and scarf, and sat for a while in an armchair beside the window. When the phone rang, he was asleep.

'Mr Hilliard?'

'Yes.'

'It's Sophie Smith.'

She left one of her frigid pauses.

Ambrose struggled for an appropriate remark. 'And how are you, Miss Smith?'

'My health is quite good, thank you. I hope you don't mind that I'm telephoning you on a Sunday.'

'Not at all.'

'I remember my brother saying that you had no religious feelings whatsoever.'

'Well . . .'

'And this is a business call.'

'Business?' he repeated, cautiously.

'I have spent the last week reading through my brother's papers from the agency. He kept a safe for his financial work, which was intact, and also his diary and several of his clients' files survived the bombing.'

'I see.'

'Sammy always shared his thoughts with me and I think that I have a very good understanding of the way he worked. It's true that I have no business experience, but I have a clear head and a great deal of common sense and nothing, now, with which to occupy myself. I've made the decision, therefore, to continue with the agency. It will still be called 'Sammy Smith's' and until I can find an office I shall work from this flat.'

'And you will be the . . . titular head?'

'I shall run the business, Mr Hilliard.'

'Oh, I see.' He wasn't quite sure what he thought about this; was any agent better than none? She might 'do' in the interim, he supposed – she might prove a useful stop-gap until he could find a real professional. 'Well, that seems rather enterprising of you,' he said.

'I couldn't, of course, run it in exactly the same way as Sammy.'

'No, obviously not.'

'My brother was a very kind man, and a very good man. He regarded his clients as friends, which I feel may sometimes have clouded his judgement.'

'Do you know, I've often thought that myself.'

'Have you really, Mr Hilliard?'

There was another wintry pause, broken this time by Sophie. 'My brother's diary mentions a possible film for you.'

'Really?'

'A small character role.'

'Oh. Is that the same role that Sammy mentioned when I called him on . . .' Not a good area, he realized, backing away. 'Is that the Baker's feature?' he amended.

'Yes.'

'How small is the role, exactly?'

'There's no completed script as yet. The story is based on a true incident at Dunkirk, in which two girls and their uncle piloted a boat across the channel.'

'That's the role? The uncle?'

'Yes.'

'He pilots the boat?'

'No. He's drunk and asleep for the early part of the story, and then I believe he wakes up and mends the engine and then dies before the end of the film.'

'Not my bag,' said Ambrose. 'Sounds more of a music-hall part. Tell them to ask Tommy Trinder.'

'You don't want me to put your name forward?'

'No.'

'There's currently nothing else for you.'

'Nevertheless.'

'I would strongly advise you to take it.'

If he hadn't been talking to a grief-stricken quasi-widow then he might have become irritated at this point. As it was, he reminded himself that she was completely out of her depth, poor woman. He thought of that narrow flat, of the dark corridor that ran the length of it. 'This is not a role for me, Miss Smith,' he said. 'But thank you.'

She sighed. 'You see, Mr Hilliard, I'm not sure what to do now. Because my brother, after a conversation like this, would replace the receiver and say, "What Ambrose doesn't understand is that the roles he is waiting for are simply never going to arrive. He's behaving as if he's thirty-five and not fifty-three." And I'd say, "Well, why don't you tell him?" I'd say, "What can you lose by being honest? Let him know that ageing, enormously conceited, moderately talented actors are ten a penny, and that he should be grateful for every part that you manage to find him." But Sammy was too kind to do that. He would never have told you, for instance, that the reason you have a good chance of getting this role is because the makers don't want star names. They've decided that, since this is a true story, they'll use faces that the audience don't immediately recognize. "Faces that look real", was the phrase they used. Sammy wrote the casting notes in his diary, here . . .' There was the dry scrape of pages. "*Playing age late fifties, early sixties. Dissipated look*" – and underneath he's written "*Try Ambrose*." He wouldn't have told you that, but I can see no reason not to. The whole point, surely, is to find suitable work for my clients and I can assure you – I can absolutely assure you – that there is nothing else for you at the moment. Do you know how many feature films are currently in production in British studios?'

Ambrose, beyond speech, shook his head; she answered anyway.

'Nine. And only twelve in pre-production, most of which have already been cast with well-known actors. If you don't take this, then you will certainly be twiddling your thumbs for the rest of this year and very probably for half of next. Of course, you are free to find other representation. Another agent *may* offer you more than I can.' Disbelief corroded her voice. In the long, long silence that followed, Ambrose heard a tiny, repetitive noise, like the tick of a distant clock.

'So shall I put your name forward?' asked Sophie.

Behind her, the ticking grew louder, the sound more complex.

Tick. Tickety. Tickety tack.

'Mr Hilliard?'

Tickety tack, tickety tackety . . .

'I—' He could barely remember the question. He raised a hand to his head. The tickety-tacks stopped abruptly and were replaced, after a brief moment, by a series of loud sniffs and then a low, salacious slurping.

'Leave it, Cerberus,' said Sophie. 'Don't be disgusting. *Leave* it. Mr Hilliard, I'm sorry for the interruption, you were going to tell me if I should put your name forward for the role of the inebriated uncle.'

Ambrose took a deep breath. Gathering the blasted fragments of his professional dignity, he made his decision, and spoke.

'I shall have to think about it,' he said.

*

Edith's cousin Verna lived in a world of wickedness. She was a pretty woman, with glossy dark hair and eyes very nearly the colour of violets. She had lived the whole of her forty years in Badgeham and had married the methodist minister, a man with a placid nature and money in the bank, and her sewing shop was doing marvellously well, but when she talked (and she talked a great deal, in a soft but insistent little voice), she glanced around warily as if corruption might, at any second, begin to ooze through the walls of her house – because (as she told Edith) sin was everywhere. The weekly dance held at the Masons' Hall was a nest of temptation, and she'd noticed women going alone to the Crown and Anchor on the village green, there, no doubt, to meet with soldiers who might, or might not, already have sweethearts or even be married, and of course that was also bad, but she reserved a special opprobrium for the cinema, not for fear of what might appear on the screen, but because it was somewhere where men and women were allowed to sit next to each other in the dark. 'If they kept the lights on then I wouldn't mind so much,' she said, taking pins from a pattern and dropping them, one by one, into a saucer. 'But you don't know what might happen in the dark. Myrtle's been on at me to let her go to

Norwich to see *Gone with the Wind* but I've told her there'll be men in that audience with only one thing on their minds. You know what I mean, don't you, Edith? I'm sure it's far worse in London.'

Edith, her eyes fixed on the long side seam of a pair of women's trousers, made a non-committal noise and pressed the treadle. Her cousin's next comment disappeared under the growl of the Singer.

The sewing-room was situated in an odd little glass-roofed lean-to at the back of the shop. It had once served as Verna's husband's greenhouse, before Verna had decided to expand the business, and when the sun shone there was still a lingering smell of tomatoes. The panes were criss-crossed with strips of anti-shatter tape, and a lattice of shadow fell across the interior. Bolts of cloth formed a layer of insulation along the walls, and on windless days it grew so warm that Verna would prop open the external door, and the neighbours' cats would slide through the gap and lie beatifically on the tiled floor. From the garden came the comfortable sound of her husband, Roy, double-digging his potato patch.

'Of course, nowhere's safe nowadays,' said Verna. 'They're sitting in the dark in the pictures and then they come out afterwards and they're still in the dark. Who's to say what's going on in bus shelters when you can't even see your hand in front of your face? You know what I mean, don't you Edith? I'm sure it must happen all the time where you live – you hear a noise and you can't think *what* it is. It could be buttons, it could be something worse.'

What could be worse than buttons? wondered Edith. Zips, she supposed, with their near-instant access to whatever they were concealing. Though, on second thoughts, the noise of a zip was unmistakeable, so perhaps Verna was implying a sort of non-specific fumbling sound, the muffled scrabble of a hand searching in a pocket. For a bus fare, perhaps, or . . .

It was Verna's repeated phrase, 'You know what I mean, don't you Edith?' that sent her thoughts along such unhelpful byways. Because, as a matter of fact – and in spite of her long-term residency on the outskirts of the bubbling Cauldron of Sin – she *didn't* know. It seemed that there were those who, like her cousin, saw sex everywhere, and there were those who, like herself, managed hardly to see it at all, and this was not through any very deliberate avoidance.

'I was coming back along Mudd Street after dark on Monday,' said Verna, 'after the salvage meeting, and I heard a noise from a doorway, not a *nice* noise, if you know what I mean, Edith, and—' There was the jangle of the shop bell, and Verna rose with alacrity. 'That'll be Mrs Campion about the skirts,' she said. 'I shan't be long.'

Edith worked on. Occasional snatches of conversation drifted through from the shop: the terrible cost of perms, the state of the chapel roof, the fall of Benghazi. After half an hour, the subject of skirts had yet to be broached, and Edith lobbed the completed trousers into the ironing basket, and stood up and stretched. A shadow by the open doorway moved suddenly.

'Hello Myrtle,' said Edith.

There was a pause, and then the figure of Myrtle Furse eased into view. 'I wasn't spying.'

'It doesn't matter. I wasn't doing anything worth spying on,' said Edith.

'I was seeing if Mum was here.'

'She's talking to a customer.'

'Good. May I sit and watch you?'

'Of course, if you'd like to. I'm only going to unpick a frock.'

Myrtle dragged a stool across the floor. She was a large girl for twelve (an 'early developer' as her mother delicately put it), and she moved with an apologetic, round-shouldered gait that did nothing to decrease her visibility. She had small hands and feet, dainty features in the middle of a wide pink face, and a great frizz of dark hair. Her adenoids were enlarged, and until their removal ('the doctor says they have to ripen') she spoke in an unlovely monotone. Verna's expression when she looked at her daughter was one of permanent exasperation, as if she had ordered a bolt of ciré marocain, and a length of canvas had turned up instead.

'How was school today?' asked Edith.

'The nit nurse came and Joyce Hodson had to go home, she caught them off an evacuee. I like the buttons on your cuffs,' she added, stroking one with a fingertip. 'They look just like liquorice drops.'

'Thank you.'

'And did you buy them in *London*?' As ever, the word was invested with breathy awe.

'I did, yes.'

'Whereabouts?'

'In a shop called Mrs Beck's in Dean Street.'

'Is that near anywhere famous?'

'It runs into Shaftesbury Avenue.'

'Shaftesbury Avenue, the heart of London's glamorous theatre land.' The phrase – one of many that she'd swallowed whole from magazines – was delivered with utter seriousness, and Edith coughed, to hide her smile.

'It doesn't look particularly glamorous at the moment,' she said. 'There aren't any lights outside the theatres, you know.'

'Yes, but it's still . . .' Myrtle shook her head, unable to express the vastness of her vision. She opened her satchel and took out the *A-Z* that a visitor from London had once left under a Badgeham beach hut. Myrtle, mooning along the sands one afternoon after school, had found it, opened it and been transported into a world where the high street didn't end at a salt marsh, and where you could take a bus from one royal palace to another, via a zoo. She consulted it daily, dipping in at random in much the same way as her mother dipped into the Bible, seeking inspirational verses. 'I was looking at the area around Piccadilly Circus this lunchtime,' said Myrtle, with easy authority. 'Did you ever go there?'

'Oh yes,' said Edith, thinking of the dreary cocoon of sandbags that protected Eros from blast damage, of the soldiers who loitered outside Lillywhite's and wolf-whistled the shop girls. 'Lots of times.'

'And have you seen any stars of stage or screen, stepping out of a taxi on their way to one of the many fashionable eating houses?'

'I'm afraid not. Though I did see Mr Gandhi once, on the steps of St Martin-in-the-Fields.'

Myrtle left a brief pause, in lieu of interest. 'I was thinking . . .' she said.

'Yes?'

'When you go back to London . . .' She looked at Edith with sudden anxiety. '*Are* you going back?'

'Oh yes.'

'I mean, I don't want you to, I wish you wouldn't go, but when you do go, well, can I come and visit you? Just for a day. I could get the train from Norwich and—'

'Is that you, Myrtle?' called Verna from the shop. 'Come here, please.'

Myrtle sighed, and put away her almanac. '*Errands*,' she said, gloomily. There were only nineteen streets in Badgeham and she knew them all.

Edith shook out the folds of a sand-crêpe dress that needed re-modelling, and took out her stitch-ripper. So when *are* you going back? she wondered, guiding the wicked little hook along the seam.

She certainly had no intention of working as Verna's junior for the rest of her life, and Madame Tussaud's had been very understanding and had said that they would hold her job open if she wanted to return. '*How's the shell-shock?*' Dolly Clifford had asked in her last letter. '*My next door neighbour told me about her uncle's cousin who was bombed out in October. He was a jeweller and he went straight back to work, setting diamonds, and then someone slammed a door and he dropped a stone worth £3,000 and it fell through a crack in the floorboards and they never found it again. He's in a mental hospital now.'* The Kings and Queens gallery had been closed for eight weeks after the bomb had fallen, but had now re-opened and there were more visitors than ever, in spite of the raids. '*Nora's fallen in love with a Polish sailor she met in the Chamber of Horrors. She says she can't even spell his name, but he wants her to go back with him after the war and live on his pig farm. I am stepping out with our shelter warden. He says we should make the most of our time, as Hitler's ordered a 400-ton bomb that's built into a glider and once that drops we'll be for it. Did I tell you that admission charges went up in January?*'

The Badgeham siren had only sounded twice since Edith had arrived, and both had been false alarms. The Londoners who'd stayed had suffered fifty-odd night raids in a row before Christmas, and a fair few sharp ones since then. God knows she was glad to have been out of it, but somehow it wasn't the thought of the raids that constricted her chest whenever she thought of returning; it wasn't even the disorder or the filth or the awfulness of having to find new accommodation. It was the insidious feeling that, war notwithstanding, she'd be returning to precisely the same spot on precisely the same road that she had left five months before.

She always thought of it as a road. Verna's mother – Edith's aunt – had owned a picture that had fascinated Edith as a child, and the title had been THE TWO ROADS – one of these the broad, slippery path to hell (lined with pothouses and gambling dens), and the other the narrow, steady climb to paradise, where the only distractions were the good deeds waiting to be done. At the centre of the picture stood two children, apparently pondering which route to take. It had implied that at some point in life there would be a choice – a fork, a crossroads, an opportunity to at least glimpse a little sinfulness, a flash of gaiety, if only from a distance. But Edith's own blameless track seemed to possess unfairly high hedges, and she'd plodded along without ever managing to catch sight of a wider view, for she wasn't like Dolly, who managed zestfully to wring the drama out of every step, or Verna who never seemed to doubt her own purpose and destination – or even Myrtle, who at least had spotted a Shining City somewhere above the hedgerows. The flight to Norfolk, the drama that preceded it, were in danger of being nothing more than a spell on the grass verge, when what she really needed was a Damascene revelation. Or even a ladder.

The shop bell rang as Myrtle left on her errands. Edith detached the dress bodice from the skirt, and began to unpick the underarm seams. She found herself matching the snap of the stitch-ripper to the scrape and thud of Mr Furse's spade; the sounds fitted together nicely: one could almost sing 'Tea for Two' to the rhythm. After a while, the nagging drone of an aircraft joined the other two noises, slightly spoiling the tune, and then, with the brute finality of someone stamping on a gramophone record, the colossal roar of the battery began, followed immediately by a tiny, dangerous whine that emanated from the glass just above her head; Edith hastily put down her sewing and grabbed a bolt of flannelette.

'I've got it,' she called, opening the door to the garden. The plane, from the local aerodrome, was flying just to the north of the village, a red-and-yellow silk target trailing far behind it on an invisible wire.

'Can you manage?' shouted Verna's husband Roy, pausing over his spade.

'I can manage.' She slid the bolt of flannelette on to the last panel of the glass roof and weighed it down with a trio of bricks. The tiny vibration stopped.

'Well done,' shouted Roy.

He straightened up, welcoming the interruption, and they both watched the plane describe a leisurely figure of eight high to the north of the village. If any of the bullets were hitting the target then they were leaving no trace.

'Ah well,' said Roy, bending to his task again, 'it'll be back again tomorrow, no doubt.'

Edith returned to the lean-to and shut the door, minutely decreasing the noise of the guns. She had just sat down again when the shop bell jangled violently, and a moment later Myrtle galloped into the lean-to. 'You'll never guess what they told me at the butcher's,' she said, panting. 'It's the most exciting thing to happen in Badgeham *ever* . . .'

March 1941

The bathroom on the first floor of the Crown and Anchor was not the ideal place in which to practise vocal exercises, but since it was the only private area available to Ambrose, he really had no choice. There was a little too much reverberation created by the large number of hard surfaces, but the ceiling was surprisingly high, and by tilting his head back he could achieve quite a decent effect. Plosives, in particular, came out well.

Bright copper kettle
Pretty copper kettle
Pretty copper kipper
Popacatapetl
Cup cot kin
Pup pot pin
Pitter patter petal
Kipper copper kettle.

Well, that was better; the words bounced back like billiard balls. Of late, he had noticed a hoarse edge to his voice – not the roughness of a throat infection, but a sort of dry creak, like that of an unoiled door. Neglect, of course, was as threatening to a delicate instrument as abuse, and there had been whole days recently (sometimes several days in a row) during which his vocal cords had rusted, unused. He couldn't risk laryngitis on the very first day of location filming.

He gargled and then began on a volume exercise, taking the syllable 'ha' from the barely audible to a ringing shout and then back again, and he was on his fourth repetition when a door crashed open somewhere along the corridor outside and a series of heavy footsteps approached the bathroom.

'It's occupied,' called Ambrose.

'I know it's fucking occupied,' shouted someone with a cockney accent. 'It's occupied by some bastard who thinks that it's hilarious to shout at the top of his fucking voice at half past six in the fucking morning.' Whoever it was rattled the handle with brutish strength.

'I'm very nearly finished,' said Ambrose.

'No you're not, you're completely fucking finished, and if I hear the fucking word "kettle" one more fucking time then I'm going to find one and shove it up your arse sideways.'

It seemed prudent to wait until King Kong was back in his den before exiting the bathroom, and Ambrose spent a useful few moments trimming his fingernails. This, then, was what happened when cast and crew were thrust into the same milieu.

'Accommodation's tight so we're all mucking in together,' the production manager had said, as if there were some sort of virtue in the idea, and what was the inevitable result? Mutual misunderstandings, and the nightly prospect of watching electricians at the very next table in the dining-room eating peas with a spoon.

All remained quiet outside, and Ambrose cautiously slid the bolt and passed quickly along the landing. He had, at least, been allocated the best room that the hostelry could offer, although this tiny victory had been undermined by the fact that another bed had been inserted into one corner. It had remained unoccupied until the early hours of the morning, when he had awoken to the sound of drawers opening and closing and the bobbing of a torch-beam across the carpet. 'Sorry,' someone had muttered, 'only just got here.'

That someone was sitting up in bed, polishing a pair of spectacles, when Ambrose re-entered the room. The blackouts had been raised and the first grey light showed a round-faced man in his thirties sporting a terrible haircut.

'Good morning,' said Ambrose.

'Oh, hello. Er . . .' The man put on his spectacles, adjusting them with stubby fingers, taking several seconds over the task as if it were a complex and skilled procedure.

'Arthur Frith,' he said, at last, extending a hand.

'Ambrose Hilliard.'

There was no hint on Arthur's face that he might ever have heard the name before.

'And in what capacity,' asked Ambrose, 'are you joining our merry little band?' He placed his mental bet on accountant, and then nudged it towards cashier. Accountants could afford a decent barber.

'I'm the special military advisor,' said Arthur, re-adjusting his spectacles all over again. 'I only found out yesterday.'

God help us, thought Ambrose, no wonder we're on the road to defeat, he looks about as bellicose as a currant bun. 'You're from the War Office?'

'The War Office?' Arthur looked amazed. 'No, no, I'm a lance-corporal storeman in the East Surreys.'

It was Ambrose's turn to slacken his jaw. 'So what exactly are you supposed to be advising us on?'

Arthur cleared his throat, paused and then cleared it again. 'I'm not altogether sure,' he said. 'It was one of those "You over there, one pace forward" jobs. Someone said something about a film . . .'

'That's right.'

'Is it a training film?'

'No.'

'Oh. I thought it might have something to do with the new field paraffin stoves we've been issued with.'

'No.'

'Well, perhaps it's a mistake. That sort of thing does seem to happen quite often.'

'It's a feature film,' said Ambrose. 'It's the true story of a cockle-boat captain who took his boat to the Dunkirk beaches.'

'Ah.'

'And his nieces came, too. Were you at Dunkirk?'

'Yes. Yes, I was.'

'Then I expect they want somebody who was actually there to check on the accuracy of the film portrayal.'

'Really?' He looked disconcerted. 'Well, it was all a bit of a muddle.'

'What was?'

'The evacuation. It was all rather . . . Which bits do they want me to remember?'

'No, no, you don't have to remember anything.'

'Don't I?'

'You simply sit and watch. And if something doesn't look right then you tell someone.'

'Do I? How long will it all take?'

'Three weeks here, and then five weeks in a studio in London. With a fortnight's gap in-between.'

'My goodness . . .' Arthur scratched his left ear with his right hand and then, after a short pause, his right ear with his left. The second gesture knocked his glasses askew, and for the third time he began the fussy process of re-adjustment. 'It makes a bit of a change, I suppose. I'm not much of a picture-goer myself, more of a hobbies man.'

Stamps, thought Ambrose, sprinting to the bookies. Fretwork. 'What sort of hobbies?' he asked.

'Fretwork,' said Arthur Frith. 'And I have quite a large stamp collection. Or rather I did have. When the night blitz kicked off I put it in the bank for safe-keeping and then Jerry blew the bank up. I had a ten-centime four-colour Mauritian peacock with a bi-wheel watermark.'

There was a note of yearning in his voice. Ambrose nodded

and then, stuck for a verbal response, took a stroll over to the window. Clapboard houses, a wedge of greensward, rooks wheeling above a row of elms – the view was almost absurdly idyllic, marred only by an ugly brick-built shelter in the middle of the grass. The miracle was that, with front-line troops of the calibre of Arthur Frith, the German tanks weren't already grinding past the duckpond. Although of course, one always thought that the enemy soldiers must surely be tougher, crueller, altogether more *military* than the jug-eared schoolboys on one's own side; somewhere across the North Sea, blinking nervously at the icy water, there would be other Arthur Friths, battalions of them. Ambrose had a sudden memory of a German dugout, unoccupied, abandoned in a hurry – a jar of warm coffee still on an upturned box and a rat scuttling away with the remains of a black loaf – and trodden into the mud, a bird-identification book, the section on finches marked with careful pencil notes.

'So what is it that you do?' asked Arthur Frith. 'Are you the fellow who works the camera?'

'No.'

'You're not in catering, are you? Because in civvy street that's my own line of . . .'

'*Actor*,' said Ambrose, crisply. 'I'm an actor.'

'Oh.' Arthur looked completely nonplussed. 'But I would have thought an actor . . . I mean to say . . .'

Ambrose waited, fatalistically. He had obviously missed the exact moment when open season had been declared on his career, but it was clear that anyone, these days, felt free to take pot shots. An ex-wife, an unqualified agent, a man who counted giant tins of sausages for a living – all were happy to load the ammunition and let fly.

'. . . I would have thought,' said Arthur, hesitantly, 'that you'd be staying somewhere a bit more . . . important. Not sharing a room with someone like me.'

The louring clouds of Ambrose's current existence parted momentarily. 'I think you'll find that we're all mucking in together on this production,' he said, warmly. 'Just as we're all mucking in together to defend our country.' Not a bad line, he thought; one to remember for the publicity feature.

There was a knock at the door. 'Ten to seven, Mr 'illiard, Mr Frith,' said someone in a soft, hoarse voice that seemed somehow familiar. 'Breakfast is downstairs and then Mr 'illiard to make-up by seven thirty.'

'Ooh, breakfast,' said Arthur Frith, visibly cheered. 'Nothing like a good breakfast. Fresh eggs, perhaps, since we're in the country.' He took off his spectacles for the fourth time in as many minutes, and began to polish them on his pyjama jacket – left lens, right lens, right lens, left lens. 'Three weeks by the seaside,' he said, reflectively. 'It's almost like being given a little holiday, isn't it? I can't think why on earth they picked me.'

The louring clouds stayed parted for most of breakfast. There were no eggs, but the porridge was hot and the bacon crisp, and it was pleasant to share a table with someone so engagingly ignorant of the whole business of film-making. One could teach so much that was of value.

'That tall man at the corner table,' he said to Arthur, very quietly, 'is called Alex Frayle and he's the director.'

'And he calls "action", does he?'

'No, more usually that's the job of the first assistant director.'

'So what does the director do?'

'That all depends. A truly great director has a vision of precisely how the film should turn out, and by nurturing the skills and experience of his cast, will endeavour to convert that vision into a reality. *That* man, on the other hand, is a jumped-up little camera assistant who's apparently been given this job on the strength of three years spent making films about fishwives and coal heavers with Grierson's lot.'

Arthur looked mystified. 'With . . . ?'

'Documentaries,' said Ambrose, expelling the word like a foul-tasting lozenge. 'Never happy unless the screen's filled with slag heaps. The man next to him is the first assistant director. He ensures that the daily schedule is adhered to.'

'Do you know him, too?'

'No, but first assistants tend to divide into Hitlers and toadies, and he strikes me as a toady.' It was the deferential way in which the man was listening to his director, like a coolie awaiting orders. 'The fellow next to him is the writer, I spoke to him in the bar last night, he's a northerner, not quite as much of a fool as he looks, and I'll concede that his script isn't entirely without merit. And this—' he added, as a stringy red-head approached the table, 'is our continuity girl. We've worked together before, haven't we my dear?' She was apparently impervious to charm, for she merely nodded and slapped a sheaf of paper in front of him.

'Today's scenes,' she said.

'I received those last night.'

'All changed, I'm afraid. Someone misread the tide chart and we'd prefer not to drown half the cast on the first day. You're up second, incidentally – just the one set-up.'

She turned to leave and realized that Arthur was standing, his hand outstretched.

'Arthur Frith,' he said. 'Pleased to meet you.'

'Phyl. Likewise.' She shook his hand briskly and whisked away again.

'I think you'll find that a film set's more informal than most workplaces,' said Ambrose to Arthur. 'First names and so forth—'

'Mr 'illiard?'

And now Ambrose knew why he'd recognized the voice behind the door; it was the third assistant director from the Home Security shorts, the one with the ridiculous name, the one built like a bollard.

'They want yer in make-up, Mr 'illiard.'

'I shall be five minutes,' said Ambrose. 'I have *just* received a completely new shooting script, and I'd be grateful for the chance to cast an eye over it.' He smiled wryly at Arthur – it was good that a neophyte should glimpse the daily difficulties and demands that an actor encountered; so many people seemed to think it an easy job – and then noticed that Chick was still standing by the table.

'Five minutes,' said Ambrose, with a smile of dismissal. Chick took half a step backward, his face impassive.

'You begin to see the essence of filming,' said Ambrose, sotto voce to Arthur. 'Never Enough Time. Now, let's see what we have here . . .' He turned to his scene. It was short.

118. EXT. SEASCAPE DAY (GLASS SHOT)

On board Redoubtable, LILY is steering, ROSE is on lookout.

UNCLE FRANK climbs on to deck from below.

119. STOCK SHOT STUKA SCREAMING OVERHEAD

(Or use RAF footage Scene 340.)

120. RESUME SEASCAPE (GLASS SHOT)

Lily and Rose duck. Uncle Frank stares up at the sky in disbelief.

UNCLE FRANK

What the devil . . .?

Uncle Frank then looks in direction of beach, and reacts with amazement.

(NB C.U. AND DIALOGUE TO 120 TO BE SHOT IN STUDIO)

'Many new lines to learn?' asked Arthur.

Ambrose looked at him sharply but there was no sarcasm in the man's tone, merely innocent enquiry. 'No,' he said. 'You'll find that most of the dialogue scenes will be recorded in studio. It's far too expensive to—'

He stopped abruptly; he could hear something – he could hear that damned noise again, that tiny, distant clock, that slowly-approaching tick-tock, tickety-tackety, up-the-dark-corridor, toenails-on-parquet, and for one wild and chilling moment he thought it must be Sammy's dog, Sammy's dog still searching for his master. He twisted round in his chair towards the source of the noise. Through the dining-room door came Sammy's dog.

'Cerberus,' said Ambrose, his voice guttural.

'Chopper,' said Chick, and clicked his fingers. The dog dropped to its belly as if shot.

'Are you feeling all right?' asked Arthur, peering at Ambrose. 'You're looking quite pale.'

'I thought I recognized the dog,' he said. 'I know a bull-terrier who's the spit of that one.' Though, now that he thought about it – now that his heart had started to beat again – he remembered that Sammy's dog had a white patch on its nose; this one was uniformly brindled. It lay at its master's feet, ears flattened servilely.

'He's very well-trained,' said Arthur.

'Die,' said Chick, pointing downward. The dog rolled on to his side, and lay with its eyes closed. Chick shifted his heavy gaze towards Ambrose.

'Shall we go?' said Ambrose. 'I think I can hear the greasepaint a-calling.'

*

Everyone had been awfully friendly to Arthur. He'd been given a cup of tea and a canvas stool to sit on, the camera chap had demonstrated his light meter, rather in the manner of a schoolboy showing off his birthday penknife, the two young lady actresses had shaken his hand, the director had looked briefly in his general direction, and a talkative man with a pair of scissors had offered him a haircut. 'On the house,' the man had said. 'Honestly, I'd be grateful for the activity, I'm kicking my heels here, the director wants everyone looking wind-blown and natural, and besides, they're all wearing woolly hats.'

'Perhaps later,' Arthur had said. He was supposed to be at work, after all.

He had found a nice level spot on the sand-bar for his stool, and after dusting the seat, and removing a few scraps of drift-wood and weed that were cluttering up the immediate area, and sweeping away a cluster of worm-casts with a rolled-up news-paper and giving his glasses a quick polish, he was ready for action. Or 'action', rather, as these film-people would have it.

Nothing happened for a good hour. The tide began to creep in. Chopper the bull-terrier passed by, busily sniffing, and one of the young lady actresses stepped on a jelly-fish and screamed a great deal. Arthur found a bigger piece of driftwood and occupied himself by drawing a perfect square in the sand around his stool while remaining seated; it was more difficult than one might think. Round about ten o'clock, a light wind began to pluck at the water and the young lady actresses were helped into a rowing-boat and taken across to a thirty-foot white-painted tub anchored a few yards off-shore. Both actresses were wearing trousers, which was just as well since they had to climb a fixed ladder and swing themselves over the gunwales. The director shouted something through cupped hands, and one of the young ladies positioned herself in the bows, a hand shading her eyes, while the other took the tiller. The director gave a 'thumbs up' sign and strolled away to speak to the cameraman. A few minutes later, a boy holding a bucket and brush waded out to the boat and started to daub the side with what looked like muddy water. The tide crept in still further. Arthur erased the perfect square and replaced it with an equilateral triangle.

'Quiet, please,' ordered the first assistant director, through a megaphone. '*Quiet*. Going for a take.' There was a cessation of movement behind the camera and an indefinable sharpening of attention. The actresses re-assumed their positions at stern and bow, the clapper-board smacked shut and the boy holding it hurried to one side. The row of spectators on a nearby sand-dune nudged one another and leaned forward. The man with the megaphone shouted 'Action!' and then for nearly half a minute one actress pretended to steer, while the other pretended to gaze at the horizon. Neither spoke a word and nothing else happened. The spectators stirred uneasily.

The director shouted 'cut', and the actresses relaxed their poses. There was a moment of consultation behind the camera, and then the man with the megaphone called 'Going again', and Arthur slowly rubbed out the corners of the triangle and began to turn it into a hexagon.

There were two more 'goes' at the half-minute-of-nothing-at-all before the director was satisfied, and then Ambrose Hilliard, almost unrecognizable in a stained jersey and oilskins, was rowed out to join the lady actresses. Some mime-play followed, during which, at a shouted cue, the three occupants of the boat looked suddenly upward at an invisible object and then ducked. They were asked to carry out this procedure a further five times, and then lunch was called. Arthur stepped over the elaborate hexagon-within-a-pentagon that now circumscribed his stool and followed the crew around the edge of the sand-dune to where a table had been set with plates of sandwiches and a tea-urn. People were eating as if they had spent the morning breaking rocks instead of standing on a beach, and Arthur waited to one side until a gap might appear in the scrum.

'Hello there,' said Phyl, glancing up at him. She had bagged a section of breakwater and was making rapid notes in a file. 'Enjoying yourself?'

'Yes, thank you,' he said, automatically.

'If you're wondering if it's always this slow, then it's not. We've fallen behind. Our director wasn't entirely happy with the performance of the waves.'

'Oh I see.' Though in fact, he'd barely registered the slowness; since joining the army he'd become used to great wedges of time spent simply waiting around, without any clear idea of what one was actually waiting for.

'We'll have to start catching up,' she said. 'The first couple of days are fairly straightforward but the end of the week's sheer hell. Over a hundred extras on Thursday, and the RAF's promised to send us a couple of planes.'

'Have they?'

'And there's Chick's dog as well, doing a couple of scenes. Did you know it had a part in the film?'

'No, I didn't.'

'Though it'll be less trouble than most actors, probably.'

'Yes.'

'No costume, no make-up, no drivelling on about the size of dressing-rooms.'

'I'm sure.'

She looked up at him with apparent amusement. 'You don't say much, do you?'

'Well . . . I—' There was, he realized, a large thumbprint on his left lens; he took off his spectacles and started to polish them. He'd come across this sort of thing before in conversations with women – all of a sudden they'd want you to talk as well as listen, and then you'd be stumped.

'It doesn't matter,' said Phyl, shrugging. 'Makes a pleasant change around here. Just don't be afraid to speak up if there's something we ought to know.'

'Oh yes. About that – I was wondering . . .'

'Yes?'

'When are you filming the part of the story set at Dunkirk?'

She raised an eyebrow. 'We already have.'

'When?'

'Those two scenes that we shot this morning. They're

supposed to be taking place just off the French coast.'

He looked at her carefully to see if she might be joking. It appeared not.

'When you see it on screen,' she said, 'there'll be a whole fleet of other ships. It was a glass shot, you see, it's like a magic-lantern slide that sits on a frame in front of the camera lens. And there'll be sound effects put on afterwards, explosions and so on. It'll all be quite different.'

'I see.'

She was glancing at her notes again, clearly keen to get on with her work, and Arthur gave an awkward sort of nod.

'Thank you,' he said, and he saw her bite her cheek. Saying 'thank you', then, was probably too formal for the current situation. He always found the beginnings and ends of conversations rather difficult to negotiate, rather ill-defined; it was a pity there wasn't a clear, impersonal signal of some kind, of the Aldis-lamp variety. *Blink, blinkety, blink: – I wish to stop speaking to you. Please move away.*

There were fewer people, now, around the refreshment table, and he took a sandwich and a cup of tea and retraced his steps around the dune. A gust of wind had tumbled the stool a few yards from its previous position, and he cleared a fresh section of sand before setting it down again.

He'd last seen an Aldis lamp on the beach at Bray-Dunes, on the fourth day of the evacuation. A driver from his unit had found one amongst the litter on the sand – though 'litter' was not really the word for it; there *was* no adequate word for it. For half a week, fifty thousand men had lived and slept among the dunes that stretched from Dunkirk to La Panne, had been shelled and machine-gunned, had nearly gone mad from thirst, had used bomb craters as foxholes and foxholes as latrines, had queued time and time again for a place in a boat, in long patient lines that ran from the land into the sea like human breakwaters, had emptied their rifles at Stukas and played cards and prayed and sworn and waited for rescue, with the German guns edging closer, and the sea that had been like grey glass for the first few days beginning to slap and heave and rock the debris on its margin. And somewhere amongst all the filth and disarray, somewhere above the tide-mark of discarded greatcoats and packs, of smashed planks and crates and smears of oil, driver Tony Pierce had found a signal-lamp.

He brought it back to the cleft in the dunes that the remnants of their unit had adopted as home, and spent the fag-end of the afternoon fiddling with the mechanism. There was nothing else to do, for whether it was down to the deteriorating weather or the German navy, or the arrival of a vast invasion force in East Anglia, or a decision by the British government to cut their losses and simply abandon the BEF (for nobody knew what was going on – rumour was piled on rumour), there were currently no ships near their part of the shore, although a speck or two on the horizon seemed to hint that more were on their way.

Arthur opened a tin of peas he'd been hoarding and counted them into an upturned helmet; it came to seven each and the men ate them as if they were cocktail olives. Darkness fell and the wind dropped a little. There was no moon visible, and the only light was from the glimmer of a thousand cigarettes, and the red-tinged pall of smoke that hung to the west, above the port of Dunkirk. Pierce disappeared for a while, and then returned in triumph, bearing a signals book. 'Borrowed it,' he said laconically. 'Shall we give it a try?'

Arthur and Pierce and Madden, and a few others too rattled to sleep, walked down the beach towards the water, where a smear of phosphorescence marked the breaking surf.

'There's a whole section on "Calls to an Unknown Ship"' said Pierce. 'What about it, chums?'

'"Calls to an Unknown U-boat", more like,' someone muttered, but no one tried to stop Pierce. Arthur thought afterwards that as the only NCO present he should have said something, but at the time the scheme had seemed no more strange than all the other strange and terrible things that had happened over the past week, ever since a motorcyclist had swung past the bakery at Merville where they'd had their billet and had told them to head for the coast 'on General Gort's orders'. From then on it had been like one of those terrible dreams where a simple task is constantly hampered by the bizarre and the unfathomable. The roads had been clogged with terrified refugees, every yard of the verge strewn with abandoned luggage and clothing and burnt-out cars; half of the unit had gone off to look for firewood one night and had never come back; a Stuka had strafed a herd of cows at a cross-roads, and Arthur had spent most of a morning helping to move bovine corpses so that the trucks could get through. Every mile had been marked by chaos and fear and dead bodies, and then, when they were still half a league from the coast, they had finally run out of petrol. After they'd pushed the trucks into a ditch and spiked the engines, the lieutenant had said, 'It's every man for himself now, chaps,' and Pierce had nipped into a nearby village and returned minus his watch but wheeling two ancient bicycles. Those last few miles had been the most serene of the journey; Arthur had never ridden a bike, so he'd perched on the back of Madden's and closed his eyes, and the breeze on his face had been almost pleasant, despite the fact that the air reeked of burning petrol.

So to find himself standing beside an invisible sea while Pierce flashed a message into the darkness was merely one more oddity to add to the list, and the fact that an answer came blinking back out of the night was pleasing but not entirely unexpected.

'They're sending a boat for us,' said Pierce calmly, and started to take off his coat, and Madden volunteered to fetch the rest of the unit, and to find a few others beside who might want a midnight rescue.

They waded out Indian file, Pierce at the front giving the lamp a blink every half-minute or so. The beach shelved so gently that they were ten yards out before the water crept as far as Arthur's groin and he realized, with a gasp, how awfully cold it was. Pierce kept going until he was chest-deep and then stopped and sent a double flash out into the darkness.

'Oi Pierce, tell Ma I'm coming home,' shouted someone from the back of the line. There was a laugh and somebody else called, 'Tell my wife to get the kettle on' and before very long the whole of the queue, except Arthur, was shouting requests for Pierce to send a message to their granny, to their dog, to their baby son, to the landlord of the Barley Mow, and Pierce was telling them to pipe down or they wouldn't hear the boat coming, pipe *down* chums, and then there was a sudden sheet of light to the far west and all noise stopped. It was a ship burning, a minesweeper, its silhouette momentarily perfect before another flash of orange broke it in half. The sound of the first explosion rolled across the water, but before the sound of the second reached them, the light had gone.

For a moment there was utter silence and utter darkness, and then Arthur heard the clop of an oar.

'Oh—' said Pierce, and there was a thud, and the man in front of Arthur cried out and Arthur himself was smacked on the shoulder, knocked sideways and then hit on the back of the head, and then he was upside-down in the water with his nose actually grazing the sand, his pack dragging him down, and he tried to push off the bottom but something hit him on the head again, and then fingers clawed at his face and grabbed him by the hair and pulled him above the surface. He heard the bark of the air leaving his lungs, and then he was being hauled painfully over a wooden ledge before tumbling face first across the thwarts of a rowing-boat. Someone fell on top of him and a boot caught him above the eye, and he wasn't properly awake then, at least not in any consistent way, until he opened his eyes and saw a feathering of pale streaks across the sky, and felt the gentle judder of planking under his shoulders and sat up to find that he was on a Thames paddle steamer, five miles out of Dover. He had a stinking headache and had lost his spectacles and his pack and a clump of hair from one side of his head, and he thought, looking around the solid carpet of sleeping soldiers that covered the upper deck, that he had lost his entire unit – until Madden found him just as they disembarked.

'Pierce?' asked Arthur.

Madden shook his head. Pierce had never emerged from the inky water, and neither had two others from the front of the line. It was possible, of course, that they'd waded back to shore, but the likelihood was that after weeks of dodging Jerry bullets, they'd been done for by the hull of a British rowing-boat.

In the special troop-train from Dover to God-knows-where, Arthur had dozed and clutched the postcard he'd been given by a lady volunteer at the station. 'Fill in the address,' she'd said, 'and we'll post it to your people to let them know you're safe,' and a stub of pencil had been passed from soldier to soldier in Arthur's carriage, and the sheaf of postcards handed back to the platform just as the train moved off. Arthur had kept his, since there was no one in particular to send it to. He still had it, propped on the mantelpiece in Wimbledon.

The afternoon of the first day of filming was very similar to the morning. By three o'clock most of the adult spectators had drifted away, and the schoolchildren who took their place needed only half an hour to realize that anything in the way of entertainment would have to be created by themselves. Shouting 'Cut' just after the assistant director had shouted 'Action' kept them amused for a while, and then one of the more enterprising started taking pot-shots at the camera with a potato gun. Chick, his face expressionless, walked over to the foot of the dune and crooked a finger. Chopper flew towards the group like a brindled bullet, and the crest of the dune was suddenly empty.

Tea and rock buns were served at four and then, as Arthur was making his way back to his own particular patch of sand, he was approached by a young man in sergeant's uniform.

'Hadley Best,' said the other, gripping Arthur's hand and staring into his eyes with disconcerting intensity. 'I'm playing Johnnie. I gather that you're our military expert.'

'Yes,' said Arthur, uneasily, 'though I don't think I'd classify myself as an *expert*.'

'I'm joining the navy myself.'

'Are you?'

'The board's allowed me three months' grace to shoot this and then I'm off. Yo ho, heave ho and all that.' He continued to stare unblinkingly from what seemed far too small a distance. Arthur took half a step backwards.

'I want you to know that I'm a stickler,' said Hadley, smartly closing the gap. 'It would cause me real pain if people came out of the cinema and said, "That was all very exciting and thrilling but in actual fact the East Surreys always salute with the *left* hand." '

'They don't,' said Arthur, relieved to find something about which he could be certain.

'Just a light-hearted example, Arthur. I'm not like other actors, you see, I'm not simply concerned with how many lines I have. I'd rather have four honest words than fifty pages of bilge.' The unblinking stare continued; Arthur took another, involuntary, step backwards, and fell over his stool.

'I want you to promise,' said Hadley, as if nothing had happened, as if Arthur hadn't landed arse over tip and wasn't now groping around in the sand for his spectacles, 'absolutely to promise that you'll tell me if you see or hear something that doesn't ring completely true. Will you promise me?'

'Yes of course, I'll do my best. The trouble is . . .'

'Any detail, however small. Any word of the script that sounds a false note. For instance, we're just about to shoot a scene on the beach where Johnnie and a few others are queueing up to their knees in water. Is that something that you actually experienced, Arthur?'

'Yes.'

'And then as the darkness drops over the French coast they start to wade back to the shore and one of the other characters turns to Johnnie and says, bitterly, "Another bloody night on the beach." Does that sound like the kind of phrase that you might have heard?'

'Yes,' said Arthur, with some feeling.

'Good. Very good. Cigarette?'

'No thank you.' The light was beginning to fade. Arthur gave his spectacles a polish, and watched as a man unwound a spool of cable across the dunes, past the remaining spectators, and along the beach towards an enormous lamp a few yards from the water's edge. A corporal was sitting on a canvas stool in the middle of the sand with a towel round his shoulders, while the barber snipped at his hairline. The two young lady actresses were performing leg exercises, using the breakwater as a barre.

'The trouble is,' said Arthur to Hadley, 'that this is all very new to me. I hadn't at all realized how much trickery was involved.'

'Trickery?'

'Well . . . glass-shots, for instance. If you can add boats to a scene, then I suppose you can add all sorts of things that I don't know about. And noises being put on afterwards, and so on. And someone was telling me that anything white, like the side of the boat, has to be dirtied down because otherwise it's too bright to photograph, so I suppose that the reason that actual dirt isn't being put on things that should really be dirty is because it won't show up. Is that correct?'

'You've lost me,' said Hadley. 'What things that should really be dirty?'

'Well . . .' Arthur eyed him critically. Apart from a light, almost artistic, spatter of mud across the breast pocket, and a small area of scuffing on the left knee (the latter looking as if a pumice stone had been passed gently over the serge), Hadley's uniform was completely pristine.

'You mean this should be dirtier?' asked Hadley, following his gaze.

'Dirtier, and also . . .' He fished for an adequate phrase, thinking of the scarecrow army that had arrived at Dover, undershirts used as bandages, jackets as pillows and stretchers, trousers striped with salty tide-marks from successive queueing in the surf. '. . . more weathered.'

'*Weathered*,' repeated Hadley, appreciatively. 'That's an excellent note, I shall pass it on straight away. I gather the director's keen on a real-life sort of look. Anything else?'

'Yes,' said Arthur, warming to his role. 'Your uniform fits much too well. Most of them are too long in the arm – like mine, d'you see? – or too short in the leg, or simply far too big.'

Hadley nodded, but with noticeably less enthusiasm.

'Honestly,' said Arthur, 'I'd say that that was as important as the weathering. Our sergeant-major said we looked like a bunch of hunchbacks after we were kitted up for the first time.'

'Mmm,' said Hadley, turning away.

'We were known as the baboon platoon,' called Arthur, but Hadley was clearly already out of earshot.

★

Before going to Norfolk, Buckley had given Catrin a typed list of instructions:

> *i) Do not attempt to tidy my desk. Any attempt at tidying my desk will result in immediate dismissal.*
> *ii) Check Parfitt for signs of life. Repeat at half-hourly intervals.*
> *Homework:*
> *i) Ask Muriel in Baker's office to dig out scripts of* Any Day but Today, Holiday in the Rain, Simpkins and Son, The Long, Long Wait *and* The Ladder Gang. *Read, mark and inwardly digest. Note clever flashback structure in* The Long, Long Wait. *That's the way to do it. Not that I got any credit, of course, since reviewers think that films are invented by the director as he goes along.*
> *ii) For Christ's sake go and see some American films. Your idea of the way Americans talk appears to be based on Louisa May Alcott.*

iii) The director's informed me that the propeller-fouling scene (studio) has too much dialogue and not enough tension. I don't agree, but better we do the rewrites than he does. You may as well have a stab at it. Don't cut any gags.

iv) Go and sweet-talk Mr Shipton in accounts. Since Parfitt won't travel (think of him as a crate of fine wine, the sediment of which needs to remain undisturbed), you might be able to squeeze a return train-fare and a couple of nights out of the production. Come and see why films should always be shot entirely in studio.

v) Don't stand underneath any thousand-pounders.

Parfitt had been left no such list, and without Buckley's gadfly presence he seemed to sink into torpor, dozing for most of the morning, chin on chest, and staring out of the window with his arms folded for most of the afternoon. Catrin wanted to ask him why he didn't just go home, but she felt oddly constrained; she realized that she'd scarcely ever spoken to him directly – all communication had been via Buckley, as if the latter were the string between two cocoa tins.

Rather than ask Parfitt questions, then, she offered an occasional commentary on what she'd been doing, in the hope of gaining some response.

'I went to see *Men Against the Sky* last night, it's about a drunken test pilot. They talk so fast, Americans, I kept thinking that we ought to give our American a bit more to say otherwise we'll end up ten minutes short.'

'Any good?' asked Parfitt, after a pause of several seconds.

'You mean the picture?'

'Yep.'

'Not bad. I could see the ending a mile away, though.'

'Flagged.'

'Sorry?'

'Flagged the ending. That's what we say. They flagged the ending.'

'Oh I see . . .'

That was one entire afternoon's conversation. On other days, she managed to extract Parfitt's opinion on the director ('picky'), the war ('lost unless we get the Russians in'), and Buckley ('best in the business'), as well as his suggestions for the propeller scene, which mainly seemed to involve cutting most of Rose and Lily's dialogue. She had the feeling that Parfitt didn't have much time for women.

By the second week of Buckley's absence, she had read a bundle of scripts, sat through nine examples of whip-crack American dialogue, obtained a travel chit from a grudging accounts department, and lopped two and a half pages from the scene in question. She handed it to Parfitt late one afternoon and he read it slowly, hunched over the desk, the breath whistling through his nostrils.

```
The 'Redoubtable' has started to drift.

   HANNIGAN
      (making his way along the deck) Hey, there — what's
      happening? Has the engine stopped?

   UNCLE FRANK
      (leaning over gunwale, trying to take a look) Ruddy
      propeller's fouled.

   HANNIGAN
      Can I help?

   UNCLE FRANK
      Know what a twin gasket screw valve is?

   HANNIGAN
      Can't say that I do.

   UNCLE FRANK
      You've just answered your own question.
```

Uncle Frank almost loses his balance. Hannigan grabs his belt.

HANNIGAN

Steady there, old timer.

LILY

(calling from wheel) What's happening, Uncle Frank?

HANNIGAN

Propeller's fouled.

UNCLE FRANK

Oh and you're the expert now, are you? Typical Yank.

Hannigan is about to reply when he and Uncle Frank hear a noise. They look up. It's a Stuka. It crosses overhead.

The bows. The deck is packed with weary, anxious soldiers. ROSE is kneeling beside JOHNNIE, bandaging his arm. The DOG is watching intently.

JOHNNIE

(in pain) What the hell's going on with the engine?

ROSE

I don't know.

The Stuka crosses again, lower this time.

JOHNNIE

(starting to get up) He's eyeing us up, making sure we've got no defences. We're sitting ducks unless we can get going again.

ROSE

(pushing him down again) You stay right where you are.

She picks her way along the crowded deck towards the stern. UNCLE FRANK has tied a bowline around himself and is climbing over the gunwale. HANNIGAN holds the other end.

ROSE

What's happening?

HANNIGAN & UNCLE FRANK

(simultaneously) Propeller's fouled. (They glare at each other.)

UNCLE FRANK starts to lower himself into the water. It's cold. He steadies himself on the propeller shaft, takes a breath and ducks under water. After a few seconds, he bobs up again, gasping.

UNCLE FRANK

It's a bloody great tangle. Webbing or some such — I'm going to need a knife.

ROSE

I'll find one.

HANNIGAN

I've got one.

HANNIGAN reaches down and takes a knife from his boot — the same knife that he took from the German shot by Johnnie in the scene with the Belgian refugees. HANNIGAN looks at the blade for a moment.

HANNIGAN

(to himself) About time it did some good.

He leans over the gunwale and hands it to UNCLE FRANK, who takes it and ducks under the water again.
— if possible we see UNCLE FRANK — or at least the knife — under the water, hacking at the tangled webbing.

SEQUENCE:

The stern, where ROSE and HANNIGAN are watching anxiously.

Point of view of the Stuka pilot – tiny boat on sea beneath.

UNCLE FRANK hacking away at the webbing.

The Stuka starts to dive.

Point of view of the Stuka pilot – diving towards tiny boat.

The bows. Everyone on deck looking up as they hear the screaming dive. Bullets rat-tat-tat.

A line of bullet holes appears beside the propeller shaft.

Everyone on deck ducks down.

The DOG jumps up on the cabin roof and barks loudly.

The Stuka wheels away.

A SCOTTISH SOLDIER in a kilt shakes his fist at the sky.

SCOTCHMAN

Missed us all, ye boss-eyed Nazi!

HANNIGAN has been gazing skyward, but now he looks down and sees bubbles coming from the water. His smile fades.

HANNIGAN

Hey! Hey there!

He pulls on the rope, and UNCLE FRANK comes to the surface, alive but wounded.

ROSE

Quick! Let me take that!

ROSE grabs the rope from HANNIGAN, and he climbs into the water and supports UNCLE FRANK. Soldiers crowd around the rail.

UNCLE FRANK

I've dropped the knife.

HANNIGAN

You've done a fine job, old timer.

UNCLE FRANK

But I've not finished yet.

HANNIGAN

You'll just have to leave it to me.

UNCLE FRANK is pulled to safety. HANNIGAN steels himself and ducks underwater.

Parfitt paused at this point, and tapped the page.

'Needs a gag.'

'Where?'

'Just before they take Uncle Frank out of the water.'

'But he's mortally wounded.'

Parfitt shook his head in irritation, as if she were a fly buzzing around his ears. 'Needs *something*,' he said. 'Something about Yanks. Leave it to me.'

Catrin sat down again, and watched him pick at the skin around his nails, his eyes fixed on the script. He was still staring at it when she left for the evening.

She opened the door of the flat and to her surprise heard the distinctive sound of Perry in mid-anecdote. He was sitting at the kitchen table together with Ellis and a nervy little painter called Conroy and a trio of beer bottles.

'I wasn't expecting—' she began, and Perry raised a warning finger so that she wouldn't leap in and ruin his story, and she took off her coat and put on the kettle and began to unpack the shopping that she'd bought on the way home. As she passed Ellis he caught one of her hands and gave it a fierce squeeze.

'. . . and then he informed me that what he was looking for was something in the Burne-Jones mode . . .' continued Perry.

Ellis was leaning back in his chair, smiling slightly, more at ease than she had seen him for months, and she could tell that he wasn't really listening to Perry, and she could see that Perry was aware of this fact and was upping the vigour of his narrative in order to attract Ellis's attention. Conroy, too, was looking at Ellis rather than at the story-teller, apparently wanting to gauge the former's reactions before deciding how to react himself.

It was strange, thought Catrin; they were like courtiers, bidding for attention.

'Has something happened?' she asked, interrupting Perry.

He threw her an irritated glance '. . . and I *suggested*,' he continued, managing to inject reproof into the word. 'I suggested to the fellow that if he really wanted a more figurative approach then he should buy a camera. At which point he left rather suddenly.' He laughed loudly, and Catrin contributed a smile and Conroy bobbed his head non-committally.

'I've had a letter,' said Ellis. He fished into his pocket and took out an envelope and handed it to Catrin. She unfolded the single sheet of paper.

Dear Mr Cole,

I am pleased to inform you that in addition to confirming the purchase of five of your blitz paintings for inclusion in the forthcoming update of the WAAC exhibition at the National Gallery, the Committee is in agreement that you should be placed on salary with the initial brief of documenting bomb damage in provincial cities, the particulars to be decided in consultation with Home Security. I would be grateful if you could telephone me immediately on receipt of this letter as the Committee is most keen to expedite the above commission,

Yours etc.

E.M.O'R. Dickey

Secretary to the War Artists Advisory Committee

'Oh Ellis . . .' she said, and he took the letter back from her and looked at it calmly, and it struck her that he'd been expecting this moment to come – had been expecting it ever since she'd known him. He had worked like the devil and never doubted his own worth.

'And did you speak to this man?' she asked, sitting down beside him.

He nodded. 'They want me to go to Coventry next week and then Bristol after that, and then other places – they're still deciding where, exactly.'

'So you'll go away to sketch and then come back to London and paint?'

He shook his head. 'Too much travelling. That's what we've just been discussing. We'll have to give up the studio.'

'This,' said Perry, raising his bottle, 'is both a celebration and a wake. Conroy had a letter last week informing him that his services are required in a camouflage unit, and today's summons means the tipping-point has been reached – as a group we can no longer maintain an adequate fire-watch at the garage. No point in seeing genius consumed by the flames.' He chinked his bottle formally against the other two. 'Au revoir to Paddington for the duration.'

Catrin looked from Perry to Ellis and then back again. 'So where . . .?'

'Perry has a place in Worcestershire,' said Ellis.

'I'm drawing on filial connections,' said Perry, '*not*, I hasten to add, something that comes easily to me, given that my family only considers a painting to be art if there's a mangled stag in it somewhere, but I have a fat old aunt with a summer cottage outside Malvern, and I think she may be prevailed upon to offer it up for the war effort. It has a garden room and it's dry, at least, and it's quite near a railway station. I'll probably join you there unless the army gets me first.'

'So . . .' Catrin tried to organize her thoughts. 'So do you think they have Sunday trains?'

'What d'you say?' Ellis was looking at the letter again.

'Because I could travel up on Saturday nights after work, I suppose, but I'd have to get back here for Monday morning. I wonder how long the journey takes?'

He raised his eyes and she saw that familiar look of

puzzled impatience. 'What are you talking about?' he asked.

'About visiting you while you're in the country.'

'No, no. You'll come with me to Worcestershire,' he said, as if she'd slightly misheard a simple statement. 'You don't want to stay in London on your own.'

The kettle began to whistle, a rising shriek like a cartoon parody of the All-Clear. Catrin rose to turn off the gas. She was feeling oddly short of breath, her mouth as dry as chalk.

'Tea?' she asked, over her shoulder as she rinsed the pot. 'Tea, everyone?'

'Aren't there supposed to be nine hundred and ninety-nine people working in the Ministry of Information?' asked Perry. 'I'm sure they could find someone else to do what you've been doing.'

'I'm not at the MoI,' said Catrin, and she found that she could barely keep her voice steady. 'I haven't been for months. I'm writing dialogue for a feature film.'

'Oh really? I didn't know.'

'Ellis,' she said, 'I don't want to leave London yet, not until the picture's finished. Not until the end of May.'

He was looking slightly past her, rubbing his top lip with a finger, his face expressionless.

'Ellis . . .'

'Hmmm?' He met her gaze. 'Yes,' he said, 'tea for me.'

She realized that she had started to tremble, not with fear but with frustration. 'No. No, I wasn't talking about *tea*,' she said, and the banal words must have held a note of derangement, some promise of hysteria, because there was the sudden scrape of chairs, and she turned to see Perry steering Conroy towards the door.

'We're off to the Malt Shovel,' said Perry. 'Join us when you're ready.'

'I thought we were having tea,' said Conroy, rather plaintively.

The door closed.

Ellis tipped his chair back and stared at her. 'Whatever's the matter?' he asked.

She drew a deep breath and then another, shocked at how panicked she felt at the thought of leaving the job prematurely, and when she spoke again her voice was more measured.

'I'd like to stay here until the picture's finished,' she said. 'It'll only be till the end of May.'

'Which picture's this?'

'The one that I've been working on since November. About the twins going to Dunkirk. I've told you about it lots of times.'

Did he nod or simply move his head irritably? She wasn't sure.

'I'll take good care of myself,' she said, 'I promise I will, I'll even go and sleep in the Underground if you think I ought to, but I don't want to leave before the end. I've been working on this from the very start, and if I'd told the truth about Rose and Lily it might never have happened at all, and they've hardly even started the filming yet, and Buckley says they sometimes do script amendments all the way through studio . . .' She was watching Ellis's face as she spoke, trying, as ever, to work out what he was thinking, trying to interpret every blink and twitch, and she thought suddenly and yearningly of the office at Baker's, where if she wanted to know something then she could ask a question, and the answer might well be rude or infuriating or just plain silly, but at least it would be an answer.

Ellis leaned forward again and rested his arms on the table. 'Well *I* have to leave London,' he said. 'You do understand that?'

'Of course I do.'

'And I'd assumed that you'd want to come with me. I'd assumed that that would be the most important thing to you, but it seems that I was wrong.'

There was a short, horrid silence.

'It would only be till the end of May,' said Catrin, for the third time, and it seemed to her that her voice sounded oddly hollow, as if repetition had scooped all sincerity from the promise.

Ellis's face was very still. She had never seen him lose his temper, and she wasn't sure whether he was angry now, but all at once she felt afraid.

'Ellis?'

'It's all right,' he said. 'You needn't worry that I'm going to drag you away by force if you really don't want to go. I'm not the type.'

'No, I know, but—'

'Stay in London if you want,' he said, and stood up and put on his jacket, and Catrin, standing beside the table, thought of the phrase that he'd used in Ebbw Vale three years ago. '*Come with me if you want*' – your choice, he'd meant, your choice and I make no promises. And she'd left Wales like a burr stuck to his sleeve, and now, three years later, she had somehow worked herself loose, and the choice was hers once again. And she looked at Ellis, handsome and foreign-looking, an *artist*, and her heart seemed to creak.

'I'll stay, then,' she said.

*

Hollywood-next-the-sea

Cries of 'Put that light out', were replaced by calls for 'Lights! Cameras! Action!' on the north Norfolk coast this week, when the cast and crew of an important new feature film (currently untitled) arrived for a fortnight of location shooting, and turned the fishing village of Badgeham into 'Hollywood-next-the-sea'. The film, produced by Baker's Productions of Soho, London, tells the story of the Starling twins, the daring distaff duo from Southsea who co-piloted their ketch across the channel to Dunkirk and rescued upward of fifty British soldiers. The brave pair are being portrayed by up-and-coming actresses Miss Angela Ralli-Thomas and Miss Doris Cleavely [see interview page 2], while their uncle is played by Mr Ambrose Gilliard, whom some of our readers may remember from that more innocent era when pictures were unsullied by sound, and also from the series of popular mystery films starring the much-missed Reeve Callaghan as Inspector Charnforth.

Helm

Taking the 'helm' on the production is director Mr Alex Frayle. With a background in 'documentary' films, we can be sure that a realistic approach is high on his list of priorities, and he has already 'cast his net' and 'caught' a few examples of authentic local fisher-folk, who have been appearing as 'extras' in some of the maritime scenes. Mr Keith Leesmith of Harbour Row, Badgeham declared, 'They said they wanted me because of my beard, but then they asked me to say some words as well. I told them I was no actor, but I had twenty-odd chances to get it right and by the end they seemed quite pleased.' When asked if he would pack his bags if Hollywood called, Mr Leesmith said, 'Not for all the tea in China. It's not what you'd call a man's job.'

War-work

Local ladies, meanwhile, have also been recruited, this time by the wardrobe department. 'The head of costume came to my establishment and said that she urgently needed help to prepare the uniforms for the large numbers of 'extras' playing soldiers on the Dunkirk beaches,' said Mrs Furse, sole proprietress of Furse Quality Dressmaking of Rope Walk, Badgeham, and wife of the Reverend Roy Furse, Minister of Bethesda and the Lamb Wesleyan Chapel. She adds, 'Although most of the "extras" will be pupils from Clidley College OTC, who will have their own uniforms, the director feels it's vitally important for the "look" of the film that those uniforms should appear weathered, as if the soldiers have been on the beaches for several days. I am helping the costume department to add wear and tear to the cloth, which is known in the film industry as "breaking down" the material. Although to a certain extent I am neglecting my own business to do this, I see it as a form of war work.'

Welcome

The distinguished veteran producer, Mr Edwin Baker, has praised the people of Badgeham for offering a warm Norfolk welcome to both cast and crew, and has said that he is very happy for local people to come and watch the filming, just as long as they 'keep still and keep mum'!

So until the director calls 'Cut' for a final time, it's 'Quiet Everybody, We're Rolling!' in 'Hollywood-next-the-Sea'!

What spinach, thought Ambrose, laying down his copy of the *Eastern Daily Press* and taking a mouthful of criminally weak tea – what utter spinach. And it wasn't even the misspelling of his own name that gave him the greatest offence, it was the use of that careless, clichéd phrase '. . . *whom some of our readers may remember from that more innocent era when pictures were unsullied by sound* . . .' Innocent? It had been the most hedonistic, extravagant, promiscuous, thrillingly *overripe* era imaginable. A bletted peach of an era, all the tastier for being so close to corruption. Did people honestly think that all those dark-eyed little houris had wiped off their make-up at the end of the day and gone home on the tram to a nice slice of seed-cake and a cup of cocoa? Did they truly suppose that the feverish demeanour that the medium demanded of its exponents, the twitchy cow-eyed gaze, the shuddering emotion that spilled over the edge of the screen and into the aisles like a roiling flood of incense, had been achieved without a soupçon of chemical help? Did they imagine that the sawdust-dry austerity of the current era, the tomboy actresses with their curls and big buttocks, the men who were afraid that the slightest facial movement would label them irredeemably queer, the awful wholesomeness of what currently passed for biographical notes ('Bunty loves her bicycle to bits, and when she's not out cycling you'll find her behind the counter of the local WVS canteen'), was in some way superior to the furs and running-boards and glamour – no, he wasn't ashamed of the word – the utter glamour of those days. People had forgotten, presumably, or else they were too young to remember. Which reminded him . . . he turned the page to see Doris Cleavely beaming at him from beneath a six-point caption.

Stardom beckons the girl from Beckenham

'I'm just a normal sort of girl,' says Doris Cleavely, 23, as she takes a swig of lemonade and waits patiently for the director to call 'Action'. 'I love going to dances, and trying on dresses and playing the giddy goat.'

'Christ!' said Ambrose, out loud, and the maid who was clearing the last of the breakfast dishes gave a little jump.

> *'When I was told I'd won the part of Lily Starling I was half-pleased and half-terrified, because I haven't worked on a full-length feature before, and I was afraid that it would all be awfully strict, but so far it's been the most terrific fun . . .'*

He skimmed the rest of the article – *thrilled, fun, fun, fun, terrific, fun, Angela, fun, director, fun, Hadley, fun,* no mention of his own name, *super, goofing about, fun* – and then he closed the newspaper, and stretched back on the hard dining-room chair and clasped his hands behind his head.

Doris was a ninny, the possessor of saucer eyes and a pretty, dimpled face that reflected every passing emotion, like that of a toddler. Watching her interpret a scene was akin to viewing a speeded-up film of the sky – the clouds flicking across the sun, a brief rain-shower, a ruffle of wind, the sun bursting out again – all in the course of a single listening shot. It was artlessness taken to exhausting lengths. Her 'twin' Angela – and they were a fair match facially, aided by congruous hair-styles and a clever identical beauty spot added by the make-up chap to each rosy left cheek – was a cipher by comparison, though she made up for any sphinx-like qualities of appearance by an absolutely uncensored approach to conversation. Her life was laid bare at every opportunity and to anyone within earshot – romance, arguments, reconciliations, bust-ups – all shared in such minute and relentless detail that the items became indistinguishable, a single linkless sausage, devoid of mustard or spice. And then there was Hadley Best, poor sap, using the word 'stickler' in every other sentence, as if military accuracy would in some way compensate for the fact that he was consistently out-acted by Chick's dog. 'Of course, I'm off to the navy myself,' he kept saying. 'Yo ho heave ho.' And behind the hard-tack-and-hornpipe jocularity, and the renditions of 'Blow the Man Down' one could almost smell the black waters of the Atlantic, the death-run that was swallowing ships whole.

They were all so *blank*, these youngsters, so pristine, so lacking in footnotes and bookmarks, their pages uncut, their margins unsullied; even Arthur Frith, peering out at the world like a tortoise newly emerged from the shell, seemed to have acquired no history over the course of his thirty-odd years.

'Mr Hilliard . . .' Ambrose turned to see the landlady of the Crown and Anchor, her hand slightly raised as if volunteering in class. 'I wonder, Mr Hilliard, if you'd be kind enough to vacate the dining-room so that the girl can tidy around. There's a very nice fire lit in the snug . . .'

He nodded, affably enough, and took his paper into the bar-room. It was a bleak morning, rain sliding down the windows and a stiffish breeze rattling the trees on the green. The big reveal sequence had been scheduled for today – Uncle Frank climbing on deck, German aircraft overhead, crowds of extras in the water, explosions – but this ridiculous business with the extras' costumes had shoved the whole thing back a week, and, instead, the crew was out shooting a scene involving Hadley, the dog and a crowd of Norfolk villagers masquerading as Belgian refugees. Doris and Angela, their own scenes postponed, had gone to Norwich for the day to look at the shops, the writer Buckley was observing his usual practice of sleeping until noon, and Ambrose himself was at a loose end until the following morning. He lit a cigarette and turned to the back page of the *Eastern Daily Press*. It was hard to believe that so little happened in East Anglia that they could devote one whole page out of a total of four to small ads and notices. Or perhaps not, he thought, as a gust of wind tumbled a rook past the window. He began to work his way through the columns – *For Sale*, a tandem in Downham Market, four white leghorns (good layers) in Holt; *Help Needed*, maid wanted, maid wanted, housekeeper wanted and good luck to them with that particular search; *Entertainments*, Hoxne Amateur Dramatic

Society tackling *King Lear*, God help the audience, Norwich Players with *Rookery Nook*, Ipswich Grand presents *The Ghost Train* by Arnold Ridley, Prince of Wales Theatre Cromer would like to announce the extension of their record-breaking run of *The Student Prince*.

He folded the newspaper. The fire seemed to be producing smoke rather than heat, and the only other occupant of the snug was a trembling ancient, currently asleep. Ambrose crushed his stub into the ashtray, looked out of the window at the sodden village green, and then checked his wrist-watch. Nine thirty; three hours until luncheon. He lit another cigarette and picked up the newspaper again. There was something tugging at his memory, something he'd seen on the back page . . .

★

Edith had never thought of herself as a passionate woman, but she was passionate now, so much so that she kept jamming the Singer by dint of over-vigorous treadling, and had several times caught herself muttering out loud, like a mad old woman, because it wasn't fair, it simply *wasn't fair* that it was Verna who had been seconded by the film people when she herself was almost certainly the only person in Badgeham, and very probably the only person in the whole of Norfolk, who already knew the meaning of the phrase 'breaking down' within the context of costume authenticity and had, in fact, been responsible for actually re-inventing the previous, rather primitive, Tussaud's method of fabric-ageing (a butter-churn filled with stones) when required to re-clothe Livingstone and Stanley for the 1937 Four Corners of the Empire exhibit, during the course of which she had even researched the colour of the mud in the Tanganyika Delta. She was the closest thing to an expert that anyone could possibly stumble across, and yet, when the woman from the wardrobe department had unexpectedly called at the shop and begged for assistance, had Verna said, 'Why, that's just the job for my cousin Edith, who at this very second happens to be out of the room?' No, she had instantly volunteered for the task herself, and when Edith had arrived back from the WC three minutes later it was to find a fait accompli, and a pile of women's overalls in saxe-blue cotton drill, pinned but not yet stitched, that she was now required to complete all on her own – presumably by skipping meals and working straight through the night – because Verna was *needed*.

'Though to be honest, it's not an exciting job,' her cousin had said, on the first evening. 'I've been given a nail-file and I'm roughening all the buttons so they don't look so shiny on camera,' but her voice, as she said it, was full of kindly condescension, and for a moment Edith had experienced the urge to pick up a fork and stick it in the back of Verna's hand, for it was not the *interest* of the work that had drawn her, it was the perfection of the coincidence, the sense that something fresh and unexpected and utterly Edith-shaped had appeared on the road ahead. 'It' had arrived, at long last, 'it' had smiled, 'it' had beckoned, and 'it' had been lassooed, hobbled and dragged away by Verna.

'And I have to say that I'm very impressed by the whole tone of the proceedings,' added Verna, in that breathy, busy little voice, 'because obviously, I was anxious that the arrival of so many newcomers from . . .' she glanced at Myrtle, who was concentrating on her sponge pudding, and then mouthed the word 'London' at Edith, 'might have a lowering effect on the village, on the local girls and so forth – you know what I mean Edith, don't you? And I felt that it was important, as a chapel-goer, to keep an eye on what was happening, that's of course why I volunteered to help, but I've been assured that the story of the film is entirely clean in every respect, and the people I've met so far have been very nice, with very nice manners. Married, most of them.' Was there a slight edge of disappointment in her voice? 'Because all the younger ones have been called up, of course.'

Had she been hoping to widen her gossip pool, to hear a few more sets of fumbled buttons on Mudd Street? Edith slapped down the thought, shocked by her own spite and prurience; still, it was infuriating to hear Verna dispensing new-found expertise over the supper table ('. . . and then there's a standby wardrobe assistant who checks the costume every time there's a take, and, of course, by the word "take" I mean . . .'), and a relief when Myrtle finished her pudding and cut straight to the heart of the subject.

'But have you met any film-stars?'

'I saw a gentleman who apparently used to be a film-star, and also a very polite and nice young lady actress called Miss Doris Cleavely who came in for a costume fitting. I don't suppose that *she* ever puts her elbows on the dining-room table . . .'

Since then, Edith's outrage had continued to smoulder. 'It's really very fortunate that you're here,' Verna had said only this morning, vigorously fanning the embers. 'Otherwise I might have had to cancel that last order of overalls.'

In the little lean-to at the back of the shop, deafened and blinkered by the ugly rattle of her own thoughts, and the drumming of the rain on the glass roof, and the chatter of the needle, and the endless line of stitching that chased across the stiff blue material, one colour scarcely darker than the other so that she needed to peer closely in the low afternoon light to check the straightness of the seam, Edith's world seemed to contract, its walls to thicken. She didn't notice the resumption of gunnery practice, nor – some time later – the tinkle of the shop bell.

*

It was only after he had knocked at the stage door and was waiting for a reply that it occurred to Ambrose that he ought to have brought something – a token – flowers, perhaps. He turned to look along the street in the faint hope of seeing a nosegay-seller emerge from the gloaming, but there was no one in view but a distant cyclist, pedalling grimly through the puddles. The rain fell in the same constant, dispiriting fashion that it had pursued all day. It had turned the landscape between Badgeham and Ipswich into a dismal blur, and leaked through the seams of his shoes as he'd walked from the station to the theatre. There was no sign of it stopping; another couple of weeks of this and the German navy would be able to float straight to London via Cambridge.

He lifted his hand to knock again, but before he could do so, the door sprang open to reveal a pretty little thing in a pixie hood, and a weak-looking chap holding an umbrella.

'Sorry,' said the girl, ducking past Ambrose; he'd seen her on the stage just ten minutes before and she was still in full make-up, her lips startlingly vivid. 'Ooh, I could murder some cheese on toast . . .' he heard her say to her companion, as they hurried away. Ambrose entered the corridor and let the door swing shut behind him.

It was a touch unfortunate that a combination of a delayed connection at Norwich, and the understandable assumption on his part that the matinee would begin, as matinees had always begun, at three o'clock, had meant that he'd missed the entire opening act of *The Ghost Train*. In fact, as the crone in the box-office had explained to him at unnecessary length (and with the inevitable use of the catch-all phrase 'owing to the international situation'), the evening performance these days began at six and the earlier performance at two. As a result, by the time he'd settled into his seat in the stalls, Cecy's character – a comic spinster, Miss Bourne – had already accidentally imbibed a flask of whisky and was lying in an inebriated sleep on the table in the station waiting-room, and he'd had to sit through another hour and a quarter of stilted nonsense before she'd awoken on cue and uttered the penultimate line of the entire play. It was lucky that he'd seen the whole thing performed once before, years ago, and could dimly remember a spot of comedy business with Miss Bourne's parrot in the opening scene; it was always best to compliment a specific moment when going round.

Dressing-room Number 5 was at the top of three steep flights of stairs, and Ambrose paused outside the door to recover his breath. 'Mrs Clyde-Cameron, Miss Robertson, Tommy', it said, rather puzzlingly, on the strip of pasteboard below the number. From inside the room came the tinkle of spoon on glass. He knocked.

'Come in, darling.'

A great belch of warm air engulfed him as he opened the door. Cecy was sitting in front of a two-bar electric fire, a black cat on her lap, a small tumbler in her hand. Her expression, as she looked at him, was one of pantomimic amazement.

'*Ambrose!*'

And although her amazement quickly gave way to what should have been a gratifying degree of delight, Ambrose felt a converse drooping of his own spirits, because ever since he'd read the notice in the newspaper this morning, and had made the connection between the repertory theatre at Ipswich and the possibility of having a conversation with someone who hadn't actually been wearing school uniform in the twenties, it seemed that he'd been carrying an image of Cecy in his head that was (as it now transpired) altogether softer, more shapely, and less toothy than the original, and the shock of seeing her in the flesh – in the too, too solid flesh – had made him suddenly start to think about what a bloody long way it would be back to Badgeham this evening.

'So what are you *doing* here?' asked Cecy, after he'd kissed her cheek, its surface as powdery and cushioned as the top of a Victoria sponge. 'And Ambrose, please don't tell me that you saw the matinee.'

'I did.'

'Oh *Lord* above, today of all days. Then you can't have missed the dry?'

'I thought you covered superbly,' he said, covering superbly.

'Really?'

'Oh yes.'

'It was the upstage turn that foxed me.'

'It would have foxed anyone.'

'He's *so* inconsistent, the boy playing Teddie – they're simply not trained, these days. And what about that fearful muck-up with the window?'

'Unnoticeable to anyone outside the profession,' said Ambrose, smoothly, 'and the parrot routine was beautifully handled. Laugh after laugh.'

'*Bless* you. So . . .' She lifted her glass, '. . . little hot toddy for you? Not the real thing, of course, just honey and hot water and the teeniest dribble of Amontillado. And while I concoct it you can sit on Jillie's chair – that's the girl playing Peggy Murdock, she's awfully good, I think, and the lisp is actually quite charming although I suspect it might cause a problem or two if she ever gets a film, those microphones are so *unforgiving* – you can sit down and tell me absolutely everything. Take Tommy, will you?'

She lifted the cat from her lap, and it dangled bonelessly, like a stole, its back claws flexing for purchase as she lowered it towards Ambrose's groin.

'He's a grumpy old thing but he generally likes men,' said Cecy, 'though perhaps you shouldn't make any sudden movements. And you couldn't just ease the lid off this for me?' she added, passing Ambrose a jar of honey. 'Marvellous, *so* strong. Now do tell all.'

She set about making the toddy, bending over the kettle so that most of his words were addressed to her generous rump, but she was a good audience (he had to concede), exclaiming at all the right places, and offering comments about the film that were both pertinent and surprisingly intelligent – 'It sounds to me, Ambrose, as if your character's a sight more complex than the others' – and the toddy, when it came, was very pleasant, and the cat sat inertly on his lap, and didn't smell, nor seem to have any fleas.

'So who's playing the American journalist?' asked Cecy, picking up a piece of knitting.

'Good question. Apparently the character was a last-minute addition to the script and they're still casting.'

'No location scenes with him, then?'

'Back of his head in a couple of set-ups. One of the ADs has been standing in.'

'Did you know that they're shooting *The Ghost Train* at Gainsborough?'

'Really?' He made a quick mental inventory of the characters he'd just seen on stage: the gun-running Bolshevik masquerading as a doctor might be a nice, meaty role. 'When are they casting?'

'Already done, darling, they've almost wrapped. The story's been changed so that it's all about fifth-columnists now, and Arthur Askey's playing the lead and Kathleen Harrison's Miss Bourne.'

'Oh.' Damn Sammy. Or Sophie, rather. Though it was possible that the doctor had been written out, the whole concept of gun-running to Russia being somewhat dated these days, and . . . it occurred to him that Cecy had stopped talking and was concentrating, in a rather obvious way, upon her knitting; he had, he realized, missed his cue. 'I always find Kathleen Harrison's comic delivery rather broad,' said Ambrose. 'I'm surprised they didn't approach you about the part.'

'Ah well . . .' Cecy smiled and shrugged, but she gave him a sharp look from under her heavily darkened eyebrows. Her needles clicked industriously, producing something pendulous and khaki. Comforts for soldiers in general, or for a soldier in particular? Ambrose dredged his memory – hadn't Sammy mentioned that she'd had twins, although surely her offspring couldn't yet be of an age for military service? And of course she'd been married to that sad old soak George Garamonde, now long since propping up the bar in the eternal lock-in.

'Tommy likes you,' said Cecy, nodding at the passive black

bundle on his lap. Ambrose raised a hand to pat it, and then thought better of the gesture.

'He travels with you, does he?' he asked.

'Oh yes, I pop him into his little basket and off we go together, and he's the most wonderful gauge of character. I'm always suspicious of people who don't respond to animals – I think there must be a tiny little core of ice at the centre of their soul. Don't you?'

'Mmm,' said Ambrose, non-committally. 'And how are your – er – twins?'

'Oh gosh . . .' She didn't speak for a while, and when she did her voice was quite light. 'Such a long, long time ago. No twinnies, I'm afraid, they were born much too early,' and Ambrose wanted to pull his tongue out by the roots.

'Another toddy?' she asked.

He managed, somehow, to nod.

'And then you must tell me all about what's been happening to poor dear old London Town. I've felt quite the deserter, skulking in the provinces. Is it true about the Café de Paris?'

He found his voice again and led Cecy through the boarded windows and sandbagged foyers of the West End, and he had just moved on to a subject very close and very dear to his heart – viz., the nightmarish difficulty of trying to find a domestic plumber – when there was a knock at the door.

'Oh – now that's sure to be Gus,' said Cecy. 'Do come in!' and a bearded man entered the room, caught sight of Ambrose and leapt back in mock-surprise.

'Egad, milady Cecilia, thou hast a visitor!'

'This is Ambrose Hilliard, Gus.'

'Nay, thou needst not vouchsafe his name, for well I knowst that visage – hath I not seen it oft a-flicker in the darkness, stretched full twenty feet from ear to ear? Greetings sirrah!' He swept a bow, and Ambrose nodded, coldly; a wag, forsooth. The fellow had played the station-master, but was not quite as old as he had appeared on stage. The paunch had been fake, the thinning hair and beard whitened with chalk.

'Do you know,' said Cecy, 'I first met Gus in 1916. I was ASM at Hampstead and he was juve lead, isn't that right, Gus?'

'And she don't look a day older, do she, what, I say?' said Gus, adjusting an invisible quizzing-glass, having leapt inexplicably from Shakespeare to Sheridan.

'And then I walked into the rehearsal room in Ipswich and there he was. He's been the life and soul, really he has.'

'And this fair lady hath been the queen of all our hearts.' Gus knelt and took her hand and laid it against his chest.

'And now you're being most awfully silly,' said Cecy, looking nonetheless rather pleased. It was a second or two before she detached her hand and resumed knitting. 'Ambrose is on location with Baker's Productions.'

'Oh really?' Instead of standing up, Gus sank back on his haunches and lolled against the leg of Cecy's chair, his posture self-consciously bohemian, though he lacked the boneless ease of youth. 'Is it a comedy?'

'Drama.'

'Oh, I thought Baker's was all slapstick and pies, and fat boys climbing ladders.'

'Not any more,' said Ambrose, lips barely moving.

'No offence, old man,' said Gus. 'Now before I forget, Cecy dearest, I just came in to ask if you had any spirit gum.'

'Right out, I'm afraid.'

'Oh *bother*.'

'Is it for the wig?' asked Ambrose. 'I noticed during the matinee that it needed patching – just at the back,' he added, helpfully. 'There's a bald area, small but obvious.'

There was a pause. Gus reddened slightly and Ambrose felt a nice jolt of satisfaction.

'I'm sure that Jillie must have some,' said Cecy, suddenly full of bustle. 'Yes, look, just here, she uses it for her kiss curl, I'm sure she won't mind if you borrow a dab. It's for the braid on your shoulder, isn't it, Gus? Keeps happening, doesn't it? I could sew it on for you if you'd prefer.'

Gus, clambering awkwardly to his feet, ignored her and fixed Ambrose with a dyspeptic eye. 'So sirrah,' he said, back at the Globe again, 'thou wast in the audience this post-noon?'

'Yes,' said Ambrose, shortly.

'And yet thou wast not – ah, conundrum!' He posed with a finger under his chin, his expression arch.

'Whatever do you mean?' asked Cecy.

'I meanst that in the blackout twixt the first and second scenes in Act Two, I hath espied a most egregious late-comer, a fellow in hat and coat a-creeping into the stalls like the veriest mousie!' Gus essayed a rodent scamper and then paused to look at Ambrose again. ' 'Twere not so, sirrah?' he enquired, pointedly.

Silence seemed the only option. Gus paused hopefully for a moment longer, then waved the tube of gum at Cecy, and said, 'Do thank Jillie for the kind loan,' and left the room.

After a long moment, Cecy picked up her knitting again. 'Well really,' she said, tightly, 'what a pair of silly boys.'

Ambrose found that he could not meet her eye. He looked, instead, at the orange glow of the electric fire.

'So you missed my scenes,' said Cecy.

'I'd thought that the matinee began at three.'

'I see.' She came to the end of a row, and shook out the length of khaki before counting the stitches in an emphatic whisper.

'Muffler?' asked Ambrose, when she'd finished.

'Ear-warmers.' She folded the knitting on to her lap. 'You know, when I first met Gus, all those years ago, he could barely speak when he wasn't on stage. He'd been invalided back from France and he couldn't keep his voice on the level, you see, it kept wavering, and as time went on he started assuming different accents and characters, I think as a way of concealing his difficulty. It seems to have stuck with him, doesn't it?'

Ambrose nodded, uncomfortably.

'No one ever mentioned anything to him, of course,' said

Cecy. 'One never did, did one? All those fellows coming back with twitches and stutters and nightmares – we all thought it was kinder to pretend that we hadn't noticed. I don't think anyone guessed that with some people the effects might go on and on and on . . .' She gave a brisk sigh. 'Still, one can't blame the war for absolutely everything, can one? Sometimes bad behaviour has an excuse, and sometimes it's simply bad behaviour, and I must say I'm awfully tired of all that sort of thing. Kindness and friendship are what I value these days. Kindness and *friendship*,' she repeated, firmly, 'and nothing more. Now . . .' she nodded towards the kettle. 'Another drink?'

'No. Thank you. I really ought to be heading back.' He shifted slightly and the cat opened an eye.

'Are you sure?' asked Cecy.

'Really. The trains . . .'

'Well, it was very kind of you to come all this way. It *was*, actually,' she added, a fraction more warmly, 'and it was very kind of you to compliment my performance, even if you didn't see it. Us thespians, we're awfully good at pretending, aren't we?'

A response was clearly called for, but Ambrose could produce nothing but a vague nod. Over the last hour and a quarter he had chalked up pleasure, depression, mortification, fury, triumph, guilt, remorse, and even – could it be true? could this really have happened? – a bizarre spurt of near-jealousy. He had nothing left in stock. He lifted the cat from his lap, and it bit him, savagely. Pain, ah yes, he hadn't yet experienced pain.

'Oh *Tommy*,' shrieked Cecy. Ambrose clutched the fleshy web between thumb and forefinger and watched the blood drip on to his trousers. Yes, pain.

*

It was past midnight and Arthur was still awake. He had always found the business of getting to sleep rather tricky, a skill unmastered, but in the army he had temporarily discovered the knack and had fallen nightly into unconsciousness like an anchor dropped into water – no dreams, nothing but a blink of darkness before the morning, and this despite the cement mattress, the barnyard smells, the snores like the grinding of machinery. Here in Badgeham, on a feather bed with no noise but the distant sea, he lay with his eyes open and stared at the pale square of the whitewashed ceiling.

It had rained all day. The crew had worn waterproofs and the camera had been protected by a huge umbrella, and for the first hour or two all had been efficiency and vigour and then, as the damp had begun to creep into both canvas and bones, the pace had slowed. People had stopped cracking jokes, and every scene had been halted before its completion, the photographer objecting to drips from the edge of the umbrella, the fellow with the microphone complaining about splashing footsteps, the actors slipping in the mud. Lunch had been taken early, in the hope of the weather easing, and in the barn in which cast and crew sheltered, the director formed a worried huddle with the other important types while the actors commandeered the hay-loft and sat with their legs dangling over the edge, their feet swinging in a free and easy manner. All around the barn little groups formed. Arthur sat on a bale of straw and ate a Bovril sandwich and listened to the hum of conversation.

'Everything ship-shape, Arthur?' called Hadley Best from the hay-loft. By way of reply – his mouth being full – Arthur gave a thumbs-up, and noticed that there was a streak of Bovril on the back of his cuff; that was the problem with sleeves that came down to one's knuckles. Of course, he was beginning to understand that no one in the picture business (apart from the actors) cared two hoots about smartness – it was, apparently, quite the normal thing for a crew to sport frayed collars, flapping ties, filthy turn-ups, patched elbows, long hair and black nails, it was part of being 'behind camera', it was almost a uniform – but at least the crew's clothes *fitted* them.

'Change of plan,' shouted Kipper, the first assistant director, clapping his hands. 'Change of plan, everybody. Blame the weather. The director's decided that we'll be leaving sequence 21 to 27, and moving on to scene 42, exterior French farmhouse with Mr Best and young Master Chopper, camera position *within* the barn, shooting out towards the yard. We can say goodbye to our extras for the afternoon, thank you ladies and gentlemen. You'll find the cashier's office in the back room of the Bull, open until half past six. In the event that we complete scene 42 while we still have some light, we'll be moving on to 87A.'

'Fat chance,' muttered one of the chippies.

'And see me if you need the new pages,' called Phyl, waving a sheaf of paper.

There was a gradual movement of bodies within the barn, the leisurely shuffle that passed for violent activity within the film world. Arthur joined the queue and collected a copy of the scene.

42. EXT. FRENCH FARMHOUSE. DAY

Start in darkness. Door opens slowly (pushed from inside) to reveal farmyard and DOG sitting in background. Trees and countryside beyond — a wide, dangerous view.

ALAN (OFF)

(whispers) Don't be a fool, Johnnie. There's a sniper out there.

JOHNNIE, crouching, steps forward into silhouette.

JOHNNIE

(whistles softly) Come on boy! (Whistles again, more loudly.)

The DOG looks at him but doesn't move. JOHNNIE

flinches as he hears the crack of a rifle. He makes a decision.

ALAN (OFF)
(shouts) Johnnie!

JOHNNIE runs over to the DOG, slips his belt through the DOG's collar, and runs with him back to the farmhouse interior.

NB – (C.S. DOG and collar action to be shot in studio.)

'OFF', Arthur had learned, meant 'not visible in shot' which, in turn, meant that the actor who spoke the 'OFF' lines didn't actually have to be present – a gap of the right length could be left in the dialogue, and the words recorded afterwards in a nice quiet sound studio somewhere in London. The scenes on location, he had found, were full of such shifts and short-cuts, all of them attempts (it seemed) to simplify the astonishing complexity of outdoor filming.

Sometimes, during a 'take', an actor moved at the wrong time, or forgot a word, or picked up his cigarette with the left hand instead of the right, or said, 'Sorry, everyone, but it's awfully distracting to have all those people standing just in my eyeline, can we go again?' Sometimes the camera needed re-loading, or the microphone dipped into shot, or a cow mooed at an inopportune moment, or the director changed his mind about the framing, or a shadow fell across an actor's face, or there was too much light or not enough light or light of the wrong quality, or a local urchin accepted a dare to run up behind the sound recordist, shout 'bugger' and then scarper – there were many, many reasons why a scene might need to be re-shot, but it was never the fault of Chopper because Chopper was eerily perfect, every time. People congregated to watch his performance. Arthur was beginning to suspect that the other actors, the human ones, found this rather irritating.

'So do I wait for the dog to turn his head before I flinch?' asked Hadley Best, plaintively, during the rehearsal. 'Or do I take my own cue?'

'I'll cue you where the sniper's shot's supposed to go,' said Kipper. 'They'll replace it with the real noise at the edit. Settle down, everybody, the director's decided we'll be taking sound for Mr Best on this one.'

'What sort of cue?' asked Hadley.

'I'll click my fingers,' said Kipper. 'That be all right for you, Dick?'

There was an affirmatory grunt from the sound recordist.

'And settle *down*,' called Kipper, for the sixth time, as if everyone were dancing a conga instead of standing around with their hands in their pockets. 'Going for a take, everybody. Slate it.'

'Just a very quiet click, please,' said Hadley. 'It's hard to explain to a non-actor, but I want to react to the sniper out there, and not the finger-snap in here, do you see what I mean? It's a matter of authenticity. In fact, there's no chance of actually firing a rifle is there?'

'No,' said Kipper. 'Quiet click it is. Now, are we all ready?'

They were all ready. The clapper-board clapped. The barn door was pulled shut.

'And *action*,' shouted Kipper.

Slowly, the door opened. Arthur, from his vantage point two yards behind the camera, could see Chopper sitting in the drizzle. Hadley, crouching, stepped forward and left a long pause before giving a whistle.

'Come on, boy!' he called, softly. He whistled again; Chopper turned his head.

The fractional silence that followed was broken not by a quiet click but by the most stupendous burst of heavy gunfire coming from immediately behind the barn. Arthur found himself lying on the ground, arms over his head, while all around him people shouted and cannoned into each other, and shrapnel clattered on the roof.

'Mind the *camera*,' shouted someone. There was a scrape, and a thud, and the muffled smash of glass and then the gunfire stopped, and only the slow drone of an aircraft was audible.

'What the bloody hell . . . ?' asked someone. 'Who was that? That wasn't Jerry, was it?'

'No, that was my bastard lens-box,' said the cameraman, bitterly.

By the time that Arthur got to his feet and dusted himself off, most of the crew had run outside and were staring upward. He followed them. A Wellington was making leisurely progress from north to south, towing, far behind it, a red and yellow target.

'But where are the guns?' asked Phyl.

'I bet it's a mobile ack-ack unit from the battery,' said Hadley. 'They're probably in that field just beyond the spinney.'

The rain was spotting Arthur's spectacles and he took them off to give them a polish, and found himself staring at Chopper. The dog hadn't moved and was sitting as if welded to the spot, its blunt, brindled face turned towards its owner. Chick had been placed by the director against the outside wall of the barn, invisible to the camera.

'Oh, incidentally, everyone, that's a cut,' shouted Kipper.

As Arthur watched, Chick shook his fist as if about to throw a pair of dice, and Chopper became a normal dog again, trotting off in a busy figure-of-eight, yawning, lifting his leg against the barn door.

'So when you shake your fist, does that mean "stand easy"?' ventured Arthur.

'Yer might say that,' said Chick.

'He's certainly a very good dog.'

'He's the *best* dog,' corrected the owner. He seemed offended by the slightness of the compliment.

Arthur busied himself with his spectacles, and found that his hands were shaking. He dropped the spectacles once, and then twice; his legs felt unstable, as if they might fold without warning, like those of an army camp-bed.

'All right, everybody,' said Kipper, 'settle down. We're sending someone to find out whether that little interruption's likely to happen again. In the meantime, the director's decided that we'll do a mute version of the scene.'

There was an upturned crate in a dark corner of the barn, and Arthur sat on it for a minute or two, and then began to wonder if he might feel better outside, away from other people, because the shaking was getting worse. He could think of nothing in the way of military expertise that he could contribute to the scene; there had been a rescued dog on the same paddle steamer that had picked him up at Dunkirk, and it had been shot dead on the quay at Dover, as a rabies hazard. He didn't think that this piece of information would be welcomed. In any case, he didn't think that he could trust his voice. He waited until Kipper shouted 'settle down' again, and then he slipped away.

It was a slow, muddy walk back to the edge of Badgeham, along a causeway between salt-marshes. The Wellington circled lazily overhead, and the guns from the field beside the barn alternated with those from the main battery; the noise seemed more bearable in the open air. Arthur breathed deeply and swung his arms in approved parade-ground fashion. He had never minded drill: the concentration required was just enough to empty the mind of nagging worries, and moreover he found the enforced neatness rather satisfying.

His father had been a military man, a career soldier until wounds sustained in France had rendered him barely able to walk, let alone fight. He had often talked about the army – not the army of boggy entrenchment and the sniper's bullet, but the Edwardian army, brutal and thrilling, all glitter and ceremony and the rumble of hooves. He had wanted to be buried in his Lancers' uniform, but he had survived too long – twenty-three years after Ypres – and the cloth had rotted before he had.

When Arthur had enlisted in 1939, a year after his father's death, he had half-expected to find a world where disputes were still settled with bare knuckles, and where tots of neat rum were drunk blindfold to the roll of a drum. He had expected, too, that he'd be seen as an oddity – the oldest, the shyest, the least soldierly, but this was a different army, and his platoon of conscripts had been stuffed with oddities, with men beside whom Arthur could pass for a Berserker. There had been nicknames for all, and his own ('Dynamite') had been no more sarcastic or cruel than any other. Life had become curiously easy – not comfortable or pleasant or even interesting, but certainly uncomplicated. There had been no empty rooms, no hours to fill, no time to sit and brood over lost years or ungrasped opportunities. Until the Germans had started strafing him, he had almost forgotten the inevitable concomitant of army service. And now he was afraid of going back to war. And now he was dreading going back to peace, if it ever came.

The rain began to fall more heavily as he reached the outskirts of Badgeham, and he took shelter under the awning of a shop. *Furse Quality Dressmaking* was written in fly-blown gold lettering along the window, *Design, Alteration, Repair.*

*

Ambrose arrived back at the Crown and Anchor at a quarter to one in the morning and had to ring the bell four times before he was let in.

'*Please* don't,' he said, as the landlord began a reiteration of the rules. 'I have been standing in a train corridor for the past five and a half hours and I can assure you that my temper is dangerously short.'

He felt cold to the marrow, his mind focused solely on the emergency hip-flask in his room and the teaspoon of Bells that he felt sure was still in there. The thought had sustained him throughout the whole appalling journey from Ipswich – the carriages full of rowdy soldiers, the shuttered buffet, the repeated, farcical platform changes at Norwich, the rumbling spectre of the east-bound freight train that had sped unheralded through the station, each of its fifty-odd open trucks piled high with bomb rubble. 'They use it for making runways,' a fellow on the platform had said, and Ambrose had thought of Sammy's office, minced, flattened and tarmacadamed, a spring-board, now, for aeroplanes carrying bombs to drop on to Sammy's relatives. It was almost, in a ghastly way, amusing.

The darkness in the bedroom was absolute, and Ambrose stood just inside the door, waiting for outlines to emerge. 'I'm still awake,' said Arthur, switching on the bedside light. 'Oh, have you hurt your hand?' he added, spotting the handkerchief that Cecy had donated as a bandage.

Ambrose was already tugging his suitcase out of the wardrobe and unbuckling the strap. 'Vicious cat,' he said, extracting the hip-flask, wedging it between his knees and unscrewing the top with his good hand. He sat on the bed and lifted the flask to his lips and – oh joy – there was more than a teaspoon, there was a good swallow, and another sip or two besides, and he thought (not for the first time) what a sad and sorry bunch teetotallers were, depriving themselves of that mouthful that changed the world. There was nothing left in the flask now except fumes. He sighed, and took out a cigarette. 'You don't mind, do you?'

Arthur shook his head; he looked somehow unprotected without his spectacles, like a welder without the mask. 'Might I have one, too?'

'I didn't know that you partook.'

'I don't usually.' He took the offered cigarette and lit it with predictable clumsiness.

'Much get done today?' asked Ambrose.

'No, not much. One scene, I think.'

'The trouble with these documentary boys is that they're used to spending weeks getting one usable shot of a brawny fisher-lass gutting a hake, but when it comes to a *schedule*, when it comes to—'

'Could I ask you something?' said Arthur.

'Something about filming?'

'Um . . . no, actually.'

There was a long pause during which Arthur's round, inexpressive face gave no hint as to what the 'something' might be . . .

'Fire away,' said Ambrose, beginning to get bored.

'I was wondering . . .'

'Yes?'

'If you were a young lady . . .'

God in heaven, thought Ambrose, what *is* this? 'Yes?' he said, repressively.

'If you were a young lady, where would you want to go to? If I were to ask you.'

'To ask me what?'

'To . . . to meet up with you. I mean, with me.'

Light dawned. 'You've met a girl?'

'Er . . .' The phrase seemed to unnerve Arthur. He reached over to the night-table for his glasses, and began the inevitable polishing. '. . . in a way.'

'And you want to ask her out?'

'Yes, I thought, perhaps, a walk . . .'

'Is she on the crew?'

'No. No, she's not.'

'She's a local girl?'

'I think so.'

Ambrose spread his hands in disbelief. 'And you don't know where to take her?'

'I thought, perhaps, a walk,' said Arthur, woodenly, as if repetition might make the prospect more enticing.

'Good God, man,' said Ambrose, 'take her on set.'

'Really?'

If it hadn't have been for the hour, the throbbing hand, the empty flask, the chastening afternoon with Cecy, Ambrose might have laughed. 'There is no phrase,' he said, 'that thrills a female of the species more than "come and watch the filming". We in the business may know that 95 per cent of it consists of sitting on our arses waiting for some inexperienced clown to make up his mind, but there's no need to tell the girl that. Glamour, man. Give her a glimpse, dazzle her, let her clap the clapper-board, look through the lens, try on the headphones, and then take her back to your . . . your . . .' He was getting carried away, whisky on an empty stomach. 'Dazzle her, man,' he said again, leaning over to unlace his shoes. 'What's her name, by the way?'

'I don't know,' said Arthur.

'Well . . .' Ambrose crushed out his cigarette, lay back on the bed, closed his eyes. 'It doesn't matter. Turn out the light, will you?' Names had never mattered, all those little stage-door Sallies: Ooh Mr Hilliard, is this your dressing-room? So you reely do have bulbs all the way round the mirror . . .

Arthur turned out the light and listened to the huff and whistle of Ambrose snoring. 'Would you like to come and watch the filming?' he mouthed, experimentally. 'You may remember, I came into the shop on Wednesday.' He had stood in the dress-maker's porch and watched the rain sluice along the cobbles, and he'd looked at the sign again and thought idly, I wonder if they shorten sleeves? The bell on the door had jangled but there'd been no one in the shop, though he'd called twice, and had knocked tentatively on the polished wood of the counter, and after a while he'd followed the noise of a sewing-machine, and had peered around the edge of a heavy curtain and seen a woman at work beneath a glass roof, her foot busy on a treadle, her hands guiding a length of dark cloth beneath the needle.

He wasn't sure, afterwards, quite what had caught and held him for so long – some sense of recognition, a resemblance to a painting he'd once seen, perhaps, or a glimpse of a room bathed in that same shifting, watery light – but for a minute or more he had stood and gazed at the scene, at the bolts of cloth in their orderly towers, at the reels of coloured thread, at the pleasing neatness of the sewing table and the quiet intensity of the woman's expression, and then, reluctant to disrupt the picture, he'd let the curtain drop back and had tiptoed towards the door. The sewing-machine had stopped just as he'd set the shop bell swinging again, and he'd waited then, one hand on the handle, and she'd lifted the curtain aside and hurried in and said, 'Hello, can I help you?' She'd looked rather anxious.

'I was just wondering . . .' he'd said. He'd held out his arms in front of him, in mute demonstration.

'Oh yes.' She'd pinched the cloth of one of his cuffs, turned it back and examined the stitching, her ringless fingers brushing his arm and hand, but impersonally – professionally – as if he were a shop-window dummy and she the dresser. 'Yes, I could shorten them if you'd like, I can do a tuck behind the cuff, but not when the material's wet.'

'I see.'

'Can you bring the jacket back when it's dried out?'

'Yes.'

'We're open from eight in the morning, Monday to Saturday.'

'Thank you.'

She'd nodded.

A brisk, clear conversation, information transmitted, information received, no awkward silences or dangling questions, everything squared off, stuck down, trimmed and sanded. When his jacket was dry, he was under instruction to return.

'Would you like to come and watch the filming?' he mouthed to the whitewashed ceiling of the Crown and Anchor. He could almost imagine saying it.

⋆

'Wondered which day you'd turn up,' said Buckley, when Catrin tracked him down to a window-seat in the Copper Kettle, a tea-shop just beside the harbour at Badgeham. He was sitting with a notebook in front of him, and an empty cup. He appeared to have put on weight. 'Just got in?' he asked.

'Half an hour ago.'

'How's London?'

'Quiet since last weekend.'

'Quiet?'

'Yes.'

'So why do you look as if you haven't slept for a month?'

She shrugged, with an attempt at insouciance. 'I was up at four to catch the train.'

'And that's the reason?'

'Uh huh.'

He gave her a long, shrewd look, and then flipped open the notepad. 'Well, you're just in time. You can do the honours, pick the title. I've narrowed it down to three.' He cleared his throat, theatrically. 'First choice . . . *Just An Ordinary Wednesday*.'

'It wasn't a Wednesday, it was a Sunday,' said Catrin.

'Sounds too religious. If it was identical vicars crossing the Channel we might get away with it. Second choice,' *Just An Ordinary Thursday*.' He glanced up at her. 'No? Don't like it? Usual tiresome objections on the accuracy front? All right, third choice, *The Sterling Starlings*.'

'I don't believe you,' said Catrin.

'What, not even for a second?'

'No.'

He shook his head, apparently disappointed. 'It's a shame, really,' he said. 'You'd have swallowed that when you first started.'

'So what's the third choice?'

'*Just An Ordinary Friday*.'

She gave a snort of laughter.

'That's a bit better,' said Buckley. He glanced over his shoulder and beckoned. 'Have something to eat,' he said to Catrin, 'you're looking scrawny. And before you say anything about my own size, I've been taking advantage of a fortunate liaison. The natives are friendly, you might say . . .'

The friendly native was a large-breasted waitress who took their order and received a lingering slap on the rear by way of thanks from Buckley.

'So how's the filming going?' asked Catrin.

'Oh, the usual. Think of a snail's pace, and then halve it.'

'What are the actors like?'

'Vain, silly, overpaid.'

'No, I mean . . .'

'I know what you mean. They're not bad, just about able to walk and speak at the same time. God knows I've seen worse.'

'And the director?'

'Seems to know what he's doing. Says what he wants in as few words as possible and then expects it all to happen. Lots of grey-faced people running around trying to work bloody miracles.'

'And what scenes are they doing today?'

'Flipping heck,' said Buckley, 'you don't want to know much, do you? It's quayside stuff this morning, and then the beach in the afternoon – big number with extras and the RAF supplying a couple of planes. No dialogue. Now, am I allowed to ask you a couple of things?'

'Yes, of course.'

'How's the propeller-fouling scene?'

'Better, I think. Shorter.'

'How's Parfitt?'

'Asleep, mainly.'

'How's your husband?'

She should have seen it coming. 'He's doing awfully well,' she said. 'He's been commissioned to travel all over the country recording air-raid damage.' And then she looked quickly out of the window, as if something on the harbour-side had caught her eye. There was, in fact, a modicum of activity there – the two girls playing the Starling twins were posing for a photographer, first smiling in gleaming unison, and then assuming a more serious expression, and shading their eyes against the imaginary glare of the sun.

'Tell you what,' said Buckley, 'they're much better at acting than you are.'

'Don't,' she said.

'Don't what?'

'Be nosy. Because it's none of your business and I'm not going to tell you anything.'

'I'll be the soul of discretion.'

'And I'll be Eleanor bloody *Roosevelt*.'

She spoke more loudly than she'd intended, and one or two diners turned to look at her.

'Oho!' said Buckley, admiringly. 'Spitfire!' He ran a hand through his hair, examined the palm with apparent interest and then wiped it on the tablecloth as the waitress approached. 'Lovely sight,' he said, as she stooped to serve them. 'Double portion . . .'

Publicity photographers were men of very little imagination. Not for them the subtle, the surreal, or the oblique. Ambrose's character, Uncle Frank, could loosely be classified as an old salt, and therefore, for the purposes of advertising the film, Ambrose was required to stand on the harbour wall with a pipe in his hand and a rope slung over his shoulder. Vain for him to protest that this was a story of redemption and sacrifice, deserving of a veil of shadow across the face, a glimpse of anguish in the eye.

'Big smile,' said the photographer, pressing the shutter. 'And now point towards the horizon. And now put the pipe in your mouth and look thoughtful.'

'How much longer do you think you'll be? I'm working this afternoon, you know, we have a very heavy schedule.'

'Couple more poses, Mr Hilliard, and then I'm done. Can we get the dog in again? That's lovely. And can you take a pace back, Mr Hilliard? And now another? I want the dog foreground, you see.'

'Oh what a surprise.'

'And another pace back, please, Mr Hilliard.'

'I'm clearly ruining the dog's shot. Would it be easier if I simply threw myself into the water?'

He was released at last, and lingered for a moment to watch Hadley being photographed. ('And now shake hands with the dog. Lovely.') The wind was picking up, and the boats in the harbour rocked in synchrony, a marine chorus line. Ambrose felt a passing twinge of sympathy for those extras who were going to be spending the afternoon up to their waists in water.

'You'll be needed at the next location at half-past one, Mr 'illiard,' said Chick.

'Then perhaps you should have some Pepto-bismol standing by, since that will give me precisely thirteen minutes for lunch.'

'You want me to getcher some at the chemist?'

'No, that was merely . . . oh, never mind.' It was like trying to banter with a boulder. Ambrose reached for his cigarettes.

'Er . . . Mr Hilliard.'

He turned to see Arthur Frith looking smarter than usual, his hair brilliantined.

'Mr Hilliard,' said Arthur, 'may I introduce you to Miss Edith Beadmore?'

So this was the local girl that Arthur had mentioned – except that she wasn't a girl, she was a woman well into her thirties, well-dressed but with owlish features and a worried air.

Ambrose took her hand. 'Charmed,' he said, mendaciously. 'Arthur showing you the ropes?'

'Yes he is.'

'Splendid.'

'That's Hadley Best over there, Miss Beadmore,' said Arthur. 'He's another of the actors, and that's a dog called Chopper who's also in the film, and that's Chopper's owner, he controls the dog with the use of various hand signals, it's really very impressive . . .'

Edith nodded, though she was beginning to feel fogged by detail. Over the past half hour she had been introduced to upward of thirty people. She had learned the definition of 'gaffer'. She had looked through the camera. She had clapped the hinged baton on the clapper-board and she had spoken into a microphone and seen a needle quaver in response. 'Would you like to meet one of the writers next?' asked her escort.

'Yes, thank you,' said Edith, politely.

'And then we should get back to the beach for the afternoon's filming. Are you able to stay and watch?'

'I am, yes.' As she followed him into the Copper Kettle she found herself smiling. How marvellous, how truly marvellous, it had felt to say to Verna, 'I've met the military advisor to the film, and he's invited me on to set.' With one stride she had vaulted her cousin's lowly connection, had transcended the pit of back-room button-filing to arrive as an honoured guest. And how sweet it had been to leave Verna (whose own stint on the picture had finished) sewing overalls at the back of the shop, to have her warn, 'Now do be careful, remember that soldiers are only after *one thing*, if you know what I mean, Edith . . .' and to feel that she was doing something, for once, both unpredicted and unpredictable. Although, so far, the experience had been rather less like a dangerous liaison, and rather more like the junior prize in a film-fan competition.

'And this is Mr Buckley, who's written the film,' said Arthur.

Edith shook hands firmly. 'I'm very pleased to meet you.'

After consuming two helpings of cottage pie, Buckley declared his intention of going back to the hotel for the afternoon. 'I'm warning you,' he said to Catrin, putting on his hat, 'if you're set on watching, they're doing a mute choreographed shot. Do you know what that means?'

'No.'

'It means hours and hours of boredom for the sake of forty feet of celluloid, it means people bellowing through megaphones, and other people shouting, "What? I can't hear you?" It means extras arranged in tasteful patterns. It means *art*.'

'So what are you going to do?'

'Make notes for my next script.'

'What's that?

'A romantic comedy set in a sanatorium for people with facial tics and it's called—'

'*Forty Winks*,' she supplied.

'Very good.' He nodded, with grudging respect. '*Very* good. You're mustard these days, aren't you? Whatever happened to Little Miss Blush? Oh, she's back.' He grinned at her discomfiture. 'Okeydokey. Well, enjoy yourself this afternoon. Don't speak to any actors if you can possibly help it.'

She walked along the harbour and over the headland, and then took a path that undulated across the top of the dunes. Choosing a spot near the apex of one of the tallest, she sat on a springy clump of marram grass. Badgeham Beach lay like a theatre stage before her, an arc of grey sand stretching from the shallow hump of the headland to her right, as far as the wire and warning signs of the minefield to her left, and sloping gently down to a choppy sea forty yards away. A fishing boat with an engine was anchored a good distance offshore, and there was activity on board, a huddle of little figures surrounding the black tripod of the camera. Three rowing-boats were drawn up on the edge of the water, and a fourth bobbed at anchor.

At the foot of the dunes to her left, just beside the coiled wire of the minefield, a tatty marquee and a couple of smaller tents had been pitched, and there was a table with a tea-urn, and a number of folding chairs. Soldiers milled around. Those who were near enough for Catrin to see were painfully young – schoolboys with pimples, their narrow shoulders hunched against the wind. They were going to be even chillier soon, thought Catrin, as she read the single sheet of script that Buckley had handed her.

LOCATION SHOOTING SCHEDULE 'DUNKIRK FILM'

---

15 March 1941

Scenes p.m. Badgeham Beach

225. EXT. BEACH. DAY

(W.S. FROM DECK OF 'REDOUBTABLE', UNCLE FRANK'S P.O.V.)

Soldiers throng the beach, and stand in long queues that stretch from the sand right out into the water. Some are being hauled into rowing boats, while others wave and call out for rescue.
Suddenly, those in the water duck, and those on land throw themselves down as the beach is strafed.

340 EXT. DAY (RAF and weather permitting)

German planes in low pass.

Ambrose, sitting on the least decrepit of the camp-chairs, watched Kipper work out a system of cues with his team. 'So it's white flags for rehearsal, red for a take,' said Kipper. 'Two above the head for smoke, one above the head for first positions, one sharp flap for action, two flags in a V for setting off the electrics and two flags flapping for "cut". And keep the dunes at the back clear between the markers, though I doubt they'll be in shot.'

'We re'earsing the extras in the water?' asked Chick.

'Yes.'

'Only they're complaining already about it being cold.'

'Stuff 'em,' said Kipper, crisply. 'They're getting paid, aren't they? And tell them to keep their bloody kit on, I just tripped on a pile of webbing, and costume keep having to pick up helmets. Any other questions?'

'I have a question,' said Ambrose, approaching the group. He held out his page of script. 'It states here that the scene is "Uncle Franks's POV". Now, correct me if I'm wrong, but I've always been under the impression that "POV" stands for "point of view".'

'Yes,' said Kipper, cautiously.

'So the camera on the fishing boat out there will be recording what Uncle Frank sees when he steps up on deck after rousing himself from an inebriated stupor in the bilges?'

'Yes.'

'I thought so. And yet, apparently, my actual physical presence is required, so I was rather wondering which part of me is going to appear on camera. My eyelashes?'

'The director feels that later on we may want you for some over-shoulder shots.'

'So *later on* you may wish to use part of the back of my head?'

'That's right.'

'And until then, I'm to remain in full costume and make-up on a freezing beach with no shelter other than an antediluvian tent reeking of mildew?'

'Yes,' said Kipper. 'I'm sorry, but if you go back to the Crown I've got no one to spare to come and get you. Not this afternoon.'

'I see.'

Ambrose sat down again, shifting his chair into the lee of the bell-tent. There was no one else there apart from Chopper, who sat as if nailed to the spot.

'Waiting for your close-up?' asked Ambrose, peevishly. He was feeling neglected; there was a lack of care on this shoot, a laissez-faire attitude towards those who should be cherished and nurtured, a kow-towing to the nabobs of accountancy that showed in every cheese-paring decision. Even in provincial rep, Cecy had been given an electric fire and access to a kettle. There had been a warmth there that had been most pleasant . . .

Chopper gazed at him, impassively. 'Die,' said Ambrose. There was no response. 'Die,' he said again, trying to remember the hand-signal that Chick used – was it a snap of the fingers? He tried it, and Chopper lay down neatly. 'No,' said Ambrose. '*Die*. Die for the King.'

*

'You're not cold, are you?' asked Arthur, as he escorted Edith across the beach.

'Not in the least,' she said. 'I used to walk here every morning in the winter. I wonder what they've done with those huge metal items that were stuck in the sand?'

'Tank traps,' said Arthur. 'They've been removed especially for this scene, they brought in a tractor to do it. There weren't any tank traps at Dunkirk, you see.'

She nodded, and he could almost have cut a caper, for this was *conversation*, a proper back-and-forth, one speaking, the other listening, a balanced sharing of thoughts and experience such as he had never previously managed in the social company of someone from the distaff side. For this was by no means the first time that he had asked a lady out.

'The large tent over there is for the use of the extras,' he said to Edith.

'And the two smaller ones?'

'Costume and make-up, I think. I'll introduce you.'

It was the sixth time, in fact. He had made a start on the wooing front a respectful two months after his father's funeral, inviting Rose Pritchett to a musical evening at Wimbledon town hall. Miss Pritchett worked as a waitress in the directors' dining room at Waring's, the factory at which Arthur was catering manager, and he had been attracted by her friendly demeanour. The invitation had been refused, with the entirely reasonable explanation that Miss Pritchett was already 'seeing' a chap from the transport department, although he'd learned subsequently that this was untrue.

He had asked Dulcie Reed next, from Waring's switchboard, and they had spent a Sunday afternoon together in South Kensington, leaving the Science Museum after only half an hour, as Miss Reed had declared the heat there to be stifling, and going instead to Farelli's Ice Cream Parlour where she had eaten a knickerbocker glory and a Key lime wafer, and drunk a vanilla cream soda before looking at her watch and exclaiming that her mother would be expecting her home at any moment. Alice Davies, secretary to the Waring's distribution manager, had accompanied Arthur to an exhibition of marine water-colours at Dulwich Picture Gallery, but had declined a visit to the tea-rooms afterwards as she was suffering from a headache. Edna Brady (pudding cook, Waring's canteen; stroll on Wimbledon Common followed by a meal at Lyons Corner House) had thanked him for a nice time, which had been encouraging, but then he had overheard her in the kitchens the next morning, complaining that if she'd known she was going to spend an afternoon with a mute, she'd have chosen Harpo Marx, since he might at least have been amusing.

Conversation, then, was important; until that point, he had thought it enough to be polite and to pay for everything.

On the next occasion (a steamer to Hampton Court with Avis Glickman from the accounts department) he'd written six possible topics of interest on the palm of one hand, but she'd spotted the list early on, and had made a joke of it, and when it came to saying goodnight, she had dashed into her parents' house before he could even shake hands. After that, he'd begun to get the impression that some of the female staff at work, previously pleasant and respectful, were starting to giggle the instant he left a room. An envelope had appeared in his pigeon-hole, containing a typed list of all the women who worked at the company, with five of the names crossed off and the hand-written addition: 'Who's next?!' Who indeed? Outside of Waring's, he knew no women.

Not long after that, war had been declared, and he had enlisted, and although his fellow soldiers had spent much of their time discussing the female of the species, Arthur had learned nothing that could ever be repeated (or even thought about) in mixed company. Certainly, none of them had possessed the worldly wisdom of Ambrose Hilliard; none of them had ever advised him to 'dazzle her, man'.

He watched Edith talking to the wardrobe mistress. 'Dazzled' would be a wild exaggeration, but she appeared animated, alert, *interested*. She was asking questions, and giving detailed responses, and although she still appeared a little anxious he was beginning to wonder whether that might be the natural cast of her features, and he almost liked her the better for it – for, as he had discovered (five times), an expression of amiability could be illusory.

'Of course, they'll all end up being dots on the horizon,' the wardrobe mistress was saying. 'You'll see what I mean if you go on the boat with the camera – there won't be a single extra in close-up, and ten days' work will have gone for absolutely nothing, which I knew would happen. I've been in the business twenty years, and I said to Kipper at the start, I said: "Before I begin attacking a hundred and twenty brand-new uniforms with a rasp, can you assure me they'll actually be visible?" But I got the usual dusty answer. Mind you, if I'd known there was someone here with your sort of experience it would have made life a darn sight easier, where on earth have you been hiding?' and Edith smiled, and threw Arthur a quick glance of what he interpreted, after a moment of surprise, as gratitude.

'And the worst of it,' continued the wardrobe mistress, a touch hysterically, 'was being lectured, hour after hour, on the evils of drink and fornication by a local woman who'd volunteered to help me out. As if I had the time for fornication! Chance would be a fine thing . . .'

A man with an armful of flags asked Catrin to move, and she walked another fifty yards, in the direction of the tents, and sat down again, a short distance from a cluster of other spectators. Near the water's edge, the extras were being formed into lines, and the stench of burning tyres heralded a column of black smoke that rose from somewhere behind the dunes. In the centre of the beach, three men were burying a length of hose, and marking its sinuous course with driftwood stakes. A wire poked up through the sand at one end, and stretched back towards a cleft in the dunes.

'Excuse me.' It was a plump, dark-haired young girl wearing a school mackintosh. She held out an opened notebook. 'I'm collecting autographs. May I have yours?'

'Mine?'

'Yes. Because you work on the film, don't you?'

'How do you know?'

'Because you're not from around *here*,' said the girl heavily, with the implication that 'here' was an unspeakable hell-hole. 'I'll bet you live in London, don't you?'

'Yes.'

'You're so lucky.'

'I wouldn't call it so very lucky at the moment.'

'Oh *bombs*,' said the girl, dismissively. 'I'm going to live there when I'm grown-up.' She proffered a fountain pen. 'Could you please put "to my dear friend Myrtle" at the top, and then your name and also what your job is on the film? My mother says it makes it more educational if I ask people that.'

Catrin bent to her task.

'So you're a waiter?' asked Myrtle, peering critically at the result.

'No, a writer.'

'Oh yes. I thought that "r" was an "a". And is Catrin Cole your real name?'

'My real name?'

'Yes, because Doris Cleavely's real name is Joy Weeks.'

'Oh. Oh, I see . . .'

'She told me it took her ages to decide what to call herself, but I've already chosen a name for if I become an actress.' Myrtle paused, delicately.

'I'd love to know what it is,' said Catrin.

'It's Deborah-Anne Duvalier.' The syllables were lovingly enunciated. 'Do you like it?'

'Very much. And where will you live in London?'

'Claridges.'

'Which floor?'

Myrtle's pink face turned pinker. 'Are you teasing me?' she asked, huffily.

'Maybe just a little bit. I'm sorry.'

'Because I don't know which floor.'

'Neither do I, but if you're a famous actress, you should probably have a town-house on Park Lane as well.'

'All right, then.' Myrtle nodded, as if agreeing to the terms of a contract. 'I will. Thank you very much.' She closed her notebook with a snap, and set off in search of fresh prey.

On the beach below, one of the assistant directors was shouting into a loud-hailer, and Catrin just caught the words 'quiet' and 'rehearsal' as they were whipped away by the wind.

She thought about the autograph that she'd just given to Myrtle. It had not, strictly speaking, been of her real name; she'd been called Cath Pugh when she'd met Ellis, but he'd said that a beautiful girl ought really to have a beautiful name (and oh, how she'd loved that), and he'd suggested 'Catrin', from a book of Welsh legend, and she'd tacked his surname on to the end, just to save any awkwardness, and had bought herself a ring in Woolworths, and had left Cath Pugh behind her in Ebbw Vale, and whatever might or might not come to pass once the film was over, she knew that she never wanted to go back to being Miss Pugh again. And, after all, it was not just actors and actresses who rechristened themselves. Catrin Cole might not be her married name, but perhaps it could be her *nom de plume* . . .

On the camera boat, a white flag waved briskly, and the lines of mock-soldiers began to shuffle into the water, and towards the four rowing boats that bobbed offshore. Further back on the beach another group of extras set off on a pre-arranged course, weaving between carefully placed crates and packs, while a third contingent made their way down one of the dunes, walking in ragged formation.

On the margins, well outside the frame of the shot, stood the other army: props men and costume standbys, sparks and chippies, the make-up artist, the art director, the location manager and his assistant, the stills photographer, the caterers, the runner. And all this, thought Catrin, from a single sentence on a page – all this from a decision, taken in utter naivety, to confirm a story that had never existed. She felt a jolt of guilt, and then a tiny, unexpected, nudge of pride. I did this, she thought. Catrin Cole (writer) did this.

'. . . to my dear friend Myrtle, and then your name,' said the girl with the catarrhal voice and the shoulders of a coal-heaver; she spoke with the local accent, an oddly-inflected mutter delivered with the mouth half-closed. 'And also what your job is,' she added.

'What my *job* is?' repeated Ambrose, acidly.

'Yes. Please. Everybody else has.' She held out her notebook and he took it reluctantly and flipped through the pages.

'Ah splendid,' he said, 'I see that you've already captured the elusive signature of the camera-car driver's mate. Surely the addition of lesser names can only dim its lustre?'

Sarcasm, of course, was wasted on the very young; Myrtle merely gave him a nervous glance and picked at one of her fingernails.

'Oh very well,' he said, finding a blank page.

'Thank you very much.' She took back the book and scrutinized what he'd written. 'I thought you were him,' she said, with satisfaction.

'Did you?'

'My mother said to look out for someone quite old. And is that your real name?'

'Yes,' said Ambrose, untruthfully. 'And now I really must get back to my *job*, which is to prepare for the next scene without being constantly interrupted.'

'Sorry. Thank you.'

He watched her lumber away, notebook in hand. The rehearsal had been halted and a procession of sodden extras was beginning to walk up the beach in search of hot tea. Ambrose returned to his former occupation.

'Roll over,' he said. 'Go on. Roll over. Or sit. *Sit*.' There was no response; the dog lay as if carved on a crusader tomb.

'Stay, then,' said Ambrose, sourly, and shook his fist at the silly creature, and Chopper, at last receiving a signal that he recognized, jumped up keenly and began to nose around the base of the tent. 'Oh, for God's sake,' said Ambrose.

'All extras in first positions for a take,' shouted someone. 'Now. Not after you've had some tea. *Now*.'

'Look through here,' said the camera operator, and Arthur bent his knees, and pressed his eye to the viewfinder, and felt his breath catch. The wide, cluttered beach had contracted to a precise rectangle. The tents were excluded, and the rolls of wire, and the trestle tables with their tea-urns, and the huge white sky above, and the spectators on the dunes, and the knots of crew who waited on the margins, so that what he saw was only a stretch of dark water and a swathe of sand pocked with litter and patterned with skeins of anonymous soldiery. A curl of smoke drifted across the scene.

'Yes,' he said, straightening up, 'that's really quite . . . like.'

The director nodded briefly, and resumed his conversation with Kipper, and Arthur returned to the stern of the fishing boat, wondering as he did so whether it was the slight motion of the deck that had caused his forehead to film with sweat.

'Was the wardrobe mistress right?' asked Edith, as he sat down beside her. 'Are the soldiers just dots on the horizon?'

'Just dots,' he confirmed, taking out a handkerchief to dab his brow. 'You're not cold, are you?'

'No, not a bit.'

'Good, good.' He folded his handkerchief carefully, suddenly aware that he had entirely run out of things to say. The pit of silence yawned. Could he ask her if she were cold? No, he had only just done that. He cleared his throat, uncomfortably.

'All right,' said Kipper, with perfect timing. 'Going for a take.'

★

The earlier wind had dropped, and there was silence on the beach apart from the soft slap of waves and the occasional sneeze. A gull flew the length of the dunes and then broke from its course and wheeled in a long curve above the lines of static figures, and Kipper, on the cabin roof, waited until the flake of white had left frame before raising his red flag and flapping it sharply.

Action, thought Catrin, if one could use such an energetic word about such a gradual progression. The extras inched into the surf or trudged along their set routes, and although she spotted the odd grin, or muttered aside, most seemed to be taking their roles with admirable gravity, looking apprehensively out to sea, or glancing up at the ceiling of smoke. Those in the water, or scrambling awkwardly into the rowing-boats, looked wholly and convincingly miserable.

The gull returned, tilting like a fighter plane above the beach, and Kipper on the cabin roof raised two flags in a V, and in an instant a chain of explosions erupted along the centre of the beach, following the curved line of the hosepipe, sending plugs of sand six feet into the air but with a noise that sounded strangely innocent – burst paper bags, Guy Fawkes bangers, party balloons – and the figures on the sand threw themselves flat, and the scene in front of Catrin was no longer a moving picture but a tableau, save for a streak of brown at the corner of her vision, a shape that darted away from the reports in a series of scrabbling runs. 'Hey!' called one of the spectators. 'Look where it's going!'

It was most peculiar, and it happened quite suddenly. Arthur had been sitting beside Edith, his arms folded tightly because his hands had started to shake again. He had seen Kipper marshalling his flags in readiness for cueing the electrics, and he was trying to prepare himself because, out of all the awfulness of those days on the beach at Dunkirk, it was the strafing that had caught on his memory like a hook – the feeling of utter nakedness, the banshee shriek of the dive-bombers, the hammer of the guns, the sand spitting – and he steeled himself and took a deep breath.

Kipper raised his arms. There were a few distant pops. Some of the extras dropped on to the ground. 'Cut,' said the director.

Arthur felt an odd internal jolt, as if he had just missed a step in the dark.

'I thought the explosions would be louder,' said Edith.

'Yes. The sand muffled them, I suppose.'

I'm *alive*, he thought, I survived, I'm here and I'm watching play-acting, I could have died on a French beach but I didn't, I came back, I was lucky.

He placed his palms on his thighs. He felt quite steady, and immensely real, and solid; he had never been so aware of his own body, of the muscle and bone, the density and heft of each limb. The bullets missed me, he thought, they *missed* me – and for a queer moment, the world seemed to dangle before him like a Christmas ornament, glistening and bright, hanging just within his reach.

'Hold that take, but we're going again,' shouted Kipper, and the words were like a draught that slammed a door shut. The bright world was gone again.

'I wonder why they're doing another take?' asked Edith.

'Oh . . .' For a second or two Arthur could hardly catch his breath. He took off his spectacles to polish the lenses, but they were already quite clean, and he put them back on again and saw Edith, neat and interested and smart in her maroon coat with ivory buttons. '. . . I suppose it might be something technical.'

Kipper was standing on the cabin roof again, holding a single flag above his head, but after a moment he jumped down, picked up a megaphone and leaned out over the bows.

'What is happening?' he shouted, the words well spaced. 'Where is everyone going?'

The occupants of the beach were drifting across to the right, and congregating between the tents and the coils of wire that demarcated the minefield.

'What is happening?' shouted Kipper again, and one of his assistants came to the edge of the water and shouted something back, through cupped hands.

Edith looked at Arthur. 'Did he say something about a dog?' she asked.

In his flight from the explosions, Chopper had plunged towards the wire and had almost found a way through, but a strand had caught around his chest and he had panicked and kept going until the loop had pulled taut into a deep 'V' and he could run no further. He stood now, some twenty feet into the minefield, panting, bleeding a little, the wire stretched into a series of stiff curves behind him, like a scrawled signature.

The growing crowd stared at him, with collective impotence. 'Here boy,' called one young fool. Ambrose turned to admonish him and saw, in the distance, the short, menacing figure of Chick approaching. The fellow had been stationed right at the other end of the beach and still held the flag he'd used for acknowledging Kipper's signals; he held it rather in the way that one might hold a rifle. Ambrose felt a flicker of personal anxiety.

The same youth opened his mouth again. 'Your dog ran away,' he called, as Chick came within earshot. 'He ran away when the charges went off.'

'My dog don't run away unless I tell 'im 'e can run away,' said Chick, without breaking stride. 'So some bastard's been muckin' abaht with 'im. Dixie, you got the nips?' One of the electricians tossed him a pair of pliers and Chick tucked them into the pocket of his overalls, threw the flag to one side, and carried on walking, straight through the gap that Chopper's run had opened in the hedge of wire.

There were gasps, and a stifled scream from somewhere in the crowd. 'Oh *God*,' said someone. 'Wait! We've sent a man round to the battery,' but Chick continued as if deaf, following with calm intent the paw-prints that jigged across the virgin sand, reaching the dog in the same length of time that it took for Ambrose to wonder whether anyone had seen him issuing orders to Chopper, and if so whether he might be called upon to give evidence at the inevitable inquest. '*Actor "must shoulder some of the blame" says coroner.*'

The watchers had fallen silent, and the dog's faint whimper became audible as Chick knelt beside it, cut through the wire with a few swift snips, and then lifted the stocky brindled form and unhurriedly re-traced his steps. He reached the gap again, passed through and kept on walking. Kipper was climbing from a rowing-boat into the shallows and he called out to Chick, 'How's the dog? Where are you taking him?'

'Bermondsey,' said Chick. 'He's off the picture. And so am I.'

'What?'

'You 'eard.'

There was a long moment during which Kipper seemed too shocked to speak, and then he rallied himself, and ran through the surf after the retreating figure.

'But we've already shot half of his scenes,' he called out. 'You can't take him now.' The answer was a brief, loud obscenity. Kipper appealed again but this time there was no reply. Chick walked steadily, inexorably across the width of the beach, and up the path and over the headland. For a brief moment he was silhouetted against the smoky sky and then he – and Chopper – were gone.

'*Actor "must bear substantial portion of cost for cancelled feature film" says auditor.*' Ridiculous, thought Ambrose, giving himself a mental shake – nevertheless, he glanced around to check for accusatory stares. Most people were looking back at the minefield again. 'They're probably duds,' said one youngster in uniform, feinting a leap over the wire.

Kipper blew a long blast on the whistle, and with a certain reluctance, the crowd shuffled round to face him. 'Never mind what's just happened,' he shouted, rather shrilly. 'Never mind standing around gossiping, let's have a bit of concentration here. The director's decided we're going again very shortly, so we need extras in first positions.' He waited for several seconds, but no one moved. 'Now!' he added, peremptorily.

A raspberry, wet and derisive, was blown as he turned to wade back to the rowing-boat and then one of the extras, soaked to the armpits, took off his tin hat and lobbed it towards the spot on the minefield from which Chopper had been rescued. It bounced harmlessly.

'I say!' called the boy. 'The wind's taken my hat. My kit's not on properly, we can't possibly shoot.'

Kipper seemed not to hear.

'Oh no! Me too,' called another young ham, flicking his own over the wire, and suddenly the air was full of flying helmets.

'Stop that!' shouted Kipper, ineffectually. 'Stop that this—'

There was a dull crump, and a fountain of sand, and a triangular piece of hat with the chin strap still attached whined past Ambrose and hit the tea-urn with a tremendous clang.

'*Actor "only able to find character work since loss of nose" says barrister.*'

Everyone had ducked, involuntarily, and as the sand ceased to patter down, there was a slow unclenching of shoulders. The silence was broken by Kipper.

'Going for a take very shortly,' he shouted. 'First positions, please.'

The afternoon light was beginning to weaken as the RAF planes began their thunderous runs above the beach. Dark crosses had been painted on the underside of their wings, and the shape of their tails had somehow been altered or added to, Edith thought, so that they looked indefinably *foreign*, but when she asked Arthur if that were the case, he only nodded vaguely and carried on staring at the sky. He had been very silent for the latter part of the afternoon, all through the excitement of the trapped dog, and the near-mutiny of the extras – very silent but scrupulously polite, and when the camera boat had docked at the harbour, he had escorted her across the gang-plank and up to the headland, and had found a camp-chair for her to sit on beside the new camera position, and had brought her tea, and had altogether behaved in a way that was so different from Verna's idea of licentious soldiery that Edith, to her shame, had felt rather disappointed. He stood now, his head tilted back as he watched the planes, and she scrutinized his thinning crown; there was, it seemed, no angle from which Arthur appeared memorable. Of course, it was dreadfully shallow of her to think in that way, especially since her own looks were so undistinguished, but she simply couldn't help it. She wasn't demanding a Cary Grant, but she wanted to find an aspect, a feature, an expression of Arthur's that was more than merely inoffensive, in the same way that she always liked the most mundane of garments to possess a cherishable trim, or an unexpectedly gorgeous lining.

If he asked her out again, she wanted to be able to accept for a reason beyond that of simple flattery, and if he didn't, then she'd like to be able to recall in future years (or even to mention, occasionally, casually, to Dolly Clifford and the others in the sewing-room once she was back in London), that the military advisor who had invited her to watch the filming in Norfolk had possessed nice eyes, or good hands or a ready wit. And she wanted that recollection to be a truthful one because there was nothing sadder than owning memories so unremittingly spartan that they had to be embroidered before display.

She blocked her ears as the planes roared over again, a beat apart, much lower this time, the noise so vast that it seemed to shake her whole body. The camera tilted and swivelled, the sky darkened briefly and then they were gone again, chasing each other across the bay, climbing steadily, a final dip of the wings and then away. The drone of their engines dwindled after them.

'Cut,' said the director, and Phyl pressed the button on her stopwatch; a tiny click, suddenly audible.

'Thank you,' said Kipper, to the crew. 'And that's a wrap for today.'

Arthur had remained staring at the sky, but at Kipper's speech he seemed almost to awaken and shake himself. 'Would you care for a short walk?' he said to Edith. 'If you're not too cold, that is?'

She realized almost immediately that something had changed. As they strolled through the fishy air of the harbour's edge, he kept glancing at her, clearing his throat, adjusting his spectacles, running his fingers across his chin as though checking for stubble growth.

'Along here?' he suggested, when the cobbles gave way to coarse grass, and they took a sandy path that wound inland, parallel with the line of stunted hawthorn that marked the coast road. The day was closing in, the light bluish-white, the colour of watered milk. 'You're not cold?' he asked again; the path was quite narrow and his sleeve was brushing hers.

'No, no,' she said, though she was actually a little shivery. He was going to kiss her, she realized – he was going to wrap an arm around her thirty-six-year-old waist and place his lips on hers, and she felt herself begin to breathe faster. 'He's a good kisser,' the juniors at Tussaud's would sometimes say about a boyfriend, and Edith had sometimes wondered precisely what they meant – were they talking about duration, frequency, lip texture? And should she lean against him when he took her in his arms, or place a hand behind his head and kiss him back, as women did in the 'hotter' sort of film, or would that appear to be over-eager? Because she was feeling suddenly rather keen: it was *passion*, perhaps, that could transform the mundane into the noteworthy, and a passionate Arthur might be a memorable Arthur. And perhaps – it occurred to her – perhaps it wouldn't stop at kissing, perhaps she should be prepared for more than that. She was a grown woman, after all, and he was a soldier far from home and wouldn't it be just a little thrilling if, when Verna said, 'You know what I mean, don't you Edith?' she was able to reply, 'Yes, Verna, I know *exactly* what you mean.' And if all this were happening too quickly – well then, she could blame the era they were living in, the 'war madness' that the newspapers loved to talk about, she'd simply be a woman of her time, she'd be acquiring a past and . . .

'Miss Beadmore,' said Arthur, stopping abruptly, so that she'd walked a yard or two beyond him before she'd realized. 'Edith,' he said, as she turned to face him. 'You don't mind if I call you Edith?'

'No, of course not.'

'Thank you. Edith.' He hesitated, and then took off his spectacles to polish the lenses and Edith waited, her heart drumming; of course, if it did go further than kissing then she'd have to *be careful*, as the phrase went, but then she'd heard that all soldiers were issued with . . .

'I realized something this afternoon,' said Arthur, staring down at the spectacles. 'You see, I hadn't thought before of how lucky I'd been. Surviving.'

His hands were beautifully clean, the nails smooth and trimmed neatly, and she caught herself wondering if his body, pressed close, would smell of soap, and she almost snorted at a thought so un-Edith-like.

'It's almost as if I've been given a gift,' said Arthur. 'I don't want to waste it.' He replaced the spectacles, and looked at her, his eyes smaller behind glass. 'Edith,' he said, and made a sudden movement and Edith moved too and then found herself flailing for balance because instead of enfolding her in his arms, he had bobbed down on the spot and she had very nearly flipped head-first over his shoulder, a fate averted only after much teetering and the use of his face as a brake.

'I'm sorry,' she said, embarrassed, stepping back. 'Are you hurt, or . . . ?'

He looked up at her, a red mark on one cheek from where she had planted her thumbnail.

'Edith,' he said. He was on one knee, she realized. 'Edith,' he said again, reaching for her hand, 'I want to ask you something . . .'

Edith stared at him.

He's not, she thought, he can't be, he *can't* be.

*

It seemed to Edith, in the astonishing aftermath of Arthur's proposal, that she had inadvertently unleashed the elements, like the girl in the fairy tale who summons the sea with a careless phrase. A single syllable, a brief glance, had changed everything, and in the tidal wave that followed she was swept along like a scrap of flotsam.

Her last entirely clear memory was of saying 'yes' – or rather, of hearing the word emerge from her own mouth, like an unexpected hiccough. The amazement on Arthur's face must have been mirrored on her own.

'Oh really?' he'd exclaimed, looking startled, and she'd felt flustered and had begun to say, 'What I mean is . . .' and then had changed it, mid-sentence, to, 'I wasn't expecting . . .'

'No,' said Arthur. 'No. Neither was I.' He seemed rather dazed, keeping hold of Edith's hand as if it were a hanging strap on the Underground, and she herself had no inclination to move, since any movement would initiate the next stage of the proceedings, and she hadn't the faintest idea of what that might be. The naked truth was, that although the 'yes' had surprised them both, it had been preceded on her part by a series of very rapid and rational thoughts – *He has just proposed, he seems sincere, he is not hideous, he has a good job in civilian life, he owns a house, he is very likely the only person who will ever ask for my hand in marriage . . . oh and won't it just knock Verna for six* – and it had been the last and most venial of these that had triggered her answer.

'Well . . .' said Arthur, eventually, letting go of her hand. He stood up, and dusted the sand from his knee, and then took off his spectacles and gave them a thorough polish.

'Well . . .' he repeated. 'My goodness . . .'

A faint mist was beginning to rise from the marshes. 'I suppose we had better be getting back,' said Arthur. They turned, and walked in awkward silence towards the harbour, and disbelief seemed to thicken the air between them – disbelief and a certain embarrassment. Perhaps, thought Edith, perhaps it would be altogether easier to carry on as if the events of the last ten minutes had never happened.

Thank you for a delightful day.

I enjoyed it.

Yes, so did I.

Good evening.

Yes, good evening.

They plodded on. The crew was still on the headland, smoking, packing equipment into boxes, winding cables, their voices carrying clearly in the chilly twilight.

'They'll just have to get a stuffed one, won't they?'

'What, a stuffed one that swims and barks?'

'They could do it in long shot.'

'They'd have to do it on wireless before that worked.'

'We lost a donkey once.'

'On what?'

'Irish comedy, *O'Hoolihan's Treasure*. We was shooting on Ealing Common, and the bugger ran off, last seen heading for Acton.'

'Did you get a stuffed one?'

'No we just put ears on the director.'

Laughter followed, and then all heads turned as Edith and Arthur emerged, self-consciously, from the gloaming.

'Oy oy,' said one of the men, grinning, 'and what have you two been up to?' There were sniggers from his colleagues.

'Now stop it,' said Phyl, 'I'm sure they've just been for a nice walk.' But there was amusement in her narrow grey eyes, and Edith felt suddenly indignant, for was it really so funny, the idea that she and Arthur might have been 'up to' something? They were not a joke, the pair of them, they were not coconuts in a shy – and besides, they had most certainly done more than just go for a *nice walk*. Defiantly, she took Arthur's arm.

'Oy oy,' said the man with the cable, again, 'so when's the wedding?'

Edith and Arthur exchanged a swift, involuntary glance – a double flinch, almost – and Arthur turned crimson.

'Oy *oy*!' said the man, in quite a different tone, and Phyl exclaimed, 'You're a dark horse, Arthur, and did she say yes?' and when Arthur nodded, she said, 'Well, I'll be damned!' and the chap with the headphones walked over and shook Edith's hand and clapped Arthur on the back, and said, 'come for a drink,' and that was just the start of it, the very start of a great surge of sentimental goodwill that bore them up and carried them off, and within minutes the bar of the Crown and Anchor began to fill with other crew members who'd heard the news, and a makeshift banner appeared between the beams, bearing a picture of intertwined hearts and the legend:

CONGRALUTIONS ON YOUR ENGAGMENT

and a man with a Ronald Colman moustache leaned beerily over Edith's shoulder and said 'None of the scenic artists can spell, that's why they draw for a living,' and the actor Hadley Best kissed Edith's hand and called for a toast and everyone raised their glasses and shouted, 'To Edith and Arthur!' as if they'd known them for years, and then the costume lady ('Call me Glenys') took Edith aside and asked her if she fancied a job as a standby wardrobe assistant, since the studio was sure to be a nightmare, they'd be using a water-tank and it would be wet, dry, wet, dry the whole blessed time, and the only girls she could get nowadays were a pack of silly gigglers, and then a bottle of champagne – actual champagne! – appeared from somewhere and Edith, who never drank, found herself taking a great gulp, and became a silly giggler herself, and the man with the Ronald Colman moustache leaned over her shoulder again and said that he was the NATKE rep and that if she was going to work in wardrobe then she'd have to join, and he needed a word about the dues, and then Glenys returned with a pink gin and said, 'Oh unions, they're *such* a nuisance,' and the chap with the moustache countered that that was a fine thing to call the greatest advance for the working man since the end of slavery and if she didn't agree with the principles of social justice then why didn't she just move to Berlin where he was sure they'd be happy to have her, and Kipper appeared suddenly and led the man with the moustache away, and Glenys put one heavily ringed hand on Edith's arm and said, 'A word of advice, my dear, *don't* have a long engagement, not during a war,' and held up the fourth finger of her left hand in order to demonstrate that there was a diamond ring beneath the swollen knuckle, but no wedding band, and then one of the actresses climbed on to a stool and sang the whole of 'Apple Blossom Time' although no one appeared to be listening, and Hadley called upon Arthur to make a speech, and there was a great assenting roar, and Arthur, who was on his second glass of champagne and beginning to look rather tight, got to his feet and said, 'Thank you, everybody, on behalf of my intended and myself, for your good wishes,' and sat down to prolonged applause before standing up again and adding, 'I would also like to thank Mr Hilliard for his kind and useful advice,' and Ambrose Hilliard, over by the window, inclined his head and smiled graciously, and then Arthur, who had just resumed his seat, stood up for a third time and said, 'Oh, I've just remembered something – Mr Hilliard, didn't you mention on that first morning at breakfast that you knew a dog who looked exactly like Chopper?' and there was a sudden hopeful movement from the corner where Kipper was standing with the director, and then all heads swung back towards Ambrose Hilliard.

'I was, of course, fully intending to mention it,' he said, rather stiffly.

*

Ensconced in a corner of the snug, Buckley drank the last of his pint and set the empty glass on the table. 'Norfolk piss,' he said, judicially. 'It should be a crime to serve ale of this quality at any public celebration other than a hanging.'

'Do you want another?' asked Catrin.

'Might as well. No – as you were, we're getting a visitor.'

Kipper was making his way between the tables towards them.

'His first words,' said Buckley, under his breath, 'will be "*the director wants* . . ." How are you doing?' he added, with false jollity.

'The director wants to speak to you,' said Kipper.

'Don't tell me, he's cancelled my fitting for the dog costume.'

The corners of Kipper's mouth stretched briefly, as if responding to a gastric spasm.

'Joking aside,' he said, 'the producer's sent a telegram.'

'Bad news? Rushes gone up in smoke?'

'It's about casting. They've found a Hannigan, some American who's been flying with the RAF.'

'Oh, I see.' Buckley glanced at Catrin. 'Get us a pint while I'm gone,' he said, 'there's a good girl.' He followed Kipper, and Catrin entered the roaring bonhomie of the bar-room.

'No spirits left,' shouted the landlady, moving like an automaton between till and beer-pumps, 'and half-pints only or we'll be dry in twenty minutes.'

There was a jeer from those waiting, and a fresh wave of importunates at the bar, and Catrin found herself overtaken and pushed aside.

'Would you like a gin?' asked a voice behind her, and she turned to see Edith – transformed, in the seven hours or so since Catrin had shaken hands with her in the Copper Kettle, from a neat, pale figure to someone who looked as if they'd just been thrown off the Waltzers for riding without a ticket. She was holding a full glass in each hand. 'People keep giving them to me,' she said, 'and I've had enough, I think. You work on the film, don't you? I'm sure that I shook hands with you at some point. Would you like one?'

'Thank you very much,' said Catrin.

'Would you like the other?'

'Thank you very much,' said Catrin again, feeling sure that Buckley would drink it. 'And congratulations.'

'Yes,' said Edith, uncertainly. Her hands free for the first time in what felt like hours, she patted her hair and straightened the yoke of her blouse, trying to impose a little order on the proceedings. At some ill-defined point, her evening had stopped hurtling forward in a continuous fashion, and had become, instead, a jerky series of encounters with one semi-recognized crew-member after another, each offering congratulations, expressing surprise, and then disappearing again, leaving Edith with yet another drink in front of her and the impression that there were more people in the room who knew her Christian name than she had met in total in the whole of her previous life. It was all so peculiar, so extraordinarily *public*, and it was only the occasional glimpse of Arthur in the crowd, his expression an entirely plausible one of vaguely-pleased bewilderment, that convinced her that what was happening was real, and not a dream of the sort in which one suddenly looks down to discover that one has left the house wearing only a pair of knickers. It was real, it was true, and she hadn't even told Verna yet.

'Who's Verna?' asked Catrin, and Edith realized that she'd voiced the thought aloud.

'My cousin,' she said. 'She's never met Arthur. Well, I've only met him three times,' and she waited for the shriek of disbelief that the statement deserved.

'I ran away with someone that I'd only known for a fortnight,' said Catrin, and Edith, who hadn't really been looking at her – had noted only that she was pretty and that one of the shoulder-seams of her primrose jumper was missing a stitch or two – turned to her hungrily.

'You ran away with him?'

'Yes. And it wasn't even a fortnight, really – I spoke to him for the first time on a Tuesday, and ten days later I packed a suitcase and met him at the station.'

'But why did you?'

'Oh God . . .' Catrin coloured, and laughed in a rather forced way. 'I was madly in love. I was in love with him and I was in love with the whole idea of him – I thought I was doing the most romantic thing in the world. I would have run after that train in my stockinged feet, I would have hung from the carriage by my fingernails.' She took a swallow of gin, and then another. 'And what about you?' she asked.

'No,' said Edith. 'I'm not in love. And neither is he.' And she knew with utter certainty that that was true, and she found the thought strangely reassuring, for it meant that there had been nothing feverish about Arthur's proposal, and therefore no shame attached to the expediency of her own reply.

'So . . .' Catrin looked at her, a little baffled. 'Why are you doing this?'

Edith thought for a long moment.

'Because I need a change,' she said.

MAIN FEATURE

April 1941

'I've got it,' said the taxi-cab-driver, triumphantly, as he waited for the lights on Regent's Street to change. 'I've been trying to work you out since Trafalgar Square, you're in pictures, you was in the one about the rich Yankee feller who comes over and builds a house for the orphans in the East End. What was it called?'

'*A New Leaf*,' supplied Ambrose. Associated Metropolitan 1931. Not one of his better-known films, and not the happiest of shoots, either. The angel-faced child who'd played 'Sonny' ('I don't know whose son I am, mister, so I might as well be yours . . .') had not only fleeced the entire cast at poker, but had turned out to be playing with a marked pack, supplied to him by his mother.

'*A New Leaf*,' repeated the cab-driver, 'that's it, and I saw it with me missis in March 1932. You know why I can put me finger right on the date?'

'No.'

'Because in April of that year I brought the Lord Jesus Christ into my heart, and I didn't never go to the pictures no more after that . . .'

Even without the subsequent eschatological lecture, the journey seemed interminable. There was a time bomb on the Euston Road, and another on Drummond Street, and a fractured gas main somewhere behind St Pancras, necessitating so many diversions along so many shattered streets made identical by ruin that Ambrose entirely lost his sense of direction, and found himself gazing out as if at a foreign city, or at one newly excavated, Pompeii under a leaden sky. It wasn't until the taxi-cab passed the stone fretwork of St David's, grimy but intact, and turned on to the Holloway Road that the map of Islington righted itself in his head, like a needle swinging to true north. There were rows of cabbages on Highbury Fields, and a pig in a sty.

'This the place?' asked the cabbie, pulling in beside Sammy's mansion block. 'Been knocked about a bit, ain't it?' he added, eyeing the timber flying-buttresses bolted to the brick of the side wall, their bulk partially concealing a crack that stretched from pavement to guttering.

'Could you wait?' asked Ambrose. 'I shouldn't be very long.'

Sophie answered the door of the flat herself. She was dressed in black, with a beaded brooch at her throat. Her dark hair was drawn back into a chignon. 'Do come in,' she said, turning away as she spoke, and leaving Ambrose to close the door and follow her into the drawing-room. The window there was boarded-up and the only light came from an oil lamp, the smell a heady leap into the past.

'We lost the windows last month, and the electricity four nights ago,' said Sophie. 'Strangely, there is still gas. Thank you, Elena,' she said, to the woman who placed a tray in front of her. There were two glasses of tea on it. 'No lemon, I'm afraid. Sugar?'

'Two please,' said Ambrose. No noise intruded through the shutter from the world outside, and the tinkle of the spoon seemed very loud.

'I'll just mention that I have a taxi waiting,' said Ambrose.

'How fortunate. They're not easy to find these days.' Sophie put down the spoon and folded her hands. 'And how are you enjoying playing this role of the uncle?'

'I can't say that I'm *enjoying* it, exactly. Until studio begins one doesn't get the chance to approach the part in any depth – location filming's awfully disjointed.'

'I see.' She picked up her glass and took a sip. 'I am still quite new to this, of course. I shall have to come to Hammersmith and watch you in a scene. You don't mind, do you?'

'Not at all.' Though it wasn't a comfortable prospect.

'My brother liked to go on set, I seem to remember, though I think that was because he found the administrative side of things rather dull. Oh, before I forget, I ought to tell you that I'm having to raise my fee to 12 per cent. Finding suitable new premises is time-consuming, and I shall have to pay office staff more than Sammy used to, since they can make double the previous wage in any munitions factory.'

Ambrose opened his mouth to protest.

'And I have had to let a few of the old clientele go, I'm afraid,' continued Sophie, 'I think the English phrase is "dead wood".'

Ambrose closed his mouth again.

'And now to Cerberus,' said Sophie. 'I have considered your request very carefully.'

'I wouldn't say that it was *my* request – I'm asking on behalf of the production.'

'But it was you who pointed out the resemblance between Cerberus and the other dog?'

'In a manner of speaking, but . . .' He broke off. It was manifestly too complicated to explain about Arthur Frith's drunken bellow across the bar-room of the Crown and Anchor. It had been heard by everyone, from the director down to the most simian of the sparks, and Ambrose had been forced to agree in public that, yes, it was a most marvellous coincidence, and that he would certainly act upon it. He'd known immediately that asking a favour of Sophie would be a sticky task.

'And what would be his duties?' she enquired, as if Cerberus were applying for the post of under-housemaid.

Ambrose tried to page through the script from the dog's point of view. 'I think there's a scene in which he's rescued with the injured fiancé, and then he's on deck, of course, and he has to bark at one point, supposedly at the dive-bombers. That sort of thing . . .'

Sophie took another sip of tea, setting the glass back on the tray before speaking again. 'It has not been easy trying to feed and protect a dog in the current climate,' she said. 'You know that most other people in London, who have pets, have taken quite a different course.'

Ambrose nodded, soberly.

'But my brother had great affection for Cerberus so I feel it is my obligation. If I were to lend him to this production, I would want him to be well taken care of. Suitable food, shelter during raids and so forth.'

'Of course, of course.'

'And it would be unreasonable to expect him to be dragged between the studio and this flat every morning and evening, it's a very great distance. He would have to stay with you.'

For a moment, Ambrose was unsure whether he had heard the sentence right – it was the closeness of the room, the oil fumes affecting his concentration. 'With *me*?' he repeated, cautiously.

'I assumed that was the proposed arrangement.'

'No, no, no, no, no. The first assistant director would be arranging for the dog's accommodation. I expect one of the props boys will take him.'

There was silence. Sophie moved her head slightly, and the soft wash of lamp-light caught the brooch at her neck so that it glittered like mica. 'Were you always so very casual with the lives of others?' she asked.

An answer or two fluttered and expired on Ambrose's lips, before he could find his voice again.

'I really couldn't look after a dog.'

'I fear that may be true,' said Sophie.

'No, what I meant was that I don't have time to . . . to . . .'

She looked sibylline in the shadows. 'To do what, Mr

Hilliard? Cerberus is quite a small dog, his needs are few and simple.'

'Nevertheless—'

'And, besides, while there are so many actors and so few roles, I think it would be foolish to miss an opportunity of this sort. Baker's need a very particular dog, and I imagine they will be grateful to you for providing one, and when another film is made then they may remember you.'

'I would hope that they would remember me for my acting,' said Ambrose, coldly.

'Yes, I would hope that, too.' Her inflexion was ambiguous. 'May I offer you more tea?'

'No thank you.' He remembered, suddenly, the taxi-cab waiting outside. 'I really must be going.'

'Without Cerberus?' asked Sophie.

Ambrose hesitated. The stately phrase 'for the good of the production' swam through his mind, accompanied by a minnow-sized twinge of conscience. 'Oh, I'll take the bloody dog,' he said ungraciously, and Sophie stood up quickly and left the room; he could almost have sworn she was smiling.

It was another ten minutes before he could leave the flat. 'His blanket,' said the maid, handing him a faded quilt, 'and also in this bag I put his bowl, his cloth I use for his feets wiping, his toy,' – this a repulsive patchwork clown with stuffing cascading out of its stomach cavity – 'his soft collar if his neck sore, his smart collar, his boot he chew, his flea powder . . .'

'He has no fleas at present,' said Sophie, swiftly.

'. . . his pillow, his new bone, his old bone what he sleep with, his medicine for when there is bomb, and his clippies for his nail. He like chasing stick in the park but he have terrible fear of pond. He have oat for breakfast if no meats, he like horse, he like potato, he like gravies, but remember to not give fish *ever*.' She fixed Ambrose with what looked like the evil eye. 'Not *ever*.'

Cerberus stood beside her, his tail swinging slowly. The white patch on his nose – the one obvious respect in which he differed from Chopper – was very noticeable.

'His lead,' said the maid, looping it round the dog's neck. She offered the end to Ambrose. 'He's good boy,' she said, stooping to pat the narrow head.

The cab started hooting while Ambrose was still in the flat, and by the time he'd manoeuvred dog, bag and blanket down two flights of stairs and through the exterior door, the cabbie had tired of waiting and had driven almost as far as the turning. Ambrose bellowed and waved and the vehicle swung in a wide loop and headed back towards the flats again. It slowed to a crawl as the driver stared at Cerberus, who had chosen that moment to defecate copiously in the centre of the pavement, and then it accelerated off again, leaving an empty road.

'And some passed by on the other side,' shouted Ambrose. He pulled at the lead, and Cerberus ambled forward a few paces before making a sudden sideways lunge at the row of salvage bins on the corner.

'Bastard,' said Ambrose, reflexly, a friction burn stinging his palm. 'Come back here. *Back here.*'

The dog continued straining in the direction of the bin marked 'PIGS' for a good five seconds longer, and then seemed to lose interest. The lead went slack, man and beast were momentarily in step, and then Cerberus spotted a small stain on the kerbstone three yards ahead, and dived forward. Ambrose felt his shoulder almost leave its socket and he dropped the lead and was seized by the urge to kick the ugly little creature straight up its filthy backside, to punt it clear across the street, and it was only the thought that Sophie might be watching (somehow, through the boarded windows) that stayed his foot. Instead, he leaned forward and smacked the brindled rump, hard, in a gesture that might, from a distance, be construed as affectionate.

'Bad dog,' he said. '*Bad.*'

Cerberus's only response was to crouch slightly, and to

continue pressing his nose to the oily mark on the pavement. It was entirely predictable, of course, that a dog owned by Sammy would lack any vestige of discipline. Edible bribes would no doubt be needed for the enforcement of good behaviour – strudel rather than the stick.

They had progressed another hundred yards together, weaving, checking, lurching, doubling back – strip-the-willow as choreographed by a drunkard – when the first person spoke to Ambrose. It was a woman with a toddler, and she asked him the doggie's name.

'Ooh, that's a funny one,' she said, on receiving the answer, 'and is he safe with kiddies?'

'No,' said Ambrose, 'he's extremely vicious.'

The second encounter was beside Highbury Corner, while Cerberus was urinating against a pile of sandbags. 'Lovely dog,' said a workman, 'oh, 'e's a lovely dog, 'e's a *lovely* dog. I love bull terriers I do, he's a lovely feller, and he's friendly too, ain't he? You're a lovely lad, ain't yer? Ain't yer lovely? Ain't yer? Ain't yer a lovely 'andsome friendly feller?' Tearing his gaze from this canine paragon, the man glanced at Ambrose. 'Tell you what, give you a couple of nicker for 'im.'

Christ, it was tempting. 'I couldn't possibly,' said Ambrose.

The workman gave him a nod of grudging respect. 'Fair enough. When your 'ome's gone, what else have you got to hang on to? Rest centre's over there, mate,' and it dawned on Ambrose that he'd been mistaken not only for a dog lover, but for a bombed-out vagrant, toting his remaining possessions in search of a nice cup of tea and a chit for a public bath.

He jerked the lead, and Cerberus trotted after him, past the rest centre, where a photographer was loitering – waiting, presumably, for a subject of the requisite crass symbolism. The yellow press seemed permanently plastered with pictures of dusty but defiant grandmothers, and bandaged urchins signing 'V' for victory. England, apparently, could 'take it', though whether she could also dish it out was a moot point, since it appeared to Ambrose that there was no corner of Europe or North Africa where she wasn't currently having her nose rubbed in the dirt. It was all an utter disaster, and yet if one were to read certain of the newspapers, one might believe that an invasion could be forestalled by a few pallid bank clerks armed with cobblestones, and that a nation could be fed on allotment carrots and the odd can of beans lobbed over by Roosevelt.

Cerberus sniffed the photographer's turn-ups, and seemed momentarily inclined to use them as a lamp-post, before Ambrose dragged him away. They crossed the road towards the underground station in relative synchrony.

'No dogs except in transit,' said a policeman, standing by the entrance. It was not yet five o'clock, but already a line of would-be shelterers was shuffling past the ticket office and towards the stairs, their arms full of bedding, their hands clutching newspaper-wrapped packages, the paper spotted with the grease of makeshift suppers.

'I am not intending to spend the night on the platform,' said Ambrose, 'I am about to purchase a ticket to Great Portland Street.'

'What's the blanket for, then?'

'It belongs to the dog.'

'And what's in the bag?'

'Also items for the dog.'

'Not bedding, then?'

'No.'

'And you wouldn't be intending to fool the authorities by buying a ticket and then dossing down on the platform with Fido here?'

'Certainly not.'

'I see.' The policeman eyed the blanket again. 'And you wouldn't rather get a *bus* to Great Portland Street, would you, sir? Only it's regulations that—'

'Leave 'im alone,' shouted a fat woman, queuing with a gaggle of small children. 'Bloody flat-foots, nag nag nag all the bloody time, regulation this, regulation that, you know where you can shove yer bloody regulations, don't you?'

'Up your arse,' said one of the children, helpfully.

'Up your arse,' agreed the matriarch, with filthy vigour. 'You take your doggie down there if you want to,' she added, to Ambrose. 'We won't tell no one.'

'Now look here—' began the policeman.

'No, *you* look here, you bloody peelers is all the bloody same, where was you when my sister-in-law 'ad her joolry pinched when 'er 'ouse come down? If you ask me it was you lot what pinched it, telling 'er she couldn't go back and get 'er bits, and then when she asked and asked and they let her in to look for 'em, the box was empty, weren't it, and the rings she got from her mum, and her cameo brooch 'er old man bought for 'er ruby wedding, and her opal-chip pin was all gone, and the bloody blue-bottles whistling with their 'ands behind their bloody backs and their eyes turned the other bloody way, so don't you tell me to look here, like I'm the one what's done something wrong, when it's you what's—' The woman's speech rolled on, magnificent and vitriolic, her voice like the clanging of a great cracked bell, and Ambrose, momentarily forgotten, hauled Cerberus across the tiled floor towards the booking office.

'Shelterers to the right hand side by the *wall*,' shouted a warden, stationed at the top of the spiral staircase, 'bona feed passengers to the *left*.' Ambrose hesitated and eyed the narrow section of tapering steps that was left to him. The dog, normally so eager to plunge ahead, sat firmly on the top tread. 'He'll have to be carried,' said the warden, just as Ambrose reached the same annoying conclusion.

It was an awkward task: there was none of the pliability, the sinuous weight of a cat's body – lifting Cerberus was like lifting a heavy box.

'Oh look,' said a girl, 'he's holding a doggie. Look, Jackie, can you see the doggie?'

'Aah, it's a dog. Aaah.'

Ambrose tilted his head to avoid having to gaze into the crusted cavern of Cerberus's right ear, and began, cautiously, to descend.

'Oh look, don't that doggie look *sweet*.'

'Oh, he's a lovely boy. Isn't he a lovely, lovely boy?'

'I wish we had a dog, Mum, can we have a dog like that, Mum, can we?'

Each slow step downward brought a fresh burst of cooing, a new face upturned, an exclamation of surprise and delight.

'Oh, he's wagging his tail, just look at him.'

'Handsome little fellow.'

'Look at him watching us. He's a clever little chap, ain't he?'

It was like a hellish parody of a premiere, the marble staircase to the foyer replaced by fissured concrete, the tiaras by headscarves, the aroma of cigars by the reek of carbolic and cold bacon and sweat and wet knickers. And there was a final difference, more unsettling even than the others: as each successive gaze slid past Ambrose, he realized that he himself was playing the role of unregarded escort. The star was on his arm.

'Just look at 'is lovely shiny nose . . .'

And while it was one thing for a fickle public to forget one's face, it was quite another to be rendered *invisible*.

'Good dog,' he said, quite loudly, and Cerberus lifted his head and swiped his tongue across Ambrose's cheek. The result was immediate.

'Ohhhhh, look at that.'

'Oh, don't he love his master!'

'Aaaah, he knows who loves him, doesn't he?'

For a moment or two, the limelight shifted and there was warmth enough for both of them, and then Cerberus sneezed and Ambrose was once again eclipsed. One would have thought, from the reaction, that Garbo had swooned.

They reached the south-bound platform at last and Ambrose lowered the dog to the floor. A few yards away, a loud argument was taking place between two families claiming the same bunk-bed, whilst beside them a small boy amused himself by repeatedly hitting a tin cup with a spoon. Ambrose felt weary and a little soiled, smeared by the unremitting coarseness of contemporary life. It seemed strange, then, that the image, specific and unwonted, that kept popping into his head during the ensuing ten-minute wait was that of his ex-wife, Anthea, preparing for a party.

He could see her dabbing Rose Bleu into her considerable cleavage. She'd been too shapely for the fashions of the twenties. 'I was born for corsets and bustles,' she'd said, rather often, 'not these silly tunics. What's a girl supposed to do with her bosoms?' although he'd always thought them marvellous, those bosoms, pillowy wonders straight out of Boucher, snowy mountains, carmine-crested, a sonnet-writer's dream.

The tube rails began to sing and Cerberus, who had been staring at the mice in the tunnel, gave a little start and looked up at Ambrose enquiringly.

'Do I *have* to go?' Anthea had said, almost every time. She had loathed film parties. 'Look at me, Ambrose, I'm all dressed up, I've plucked my eyebrows till they bleed, I've bathed and shaved and creamed every last inch, and all for nothing. When we get there those awful hangers-on will give me one glance and then fawn all over you. I don't think you realize how utterly pointless and insignificant it makes me feel.'

'And how *ungrateful* it makes you sound,' he'd added, sharply.

He'd thought her a fool to leave him.

The tube carriages were standing-room only, and once again Ambrose found himself carrying Cerberus.

'And isn't he handsome?' said a young woman, her soft, pink face lighting with pleasure. 'And isn't he a clever little man?'

⋆

There was new linoleum in Rose and Lily's kitchen, and a lovely Welsh dresser, and a gas-powered refrigerator, and a polished brass jug filled with roses on the window-sill, and a pair of crisply-starched gingham aprons hanging on a hook by the double sink. The front room, stuffed with nautical nick-nacks, offered a choice of stylish sofas and the use of a wireless and a telephone. Next to the latter stood a picture of Errol Flynn, clearly cut out of a fan magazine and stuck into a sweetheart frame, and Catrin, peering in through the unglazed bay window, was glad to have found something – *anything* – that linked this gleaming palace with the real Rose and Lily.

The entrance hall of the house was parquet-floored, though the parquet pattern was painted on, and there was carpet on the stairs, but the flight led to a blind landing and the twins' bedroom was twenty yards away, right at the other end of the studio. Three of its walls were papered with lilac sprigs and the fourth was entirely absent. It faced, at a distance of a few yards, the set of a pub interior, and the effect was vaguely indecent, as if the locals might line up for a nightly view of the girls getting ready for bed.

'Can you move, Miss?' shouted a man in overalls, and Catrin ducked to one side as an enormous flat was carried past. It was marked with odd splashes and dabs of grey and white in a seemingly random pattern that magically assembled itself, as it moved away from her, into a rough-cast stone surface of ancient pedigree; the wall of a French farmhouse, she realized, and wanted to applaud the cleverness of the illusion. There were feints and contrivances wherever she looked – painted views to be glimpsed when a door opened or a curtain was drawn, and hedges made from crêpe paper, and rooms without ceilings, whose light fittings dangled from a spot-rail forty feet overhead – and it felt almost illegal to be wandering round unchecked, as if she might at any moment be arrested for spying, although no one so far had taken the slightest notice of her. 'Pay a visit the day before shooting starts,' Buckley had advised, 'when it's all looking spanking new and bursting with possibility, and for a moment or two you can dream that they're actually going to make a film that'll treat the script with the respect it deserves . . .'

In the studio wall behind the pub there was a pair of weighted doors, and beyond them a short corridor with rooms leading off on either side. At the far end another pair of doors led to the second sound-stage, and Catrin entered cautiously, and saw not a jigsaw of sets but an enormous wooden water-tank, its buttressed sides taller than a man. The *Redoubtable* floated within it – a scaled-down version, she judged, a good ten feet shorter than the one on location.

The first sound-stage had smelled of Ellis's studio – of glue for the canvas, of freshly sawn wood and linseed oil – but the second reeked improbably of high summer. Catrin sniffed again, and thought of tarry pavements melting in the heat, and at the same moment spotted a workman holding out a bucket and a dripping black brush towards a hand that was reaching from within the tank. Even on tiptoe she was too short to see who the hand belonged to, but there was a thirty-foot scaffolding tower at one end of the studio, with a ladder lashed to its side and nobody in particular watching it, and she climbed up as far as the first platform and saw that the *Redoubtable* was not floating, but standing on stilts, and that its 'sides' ended just below the waterline – or just below where the waterline would be once the tank was filled. Currently it was crawling with workmen engaged in applying a coat of pitch to the interior.

Beyond the tank, at the far end of the studio, she could see yet another version of the *Redoubtable* – a truncated one, this time, consisting only of the wheel-cabin and a section of deck, the whole mounted on wooden rockers so that it could be wobbled around in imitation of a heavy sea-swell. Behind it, a giant canvas leaned against the wall, its top half painted a pale grey-blue, the bottom half just a shade or two darker and a misty, indeterminate transition between the two.

Or perhaps the mist had another source – for as she stood there, one hand grasping the ladder, it seemed to Catrin that a ragged veil had begun to drift across the studio, a veil that appeared to be emanating from an enormous door that split the side wall from ceiling to floor. She stared, trying to understand what she was seeing; it was not smoke, but something wispier, more ectoplasmic . . .

'Fog,' said a man in overalls, standing at the foot of the ladder. 'It gets in through the scene dock. Now we've a bloody great brute of a lamp to fix up there, so can we have our tower back, or was you wanting to rent it?'

An hour earlier, when she'd walked from Hammersmith tube station, there'd been no more than a trace of haziness in the air, and she'd been able to see the chain of barrage balloons that wallowed over South London like a school of hippos; now as she left the studio, the world outside was a blank. From the river wall, she could hear the slap of water but there was nothing but a shifting sepia curtain where the Thames should be, and she realized, with a rush of relief, that there would be no bombers over London tonight.

Lately, the fear had begun to creep up on her. In the autumn, when the Luftwaffe had scarcely missed a night in three months, she hadn't been nearly so scared, but there had been a kind of grim routine, then: the scramble to buy groceries, to catch the bus, to get through the front door before the siren sounded. One had expected a raid, and a raid had come. Now it was unpredictable, and that was somehow worse, and rather than wait powerlessly in the flat, straining to catch the first popping of the guns, she preferred to be somewhere else in the evenings – rolling bandages at the Red Cross post in Marylebone High Street, or fire-watching in Soho Square, or sitting through a full supporting programme in the stalls of the Odeon – anywhere where there was noise or activity. She was not yet used to the *Mary Celeste* feel of a home with only one occupant, where the door opened each evening on an unaltered scene, where nothing ever changed unless she changed it.

When she'd left the office to go to Hammersmith, Parfitt had been dozing after a lunchtime visit to the White Horse, and Buckley had been reading the *Daily Mirror* while cleaning his fingernails with a matchstick. In the interim, he had switched newspapers and was using what appeared to be the same matchstick for picking his teeth.

'Been busy?' she asked, innocently.

'Lull before the storm,' he said. 'Wait till next week, it'll all start then.' He lifted an imaginary receiver to his ear. '"Hello, is that Mr Bewkerley? The director's decided to shoot Scene 327 with Johnnie hanging upside down from the mizzen mast. He says it's visually more striking, but he wants you to cut three-quarters of the lines and add a song."'

'There's no mizzen mast on the *Redoubtable*.'

'Welcome back, Miss Gradgrind. So what did you think of the sets?'

'They're wonderful.'

'Accurate?'

'Not in the slightest.'

'Good girl.'

'So what do you say when you're asked to cut three-quarters of the lines and add a song?'

'What do I say? D'you mean, do I launch into an agonized defence of the original wording, my eyes brimming with the impassioned tears of a thwarted creator?'

'I don't know. Do you?'

'Not unless there's a knock-on effect on the storyline that some clot hasn't noticed, and which would mean re-shooting half the film.'

'And if there isn't?'

'I grumble a bit, and when that doesn't work I get on with it, and try and minimize potential damage. If *I* don't do the rewrites then you can guarantee that somebody less talented will.'

'But—'

'You're still mixing this up with art, aren't you?'

'I—'

'This is commerce. Speaking of which—' He closed the paper he was reading and held it out to her. 'Edwin Baker dropped this by this morning, someone sent it to him from New York. There's a little piece about the film in it, he's as pleased as punch.'

She took the copy of *Variety* over to her desk, and started to look through it, at first quickly, and then with slow fascination. Compared to current British newspapers, with their meagre four sides and cramped print, it seemed an extraordinarily luxurious object, its eighty-odd pages filled with well-spaced and largely impenetrable show-business news.

Arnaz Cancels Roxy, NY To Accomp Bride West

Citizen Kane *Release Still Indef. as Hearst Blasts RKO*

There was vaudeville gossip, and lists of which actors were flying from New York to Los Angeles, and which from Los Angeles to New York, and occasionally – very occasionally – there was a tiny mention of the war taking place on the other side of the Atlantic.

Show Biz Names on 6 London Ambulances.

Show business is well represented by the ambulances that clang through London streets during air raids to give succor to the injured. First six of them bought by contributions to the American Artists Ambulance Association are now on the street and have been christened with the names of show biz personalities. They are Fred Astaire, Laura and Irving Asher, Gilbert Miller, Phoebe Foster, Sam Eckman Jr, and Lou and Bernie Hyman.

It was as if the blitz were a dreary party only noteworthy for its American guests. Catrin felt a surge of dour patriotism.

'Got it yet?' asked Buckley.

She started to turn the pages more quickly, and found the Baker's reference ringed in red crayon.

Eng. Sea Epic enlists US Flyboy

British war films may be BO poison to US femmes –

'What does BO stand for?'

'Box Office.'

– but clever casting may tip the balance in a true-life story by Baker's of London for potential UA distrib.

Carl Lundback debuts as a US reporter trapped in France and rescued by twin fisher gals. The Eagle Squadron flyer, who volunteered for the RAF after steering crop dusters back home in Illinois, and bagged a Brit medal to boot, is non-profesh but is said to have acted plenty in legit. Pic offers no headliners –

'Legit?'

'Theatre.'

'Headliners?'

'Famous actors.'

– but with a genuine hero aboard, it could be heading for real coin.

'Good, eh?' said Buckley.

'How did Baker's find him in the first place?'

'Someone at the Ministry saw his picture in the paper, read that he'd done some acting and tipped us off.'

'And what does he look like?'

Buckley shrugged, and it was Parfitt who answered unexpectedly, lifting his head from the desk.

'He looks,' he said, 'like a gen-u-ine hero.'

★

Smart, thought Arthur, as he waited for Edith to sign the register, all the ladies looked awfully smart – but then, of course, they were all dressmakers. Edith's friend Miss Clifford, from Madame Tussaud's, was in blue with a picture hat, and Edith's cousin Verna was wearing a wine-coloured costume with matching daughter, and of course Edith looked especially smart in a dark cream frock with coffee trim, with the pearls that he'd given to her showing at the neckline. He himself, of course, was in khaki, and Mr De Groot, his next-door neighbour, was wearing a tweed suit with a 'V' for Victory tie-pin and a Home Guard arm-band. Mr De Groot was not exactly a friend – in fact they had exchanged about ten sentences in as many years – but he'd kindly kept an eye on the house while Arthur was away, and had boarded up a couple of broken windows and picked the shrapnel off the front lawn, and Arthur had hoped that asking him to be best man might be construed as a gesture of thanks. It was not an onerous role, after all – there was no transport to organize, no dancing to encourage, and Arthur hoped very much that there would be no speeches. 'Just a quiet wedding,' he'd explained. He'd not met Dolly Clifford then, of course.

She'd brought a box brownie, and after the ceremony took a photograph of Edith and Arthur on the steps of Wimbledon town hall, under the notice which read, '*Due to current Ministry of Food regulations, the throwing of rice is forbidden*' and the sun came out for a moment or two and gilded the pale yellow broom in Edith's bouquet. 'And what about one with a kiss?' suggested Dolly, just as Myrtle extracted a handful of dried sea-lavender from a paper bag and hurled it at them, and for the next minute or so, Edith was engaged in extracting small bits of salty chaff from the neck of her dress, and then the sun went in again, so there were no more photographs.

'I was praying the whole time that the siren wouldn't go off,' said Dolly, as the guests formed a loose crocodile and started the ten-minute walk back to Arthur's house. 'Because you know it's bad luck, don't you?'

'Is it?' asked Edith, vaguely; there was a piece of lavender stalk working its way into the left cup of her brassiere.

'My cousin's niece was at a wedding where there was an alert, and the groom's father was hit by a tram on his way home from the reception. Didn't you used to live on this street?'

'Yes. At Number 40.' It had been disconcerting to find that her old lodgings were so close to her new home. Her marital home. The home where she would shortly be installed as Mrs Edith Frith, a name unpronounceable to all but professional linguists.

'I wonder if your landlady still lives there,' said Dolly. 'I know they say that bombs never fall in the same place twice, but Pearl told me that her aunt's had two in her back yard, they were both delayed-action and the second one's still there, it's lodged somewhere under the lavvy. She says the ARP don't believe her but every time she sits down she can hear it ticking . . .'

Thank goodness, thought Edith, for Dolly's chatty litany of death and portent, since no one else in the little procession was saying a word. Myrtle, having spent the last three weeks talking of nothing but her prospective day-trip to London, seemed oddly subdued, Mr De Groot was clearly not a conversationalist, and Verna appeared locked into a disapproving silence. She had decided, from the first, that Arthur was an unscrupulous libertine who had snared Edith with an insincere offer, and who would hurl her aside once his warrior lusts were sated, and nothing – not even meeting him – had dissuaded her of this opinion. She had watched the ceremony with the knuckles of one hand pressed to her lips, as if to stifle involuntary cries of protest.

'Not much further,' said Edith. 'It's just round the corner.'

The arrangements had been simple, and quickly accomplished. Arthur had applied for a licence, and Edith had sewn herself a dress and bought new underwear in Cromer and then, just a fortnight after the proposal, she'd left Norfolk for Clapham, where she'd slept on Dolly Clifford's sofa for three nights and spent the days at Arthur's house, trying to turn his dining-room into a suitable place for a wedding breakfast – though it was more of a wedding afternoon-tea, really, the ceremony being at two o'clock. She had washed the curtains and scrubbed the floor, and Arthur had moved furniture and cut the ivy that crawled across the window, and they had worked in pleasant harmony and talked only of practical things, of tea-towels and saucepans and milk deliveries. It was as if neither wanted to discover any more about the other before the wedding, for that might raise doubts, and there could be no going back. It was, Edith thought, a little like the arranged marriages of the Hindoos. A self-arranged marriage.

'Here we are,' she said. The exterior of Arthur's house looked quite normal; the peculiarities began inside the front door.

'What are all these rails along the wall?' asked Myrtle as they entered the hall.

Arthur cleared his throat. 'My father was crippled in the war,' he said. 'In the last war. I put these up to help him to get about.'

There were no mats or rugs, either, as his father had tended to trip on them. The guests' footsteps clattered on the bare floorboards.

'You'll hear any burglars coming,' said Dolly, 'and that's a blessing. I knew a man, once, he had a big win on the dogs, and his wife had the whole house done out in Turkish carpeting – she'd always dreamed of it – and it was as thick as *this*,' she held out a finger and thumb, an inch apart, 'and the very next night they were robbed while they were asleep. Four men with sacks, trampling all over the place, and they didn't hear a thing!'

'Just through here,' said Edith.

The dining-room smelled of floor-polish and bay leaves, for she had collected every jug and vase she could find, and filled them with evergreen cuttings from the garden. She had draped the makeshift table with a starched cloth and tied the curtains back with ribbon and just before leaving for the town hall she and Arthur had brought in the food from the kitchen and covered the dishes with tea-towels. There was salad and spam, and rolls and new potatoes and jellied chicken, and a fruit-cream for dessert, and a wedding cake that was a plain sponge but with real chocolate icing, made from their pooled ration, and decorated with crystallized violets, and even Verna looked faintly pleased by the largesse on offer, though she refused a glass of madeira with the expression of someone offered arsenic.

It was Dolly who proposed a toast to the happy couple, which was kind, given that the shelter warden she'd been seeing since Christmas had recently turned out to have a wife in Swindon, but it was also Dolly who rapped on the top of the table with her knuckles, and then lifted the cloth to reveal the subterfuge beneath.

'Ooh, it's a Morrison shelter,' she said.

'It's Mr De Groot's,' said Arthur. 'He loaned it to us because I don't have a dining-room table.'

'Why don't you?' asked Myrtle, her mouth full of chicken.

'Because this was my father's bedroom,' said Arthur. 'He was very ill for the last few years of his life and he couldn't climb the stairs.'

For a minute or so, the breath of the sick-room seemed to thicken the air, and the only sound was the clink of cutlery on plate. It was Dolly who broke the silence.

'A man I know who's in the fire service says he wouldn't get into a Morrison if you paid him a thousand pounds, he says if the house came down and then there was a fire, you'd be trapped in there like a roast in an oven, there'd be nothing but charred bones the morning after and he says he'd rather take his chances and die in his own bed.'

Edith risked a glance at Mr De Groot. He had stopped eating.

'Did I mention that we'll be starting in studio on Monday?' she said, hurriedly, to no one in particular. 'In fact, I've been asked to go in tomorrow, the wardrobe mistress is measuring the London extras.'

'I didn't realize that you'd be going out to *work*,' said Verna, managing to imply, in a single word, that Arthur was unable to provide for his new wife and was therefore forcing her to take employment, possibly of a dubious nature.

'I did say,' said Edith, mildly. 'It's only for five weeks and then I'm sure Arthur and I will have a talk about what to do next.'

'Everyone works now,' said Dolly. 'Tussaud's never used to employ married women, but even they're thinking about changing their mind.'

'You work, Mum,' said Myrtle.

'I work inside the home,' replied Verna, with a modest lowering of the eyes. 'It's more in the nature of a little hobby. I certainly don't have to go out in the blackout. Or on a *Sunday*,' she added, pointedly.

'Well, I think it's smashing,' said Dolly. 'Husband and wife going off to work together. After all, Arthur'll go back to war when the film's finished, won't he, and who knows if they'll see each other again?' There was a tiny silence. '*When* they'll see each other again, I mean. Obviously.'

'Cake, anyone?' asked Edith. It was several months since she had had a headache, but she was getting one now.

Her cousins were the first to leave, the long train journey back to Norfolk ahead of them.

On the doorstep, Verna took Edith's hand. 'Of course, I hope that you'll be happy,' she said. 'Those whom God hath joined let no man put asunder, not that it was a religious ceremony. And I won't say "marry in haste, repent in leisure", but if you *do* find that you're . . .' she paused, significantly.

'Repenting?' suggested Edith.

Verna nodded. '. . . then remember that we're your family and there's always a place for you with us.'

Edith squeezed her cousin's hand, touched in spite of herself.

'Mum still can't find anybody else for the shop,' said Myrtle, trampling the moment. 'I want you to come back, as well. I miss you.'

'And I miss you, too.' She kissed Myrtle's round cheek and wished she could have designed the child's outfit herself; the burgundy dress and coat made her look middle-aged – a dumpy, plain version of her mother. A sugar-almond colour would have been prettier, and a full skirt with a swing to it . . .

'Is this *really* London?' whispered Myrtle, suddenly, desperately.

'It's a suburb of London.'

'But it's just houses.'

'I know.'

'Just house after house after house. I thought there'd be things to look at. I thought it would be exciting. I told everybody at school I was going to see film-stars. I even brought my autograph book, but it just looks like *anywhere*.'

'I know,' said Edith, 'I'm sorry.'

Dolly was the next to go, giving Arthur a great smacker of a kiss, and hissing 'enjoy the honeymoon!' in Edith's ear, and then Mr De Groot shook hands with them both, and said that they could keep the Morrison shelter as a wedding gift. He disappeared along the side alley, and Arthur closed the front door.

'Well . . .' he said, taking off his spectacles and giving them a polish. 'My goodness. Goodness me.' When he replaced them, he could still see Edith standing in the hall with a wedding ring on her finger, so it seemed likely, now, that this was all real and that he wouldn't wake up in hospital with a lump on his head. 'Well, I thought it went very . . .' He paused to consider how it had gone. Everything had been eaten, which was always reassuring.

'Dolly's good-hearted,' said Edith. 'She means well, even if she sometimes puts her foot in it.'

'Yes.'

'And I'm very fond of Myrtle.'

'Yes. Do you think we should start clearing up?'

'We could have a cup of tea first,' said Edith. She felt

exhausted, as if she'd spent the afternoon digging trenches instead of handing out cake.

'I think,' said Arthur, 'I ought to begin on the blackouts. It'll be dark soon.'

Edith waited for the kettle to boil, and listened to Arthur's footsteps as they moved through the house, from the bare boards of the ground floor to the carpeted rooms upstairs – the box-room where he slept, the sunny spare room overlooking the back garden that he used for his hobbies, the square bedroom at the front that had been his parents'. There were twin beds in the latter, and pretty, faded, old-fashioned decor – matching rose-pink quilts, a dressing-table runner with cross-stitched flowers and tatted edging, a rag rug in shades of blue. She'd seen it for the first time only this morning, when Arthur had carried her suitcase up the stairs. 'I expect you have things to do,' he'd said vaguely, edging out of the room again, and she had hung her clothes in the empty wardrobe, and changed into her wedding outfit, and tilted the cheval glass, so that she could see herself, head to toe. Smart, she'd thought, with a slight feeling of disappointment. Not bridal, nor blushing, nor a heart-stopping vision of nuptial loveliness, but Edith Beadmore in a smart dress, and wearing lipstick. Dolly had offered her a choice between Crimson Dawn and Sunset Glow and she was glad that she had chosen the paler shade.

Arthur had been standing in the hall when, self-consciously, she'd walked down the stairs, and he'd said, 'You look very nice,' and then diffidently asked whether she'd like to wear his mother's pearls, and of course, she'd accepted, and whilst he was getting them she had braced herself for salmon-pink misshapes, or a rope that hung down to her navel, and when she'd opened the mauve quilted box, and pulled aside the tissue to reveal a double strand of ivory perfection, she'd been speechless. The necklace felt warm against her skin; she'd never owned anything as beautiful.

He was taking an awfully long time over the blackouts. She

went into the dining-room and started to stack the plates. There was a crystallized violet left and since it was, after all, her wedding day, she placed it on her tongue and let it dissolve, and it was bliss, and on the way back to the kitchen she called a cheerful, 'Tea's brewed, Arthur', up the stairs, but there was no response.

In the hobbies room, Arthur had been snared by the Christmas copy of *The Woodworker* lying open on the work-bench. He'd forgotten to cancel his subscription when he joined the army, and every time he came home on leave there was another pile of magazines waiting for him, and he hadn't nearly caught up to date. The contents had acquired a wartime slant and he was rather taken with the short, squat standard lamp that cast its light across the floor, and could therefore be used without the curtains first being drawn. He heard Edith call, and it took a moment for him to move into the present, to understand that the voice belonged to his wife who was in the kitchen.

Ridiculously, he still found himself thinking of her as 'Miss Beadmore'. 'Edith,' he said, quietly, testing the word on his tongue. 'Dear.' What else did people call their wives? There was 'darling', of course, and 'My Old Dutch', and 'the wife', and other, much uglier terms that he'd heard in the army. He had a very dim memory of his father calling his mother 'Sally-girl' before the Great War. After it, of course, there hadn't been very much in the way of husband-wife conversation – his father curled in the clumsy wheeled chair he'd been issued, roaring for something to take away the pain. 'Woman,' he'd called her, sometimes. 'For God's sake, woman, don't measure it in those bloody little spoonfuls.' Later, when his mother died and Arthur was in charge of the medicines, he'd had to hide them before he went to school, each day in a different place.

'Would you like me to bring a cup up to you?' It was Edith again.

'No, I'll come down very shortly. Dear. Thank you.'

Perhaps when he went downstairs, they could sit together in the lounge. Edith could sew and he could read – except that he wasn't much of a reader – so perhaps Edith could sew and he could look through back copies of *The Woodworker*. Or they could sit either side of the wireless, and listen to a play or a concert and then discuss it afterwards, like a couple in an advertisement for cocoa. And then they'd switch off the lights, and he would check the back-door bolts and they'd go upstairs together, and Edith would use the bathroom first, and then . . . and then . . . his imagination seemed to judder to a halt. He had, he realized, been viewing the wedding as an end in itself, but now there was this whole new set of difficulties to consider. He took off his spectacles in order to clean them, and noticed that one of the arms was a little loose, and it was quite a hunt to find the tiny jeweller's screwdriver that he used for such emergencies, and then it seemed expedient to tighten the screws on the other side as well. After that, of course, the lenses needed cleaning again.

Downstairs, Edith drank her own tea, and then Arthur's as well. She re-filled the kettle, and pondered whether to start the washing-up, and it seemed silly to wait, so that before she knew it she had finished it all, and was hanging up the dish-towels, and there was still no sign of Arthur, and the slight headache she had noted earlier was back again. She turned off the light in the kitchen, and stood in the hall and listened for any noise from upstairs.

'Arthur,' she called, tentatively.

'Yes, I'll be with you very shortly.'

She put a hand to her head, recognizing a sensation within it, and went over to the convex mirror that hung beside the front door, and looked at herself. She could see only the right hand side of her face. The left had disappeared, its place taken by a jagged black line that flexed and extended like a caterpillar. Behind her invisible left eye she could feel a balloon beginning to inflate, each caterpillar extension adding a little more air.

'Arthur . . .'

He must have heard something different in her voice, for he came to the top of the stairs with a chisel in his hand, and looked down at her, his spectacles catching the light so that they flashed unbearably.

'I'm getting a migraine,' she said. 'The sugar violet that I ate. Stupid of me,' and she started to climb the stairs because very soon the cleaver would fall, and lying down would become imperative.

'Can I fetch you something?' he asked. 'A drink . . .'

'No.'

'I think I might have some Beecham's powders.'

'They don't help, I'm afraid.'

'A cold compress?'

'Yes. Yes, thank you. I'm going to have to go to bed.'

As they passed on the stairs she caught a whiff of fresh sawdust and wondered what on earth he had been doing, but the thought slipped away and she undressed hurriedly, tugging at the tiny buttons, each one covered with the same champagne crêpe she'd used for the bodice, the material so pale that she had carefully washed and dried her hands each time that she'd sat down to sew.

She stayed upright long enough to hang the dress in the wardrobe, and to fold her underwear – the French-style knickers, the matching brassiere, the silk stockings that had been Dolly's wedding present – 'I've heard that a way to drive a man wild is to take off everything except those and then unroll them, one at a time, ever so slowly,' Dolly had said, and Edith had been unable to meet her eye, though she'd stored the tip away for possible future use – and then she opened the drawer where she'd folded her night things, and instead of the eau de Nil satin slip with parchment piping, she put on her old winceyette pyjama suit and climbed into bed, and closed her eyes.

She barely heard her husband returning, though the cold compress was welcome, and gently applied.

'I won't disturb you,' said Arthur, quietly, solicitously. 'I'll spend the night in my old room.'

*

Pinewood, Denham, Shepperton – all had purpose-built projection rooms, the seating raked, the chairs upholstered, space enough for all so that one could choose, say, not to sit directly between a mouth-breathing scene-painter and an electrician who'd lunched on baked cabbage. The projection room at Hammersmith, however, was a boxed-in corner of the canteen and roughly the size of a coal-hole so no such choice was possible. Ambrose, wedged at the centre of the back row, his head tilted at an angle of 45 degrees in order to gain a view of the screen that didn't include the gaffer's right ear, tried to concentrate on the footage.

Watching the rushes was always purgatorial, the unedited scenes painfully raw, the chosen takes inevitably the ones that Ambrose himself would not have picked, since considerations of sound and picture always ranked far above those of nuanced performance. The merest camera assistant had only to inspect the lens and then suck his teeth doubtfully for yards of subtle roleplay to be binned, whilst the most courteous request from an actor that a particular take not be printed because his characterization had yet to achieve its zenith was almost certainly a waste of breath. Nevertheless, one had to attend, one had to know the worst.

Here, then, were the location scenes, strung together in the order in which they'd been shot: here the *Redoubtable* arriving at the coast of France, the sea beyond dotted with other ships; here Uncle Frank stumbling through the twilight from public house to the quayside; here were the girls casting off; here the muddy back-roads of France, thronging with refugees; here was that bloody dog Chopper stealing the bloody show as bloody usual; and here the beach at Dunkirk, black with figures, bullets peppering the sand – all without sound-effects or music, half the shots mute and half played-out far too long, and yet the overall impression . . . and it took Ambrose a while to digest this thought, since it was so unexpected . . . the overall impression was that it was really rather good. One could even feel it from the atmosphere in the room, from the alertness and the odd murmured aside. In each scene the camera seemed to be in the right place, the lighting apposite, the performances rather better than might be expected from the calibre of the actors. As for his own appearance, he was struck by how cleverly the make-up chap had aged and roughened his skin, giving Uncle Frank a gravitas that transcended the comedic element of the role. This was no drunken sailor out of a Crazy Gang romp; this was a man who had lived, who had suffered.

A forest of scratches replaced the final images of Hadley Best wading through waist-high water, and the lights in the room went up again.

'Marvellous,' said Edwin Baker, rising from his seat on the front row. 'Blinking marvellous, best work I've seen in a month of Sundays, congratulations to one and all. I'd say that if we carry on in the way we've started then we're looking at a sure-fire success, an absolute sure-fire success.' And although Ambrose had never been present at a rushes screening where the producer had failed to imply that the film in question was about to break all box-office records and win a shelf-load of Academy Awards to boot, nonetheless he had a feeling that on this occasion there might be more than a little truth in the praise, and by God it had been a long time since he'd had that feeling, a long, cold time. The catalogue of fourth-rate drivel in which he'd been forced to appear over recent years seemed to flutter before his eyes like the pages of a penny dreadful.

'Mr Hilliard?'

It was the new third AD, a beanpole of a boy with an Adam's apple like a half-swallowed rock bun.

'You're needed in make-up, Mr Hilliard, and then on set, Scene 42, sound stage one.'

'Very well.'

'I thought the rushes were awfully good, Mr Hilliard.'

'Did you?'

'I thought they made it all look true, like a newsreel.'

'Yes indeed.'

'And I thought you were awfully good in particular, Mr Hilliard.'

'Thank you.'

'I laughed like stink when you fell over on the quay. Do you want me to show you the way?'

'No, that won't be necessary.'

In the make-up room, Cerberus was still sitting on the folded blanket in the corner where Ambrose had left him twenty minutes earlier, but the white patch on his nose was now the same colour as the rest of his coat.

'Success!' said the nancy-boy with the brush. 'One part boot polish to two parts So-Bee-Fee gravy browning, with a touch of eyebrow pencil for the darker pattern. We tried cocoa powder at first but it kept making him sneeze. Oh, look how he worships you!'

Cerberus had lumbered across the room and was standing at Ambrose's feet, gazing upward with a convincing facsimile of adoration.

'Aaah,' said the girl assistant, 'he lubs oo, don't oo?'

Ambrose bent down to pat Cerberus and the dog licked his hand.

'Aaah,' said the girl again, with a pretty glance, 'you've a real way with him, Mr Hilliard,' and Ambrose nodded modestly and slipped a hand into the pocket where he kept a lump of meat wrapped in oilcloth. Black market, of course – obtained nightly from the kitchens of his local French restaurant – and horribly expensive, especially bearing in mind that it had almost certainly been gouged from the rump of a diseased carthorse, but nevertheless worth every penny for the instant devotion it conjured from Cerberus. Christ, the animal would follow him over a cliff just for a sniff of his fingers.

'By the way,' said the make-up chap, as Ambrose left the room with the dog at his heel, 'I heard the rushes were tickety-boo, they're all saying it could be a smash!'

Scene 42 did not feature Uncle Frank – nor, in fact, did the character appear in any other of the scenes being shot on this, the first day of studio, and yet here was Ambrose being treated with all due deference, given his own chair, his own ash tray: 'Sugar in your tea, Mr Hilliard?', 'Another garibaldi, Mr Hilliard?', 'Are you ready, Mr Hilliard?', 'Take your own cue, Mr Hilliard,' and since one ought really to give credit where it was due, he was fully prepared to admit (if asked) that it had been Sophie who had proposed that he be paid a handler's fee for Cerberus and who had, moreover, wrung a rather decent day-rate out of Baker's. Through her aegis, Ambrose had declined the offer of an extra credit ('animal trainer'), but had confirmed with the publicity department that he would be willing to speak to any journalists who might be attracted by such a charming story of thespian versatility, though so far only *Dog Breeder Bi-Monthly* had expressed any interest.

In consequence, he no longer felt quite the same urgency about seeking new representation. After all, if the film were a hit, then he would have his pick of agencies; a flop, and Sophie was proving herself at least adequate.

'Just a close-up of the dog next,' called Kipper. 'Mr Best also in shot.'

The American actor, Lundback, was on set again, watching from behind the camera. He had been accompanied into the studio that morning by Edwin Baker, who had paraded him around cast and crew like a prize bull. His photograph had been taken with Baker, with the actresses playing Rose and Lily, with two fellows from the Ministry of Information, and with the American Deputy Ambassador, whose gigantic waist circumference seemed to confirm rumours that while Londoners queued for whale-meat, all was steak and doughnuts within the embassy walls. Lundback himself had smiled throughout, a smile that had sent all the women into a frenzy of hair-patting and necklace-adjustment. He looked ludicrously boyish, *freckled* for Christ's sake, a sun-tanned farm-boy who just happened to have talked his way into the RAF and then shot down twenty-four German fighters and been awarded a DFC, and it was clear from the female reaction that even if all the other men in the studio stripped naked and ran around with their privates flapping, they wouldn't be spared a second glance.

Ambrose had noticed Hadley Best looking slightly sick (his leading-man status draining briskly down the plug-hole), and then rallying again as Lundback was introduced to him, and then it had been Ambrose's turn and Lundback had shaken his hand and said, 'Hi there' – his speech slow, his voice unexpectedly deep and velvety, so that one might almost have expected him to break into a chorus of 'Old Man Ribber' – 'Hi there. Good to meetcha, sir,' and it had been the damnedest thing, but there had been something so unaffected about the man, so good-natured, so entirely lacking in the usual actorish caution, that Ambrose had very nearly found himself smiling back.

And now Lundback was in costume, ready for his role as Hannigan, the American newspaper-man caught up in the Dunkirk evacuation. His freckles had been blotted out and a set of crows' feet added, with the result that he was now looking at least twenty-five years old. He seemed at ease, hands in pockets, smile still in place, as he watched Cerberus having his make-up re-touched, and Ambrose was reminded of the time – decades ago, now – that he'd first seen the young Ronald Colman strolling around the floor at Elstree, stardom adhering to him as if applied with the greasepaint. Sometimes one just *knew*, bugger it, and since there was so little room beneath the spotlight, each time that a golden newcomer shouldered his way onstage there was inevitably some poor bastard being shoved off the other side. Hadley, in this case. What a bitter, cruel, profligate profession it was . . .

'Going again on 42,' said Kipper. 'Mute close-up of the dog. And *action*.'

Cerberus, sitting in front of a backdrop of French countryside, looked round vaguely, as if puzzled by the number of people staring at him. Superficially, he was a good match for Chopper, but there was an absence of brain that showed in every reaction and pose. For Chopper, *sitting* had been as physical an act as running, the pose held with tension and concentration. For Cerberus, sitting was a rough alignment of arse and floor, performed reluctantly and interrupted by sporadic bouts of scratching.

'And *now*,' said Kipper, and Hadley Best ran towards Cerberus, slipped a belt through his collar and pulled him out of shot. This was the third time in a row that this had happened, but Cerberus's look of half-witted amazement was as fresh as on the first occasion.

'And Cut,' shouted Kipper. 'The director would like to print that one. Moving on to Scene 91.'

The crew began to drift over to the pile of sand in the corner that represented the beach at Dunkirk, and Ambrose checked the page of script he'd been given.

91. M.S. FOXHOLE IN DUNES. DAWN

JOHNNIE – anxious and exhausted – is scanning the horizon through a pair of binoculars. HANNIGAN is asleep, smiling slightly, his hands clasped behind his head, his hat tipped over his eyes – he looks like someone taking a siesta in a deckchair. The DOG lies beside him on the sand.

JOHNNIE

(still looking through the binoculars) Hannigan – are you asleep?

There is no response.

JOHNNIE

(more loudly) Hannigan!

HANNIGAN

Wha . . .?

JOHNNIE

Are you asleep?

HANNIGAN

Not any more. (He yawns and sits up.) And you better have a pretty good reason for waking me.

JOHNNIE

Why's that?

HANNIGAN

Because I was just sitting in a nice little bar I know, and Betty Grable was bringing me an ice-cold beer.

Another page and a half of dialogue between Johnnie and Hannigan followed, but there were no further stage directions that mentioned the dog and Ambrose felt relieved, since *lying down* was something that Cerberus could manage with very little difficulty. During the first few days after bringing the bloody creature back to his house, he'd despaired of getting it to perform a single action to order but then Sophie's note had arrived in the post – *I think I may have omitted to tell you that my brother trained Cerberus to respond to Yiddish commands* – and since she had also omitted to put any of them in the note, and her telephone was once again on the blink, Ambrose had received instruction on how to say 'sit', 'stay', 'come here' and 'lie down' from ancient Mrs Greenbaum of the tobacconist's on Clipstone Street, who'd laughed so hard when she heard his request that he'd been able to count all five of her teeth.

'Leyg zikh,' he said to the dog, over at the sand-pile. Gracelessly, Cerberus obeyed, lolling on to his side in a way that would afford the camera a splendid view of his under parts.

'Rehearsal,' shouted Kipper, 'and then we'll light with stand-ins. Mr Best and Pilot Officer Lundback, could we have you on the dune please, rehearsal everybody, let's have some quiet. *Quiet!*'

For the first time, Lundback seemed a little nervous. He cleared his throat a couple of times, and glanced at the assembled crew. 'You can't see the audience when you're on stage in the theayter,' he said, *sotto*, to Hadley, and his speech had a gentle, homespun rhythm, like the beat of a butter-churn, and Hadley replied, 'Oh, don't worry, they're fearfully good chaps,' and then Kipper called for action.

When the dialogue began, Ambrose was watching the dog and wondering idly how Mrs Greenbaum might respond if he went back to the shop and requested the Yiddish for 'stop licking your cock', and a couple of exchanges went by before he realized that something was very wrong. It was like hearing a piece of music scored for two pianos, in which one of the parts was being played on a washboard. He glanced sharply at Lundback, and then at Hadley; the latter was looking a touch panicky.

'*Why's that?*' asked Hadley, in character.

'*BECAUSE I WAS* ***JUST*** *SITTING IN A NICE LITTLE* ***BAR*** *I KNOW AND BETTY* ***GRABLE*** *WAS BRINGING ME AN ICE-COLD* ***BEER***,' said Lundback, delivering the line as if to an audience of stone-deaf half-wits seated forty yards away, the rhythm no longer gentle, but reminiscent of a navvy with a sledgehammer.

Hadley paused, and flapped his lips a couple of times. 'I'm sorry . . .' he said. 'I've dried completely . . .'

There was a moment's silence, heavy with portent, and then

Kipper said, 'We'll go again in just a moment. It's only a rehearsal, remember,' and then huddled with the director for at least a minute before issuing an inaudible instruction to the third AD that sent the boy scurrying out of the studio.

'Let's take it again from the top of the scene,' said Kipper. 'And, er . . .' he took a couple of paces up the dune towards Lundback, and lowered his voice, 'the director says to remind you that, of course, all the men on the beach would almost certainly be speaking quite softly.'

'Enemy all around,' added Hadley, encouragingly.

'And, of course, when we shoot the scene there'll be a microphone,' added Kipper.

Lundback nodded. 'I see. Thank you, sir.'

'And off you go again,' said Kipper.

It was slightly worse the second time. Though he spoke more quietly, Lundback added a number of illustrative gestures, helpfully illuminating such words as 'drink', 'look' and 'small boat' for the benefit of observers who might have only a rudimentary grasp of English. A discreet word from Kipper followed, and then a third rehearsal during which Lundback appeared to have lost the use of his arms entirely. The producer arrived in studio halfway through the fourth run-through, and was therefore able to witness a bravura melding of all the techniques so far displayed, so that Hadley Best appeared to be having a conversation with a stentorian tic-tac man, and then a break was called 'for lighting' and Ambrose turned away.

He could hear, through the clatter and hum, the cruel laughter of the gods. Fool that he was, he had dared to hope. He had been so close, so close to being in a half-decent film, and then the hand of disaster had clamped around the slender throat of promise, and if they adjusted the lighting till doomsday it would all be to no avail, for even pitch darkness could never disguise the presence of an *amateur*.

*

When the call for the emergency meeting came, late in the afternoon, Buckley collected his fags and his hat, woke Parfitt by rapping his knuckles on the desk just beside his head and then, apparently as an afterthought, looked at Catrin and jerked his thumb towards the door.

'Me?' she asked.

'About time you came to one of these.'

'What's it about?'

'Don't know yet.'

'Who's going to be there?'

'No idea.'

'Am I allowed to speak?'

'No.'

'I could take notes.'

'Parfitt does that.'

'So why am I going?'

Buckley regarded her for a long moment. 'Educational purposes,' he said, enigmatically. 'Besides, I bet you weren't doing anything else this evening, were you?'

'No,' she said, reluctantly.

'Well, then.'

They found a taxi at Piccadilly, and arrived at the studio just as dusk was thickening. Parfitt paused outside the entrance, and looked east along the river towards Battersea, where a crescent moon dangled between the chimneys of the power station as if slung on a wire.

'Do you think they'll be over tonight?' asked Catrin.

Parfitt shrugged. 'Maybe. They're tricky bastards.'

She hung back as they entered the little office next to sound stage two. Edwin Baker was already there, and the director, Alex Frayle, the latter sitting with elbows on knees, his head bowed, and there was tension in the room, the air thrummed with it.

'Come on in, come on in,' said Baker. 'Sit down, Parfitt. You too, Mrs Cole.' Catrin was startled that he knew her name. He was a short man, in his sixties but broad-shouldered and strongly built, his tone hearty yet deliberate – she could just see him behind the counter of his butcher's shop, cleaver in hand, one eye on the queue and the other on his profits. 'We have a problem to solve,' he said, slapping the desk with both hands. 'First day in studio's always a chancer, but we got off to a top-notch start this morning, didn't we, Alex? Two pages completed?'

There was no response from the director. Baker hammered on. 'And of course, we showed the rushes at lunchtime, and they were first-rate, went down a treat, all credit to you, Alex, and then we ran into a bit of difficulty in the afternoon. I'm laying some of the blame on the scheduling, I'll have to have a word with Kipper. If we'd started with a nice, short scene then the fellow might have got into his stride, but as it was he didn't er . . .' For the first time, he hesitated. 'He couldn't er . . .'

'Act,' said the director, very quietly, still addressing the floor. 'He couldn't act.'

'Who're we talking about?' asked Buckley.

'The Yank,' said Baker. 'Lundback.' He tapped the ends of his fingers together, suddenly thoughtful. 'Of course, his screen test was excellent.'

'I wasn't there,' said the director, his voice a tiny steel thread.' 'I was in Norfolk.'

'Granted you were in Norfolk, but *I* was there, and pardon me for only having produced five dozen films, and the American Ambassador was there as well, and a couple of admirals, and a chap from the Air Ministry, and another from the MoI, and Laurie Silverman from United Artists, and what we all saw was potential, enormous potential. And believe me, when someone like Silverman uses the phrase, "He looks a million dollars", then you don't start arguing. And do you know what? Do you know why I was so blinking confident about tapping that potential? I was confident because I knew that the director of our film was in documentaries before he came to us, which means he's had years of working with amateurs.'

'Non-actors,' said Alex Frayle. 'I've had years of working with non-actors.'

Baker grimaced at the delicacy of the point. 'I saw you in Norfolk doing twenty-odd takes with that fisherman chap and it looked perfect in the rushes.'

'He had one line,' said Alex, 'and he was playing a *fisherman*.' He raised his head for the first time, his pale gaze sliding in the direction of the producer, but stopping short of meeting his eye. 'If I'd had some rehearsal time with Lundback, then—'

'Look—' said Baker, sharply, and then stopped and took a breath; when he resumed speaking, his voice was steady, his expression grim. 'The RAF said they'll release Lundback for five weeks and that's our lot, and we're lucky to get it. What I need now are solutions, not more misery. I'm not denying that this afternoon was poor, the boy was nervous, and he's even more nervous now. We can move the schedule around, push his scenes back until he's had a bit more time to get used to the part, and we can make some changes to the script. What do you say, Buckley, cut a line or two?'

'Cut them all,' muttered the director.

'We'll have a think,' said Buckley. 'Do you want him out of some scenes altogether?'

'Do I heck,' said Edwin Baker. 'We could get US distribution on this, the more they see of their man, the better.'

'So keep him centre stage, but shut him up.'

'That's the ticket. And don't for pity's sake alter any of the main plot, or the Ministry'll be on our necks again – we'll have to run it past them, anyway. Can you get us something by Wednesday?'

Buckley nodded easily, as if he'd been asked to tweak a couple of commas. 'We'll get stuck in,' he said.

Parfitt, who always seemed to know of a little place just round the corner where you could still get a decent drop of wallop, led them down a steep flight of steps near Hammersmith

Bridge and into a cellar tap-room, and though the ceiling there was low, and the air chill and smoky, and the other drinkers hard-faced men with liverish complexions who studied Catrin over the rims of their tankards as if they were anthropologists who'd caught their first glimpse of a fabled tribe, there was a sense of safety in the vaulted brickwork, and when the siren began its dreary call, just as Buckley was ordering a round of drinks, it sounded muffled and irrelevant.

'Chin chin,' said Buckley, settling himself on to a stool. 'You can say it now,' he added, in Catrin's direction.

'Say what?'

'That we can't *possibly* change Hannigan's lines at this late stage in the proceedings.' His attempt at a Welsh accent was dreadful.

'I wasn't going to say that, actually.'

'Weren't you?'

'No.'

He raised his eyebrows. 'What were you going to say, then?'

'Nothing, yet. I was still thinking.'

'Well God forbid that I should disturb that process. Parfitt, your thoughts?'

'Nice drop of ale, this,' said Parfitt, taking a pull at his glass.

Catrin was thinking about Hannigan's dialogue, crisp and cynical – about how it had been inserted into the original structure of the film like a pickled onion into a sandwich. It could be removed again – she knew it could – but the tang of it would be missed and Hannigan himself would become a bland cipher, drifting about with his reporter's notebook and occasionally venturing the odd, heavily directed remark. The character's gradual shift from hands-in-pockets American neutrality to rolled-up-sleeve support for his British rescuers would be utterly lost. The whole *point* of the character would go.

'How would it be,' she asked, suddenly, 'if we could see the pages of his notebook? On screen, I mean. We could see him writing about what he's thinking.'

Buckley shook his head. 'Too slow. Besides it's a well known fact that audiences won't read.'

'Picture house, not a library,' added Parfitt.

'You might be barking up a useful tree, though,' said Buckley. 'Keep thinking. In fact you can think all the way to the bar and back if you like.'

'I've only drunk a quarter of mine.'

'And there's your trouble, you'd write it quicker if you drank more liquor. A fresh idea with every beer.'

'Work it out with a pint of stout,' added Parfitt, as Catrin made a hasty escape. 'Make it shorter when you sink some porter.'

She was served by the only other female in the pub, a wan adolescent who gave Catrin the same look of guarded speculation as had the male drinkers.

'Two shillin' an fruppence,' she said, in a voice like the cheep of a baby bird, and for a second, Catrin was back in Whiting Walk, listening to Rose Starling speaking to her from behind a broken front door.

'Two shillin'and fruppence,' repeated the girl; that same tiny doll's voice, but issuing from someone quite different.

'I've had another thought,' said Catrin to Buckley, edging the glasses on to the table.

'Fire away.'

'In the Ministry, we were always using shots of the back of people's heads and then putting new voices on them and I wondered if we could find an actor who sounded just like . . .' The idea seemed to crumble away even as she spoke; no one would pay money to see the back of Carl Lundback's head, however good the lines.

'The peculiar thing is,' said Buckley, 'that while you were away at the bar, Parfitt and me have been edging towards much the same solution.'

'Voice impersonator,' said Parfitt.

Buckley nodded. 'Not for dialogue, though. We'd use him as

a narrator. Hannigan can say the odd line in shot, plenty of our flyboy looking pretty, but we'll save all the good stuff we've written for the voice-over.'

'It could be Hannigan's newspaper story,' said Catrin.

Buckley was still for a second, and then gave her a look, a nod, a finger pointed in approbation. 'Bang on. Have his finished article as a framing device. Yankee perspective, they'll like that, and it means we can use the voice long before we see him – "*I wasn't there at the beginning of the story but it all started in a liddle Briddish seaside town where nuthin' much ever happens.*"'

'Enough coverage for it?' asked Parfitt.

'Well, there we've struck lucky,' said Buckley. 'No one shoots more unneccessary bloody footage than a documentaries director. I'll bet there are yards of seascapes and village rooftops to stick the narration over.' He lit a fag and leaned back. 'Good. I'll talk to Edwin Baker first thing tomorrow and then we can get started. Some long days ahead, mind.'

Parfitt checked his watch, then sank his second pint in a couple of swallows, swiped a hand across his mouth and stood up. 'Got to get home to Dilly,' he said, and made for the stairs, head lowered bullishly. As he disappeared behind the heavy curtain that covered the door, there was a distant crump, a faint shiver of the cellar walls.

'They'll be after Battersea,' said Buckley. He took his drink more slowly, sucking the suds through his teeth.

'Who's Dilly?' asked Catrin. She thought of a tabby cat, nose pressed to the window.

'Parfitt's wife.'

'Parfitt's *married*?'

'Thirty-odd years.'

'Have you ever met her?'

'No, she doesn't go out. She's an invalid. Her sister looks after her until Parfitt gets home, but he and the sister can't stand the sight of each other, so when he gets there he gives six knocks on the front door, and the sister leaves through the back. They haven't spoken since 1926.'

'Why not?'

'They had an argument about the General Strike. She said they should shoot the lot and Parfitt's a communist.'

'Is he?'

'And a pacifist. You know, he was a conchie in the last war. Served four years in the Scrubs.' He grinned, pleased as usual to have shocked her, and she thought of Parfitt with his marbled complexion and sparse conversation, Parfitt whom she'd come to regard as not so much a person as a rusty-hinged box containing no more than a scattering of punchlines and a little peppery dust.

'Hotting up outside,' said Buckley, as the floor shuddered again. His grin had faded, but he was still looking at Catrin, smoke climbing from the cigarette between his fingers. 'What are you doing next?' he asked, abruptly.

'Going home on the tube,' she said.

'Next after you finish on the film, I meant.'

'Oh. Back to the Ministry of Information, I suppose.'

'You're staying on in London, then? All by yourself?'

'Yes.' Although she couldn't remember actually having arrived at the decision; it seemed to have slid into place when she wasn't looking. 'Yes, I am.'

Buckley was silent for what seemed a very long time. 'So, do you want to hear about the new commission?' he said, at last.

'What new commission?'

'MoI have asked Baker's for a sixty-minute supporting feature about air-raid wardens, full cooperation from civil defence, a star name or two if we can get them. Do you want to write for it?'

'Me?'

'No, Uncle Joe Stalin. Yes, you.'

'Of course I do. Is there slop in it, then?'

'Might be. They want a dash of comedy, but I daresay they'll go for some glamour as well. Glynis Johns in a tin hat making cow-eyes at a fireman. Besides . . .'

'What?'

'It's possible that at a pinch you might just about be able to come up with an adequate line or two of non-slop.'

'Oh . . .' She found herself smiling; she had never been offered a compliment that she valued more. 'Thank you very much.'

'Good,' said Buckley. 'I'll square it with the ministry. *Yacky dar.*'

'*Iechyd Da.*' She took a couple of gulps of beer, trying to swallow without tasting its sour soapiness. 'Do I get a proper desk this time?'

'You stick with your card-table and be grateful. Another toast—' He raised his glass, 'Hitler's haemorrhoids, may they blossom and flourish.'

'Hitler's haemorrhoids!'

'My round this time,' he said, and was on his feet before she could protest. She was beginning to feel rather tight. He was back within seconds, it seemed, with too many glasses.

'I shouldn't have any more,' she said.

'Another toast won't do any harm. Your turn.' He looked at her expectantly.

'All right then, last one.' She lifted her own glass. 'To the success of *Just an Ordinary Wednesday*.'

Buckley shook his head. 'Distributors want to change the title.'

'They don't!'

'They do.'

'Why's that?'

'Because nothing's ever allowed to be ordinary in America. It'll have to be a whoop-de-do yee-hah astounding Wednesday that's more than twice the size and three times as shiny as the Wednesdays we have in England, and never mind the irony in the original title. No – don't drink to that,' he added, shooting a hand across the table and trapping her glass. 'Don't drink to that, drink to something better. Drink to the new Baker's writing team – you, me and Parfitt.'

'All right, then.'

She tugged at the glass, but he held fast, his fingers pinning her own.

'No, scrub that.' He paused, and took a sharp breath. 'Just drink to you and me,' he said, so quickly that she barely heard him.

'What?'

'To you and me.' He tightened his grip, his eyes fixed on hers. 'Catrin . . .' he said, and he was on his feet and leaning across the table towards her, smelling of brilliantine and beer. He was going to kiss her on the lips, she realized, and she reached out her other hand towards his chest and gave him a good-humoured shove.

'Don't,' she said. He sat back on the stool with a thump, his grip jerking the glass towards him so that a sheet of beer hit him in the face, and Catrin heard herself starting to laugh – an involuntary noise, feathery with nerves – and Buckley looked away, his sallow skin slowly darkening, a fringe of droplets hanging from his moustache.

'That'll teach me,' he said.

'Do you want a hanky?'

He took it from her and slowly wiped his face. 'You think I'm an old fool,' he said.

'No, I don't.' Other drinkers were staring.

'I'm just a bloody old fool to you.'

'No. Honestly. Let's forget it ever happened. It doesn't matter, really it doesn't.'

'It matters to me,' said Buckley. 'It matters like hell to me.' He looked at her for a moment, and then down at the sodden handkerchief, his expression heavy, the usual wolfishness gone, and Catrin suddenly understood. A drunken lunge, she'd thought – a drunken lunge, quickly dealt with and then back to the usual cross-talk, intrusive but ephemeral, that striped their days. But though *she* was drunk, Buckley was sober, or as near as dammit, and this hadn't been his usual bottom-pinching, chase-around-the-desk brand of shallow flirtation, but something from the depths, a kraken with a rose in its beak.

'Oh dear,' she said, and then wanted to cross the words out again, to run a pencil through the whole bloody scene, but they'd shot it now, it was in the can.

★

'All ready?' asked Arthur, door-key in hand. The question was redundant, since Edith was standing just beside him in the hall, headscarf tied, gas-mask over her shoulder, handbag in the crook of her elbow, but the asking of the question had become part of their routine, as had the reply.

'All ready,' said Edith, knowing precisely what would come next.

'I'll just double-check that the gas is off,' said Arthur. She watched him open the door of the cupboard under the stairs, disappear briefly from view and then re-emerge. 'Yes, it's off. All set then?'

This time she nodded, and Arthur opened the door for her, paused on the step in order to clean his spectacles, and then looked up at the sky; it was clear, and as blue as a harebell. 'It might be a mistake, though, not to bring the umbrella,' he said, reflectively. 'What do you think?'

'Oh, I think we could risk it,' said Edith.

He pulled the door shut, and it closed with a solid click and a little after-snap from the letter-box, and then it was five steps up the path, and the rattle of the gate latch and out on to the pavement of Cressy Avenue. 'We're in good time,' said Arthur, checking his watch. 'Off we go. Edith.'

He still tended to enunciate her name, she thought, as if it were a code-word that had to be inserted into an otherwise ordinary sentence. 'I used to be called "Edie" at school,' she said, as they turned left along Agincourt Road. 'I quite liked it. Did you ever have a nickname at school?'

'A nickname?' The long list sagged in his memory: Farty-Artie, Gig-lamps, Four Eyes, Sissy-boy, Specky, Bottle-tops, Milksop, Goggles, Nursey – Nursey had been coined by the one boy in whom he'd confided about his duties at home, and it was Nursey that had stuck. Nursey Frith. '. . . no, not really. Nothing to speak of,' said Arthur.

They crossed into Cherry Grove; two houses were missing along the row, one site recent and raw, clay lumped on splintered rafters, the other softened by a haze of green. There were boarded windows and chipped bricks and missing slates on other houses along their route and, in addition to the war damage, Edith had noticed since her return an encroaching shabbiness – neglected paths whiskery with weeds, hedges topped by a frill of unchecked growth, peeling paint on gates and doors – evidence of absent husbands and fathers, of families who had fled London for the duration. Those who had stayed were more concerned with growing onions than pulling dandelions. A cockerel crowed from a back garden somewhere.

'I'd rather like to keep hens,' said Edith.

'Hmm?' He was checking his watch. Arthur always checked his watch at the end of Cherry Grove. He would check it again, Edith knew, just as they arrived at the station, and again as the train was announced, looking up at her with a smile and saying, 'That should do it,' or 'Plenty of time, still.'

It was a nice smile, albeit diffident, at one with a manner that seemed unfailingly equable and polite. Edith had been Mrs Frith for over two weeks now, and she had encountered no unpleasant surprises, no locked room à la Bluebeard, no flashes of temper or temperament. There had been no surprises at all, in fact, unpleasant or otherwise, and each day served only to reinforce the routine into which they'd quickly fallen, and

Edith (though she could hardly bear to admit it to herself) was beginning to feel awfully flat. It wasn't that she'd imagined a life of wild, free spontaneity, it's just that she hadn't thought that there would be so very little to discover about marriage, about her husband. It was like jumping into an opaque pond and finding it ankle-deep.

It might have helped if they'd seen rather less of each other – a daily separation of some kind, so that they had news to exchange, experiences to recount – but not only did they travel to the studio together, but once there, Arthur stuck to her like a piece of lint on a cardigan, which in one way was flattering and extraordinary and wonderful (for who would have thought that she, Edith Frith née Beadmore, would ever meet a man who didn't want to let her out of his sight), but in all other ways was completely maddening, for she was enjoying the work enormously, but it was work that took concentration and care, and since she couldn't actually ignore the fixed presence of a husband at her elbow, she found her attention constantly split. And she could hardly ask him to *go away*, could she, since in only four weeks' time he'd be doing exactly that . . .

'I said that I rather fancied keeping hens,' repeated Edith. 'It would be lovely to have eggs more often.'

'Yes it would,' said Arthur. 'I like an omelette.' It had been such a long time since he'd made one. He thought with sudden yearning of the hiss of the butter, the plateful of airy gold that emerged like a conjuring trick from the pan. 'And they're awfully nutritious,' he added. 'At Waring's we used to serve an egg savoury twice a week.'

A salvage truck passed them, bins rattling in the back, and then the road was empty again and they crossed into Willow Walk and Edith glanced at Number 40, wondering if she'd see her old landlady Mrs Bailey, or Mrs Bailey's daughter Pamela, but as usual the door was shut, the windows blank.

'I wonder if they've moved away,' she said, and saw, as she spoke, a couple standing in the middle of the pavement twenty yards ahead, the man with one arm extended, bracing himself against a cherry tree, and the other wrapped around his girl, lifting her so that only the toes of her shoes were touching the pavement, leaning her over backward so that his face was above hers, his mouth pressed on her mouth, and Edith saw with no particular surprise that the girl was Pamela, her early promise fulfilled, school hat halfway down the back of her head, eyes closed in apparent ecstasy as she kissed a Polish airman. And kissed him. And kissed him. There was no sign of an end to the embrace.

'Perhaps we should cross over,' said Edith to Arthur.

'Yes.'

And that was the other thing, of course. She couldn't ignore it or pretend that it wasn't happening – or, rather, that it *was* happening. Her wedding-night migraine had lasted for twenty-four hours, and as usual she had felt like a chewed string for a day or two afterwards, and Arthur had been kindness itself, and had continued to sleep in his old room, just in case (as he'd said) his snoring disturbed her. And then, just as she'd begun to feel better, her monthly had started, so that yet again, the eau de Nil satin slip with parchment piping had stayed in the drawer and Arthur, on being informed of her condition, had disappeared downstairs for ten minutes before returning with a filled hot-water-bottle for her cramps, which was a thoughtful gesture, and one that made her feel like an elderly maiden aunt, lumpen and chaste in tartan dressing-gown and sanitary belt. After which he had gone back to his own room again.

More than a week had passed since then. Each evening, Arthur would formally kiss her goodnight, one hand on her shoulder, his body at least six inches from hers, and they would retire to their separate rooms. It was as if they'd somehow skipped forty years of marriage, leap-frogging early fervency and arriving directly at Darby and Joan, all passion spent, and Edith hadn't yet summoned up the – the what? the courage? the vocabulary? – needed to raise the subject. I'm a modern woman, she wanted to say. I took life-drawing classes at art college, I am fully au fait with the anatomy of the masculine form, I will not be shocked, I shall not be a shrinking virgin. But the trouble was that she had always assumed that if the time ever came, then she wouldn't be the one taking the lead. And now it seemed that there were two of them jostling for second place.

'We should do it,' said Arthur, startling her considerably. 'Of course, we'd have to go to a reliable breeder.'

'Hens,' said Edith, after a moment.

'And I could make the coop.' He had seen a plan for one in a copy of *The Woodworker* and after he'd finished his current fretwork project he could give it a go; it wouldn't be easy to find the materials, but there was chicken wire over the windows of the shed that he could re-use, and it was something concrete that he could do for Edith, something husbandly, something manly and useful, and he wanted to please her, he really very much wanted to please her. 'I could do that for you,' he said, 'if you'd like.'

She seemed to hesitate before answering. 'What I'd like . . .' she began. 'What I'd like is . . .' but the end of the sentence never came and they walked in silence the remainder of the route and waited side-by-side on the crowded northbound platform.

It's impossible, thought Edith, and for the first time she felt a little frightened, for she had married someone who was neat and punctual and efficient and reliable, someone who spoke less than other people, someone unobtrusive, someone wholly used to their own company. And she found herself thinking of science lessons at school, of the identical magnets that, freakishly, could never touch, since their similarity repelled rather than attracted, and then she heard the scrape of the rails as the train approached and she knew *exactly* what was going to happen next, she knew exactly, and she watched with a kind of weariness as Arthur checked his watch and looked up with a tentative smile.

'That should do it,' he said.

*

Some days of filming felt productive and purposeful, while on others one could sense the schedule slipping backward like a bread-van with a faulty hand-brake. There had been an ever-increasing number of the latter on the current production, and today was a case in point: fourteen set-ups on the shot-list and by midday only four completed, with Kipper appearing to have aged ten years since breakfast. Attempts had been made to blame the inadequacy of the generator, the stiff breeze that poppled the water, the clouds that kept sliding capriciously in front of the sun, but the bulk of the time had been lost in the usual struggle to make Carl Lundback sound like a member of the human race. Nine takes of him shouting, '*Over here*', seventeen of '*Help me get this feller out*', and it was very nearly time for luncheon, and Ambrose had done little except sit on a slatted bench next to the changing-rooms with Cerberus cringing beside him.

Parliament Hill Lido was doubling as the English Channel for one day only, and the camera had been placed on a small platform built over one corner of the pool. With its lens pointing slightly downward, it was apparently possible to shoot a much wider expanse of water than was achievable in studio, and Hadley Best and Lundback and sundry extras had been immersed up to their armpits for most of the morning. The dog was supposed to be in there too, nobly supporting his injured master until rescue came, but Cerberus had absolutely refused to enter the water, even when bribed with fresh mince from the catering wagon, and Hadley Best was having to make do with a substitute hastily run up by wardrobe and consisting of a stuffed sack with wash-leather ears. It had apparently passed muster in the wide shot; the close-up had been abandoned.

'Little bit of concentration,' shouted Kipper. 'Just one more set-up before lunch, Scene 114.'

There must have been (Ambrose surmised) a great deal of shrieking panic behind the scenes after the calamity of the first day in studio. The filming schedule had altered completely. Lundback had scarcely been seen for a fortnight, and when he'd returned, most of his lines had mysteriously disappeared, his witty quips replaced by long takes of the character gazing at the horizon, or smiling quietly to himself, or writing in his reporter's notebook while looking quizzical, or as near to quizzical as Lundback's mastery of facial expression would allow. Other members of the cast had actually gained lines, Ambrose himself acquiring a few nice nuggets of exposition, as well as a page of banter with a rescued Scottish soldier about the potential buoyancy of bagpipes, but there were moments, unfortunately, when it was still deemed necessary for the American to speak, and here, plumb in the middle of Scene 114, was another of them.

HANNIGAN

(calling jauntily to Rose and Lily) Morning, ladies – you wouldn't happen to be heading for England by any chance?

'We'll go again,' said Kipper, after Lundback's pancake rendition on Take 1. 'And er . . .' he lowered his voice, 'the director asks me to remind you that it says "jauntily" in the script.'

Clearly 'jauntily' in the United States was a synonym for 'leaden', since moribund reading followed moribund reading, with Kipper issuing a prissy little director's note after each, like someone trying to revive an unconscious elephant by fanning it with a lace handkerchief. Eventually, Alex Frayle knelt at the side of pool and engaged in a long whispered conversation with the American during which Ambrose distinctly heard the words 'transatlantic brio' and then – surely by coincidence – Lundback gave a performance fractionally less dreadful than before and luncheon was called.

'Dry clothes and hot-air heaters in the boiler room,' said Kipper. 'Back on camera at one thirty.'

Behind the lido, a path meandered across Hampstead Heath and around a thicket of hawthorn before heading rather more purposefully towards the crest of Parliament Hill. Cerberus trotted briskly along the grass, urinating on every third clump, and Ambrose walked some distance behind, his stomach churning uneasily.

Rather than face his umpteenth plate of mince of the war so far, he had plumped instead for fish in parsley sauce. 'It's cod,' the fat woman with the ladle had said when he'd asked, an obvious lie given the cheapness of the catering, and confirmed when Ambrose had scraped away the sauce to reveal what looked like a section of black mackintosh. Beneath this integument lay the grey flesh, clinging to a giant vertebra of a type more usually seen in a case in the Natural History Museum. It had tasted predictably vile and it had taken a bowl of fruit jelly with custard to wash away the lingering tang, and there, in a nutshell, was the damage that rationing had wrought – scouring clean a palate attuned to the silky piquancy of foie gras and replacing it with one that slavered at the thought of strawberry-flavoured gelatine. One might as well play jigs on a Stradavarius.

'*Kim aher*,' he called as Cerberus began to drift away from the path, nose to a scent trail that led him zig-zagging through a clump of thistles. It was a true spring day, the new leaves on the hawthorn a brilliant green, the sun (when it appeared from behind the clouds) truly warm for the first time that year, and there were soldiers everywhere, sleeping their leave away on the grass, kicking a ball around, sitting on benches watching for a girl to walk by. The boredom was almost palpable. Near the top of the hill, there was even a Welsh Guardsman flying a home-made kite, the newsprint still visible through a coat of black paint, and Ambrose paused to watch for a moment or two, before tackling the last, steep, thirty yards and turning to look at the view.

And he was shocked. He had expected devastation, but what amazed him was that London appeared so little changed. Half a year of bombing, of fires that had lit up the night and burned for days, and yet the most noticeable difference was the presence of the barrage balloons, their wires rendered invisible by distance so that they seemed to have chosen their berths high above the city. And *what* a city! A sprawl that reached almost to the far horizon, a blind-man's mosaic of grime-edged grey and pinkish buff, broken only by the grassy tump of Greenwich and the treetops that marked the Royal parks; and it seemed to Ambrose suddenly obvious that the blitz simply wouldn't work, that Goering had underestimated the sheer size of the place, and that the Luftwaffe could pepper London till Doomsday and not make a dent in the vastness. Though as he scanned the rooftops he began to see sign after sign of the barrage – cranes tilting above open rafters, the oddly uncluttered view of St Paul's, the charred skeleton of a warehouse behind St Pancras, glints of water from static tanks, raw red splashes of powdered brick interspersed among the duller hues, concavity where there should have been profile, an absence of spires where spires had soared before. Changed, then, but not changed utterly.

'No,' said a woman's voice behind him, above the rising wail of a child. 'Get *away*, get *away*,' and Ambrose turned to see Cerberus dancing along the sward with half a biscuit in his mouth, the other half still in the hand of a toddler.

'Whose dog is that?' shouted the woman, an Irish type with a jaw like a bottle-opener and an air of barely repressed violence. 'Is that *your* dog?' she added, staring at Ambrose.

'No it isn't,' he said coldly. He turned away again and found himself looking directly at Carl Lundback. The man was walking up the path towards him, looking – as usual – like an artist's projection of the adult Tom Sawyer.

'Mind if I join you, sir?'

'No, no,' said Ambrose. 'I was just stretching my legs.'

'Yeah, me too. They told me I could see the whole way to the Tower of London from here. Cigarette?'

'Thank you.'

Lundback reached into his breast pocket and took out a packet of Players, and Ambrose almost did a double-take. *Players! Unobtainable* for the past bloody year. So where had they come from? Stockpiled in a warehouse for the sole use of visiting Yanks? And would they taste as good as they always . . . ? Yes. Yes, they would. He inhaled with a mixture of pleasure and pique.

'It's quite a view,' said Lundback.

'Yes, I think you'll find that earth hath not anything to show more fair.'

There was a pause.

'So which one's the Tower of London?' asked Lundback. 'Because I promised my—'

There was a roar from the sky that momentarily drowned all speech. Three silhouettes passed swiftly overhead, travelling east.

'Hurricanes,' said Lundback. He stayed with his face tipped to the empty sky. 'Sure wish I was up there now.'

'Really? You'd rather be flying than making the film?'

'*Sure* I would.' He sounded utterly sincere. 'That's why I came here,' he added, looking at Ambrose with blue-eyed candour. 'To fly. To fight for Finland.'

'For *Finland*?'

'My mom and dad are from Oulu. My mom cried for a week when Finland was invaded.'

'But Finland was invaded by Russia. We're not at war with Russia.'

Lundback acknowledged this with a duck of the head. 'Yeah,' he said. 'I only found that out when I got here. And then I spent a night in London and I saw what Hitler was putting you guys through, and I figured that maybe you could do with a little help as well.' He gave a smile of such disconcerting sweetness that Ambrose had to fight the urge to start thanking him. Though, of course, it would come to that eventually. America would enter the war at some point, and then for the next fifty years would expect unceasing gratitude.

'Maybe I'll get to fight Russia later on,' added Lundback, almost wistfully.

'So I don't understand,' said Ambrose, 'if you'd rather be flying, then why are you in this film?'

'I'm under orders, sir.'

'The RAF ordered you to do it?'

'Yes sir. They said they hoped it'd be good for Eagle Squadron recruitment. They said to regard it as a temporary posting, sir.'

'For heaven's sake, I'm not your squadron leader, there's no need to call me sir.'

'Yes sir, I mean no. OK.' Lundback grinned and was instantly a publicity department's dream, the sunlight bouncing off his teeth – '*He's looping the loop in the hearts of a million girls*' – and as long as henceforward he stuck to playing deaf-mutes and wordless loners then his future in Hollywood was assured, though it was a pity that he'd had to begin his film career by ruining a perfectly good feature.

'So tell me,' said Ambrose, 'what acting experience have you actually had?'

'Well . . .' Lundback looked all at once rather sheepish. 'I wouldn't call it *acting*. Like I tried to tell the guy from the newspaper, it was just fooling around, you know, for fun and all.'

'What was just fooling around?'

'Well, me and the fellers from the airfield back home, we're in a – well, I think you call it a concert party over here, doncha?'

'So, singing?'

'Yeah, singing. And impersonations.'

'Impersonations of whom?'

'Jolson.'

'*Jolson?*'

'Yes, sir.'

'*Al* Jolson?'

'Yes sir. We called ourselves The Burnt Cork Barnstormers.'

'I see,' said Ambrose. The peculiarities of Lundback's technique were suddenly explained – the illustrative hand-movements, the vocal projection sufficient to reach to the back of a barn full of plaid-shirted hayseeds, the inability to understand any piece of direction more complex than 'speak softly' or 'move to your left'.

'So when did you speak to this member of the press?'

'When I went to get my, uh . . .' Lundback glanced bashfully down at his chest.

'Your medal,' said Ambrose.

'Yeah.'

'And a reporter interviewed you about your background and interests?'

'Yeah.'

'And – let me hazard a wild guess, here – when the article came out it bore little or no relation to the information that you had conveyed to him?'

'Yeah, that's right.' Lundback seemed impressed by Ambrose's perspicacity. 'It said a whole bunch of things that weren't true. And then a coupla weeks later I find I'm under orders to go for a screen test, and there's all these important guys and the US Ambassador's there and he shakes my hand and says that the President's real proud of me, and I couldn't . . . you know . . . I didn't want to—'

The end of his sentence was curtailed by a series of feminine bellows, among which the words 'bloody' and 'dog' were audible.

This time, Ambrose didn't turn around, but Lundback glanced over his shoulder, and said, 'Hey, will you look at that?' just as Cerberus ran past them, a whole packet of rusks in his mouth. The harpy with the jaw was not far behind, toddler on hip.

'If that's your dog—' she began, rounding on Ambrose, standing so close to him that the infant was able to reach out and make a grab at his tie.

'I can assure you that it's not my dog.'

'Well, it seems blooming funny that he got here when you got here, and he's stayed here the whole time that you've been here, and now when he's run off, he's run off right in your direction.'

'Madam,' said Ambrose with calm gravity, fending off the child's filthy little fingers with one hand, 'I can only say in all honesty that I have never seen that dog before in my life.'

There was a tiny pause. 'Well, whose dog is it?' she asked, suspiciously.

'I wish I could help you, but I really don't have any idea.'

'Well then you're a *fat* lot of good.' Glumly, the fight draining out of her, she looked towards the thicket into which Cerberus had disappeared. 'They were on points, those rusks,' she said. 'I had the last packet on the shelf.'

Ambrose felt Lundback's gaze upon him, like a moral spotlight.

'Here,' he said to the woman, reaching into his pocket and unluckily finding a half-crown rather than the sixpence he was hoping for. 'Buy the little chap something else. And now we really should be going.'

Cerberus re-joined them when they were halfway down the path to the lido, veering nose-first towards the pocket in which Ambrose usually kept a meaty treat, and then swerving away again upon finding it devoid of interest.

'So it *was* your dog,' said Lundback, sounding amazed.

'Yes, of course it was.'

The American shook his head in apparent wonderment. 'So how did you do that?'

'Do what?'

'Well, I sure as hell believed you when you told her you'd never seen him before. I thought it was some other mutt.'

Ambrose cast his eyes heavenwards.

'It's called acting. I *acted*.'

'Yeah, but if I'd tried that, she'd have . . .' Lundback mimed a right-and-a-left, and then chuckled and shook his head again. 'That beats all,' he said. 'Can you teach me to do that?'

Ambrose heard a kind of choking noise and realized that it was coming from his own throat. *Can you teach me to do that?* As if acting were a species of parlour-trick performed with three coins and a banana. 'Perhaps I could,' he said, distantly, 'if you had thirty years to spare.'

'Thirty years?'

'Or possibly less in the presence of innate ability. It is certainly not something that one can pass on over the course of a lunch-hour.'

'You can't just teach me a little bit of it?'

'Which little bit of it?'

'Well . . . how to say things the way I'm supposed to. So I don't keep having to do every line twenty times.'

'Again, that's acting. You're talking about the fundamental interpolation of skill and experience.'

'But . . .' Lundback looked up at the sky again with an expression of pained concentration, like someone engaged in teasing out a grape-pip from between two teeth.

'OK,' he said at last, 'say I took you up in a Miles Master. That's a trainer, handles kind of like a Hurricane. Say we just had three minutes up there. I couldn't teach you how to do a slow roll or a stall turn and I couldn't teach you how to pull out of a spin or what to do when a Messerschmitt's on your tail, but I could teach you to fly level. And I wouldn't do it by reading you an instruction book, I'd just *show* you how to do it, and then you'd do it yourself. And then you'd be flying level. You wouldn't be a pilot, but you'd know that much. D'you see what I mean?'

'I'm not sure that I do,' said Ambrose.

'Well, could you do that for me when I have a line? Show me how to do it?'

'You're asking me for a line reading?'

'Does that mean that you'd say the line just the way they wanted me to say it and then I'd say the line so I sounded just like you?'

'Yes.'

'OK. Then I'm asking you for a line reading. Sir? If you wouldn't mind?'

It seemed politic to appear to ponder the question for a few moments, although Ambrose knew instantly what his answer would be. Acceding to Lundback's request would be, of course, an utter prostitution of the thespian art, but on the other hand it promised rich interior rewards, for on how many occasions during his career had etiquette forced him to sit dumbly in the shadows while some cloddish 'friend' of the producer ruined yet another scene? On how many occasions had he longed to stand up and bellow, 'Oh for God's sake, man, don't say it like that, say it like *this*'? And now to be asked, to be *begged* to do precisely that, to be given the chance personally to winch this film back from the edge of disaster; it was an opportunity that simply couldn't be missed. And besides – it occurred to him, still tasting the mellow smoke on his tongue – there might well be other, more tangible rewards.

'Sir? If you wouldn't mind?' repeated Lundback.

Ambrose smiled magnanimously. 'Let me think about it,' he said.

*

Sitting at her card-table in the corner of the office, Catrin listened to the rattle of Buckley's typewriter.

'Just to remind you,' she said, 'I was hoping to leave a little early this afternoon.'

Buckley nodded, and then cursed under his breath as the keys jammed.

'So you don't mind if I go in about ten minutes?' asked Catrin.

'No.' He separated the clot of keys, wiped his finger on the desk top and then carried on typing.

'All right,' said Catrin, after a moment. 'Thank you.'

Until it ceased, she hadn't realized how much she'd grown used to the rigours of conversation with Buckley, the expectation that every passing remark would be pounced upon, prodded, buffed and analysed. Now when she spoke, the words seemed to hang suspended, like pebbles dropped into treacle.

'I've almost finished reading that article,' she said, raising her voice above the hammer of the keys. 'It's not half bad.'

There was no response beyond a distracted nod. She picked up her pencil and turned again to 'A Night in the Life of a Warden', and underlined the passage about an old lady refusing to go to the shelter without first putting on her corsets.

She would have liked to have read it out loud. She might have said, then, 'Is that the sort of thing we're looking for?' to which Buckley would almost certainly have replied 'Corset is.' Or 'Keep boning up on the subject', or 'As long as it stays in the mind.' Strange how one could crave terrible jokes.

It was hard to tell what Parfitt thought about the silence in the office, or even if he'd noticed it. As before, he spent much of his day asleep, or staring out of the window at Soho Square, and if he missed the acrid comments, the endless questions, the chains of dreadful puns to whose length he'd so often contributed, then he gave no hint. Perhaps when he and Buckley went to the pub together at lunch-time they resumed their usual form of conversation, an invigorating round of parry and thrust to go with the mild and bitter. Catrin herself had taken to eating lunch in a café in Dean Street filled with Free French, where everybody talked all the time and the coffee machine hissed like an incendiary.

It would have been easier if she could have convinced herself that Buckley was sulking, but there was no petulance in his behaviour. He talked when necessary. He was no ruder than usual. He was . . . muffled. The snap and fizz of his company had gone, and he looked older, the contours of his face less-defined, as if the pungency of his usual manner had acted as a preservative.

You think I'm an old fool.

And she found herself constantly re-playing the scene in the cellar in Hammersmith, checking each exchange to see if there had been a point at which she should have realized what was happening, and finding each time that the sequence rattled so quickly from inconsequence to farce that there was never a moment for reflection. Buckley had opened his heart and she had mistaken it for his liver. She could think of no way to return to the time before.

'By golly it's quiet in here,' said Phyl, walking in with an armful of paper.

'Finished in studio?' asked Catrin.

'Very late lunch, I'm going straight back. Mr Baker wanted the progress reports, or lack-of-any-discernible-progress reports as we're coming to call them.'

'Slow?'

'Deadly. Kipper's just pushed the schedule back again – thought you might like to know that on the final week we'll be working straight through from Monday to Sunday. Everyone's absolutely thrilled, as you can imagine. And the director asked me to enquire if the Scene 145 rewrites are finished.'

Wordlessly, Buckley held up a typed sheet, and after a moment's hesitation Phyl reached forward and took it.

'Thank you very much,' she said drily, and turned to leave the office.

'Hang on, I'll come with you—' Catrin grabbed her coat and bag and followed her down the stairs.

'So what's going on?' asked Phyl. 'Buckley's very subdued. Does he have toothache?'

Catrin shook her head. 'It's a bit more complicated than that.'

'He's a man. Food, sex and someone to nod admiringly when they're gassing on, that's all they require.'

Catrin gaped and then laughed. 'You're speaking from experience?'

Phyl gave her the briefest of sideways looks. 'Observation only, since you happen to ask. My interests lie elsewhere.'

There was a pause.

'Oh!' said Catrin, catching on rather slowly.

'Not, I'm sure, that you'll feel the need to repeat that last remark to anyone.'

'No, no of course not. No, I never would.'

'And where are you off to so early?'

'The National Gallery,' said Catrin. 'The War Artists Exhibition. They're opening a new room and my husband's one of the exhibitors. He's . . .' She looked at Phyl's candid grey eyes, and then down at her own hand, at the ring that she'd bought from the jewellery counter in Merthyr Tydfil. 'As a matter of fact he's not actually my husband,' she said. 'We're not married.'

'No?'

'No.'

'Your choice?'

'Well . . . not really. But then I decided that it was even more romantic, running away with a lover. And then I was too shy ever to admit it to anyone. Too chapel.'

Phyl laughed. 'Well, you're not quite so chapel these days, are you?'

'No. No, I suppose I'm not.' She twisted the ring a couple of times.

'And you're going to meet him there?' asked Phyl.

'I think so,' she said.

Though in truth she had no idea. Not long after he'd left

London, Ellis had sent her a postcard, brief and factual, giving the address of the cottage in Worcestershire, and she had sent one in reply and had scarcely known what to write. '*I hope that your work is going well, I am keeping safe, the gas was off for most of last week but is back on again now, the studio filming starts in a fortnight, the news from Greece is horrible, isn't it . . .*' She had almost put *I miss you* and then had checked herself. She missed his physical presence, an arm around her, the distinctive smell of his skin, the warmth and weight of his body on hers, she missed having someone of her own in London, someone to look after, but *him*, did she miss *him*? There had been a time when he had filled her thoughts to the exclusion of all else, when every fresh topic had been a path that looped straight back to Ellis, but now her head was packed with all manner of things, and he was only an item that she delved for now and again, and took out and puzzled over. She thought of their juddering conversations, she saw herself running along behind him, longing to be included, forever straining to be heard.

After the first card, he had sent another, this time from Coventry, and a third from Sheffield, and she had matched him postcard for postcard, dry fact for terse enquiry, and then, in reply to his three lines from Hull, she had scribbled an excited sentence or two about the new film for which she'd been asked to write and in return there had been nothing, not for weeks and weeks, and a sudden anxiety had led her to telephone the War Artists Committee, to check that he wasn't lying injured in a hospital in Hull or Swansea or Sunderland. The man in the office had said that as far as he was aware, 'Mr Cole is progressing satisfactorily with his commission', and he had kindly put Catrin's name on the guest-list for the opening of the new exhibition room. 'But will he be there?' she'd asked. 'We would expect all our artists to attend,' had been the crisp reply.

In Trafalgar Square, a group of African soldiers had clustered around one of the stone lions in order to have a photograph taken, and nearby a tea-van was parked, from which stretched a long queue of green berets. Catrin was wolf-whistled as she hurried towards the steps of the National Gallery, and one of the commandoes shouted, 'Where are you off to, darling?' and she called back, 'The pictures, of course', and was pleased to get a laugh.

The gallery was all war art now – the gods and goddesses, saints and Madonnas crated up and hidden safely somewhere outside London. She walked through rooms hung with portraits of factory workers and land-girls, the old palette of gold and azure replaced by drabber shades, but further on there were blitz paintings, crimson flame on black, and a canvas the length of one wall, showing shipbuilders at work, a sepia world lit by welders' torches and the glitter of metal.

She could hear the hubbub of the reception before she reached it, and she gave her name to the attendant, and paid sixpence for a guide booklet. Her heart had begun to beat rather fast, but once inside the room, she looked around the knots of well-dressed people and saw no one that she knew.

'Powerful,' someone was saying, 'awfully powerful.'

Even between the shifting figures she could instantly spot Ellis's work. 'A new urban anatomy,' is how she'd heard him describe it to Perry, 'flesh, bone and organ exposed,' and here were the sightless eyes of a row of houses, here a seared and blistered wall, here the skeleton of a factory, its steel girders contorted by the heat – stark images, instantly memorable, the colours raw and vivid. People would still be looking at these paintings in a thousand years, she thought; this is how the night blitz will be remembered, for ever and for ever. She moved closer and stared at the clotted darkness, the brilliant splinters of light.

In the hum of conversation behind her, one voice, emphatic and aggrieved, seemed to detach itself: '. . . and the chairman told me that the reason that it had been rejected was because the figures that I'd drawn were looking *panic*-stricken, and that the committee didn't want to imply that the raids were causing *panic*, and if I wanted to show *panic* then could I do it in some way obliquely or metaphorically. And I said, "Well what would you suggest? A full-length study of Chicken-Licken?" and he—'

'Hello, Perry' said Catrin, turning.

He stopped speaking and looked startled – aghast, in fact. His companion, an elderly woman, seized her opportunity to nod, smile and escape.

'This is a surprise,' said Perry, regaining his composure, and planting a rubbery kiss on Catrin's cheek. 'Good crowd, isn't it?'

'Very good. Is Ellis here?'

'No . . .' said Perry, with an attempt at casualness, but his eyes darted nervously about the room.

'Whatever's the matter?' she asked.

'Nothing.'

It was so obviously a lie that for a moment she simply goggled at him. He gave her a bright and unconvincing smile.

'Perry, I'm not a fool,' she said. 'Tell me what's wrong.'

'Well,' he shrugged, uncomfortably, 'I don't think that Ellis was expecting to see you here. Aren't you supposed to be working in a film studio somewhere?'

'Writers don't go to the studio,' said Catrin. She thought of all the times that she had tried to talk to Ellis about her work. Her heart was racing now. 'Tell me what's wrong,' she said again, more sharply this time.

'Er . . .'

'*Perry*.'

He cleared his throat. 'Ellis has brought a guest,' he said.

It took her only a fraction of a second to grasp his meaning, and then she was rushing towards the door, knocking into elbows, cracking her shoulder against military torsos, whisking booklets to the floor in her haste to get out of the room before Ellis and his guest could come into it, and once in the galleries she walked blindly back towards the main entrance, turning left at a burning church when she should have turned right, and finally reaching a dead end, a doorless wall hung with a picture of a bright blue sky scored by vapour trails.

She turned back and tried to find her way out again, and rounded a corner to see Ellis standing twenty yards away, talking to a man with a notebook. And just beside Ellis, unmistakably, was his guest. She was young, very pretty, dressed in her best, but a best that had been bought cheaply and washed many times, and she was watching Ellis as if he might evaporate if she broke her gaze for just one second.

Catrin took a step back, so that she was almost hidden by the corner, but she kept her eyes on the little scene. The panic that she had felt just a moment ago had gone entirely, replaced by a chilly fascination.

Ellis talked. The journalist nodded. The girl watched. Once, she rested a hand on Ellis's arm and then rather awkwardly took it away again. She smiled when he smiled, she turned to look at what he looked at, and when the journalist closed his notebook, and Ellis walked away, she pattered after him.

Catrin watched until they were out of sight, and then realized that she'd been holding her breath for far too long. Her vision was filled with sliding pin-pricks, and she closed her eyes for a moment and saw Ellis's painting of a ruined street, the cobbles empty except for a single figure, too distant for its features to be distinguishable. He rarely peopled his canvasses. The figures that he drew were only ever there to serve a purpose, to convey scale or to add contrast, and one looked much the same as another; if they failed in their function, they could always be painted out.

She walked slowly to the main entrance and down the steps into the twilight. The pavements were full of office girls hurrying homeward, all chatter and vim, and rather than be jostled, Catrin picked up her pace to match theirs and reached Regent Street at a smart clip. Instead of squeezing on to a bus, she carried on walking, faster, as fast as she was able, and she felt gripped by a strange excitement, as if she were charging towards something rather than running away, and at Marylebone High Street she saw a static water-tank ahead of her and without breaking stride, without even really thinking what she was doing, she pulled off the ring that she'd bought for herself in Merthyr Tydfil and she dropped it into the water. It barely made a splash.

*

During the lunch-hour on the penultimate day of filming, Arthur was sitting eating cauliflower cheese in the studio canteen when Phyl came over to his table with a notepad and asked him in what form he would like to see his name on the opening titles of the finished film. He didn't quite understand her question, and she explained (with her usual disconcerting half-smile, so that he wasn't sure whether she was pulling his leg or not), that some people were very particular about how they were styled. He might, for instance, after the words 'Special Military Advisor', wish to be credited as 'Lance Corporal A. Frith' or 'Lance Corporal Arty Frith', or – depending on his middle name – 'Lance Corporal Arthur Z. Frith' or . . .

'Arthur Frith' would do very well, he assured her, and then after she left he sat for a good three minutes with the knife and fork resting on his plate and the pallid sauce beginning to wrinkle, while a sense of guilt slipped over him, for it appeared that his name would be permanently and legibly attached to a film whose accuracy he had long since ceased to monitor.

His last attempt at intervention had been several weeks ago, at the very beginning of the studio shoot, after Lundback had played his first scene. Arthur had mentioned in a quiet aside to Ambrose Hilliard that he hadn't been aware of any Americans at the Dunkirk evacuation, and Hilliard had exclaimed, 'Good heavens! Is that really the case? Then it's imperative that you make the fact more widely known!' but in a tone that implied heavy sarcasm rather than genuine surprise. So there hadn't seemed very much point in keeping a close watch on the proceedings after that. Instead, he had tried to stay near to his wife at all times, just in case she required help, or perhaps a few friendly words between takes. Though on the whole she hadn't, of course. She really was awfully busy.

And that afternoon on 'B' Stage, as he watched Edith go about her work, consulting her notes and then adjusting collars and buttons and hats and belts so that they would look exactly as they had looked in the very next scene, which had actually been filmed a fortnight previously – and as he listened to the shouts of the electricians, and the murmured consultation between director and cameraman, and the muttered rehearsals behind him, where Ambrose Hilliard was teaching Pilot Officer Lundback how to say 'Steady there, old timer', in a way that seemed to put a great deal of emphasis on the word 'steady'and none at all on the word 'old' – Arthur couldn't help thinking (and not for the first time) that he himself was a useless sort of stick, hanging around on full pay while others laboured, and he tried to think of a pertinent point that he could offer, a helpful note that might finally justify not only his presence but his grandiose title. After all, the next scene was one in which the boat was strafed, and that was – it truly was – something he knew about, something he still saw, still *heard* every night when he closed his eyes: the shrilling plunge of the aircraft, men diving to the ground, hands clasped over heads, as helpless as worms under a spade. And afterwards, the lucky ones cautiously standing again, the unlucky ones scattered like stepping stones across the sand. And always, always a hot-head (or two) who had stayed on his feet and fired a gun at the plane and swore that he'd clipped a wing with the second bullet.

'Need to get the brute up, then,' said the cameraman, cryptically, and went off towards the scaffolding tower at the far side of the water-tank, and the director glanced around with his usual distracted frown and caught Arthur's eye and gave a minute nod of acknowledgement.

'I wonder,' said Arthur, straightening his spectacles, 'if you have just a moment . . .'

'*Steady* there, old timer,' said Lundback, sticking out his jaw at the end of the sentence so that he looked like Tom Mix confronting an outlaw, but otherwise giving a reading that was at least 80 per cent better than his first effort, if still a good 20 per cent below professional standards.

'And I think we should move on to the next line,' said Ambrose. 'It's a short one.'

'Propeller's *FOULED*,' supplied Lundback, who at least had a decent memory.

'Try the emphasis on the second syllable.' Ambrose tuned his own voice to a mid-west baritone. "Prop*ell*er's fouled." And more quietly, of course.'

'Mr Hilliard, do you have a moment? There's a telephone call for you.'

Ambrose followed the weedy figure of the third assistant director along the corridor and into the studio manager's office. It was an afterthought of a room, not much larger than a broom-cupboard, with one tiny window overlooking the river and a desk covered with files. The studio manager, a man who seemed to sweat with a facility that would have had Phineas T. Barnum reaching for a contract, smiled moistly and passed across the receiver.

'Hello? Ambrose Hilliard speaking.'

'Ah, Mr Hilliard.' Sophie Smith, her voice clear but very distant. 'I have tried several times to telephone you at your residence.'

'My line's been down since mid-April.'

'While my own has at last been repaired. However I'm sure that if all were not as it should be with my brother's dog, you would have found means to inform me.'

'Cerberus is extremely well,' said Ambrose stiffly.

'Is he with you now?'

'He's in make-up.'

There was a tiny noise from Sophie, a kind of squeak, possibly nasal in origin. 'And you yourself, Mr Hilliard?'

'Also well.'

'And proving indispensable, I understand. Only yesterday I was speaking to Mr Baker's casting director about the range of your talents.'

'Oh yes?'

'He has suggested an interesting role that I would like to talk to you about in person.'

'A role in a feature?'

'As I say—'

'A *leading* role?'

'As I say, I would like to talk to you about it in person.'

'It's character again, isn't it?'

'And of course,' continued Sophie, inexorably, 'I have been so very busy that I have not yet visited the studio, so it occurred to me that tomorrow I could kill the two birds with a single stone. So to speak. I would like to see a little of the film being made.'

'Oh, but really, the last day of shooting is always so piecemeal, and besides, wouldn't it be better if we had our talk at a restau—'

He was interrupted by a series of hollow clicks, followed by a burst of speech from a crossed line ('. . . honestly, Beattie, I was livid, I said "that's never four ounces, you're leaning on the scales, you are . . ."), and then nothing but a faint whizzing noise. Ambrose glared at the receiver. Bloody hell. What on earth was the point of seeing one's agent if one didn't even get a decent meal out of it? And the phrase 'interesting role' had a nasty smell; fourteen lines and a false beard, no doubt. And to top it all, he would be spending half of tomorrow up to his shoulders in water and there was something deeply emasculating about being hauled, dripping, out of a tank in front of gaping females. It was the sort of thing that one had nightmares about.

'Mr Hilliard . . .'

Ambrose dragged his gaze round to the manager. 'Yes, what is it?'

'I'm ever so sorry, Mr Hilliard, I've just remembered something.' The man pawed through a wire tray stacked with post. 'Baker's sent it on last week, I think,' he said. 'I'm afraid that I've only just remembered, what with one thing and another . . .'

He held up an envelope, and Ambrose's brief, hopeful supposition that it might contain a cheque dwindled on sight, for the envelope was pale mauve, a vehicle for correspondence rather than cash, the handwriting floridly feminine.

'Fan mail?' asked the manager, ingratiatingly.

'Oh, I expect so,' said Ambrose. 'It usually is.' He took the envelope; there was a large, damp, managerial thumbprint smudging the post-mark, and no return address. He felt a slight stir of anticipation; it had been a very long time since he'd received such a missive, though somewhere, still, within his house was a cabin trunk full of the things.

Dear Mr Hilliard, I have seen The Eye of Flame *five times and I think you are simply wonderful, so thrilling and handsome . . .*

Dear Mr Hilliard are you maried becuase if you arnt maried then will you mary me . . .

Dear Ambrose, if I may be so bold as to call you that. Oft within my chamber in the shadows of the night have I whispered your name, and . . .

He slipped a thumb underneath the gummed flap, and had partly withdrawn the single sheet of folded paper within before he realized that the envelope contained another item, a photograph clipped from a magazine. He was looking at it upside-down, and it took him a moment to recognize the subject.

'Anything wrong, Mr Hilliard?' asked the manager.

'No, no, nothing at all. If the third AD comes looking for me, just tell him I'm taking a breath of fresh air, would you? I'll only be five minutes.'

Though there was nothing very fresh about the air outside today. It stank of mud. Ambrose had never seen the tide so low – the narrow ribbon of water running beneath Hammersmith Bridge looked like a village stream. He leaned against the river wall and studied the photograph for an outraged moment or two before reading the letter that had accompanied it.

My dear Ambrose,

How I hope that this reaches you. I am writing in haste, having only an hour or so ago chanced upon the enclosed in Picture Post, *quite accidentally, while I was waiting to see my dental surgeon (only a crown replacement!). What a dreadful time of it you must have had – and yet what a blessing that both you and your dear pal survived unharmed. Of course, I've no idea when the photograph was taken. By now, perhaps, you're living somewhere comfortable, and among friends, but I've heard so much about the horrors of finding decent accommodation for those who've been bombed-out, that I wanted to extend an immediate invitation to you both, should you still be in need. My little house is not very large, but it's sufficient to offer a cosy refuge to a fellow thespian, not to mention an old friend. Our mutual profession is already perilous enough, without abandoning those in true difficulty.*

My telephone line is rather temperamental at present, but until the end of April I may be contacted at the Theatre Royal, Windsor (playing Annie Parker in When We Are Married. *Nice little review in the local rag, and marvellous audiences, despite everything that*

That Man throws at us!!!) Hoping that I hear from you, if only to be reassured of your safety.
With heartfelt good wishes,
Cecy Clyde-Cameron
PS My darling Tommy departed peacefully for happier hunting grounds just after we came home from Ipswich, so you need have no worries about a little pussy-cat's objection to my offer.
PPS I hope that all is 'ship-shape' with the film!

It was, thought Ambrose with an effort, kind of Cecy. It was a kind letter, a kind offer, devoid, it appeared, of ulterior motive. A kind offer to move to . . . he checked the address. Thames *Ditton* – for Christ's sake! It would take considerably more than a direct hit (had that actually happened) to lure him to Thames Ditton. And the house was called The Ducklings. He could just picture it – one of those frightful, leaky shacks thrown up in the twenties as weekend cottages, and now occupied all year round by impoverished theatricals, trying to pretend that the bi-annual floods, the Arctic winds howling through the cracks in the clapboard, were part of its charm. Not to mention the drunken trippers gesturing lewdly through the sitting-room window as they floated by in their hired rowing-boats.

He ought, he supposed, to reply to Cecy. A brief thanks, perhaps, assuring her that the photograph in question had been labelled erroneously and had, in fact, been a still from a yet-to-be-released short. Or something of that kidney. He gave the picture a valedictory glance, before dropping it over the wall. The breeze took the slip of paper, and spun it like a leaf towards the plains of grey mud, but the image and its caption seemed to hang before him still. It must, he realized, have been taken by the photographer who'd been loitering outside the rest centre on Highbury Corner on the day that he had collected the dog, for it showed the two of them walking along the pavement, Cerberus with his head hanging, Ambrose laden with blanket and shabby carpet bag, the unflattering angle conjuring a wattled jowl from an innocent neck-crease, the harsh contrast painting a series of deep lines and furrows across his face. '*HOMELESS BUT NOT HOPELESS*' announced the print beneath. '*His wordly goods in a sack, his tired legs fading beneath him, an old fellow and his only friend find refuge at last.*' Bastards. Was it, he wondered, possible to sue? But then, of course, he'd have to show the photograph as evidence in court. And it could have been worse, he realized suddenly, with a chill of horror. Just imagine if the caption-writer had actually recognized him . . .

⋆

When, late on the Saturday afternoon, Mr Baker's secretary shouted 'wriiii*tah*!' up the stairs, it was Catrin who answered, since she was the only person of that description still left in the office. Parfitt had gone home not long after waking from his post-luncheon nap, and Buckley had stayed for an hour or so after that, grimly re-reading his first draft treatment of the ARP film and then throwing down the sheaf of paper with an expression of disgust. The pages had slid off the edge of the desk and fanned elegantly across the floor.

'Don't bother,' he'd muttered, as Catrin had bent to pick them up, 'they're not worth it.' He had jammed on his hat, re-lit a cigarette stub that he'd extinguished only two minutes before, half-nodded to her, and then stumped along the landing and down the stairs, a thread of smoke trailing behind him. Catrin had gathered up the pages and straightened the edges and stacked them on his desk again. Then, after a moment's hesitation, she had read the whole thing, and it was Buckley's usual prose, clear and purposeful, but somehow missing its characteristic zest – steak without salt, she thought, chips without vinegar: a story that failed to stick in the mind, and characters who didn't seem to matter, a lustreless treatment from a master of polish. She had sat for a while, a little shaken, drumming her fingers softly on the desk top. *It's because of me*, she'd thought, and the idea was preposterous, unprecedented – imagine Ellis spoiling a single brush-stroke or smudging a line on her account! And she'd nibbled on the thought, and revolved the image of Buckley in her mind, studying him from every viewpoint, wondering if there was an angle from which he might ever make her heart beat faster . . .

And then came the shout of 'wriiii*tah*!', on a rising note, as if a skivvy were being summoned, and Catrin hurried down the stairs to take a phone call from studio.

'You'll never guess . . .' said Phyl, archly.

'A rewrite?'

'More of a tweak, actually. Scene 303.'

'With the dive-bomber? But I thought that was supposed to be all finished this afternoon.'

'All finished bar a couple of crane shots tomorrow morning, to which the director's just come up with the tip-top idea of adding artillery.'

'What?'

'As a matter of fact, he's already drafted the new line himself. Do you have a pen? It's the Scotch soldier's speech – the one who stands and shouts at the plane, only now he's not only going to shout, he's going to fire a rifle as well. And according to the director, he's going to be saying: "*Here's a Glasgae bullet for ye, ye Nazi bastard. And here's anither. Tell them in aul' Jairmany we'll no give in to ye, ye squeer-heeded bawbag.*" '

'What's a bawbag?'

'Dialect, apparently – our director made a documentary about Glaswegian welders the year before last, so he's rather the expert. What do you think of the line?'

'Flabby.'

'Yes, well I've heard that the Board of Censors only allows through one "bastard" a year and that's already been used up, so you have a perfect excuse for rewriting the rewrite, so to speak. Are you coming to the studio tomorrow?'

'I think so. As it's the last day. I'll promise to bite my tongue and stand in the shadows.'

Phyl laughed. 'Quite right, too. Could you be here by eight, then, with the new line? Unless Buckley says he's happy with the *aul* one, of course.'

Unlikely, thought Catrin. Back at her desk, she leafed through the script, and found the original wording: '*Missed us all, ye boss-eyed Nazi.*' The easiest thing would be to cut '*Missed us all*,' and substitute '*Take that!*', but it was a Buckley maxim that no one outside the writing profession understood that even tiny, subtle re-wordings required considerable skill, so it was therefore vital to make any changes look flamingly obvious otherwise no one would ever give you any credit for having done them. On the other hand, he also stated that in the event of a director coming up with a line, it was always best to try and save some of it, however dreadful, 'because then the cloth-eared twerp will think it's the one that he wrote, and he'll probably use it'.

She stared at her notebook. 'Bloody hell, Buckley,' she said, out loud, and she was suddenly desperate to speak to him, to hear that rasp of a voice from the corner, badgering, hectoring, prying, making her laugh, infuriating her, offering advice that was occasionally helpful and frequently impossible – her waspish mentor, her daily companion, sorely missed.

There were footsteps on the stairs and she turned quickly but it was only Shipton, the accountant, carrying a bucket of sand and wearing a tin hat. 'Still here?' he asked.

'Yes, for a bit longer.'

'Well just to warn you,' he said. 'It's going to be a full moon tonight. There's sure to be trouble,' and he unhooked the ladder that led to the roof, and climbed up. She could hear him shuffling round on the leads, preparing for his stint as fire-watcher.

She wrote, '*Missed us, ye boss-eyed bawbag, now here's one from the folks in Glasgae,*' and then, on a separate piece of paper, she wrote, '*I don't in the least think that you're an old fool. Quite the reverse, in fact.*' Though what was the reverse of an old fool? You could guarantee that Buckley would want to know . . .

She tried again. '*Truly, I don't in the least think that you're an old fool.*'

Wordy.

'*I don't think you're an old fool.*'

Bald.

'*You're no fool, old or otherwise.*'

And now it sounded like a line from *Duck Soup*. Unbidden, another Buckley aphorism swam to mind. 'For God's sake, don't keep hammering away at the same sentence, like a bloody woodpecker. Write the whole damn scene and then go back over it with a pencil.' The whole damn scene; she took the cover off Buckley's Remington, and wound a sheet of paper in place, and started to type.

INT. PUBLIC HOUSE CELLAR . EVENING

Distant gunfire is audible, but is being ignored by the drinkers. Most of them are male, but at a table in one corner sits a young woman. She is holding a half-empty glass of beer. The rest of the contents are dripping from the hair and clothes of the man sitting opposite her. He wipes his moustache.

MAN

You think I'm a old fool.

WOMAN

No I don't. Not in the least. It's just that it was so . . . unexpected. I didn't realize until too late that you were serious.

MAN

I should have given more warning?

WOMAN

It might have helped.

MAN

Rung a bell, maybe?

WOMAN

Perhaps a—

MAN

Klaxon? Gong? Foghorn?

WOMAN

Hint, I was thinking. You could have given me a hint.

MAN

Oh, a hint – you mean six oysters, a candle in a bottle and a gypsy violinist sawing away at 'Last Rose of Sorrento'. And if you'd had all that, then what would you have done?

WOMAN

I don't know. But I wouldn't have smacked you in the chest and said 'Let's forget it ever happened.'

MAN

Wouldn't you indeed? (A beat.) Want another drink?

WOMAN

No thanks. You can have the rest of mine if you'd like. And I just wanted to say . . . (She hesitates.)

MAN

Yes?

WOMAN

I just wanted to say that I . . . (She hesitates again.)

MAN

Hear that noise? It's your audience getting restive. They're wishing they'd gone to see that cowboy picture instead.

WOMAN

I just wanted to say that if we ever stopped having these conversations I'd miss them so dreadfully. I'd miss talking to you — I'd miss it more than I can possibly say.

MAN

Is that a fact? (He takes a long and thoughtful pull at his beer, and then looks at the glass.) You know, they've got a bloody nerve charging for this. I've seen stronger eyewash.

'If you're staying can you do your blackouts?' called Shipton, from the roof-hatch, and Catrin realized that the dusk was creeping in, and she was sitting with her nose six inches from the paper, and she rose – a little stiff – and went over to the window. The sky was a deep violet, and cloudless. She drew the blinds, and pulled the heavy curtains across, and switched on the light and looked again at what she'd written. She took a pencil and altered a word or two, and then rubbed out the alterations and left the pages on Buckley's desk, together with the Scotchman's new line. The siren sounded before she had even reached Oxford Street.

Edith was rubbing almond oil into her cuticles, and thinking about how bony the backs of her hands were looking. The skin was white and smooth, but the sinews protruded like the ribs of an umbrella – old hands; they seemed to have aged overnight when she wasn't looking. And she had found a white hair in her comb the other week. So that was the pattern from now on, she supposed: one white hair after another and then the slow creep of liver spots across her knuckles. She replaced the stopper on the bottle of oil, and reached for her cold cream. From somewhere outside she could hear the odd pop of distant shell-fire – not near enough, yet, to worry about. Inside the house, Arthur had been busy in his hobbies room for most of the evening; she'd heard the tap of a hammer and there was a strong smell of varnish permeating the upper floor. She had called to ask what he was making, but his reply had been rather vague.

She applied a dab of TCP to a pimple on her forehead, tucked her hair into a stockinette cap, put on her night-gloves, and was just about to switch off the light when there was a tentative knock on the door.

'Edith, dear . . .'

'Yes?'

'You're not asleep?'

'I was just about to go to bed.'

'Oh, were you?'

'Is anything the matter?'

'No, no. I just wondered if I could come in to see you.'

'Oh.' She looked at herself in the mirror, her head resembling a boiled egg in a cosy, her face as shiny as a plate, every inch of her body covered with sensible, hard-wearing fabrics, and she thought of the nights that she'd put on lipstick and brushed her hair and smelled of French Lilac as opposed to antiseptic. 'Yes, if you want,' she said, reluctantly.

Arthur poked his head around the door. 'You don't mind?'

'Mind what?'

'Being disturbed?'

'No, of course not.' There was no hint from his expression that she was looking in any way different from usual, a fact that she found exasperating. He was fully dressed and had a smear of varnish across his nose; this did not appear to be the long-awaited conjugal visit.

'I've got a present for you,' he said.

'A present?'

'A surprise. I've been working on it for quite a few weeks. Would you like to see it?'

'All right,' she said, ungraciously.

He opened the door more widely and disappeared back into the hall for a moment before re-entering the room with an object in his arms. It was a plywood box, about a foot and a half tall and a foot wide, with a solid top, and a shallow arch cut into the bottom of each of the four sides.

'What is it?' she asked.

'I'll show you.' He placed it on the floor and plugged it in and turned off the bedroom light. In the sudden darkness, the guns seemed louder, and then there was the snap of a switch, and a dim blue light appeared around the base of the object, illuminating a yard or so of floorboard on each side.

'It's a safety-lamp,' said Arthur. 'You can leave it plugged in in the downstairs hall, you see, and then if you get back after dark when I'm not here, you'll have a source of light even before you put up the blackouts.'

But I carry a *torch*, she thought, and was seized by the urge to laugh hysterically, for it appeared that while she'd been waiting (evening after evening) for her husband to come and make love to her, he had been engaged in the manufacture of something that looked like a sentry-box designed for a gnome, and then she felt her throat contract and found that she wasn't laughing at all.

'Edith?' said Arthur. 'Whatever's the matter?'

She took off her night-gloves and wiped her eyes. 'Nothing,' she said and sat down on the bed because she was suddenly crying so hard that she could hardly breathe. The main light went on again and there was Arthur, his kind, round face lengthened by worry, and she wanted to strike him for failing to understand, for thinking that she might want a fretwork lamp instead of a husband.

'Can I get you a hot-water-bottle?' he asked. 'A cold compress? A . . . a . . . a cup of cocoa?'

She could only shake her head.

'A glass of water?' He reached for the tumbler on her bedside table, and as he did so it seemed to shiver away from his grasp, and the curtains bulged inward and barked glass across the floor, and it was only then that they heard the tremendous smash of the bomb that seemed loud enough to have landed on their doorstep and yet which must have been a good quarter-mile away, since only the windows had gone, and the whole sky was full of engine noises, and Arthur shouted 'downstairs' and made a grab at her arm. He turned off the bedroom light as they left the room, and Edith glanced back and saw the blue glow of the gnome's watchtower, and beyond it the gaping hole of the window and the moon like a dish of milk above the rooftops.

As Catrin hurried up the steps from the tube, three fire-engines tore past, one after another, and the AA guns were hammering full pelt, and she hesitated and almost turned back, except that she hated being underground during a raid. If she couldn't hear any noise at all then she was always half-afraid that when she re-emerged there would be nothing left – a smouldering plain. Instead, she ran for the sandbagged entrance of the Odeon, and handed over one and ninepence without even asking for the name of the main feature, and was ushered to a place in the packed stalls between a girl who was knitting and a sailor who squeezed her thigh as soon as she sat down, apparently by way of greeting. He said, 'Oh, don't be like that' when Catrin shoved his hand away, and then he offered her a cigarette, and she took it and looked up at the screen and saw James Stewart stepping out of a stagecoach holding a canary cage in one hand and a parasol in the other. There was a shout of laughter from the audience, and the girl who was knitting said, 'Oh I *love* him, honestly I do', and then turned and kissed her boyfriend, as if to assure him of her fidelity.

'What's the picture called?' whispered Catrin to the sailor.

'It's called "Are you doing anything afterwards, darling?" '

'It's called *Destry Rides Again*,' supplied someone behind her, and Catrin swivelled to mutter her thanks and realized that people were still drifting into the auditorium, filling every seat – standing, even, at the back – and that each time the heavy doors were pushed open, they admitted a burst of noise from the streets. Something colossal was happening out there, a night to rival the worst of nights, and she kept staring at the doors, unable to break her gaze until a roar from the screen pulled her round again, a roar that was taken up by the audience and spiced with wolf-whistles as Marlene Dietrich rolled across the floor of a saloon engaged in a cat-fight of fantastic length and vigour.

'Oh, that's the biz,' said Catrin's neighbour, slapping his own leg this time. '*That's* the biz, that is,' and someone shouted, 'It's Gert and Daisy!' and the new Sheriff of Tombstone, mild but determined, waded through the chaos and tipped a bucket of water over the brawling women, and the fight was over, and a voice from the balcony called 'Shame!' And the audience erupted again, and Catrin felt herself being pulled along by the crowd, caught up in a vast and vocal caravan determinedly heading Westward for the evening, and for an hour or two there was enough applause, there were enough celluloid gunshots and gusts of laughter and galloping music, enough songs and fist-fights, enough glamour and wit and plot and spectacle to blot out the real barrage, and for a short while, the theatre seemed safer than any shelter, and the noise inside was like a shield, keeping the night at bay.

'Oh, for Christ's *sake*,' said Ambrose. He upended the carpet bag over the kitchen table and picked through the repulsive contents – a tangle of doggie necessities all coated in a slippery mixture of hair and flea powder – but there were no loose pills sifting between the litter, and no spare bottle of Bob Martin's Tablets for Canine Fits and Hysteria, and since there was nothing remaining in the first bottle but a plug of cotton wool, it signalled an absolute bloody disaster, as the only way of getting Cerberus through a raid was to administer two tablets hidden in a piece of sausage, and thus render him unconscious until the following morning. Without this medicinal cosh he was an utter liability, squeezing into one hiding place after another and disgracing himself on the lino.

Ambrose scraped the rubbish back into the bag, and as he did so, there was another rattle from the skies, like the lowering of a vast Venetian blind, and then a trio of crumps, not all that far away. The few remaining glasses in the cupboard tinkled in unison.

'Cerberus?' called Ambrose. For a moment he could hear the clatter of toenails on the stairs before they were drowned by another burst of shell-fire and another stick of bombs, the last of them so appallingly near that the whole house seemed to give a little jump. The kitchen door swung open of its own accord, and when Ambrose pushed it closed, it thudded against the jamb instead of latching, and when he tried the door of the larder, it took a considerable tug to open it at all, which meant (almost certainly) that every single frame in the house had sprung – again – and probably half the roof slates were gone as well, and oh! he was sick of it, the loathsome repetition of it all, and thank God he had had the foresight to agree to Lundback's request for tutelage, since it was only the ruby presence of the bottle of port under the sink and the topaz glint of its peaty neighbour that lightened the current darkness. Gratitude could be a truly marvellous thing.

He poured himself a generous whisky, and drank it rather quickly. The kitchen floor was shaking beneath his feet. He had never heard a night like it, one explosion after another, as if Goering had built a platform above the city and was simply rolling the canisters over the edge, bang, bang, bloody bang.

He poured another measure, and this time tried to savour it, but there was a noise that kept catching his attention, one noise in a night full of noises, a strange, high warbling on a note quite different to the usual falling whistle of the bombs. He went out into the hall and cocked an ear and realized that it was coming from inside the house, and it was a horrid sound, a ragged shriek. And, oh hell, it had to be Cerberus, Cerberus flattened by a toppled tallboy or Cerberus eviscerated by a shard of glass, and though both of those images passed through his mind as he hurried up the stairs, they were superceded by a vision yet more horrific, that of Sophie receiving the news.

The noise was coming from the box-room. The door was slightly ajar but Ambrose had to give it a violent shove to gain entry, carving a furrow across the floorboards. He hardly ever used the room – had never bothered to put up blackouts – and the first thing he saw was a glassless window full of light: search beams interlacing, and the wink of shells, and in the middle distance, the leisurely fall of a flare, its phosphorous cluster turning darkness into brilliant noon, so that Cerberus, standing below the window with his head tipped back and that unearthly yodel issuing from his mouth, cast a stilt-legged shadow as long as the room.

Back in the kitchen, Ambrose examined the dog from nose to tail, wetting a finger to lift away fragments of glass that glinted in the brindled coat, but finding no trace of blood and no obvious injury. The howling had stopped, but Cerberus's body was vibrating like an idling engine. He was panting, open-mouthed, and shifting from foot to foot as if standing on a heated surface, and although his gaze moved restlessly, nothing seemed to catch his eye (or nose) – not a piece of bacon, nor even a square of chocolate – and when Ambrose rubbed a little whisky on to the piebald gums it might have been water for all the response it produced, and it was strange, it was very strange, to see an animal in such a state, for God knows one had seen men like this, standing blank and shivering on the Salient.

Fear; it had been fear, of course – or, rather, a stage beyond fear, an involuntary shift to a place in which the blast of a whistle, or an officer's shout, or even a pointed revolver were meaningless; it was as if the mind itself had gone into hiding. There'd been nothing at all that one could do for such men apart from getting them away from the front line. The lucky ones had been labelled shell-shocked. The others . . .

Ambrose peered into the dog's bulging eyes. 'Good chap,' he said, experimentally. '*Tayer hintele*.'

Jerry was still hurling it down outside, no end to it, and the quietest possible place seemed to be the cupboard under the stairs, and Ambrose cleared a space, and wrapped the dog in a coat and tucked him between his knees, and sat on the floor in the utter blackness with a cigarette in one hand and the bottle of whisky in the other. It was, indeed, a little quieter in here, but the extra layers of wood and plaster had the odd effect of filtering out certain notes, and heightening others, so that for the first time that evening he could hear the machine-guns of the night-fighters as they chased a thousand feet above his head. Lundback would be up there again next week, hurtling through darkness, defending Finland against the Russians. Ambrose raised the bottle to him, and then took another nip.

Time passed. For a while there was a lull, and Cerberus seemed to settle down, but then the ack-ack started up again, and so did the canine quivering, and what was really needed in these circumstances, thought Ambrose, was a gramophone. There had always been music playing in the dugouts – Gilbert and Sullivan and Nellie Melba and the dripping notes of the Gymnopédies, and comic songs, *always* comic songs, raucous and invigorating, a coarse bellow of defiance. Ambrose cleared his throat and tried to remember the words of 'The Spaniard That Blighted My Life', and failed to get beyond line three, but the effect on the dog was immediate – a cessation of the shaking, an interested shift in position, a hot dry nose shoved into the palm of his hand.

'Oh, you like that, do you?' asked Ambrose.

He had another bash at 'The Spaniard That Blighted My Life', more successfully this time, and followed it with 'The Galloping Major', 'Oh! Oh! Antonio' and 'Stop Yer Tickling, Jock!' before shifting the mood with a reproachful chorus of 'I Was a Good Little Girl Till I Met You'. By this time, Cerberus was resting his chin on Ambrose's chest, and had accepted, with some light lip-smacking, a second application of whisky to the gums.

'You'll appreciate this one,' said Ambrose. 'It has canine interest, one might say. You'll know Keating's, of course, the flea powder?'

There was a response, of sorts, a slight snuffle.

'What I'm about to sing was known as the Keating's song. For reasons that shall become obvious. You know, we used tins of the stuff at the Front. "Dear Ma, please send chocolate, Punch and Keating's." Just a moment.' Ambrose wet his own lips from the dregs of the bottle. 'It's to the tune of "Let Us with a Gladsome Mind",' he added. 'Altogether, now –

Keating's powder does the trick,
Kills all Bugs and Fleas off quick;
Keating he's a jolly brick,
Bravo! long live Keating!

Keating he's the man who knows
How to bring us sweet repose
When in sleep our eyelids close!
Stop the Fleas from biting!

So if you would soundly sleep,
Keating's Powder always keep;
Peace and comfort you will reap!
Is not that inviting?

If all folks would use the same
See each tin bears 'Keating's' name

Fleas would stop their little game
And their midnight meeting.

Ambrose repeated the last line, drawing out the final note plangently. There was a moment of silence and then a long, moist snore from Cerberus.

'Tins of the stuff,' said Ambrose. 'Simply tins of it.'

Arthur could hear Edith, but not see her. She seemed to have stopped crying, but there was an occasional catch in the rhythm of her breathing. The Morrison shelter was nearly five feet wide and she was lying quite a long way away from him. If he wanted to place a comforting hand on her shoulder, there was a sort of no-man's land to negotiate first, a commando crawl across the bedclothes that seemed rather more dramatic a preamble than the subsequent gesture would warrant. Instead, he stretched out an arm towards her and found that he could just about touch her elbow with his fingertips. He wriggled them slightly, in what he hoped was a sympathetic fashion, and in response, Edith moved her own arm out of reach.

He wished he could think of something to say. Outside, it had gone rather quiet, though the all-clear had not yet sounded. He could remark on that, perhaps. Or he might talk about the windows, venturing the sort of comment that the chaps at the studio made: 'Stinking bloody windows have gone again'. He mouthed the words, and knew that he'd sound foolish speaking them aloud; that sort of square-jawed utterance had never fitted well into his own mouth. So he stayed silent, three and a half feet from his wife, and he thought of Norfolk and of the conversational back-and-forth that they'd achieved so quickly, and which almost as rapidly had gone again, and he felt as if he'd been given a present and had inadvertently, clumsily, broken it.

Edith heard him take off his spectacles and start to polish them. 'I can't think why you're doing that,' she said, sharply. 'It's pitch dark. How on earth are you going to tell if they're clean?' and she could hear a nasty needling tone to her voice, and she had never felt like this before, had never possessed the desire to deliberately goad someone, and there was a horrid sort of satisfaction to it. She could hear Arthur breathing cautiously.

'You clean them at least forty times every day,' she said.

There was the tiny sound of Arthur's lips meeting and then parting, once and then twice, as he shaped an answer.

'I suppose it's just a habit,' he said. 'But they do get smudged.'

'They only get smudged because you keep fiddling with them. You're always adjusting them and putting them on and off and wiggling the arms – it's completely pointless, you do it all the time, and that's why the lenses are always covered in fingermarks.'

There was a pause. 'Oh,' said Arthur, and his tone was that of someone receiving an interesting and welcome piece of news. 'I had no idea. I shall certainly try and stop it, in that case,' and Edith felt a rush of shame, for how could she choose to hurt someone who took nastiness and converted it into useful and beneficial information? Spite required a victim, and he was not one of those; he would never fight back, but neither would he crumble. She could say anything. She could say anything at all to him.

'The all-clear's not sounded yet,' said Arthur.

Edith shifted on to her side, so that she was facing towards her husband.

'Windows have gone again,' he added. 'Lousy things. Lousy blooming things.'

'Arthur . . .' said Edith.

'Yes?' He sounded eager, delighted to be addressed.

'I would like to discuss why we haven't yet shared a bedroom.'

In the tremendous pause that followed, she could hear the guns on the common starting up again.

'Yes . . .' said Arthur, at last. The word was almost a sigh.

Edith waited a moment longer, hoping that he would say more, but it was clear that, having launched the topic with a statement whose frankness had stunned even herself, she was obliged to continue.

'I didn't ever imagine that you'd be the type of man who . . . who had . . . had sexual intercourse with a great many women. So if you're not, then it doesn't matter in the least bit. You needn't think that I mind. Because I haven't, either. With men. Or a man. At all, I mean. So it's not that I have any . . . any . . .'

She was becoming aware of a series of furtive sounds coming from Arthur's side of the shelter; he was cleaning his spectacles again, she realized, and she reached across and carefully took them from his hands.

'Sorry,' said Arthur. 'Perhaps – I was thinking – perhaps I should take up cigarette smoking instead.'

'So what I was saying,' continued Edith, determinedly, holding the spectacles to her chest as if they were a talisman that might help her to get through this ghastly conversation, 'is that we shouldn't worry about not being as experienced in these matters as—'

She stopped. Her ears were popping. There was an odd, abrupt shift in the air, a mute percussion, and then the most extraordinary noise: a slithering and cracking as if an enormous pile of plates were gently toppling over in the room above.

'What's . . . ?'

And then a gentle, insidious rustling and a series of innocuous thuds, like apples dropping on to grass, and then a whole avalanche of apples, and the squeal and rip of timber and the thunderous slide of masonry as the house, with dreadful slowness, settled on top of them.

Coughing, she couldn't stop coughing, her throat was lined with stinging grit. Her nostrils too, and her eyes were full of it, and she could hear Arthur just beside her, coughing too, and they coughed and retched together and wiped their eyes with filthy fingers, and banged their heads on the buckled ceiling of the Morrison, and tried to catch their breaths in an atmosphere that seemed more dust than air. And when, after minutes, or possibly hours, Edith managed to open her eyes, she could still see nothing at all. She stretched out a hand, and touched a broken lath, sharp as a skewer, that was poking in through the wire-mesh of the side-wall, and she pushed her fingers between the wires and felt a jumble of plaster shards.

'I didn't hear it,' she said, hoarsely, 'I didn't hear the bomb,' and Arthur coughed halfway through his answer so that she only heard the words 'directly overhead' and 'sound-waves', and it didn't matter anyway, because here they were, sealed into the remains of 12, Cressy Avenue, like King Tut into his tomb, and she could feel panic creeping under the skin of her forehead and encircling her neck, and then Arthur said, 'They're certainly awfully well-made, these shelters,' in the tone of a house-agent talking to a client, and the panic ebbed very slightly.

'But how will we ever get out?'

'Oh, I'm sure that the rescue services will be on to us.'

'But what if we run out of air?'

'It's actually quite difficult to make an air-tight seal, even if that's what you're trying to do. You'll find that there are always little gaps and—'

'And what if there's a fire? That's what Dolly warned us about.'

'This wasn't an oil-bomb, though, it was a high-explosive, so we should be—'

'Did you turn off the gas?'

'Yes.'

'Are you sure?'

'Yes, definitely.' The final word turned into a series of rusty coughs, and then into some painful heaving, and Edith tried to pat him on the shoulder and instead whacked him on the nose, and by the time that it had stopped bleeding (Arthur used her stockinette cap, turned inside-out, to staunch it), she was feeling a tiny bit more like her usual self.

'I wonder when they'll start digging for us . . .' she said. There was absolute silence without their metal cage. 'All of our things gone. My clothes. Your mother's pearls.'

'Your pearls,' corrected Arthur.

'My pearls. Your *house*.'

'Our house. Doesn't batter,' he said, dabbing at his nose again, 'still alibe. Thad's the main thig.'

'But this is my third bomb. *Third*. They're never supposed to fall in the same place twice. Perhaps it's the person and not the place, perhaps it's – I can smell something,' she added.

'Gas?'

'No, not gas.' It was a rich smell, not unpleasant, and it was beginning to edge aside the vinegar reek of the explosive. 'Pipe tobacco,' she said, in disbelief. 'It *is*. Can you smell it?'

Slowly, Arthur took the balled-up cloth from his nose. 'Yes,' he said, his mouth barely moving.

'It is, isn't it?' said Edith.

'Yes.' Wills's Pirate Flake – red and yellow packets with a picture of a villanous-looking buccaneer on the front.

'Is it a rescuer?' asked Edith, hopefully.

'No.'

'Then who is it?'

'My father,' said Arthur. And yet when the old man had died he had scrubbed and scrubbed the walls and ceiling to rid them of their sticky amber coating, and had painted them with two coats of white and then two of pale blue emulsion; he had made the room fresh and clean again, and yet . . . 'It must have been in the plaster,' he said. 'All the smoke from his pipe. Years of it.'

'You hadn't told me that he smoked a pipe.'

Arthur moved to adjust his spectacles and found that they weren't there. The smell of tobacco was very strong, and in the utter darkness it was easy to think that his eyes were shut, and that when he opened them, the sick-room would be there again, the bed occupied, a tray to be collected, a basin emptied, the curtains opened, the curtains closed, a broken cup picked up, sheets changed, floor mopped, tea wiped from the wall . . .

'You could tell me, you know,' said Edith, quietly.

'Oh, well, there isn't . . .'

The silence was complete; the compacted layers of his house were shutting out the night, and he and Edith might be the only people left in London.

'He had awful pain,' said Arthur.

The German shell had fallen into the dugout and burst directly in front of his father, and had shattered his pelvis, and filled his bowels with shrapnel, and so it was not like the bandaged heroes in the newspapers, nor like the boy at school whose father had lost an arm. It was a dismal, whispered, never-healing injury, with consequences that were daily and excruciating, and which only worsened over time.

'He hated being crippled,' said Arthur. 'He was often angry.'

And that, already, was more than he had ever told anyone.

'In the end he wouldn't have a nurse. A professional nurse, I mean.'

His father's voice a gurgling roar: *Get that fucking bitch out of the fucking house, the fucking little whore is laughing at me, damn her fucking blue eyes.*

'So I nursed him,' said Arthur.

And behind the tobacco smoke was the whiff of feculance and of soaked sheets, and the whole of it was the smell of his father's utter humiliation. And once in a hundred days he would thank Arthur, and weep with remorse, and on the other ninety-nine he would curse him to bloody hell.

'I should think you were a very good nurse,' said Edith. 'I should think—'

'A pansy,' said Arthur, the words bursting out of his mouth, 'he said I must be a pansy, because only pansies are cooks and nurses, he said that I shouldn't bother looking for a wife because what I needed was a husband.' And his father had said other things far worse than that, far, far worse than that, and confession was not the relief it was supposed to be, it was like releasing a cloud of hornets, and Arthur felt stung all over, and heavy-eyed and dreadfully sorry, suddenly, for Edith – smart and wonderfully clever Edith – who had agreed to marry him and who had received nothing in return except a house that was no longer a house, and who surely could have found somebody better, could have found fifty better men who would have married her in a moment, and he reached out a hand and met Edith's hand, reaching for his, exactly matching, palm to palm, their fingers dovetailing like a well-made joint.

'You're a good man,' said Edith.

He drew her hand towards his face. 'Almonds,' he said, wonderingly, 'you smell of almonds, Edie,' and one by one he kissed her nails.

*

There was a red-eyed jittery brightness about the film-crew; no one had had more than an hour or two's sleep, and no one could quite believe that they had arrived at the morning intact, and in the queue for the tea-trolley there was a thread of competing stories, both thrilling and bathetic, of thousand-pounders and parachute bombs, of fires raging unchecked, of a flustered hen spotted in Leicester Square, of ceilings gone, of a privy blown across the garden, of the smoking tail of a Heinkel seen from the bus window.

'And that's the last of the milk,' said the tea-lady, triumphantly, just as Catrin came to the head of the queue. 'The milkman said a great lump of a building came straight down on the float just as he was passing the Palais, and do you know what the strangest thing of all was?'

'No,' said Catrin.

'Fifteen bottles *didn't* get smashed. He said every cat in West London was there in seconds. Next!'

And two of the extras had yet to arrive, and one of the

chippies, and the props master who lived in Bethnal Green, and the newly-weds Arthur and Edith, who were never, ever late, and the make-up artist who had already been bombed-out twice. And Catrin, her head ringing from the bitter kick of the tea, picked her way between the doom-laden whispers, and found a corner of Sound Stage 2 to stand in, just beside the screen of the painted sky, and reminded herself that since Buckley never came to the studio unless actually summoned, his absence was entirely to be expected, and not in any way worrying.

All around her, preparations for the day's shoot were inching towards what passed for a state of readiness. The sparks had slotted the stem of an enormous light into a socket at the top of the scaffolding tower, and the camera had been mounted on what looked like a giant Meccano see-saw, so that it could be raised, together with its operators, to a position high above the water-tank. Extras were lethargically arranging themselves on the deck of the *Redoubtable*, a kilted actor was miming firing a rifle up at the gantry, and Ambrose Hilliard, who had been standing with his eyes closed while a make-up assistant dusted his face with powder, made a sudden break for the back of the studio, and retched unproductively into an ash-bin behind the painted screen. He straightened up and noticed Catrin looking at him. It took him a moment to place her.

'Can I get you a glass of water?' she asked.

Welsh, a Welsh female writer; well thank God that no one of any importance had witnessed his shame. 'I think not,' he said, with dignity, and managed a steady walk back to the make-up girl, but – oh Christ! – he felt terrible, terrible, his head a snare-drum full of gravel, his stomach a crumpled wash-bag. He wanted to lie prone upon the nearest flat surface; no, he wanted *oblivion*.

'Oh, love him,' said the make-up girl as Cerberus skidded across the floor and plastered himself to Ambrose's legs. 'Have oo been getting oo's face painted? Look at him looking at you,

Mr Hilliard! Doesn't he look just like that dog in the gramophone advertisement?'

Ambrose risked a glance downward; the dog was staring at him with the same expression of melting devotion that he'd maintained since first light this morning.

'No food,' said Ambrose, patting his pockets feebly. 'No food in here,' but Cerberus continued to gaze up at him, dribbling slightly.

'You're awfully pale, Mr Hilliard,' said the assistant. 'Let me just get some Number 3 to pick you up a bit.'

And then came a whistle blast, and Kipper's voice like the clang of an iron triangle, and Ambrose found himself on board the *Redoubtable*, taking an upward eyeline in the direction of the brightest light in the history of kinematography, and he might as well have rammed a brace of pencils into his eyeballs, it couldn't have been any more agonizing, and he ventured a suggestion – 'Wouldn't Uncle Frank be more concerned with looking down at the engine at this point?' – which was, of course, ignored, so that by the time a satisfactory take had been secured he was as good as blind, and stumbled twice over Cerberus as they made their way back down to the floor, occasioning several jocular remarks about guide dogs from the extras – and at what point, incidentally, had extras decided that it was in any way appropriate for them to converse with the actors in the cast? In the old days they'd stood aside in a quiet and respectful way. In the old days they'd had to bring their own sandwiches and wait in the back lot during scenes in which they weren't involved, even if it were raining, even if it were blowing a bloody sideways blizzard, and quite bloody right too.

'Top shot of the dog barking at the Stuka,' shouted Kipper – everyone was *shouting* today – 'Just the dog in frame. Mr Hilliard, could we have your help, please?' and back Ambrose had to go again, up the steps, across the little gang-plank to the deck of the *Redoubtable* and into the cruel yellow light.

'The director's shooting down at the cabin roof, and he'd like the dog to bark at a point just to the left of camera,' said Kipper, gesturing upward. 'And we need to take sound on this, of course, so could you use a sign rather than a command?'

'A sign?'

'Yes.'

'What sort of sign would you suggest? The word "woof" written on a piece of card?'

Kipper frowned. 'Well I thought, perhaps . . .'

'Cerberus can sit, he can lie down, and with sufficient bribery he can beg, but those are the limits of his thespian ability.'

Kipper nodded unhappily. 'Just a moment,' he said, and went off to talk to the director again, and Ambrose leaned against the rail and looked down at the water. Loathsome to think that this afternoon he would actually be immersed in it. The surface was scummy with dust, and he watched the slow drift of a spent match, until it suddenly seemed to him that the water was standing still and the deck of the *Redoubtable* was moving, and he straightened up hastily and emitted a prolonged whisky-flavoured belch with a strong aftertaste of acid.

Kipper hurried back along the gang-plank. 'The director wants to know if the dog ever barks. Under normal circumstances.'

'He barks at other dogs,' said Ambrose. 'He barks at horses, he barks at cats, he barks at pigeons – is this helpful? Shall I go on?'

'Please,' said Kipper.

'He barks at doorbells, at fire-engines, at passing motor cars, at small children with toy trumpets, at butchers'-shop windows, at any delay between seeing and actually receiving his food, at women in large hats—'

'Just a moment,' said Kipper, disembarking again.

Cerberus, who had been sniffing around the deck, came back and sat heavily on Ambrose's left foot. Ambrose closed his eyes against the light, and for a wondrous fraction of a second he was lying on a terrace in Capri, with the Southern sun stroking his upturned face and his limbs suffused with sleepy warmth, and then Kipper's voice jerked him awake and into the bilious present again.

'The director's had an idea,' said Kipper.

As director's ideas went, Ambrose had to concede, it wasn't a bad one. A makeshift fishing rod was constructed, and one of the props boys took it and climbed halfway up the scaffolding tower and dangled a sausage on a string a yard out of Cerberus's reach, and it really should have worked, it really should have resulted in a prancing, yelping dog who couldn't help but take an upward eyeline just to the left of the camera. But unfortunately Cerberus ignored the bait and looked instead for Ambrose, scanning the studio floor until he spotted him sitting just beside the tea-trolley, and then moving to the very edge of the cabin roof and whining desolately in his direction, the tip of his tail beating the air.

'Cut,' said Kipper, after two useless takes, and went over to talk to the director again and Ambrose looked around to see whether there might be a biscuit within reach, something dry and plain that might help settle his stomach, and instead saw his agent walking towards him. He struggled to his feet.

'Sophie . . .'

'Mr Hilliard.' She offered her hand and then withdrew it almost as soon as his fingers touched hers. 'Did you forget that I was coming?'

'No, not at all.'

'You don't look very well, Mr Hilliard. Rather pale for a fisherman. Green, almost.'

'Lack of sleep. Have you been here long?'

'Five minutes or so. Long enough to observe that Cerberus appears devoted to you.'

'Yes, well . . .'

'My brother would have been delighted. As am I. It's always pleasing for an agent to see a client extend his range,' and she smiled fleetingly, the first time that he had ever seen her do so, and it gave her face a rather chilly beauty.

'Speaking of which . . .' said Ambrose, ignoring the convolutions of the remark. 'You mentioned a role that I've been offered.'

'Yes. Although I think perhaps we should wait until luncheon before we discuss it.'

'But—'

'This is all fascinating to me, this business of filming. What, for instance, is the role of the little man crouching just beneath the camera?'

Was there a little man crouching just beneath the camera? Ambrose glanced over to check. Yes there was. 'Sprocket assistant,' he said, randomly.

'And what does that job entail?'

He was saved from having to invent an answer by the arrival of Kipper.

'I'm sorry to interrupt you, Mr Hilliard, but the director has a request.'

'And what would that be?'

There was a certain reluctance in Kipper's demeanour. 'The director wonders whether you might help with the dog's eyeline . . . if you could perhaps climb a few feet up the tower. Just a few feet, hardly more than halfway. It would be the most tremendous favour and the director would be most terribly grateful . . .'

And as Ambrose was drawing breath for a firm but fair refusal, encompassing a reference to his contract, his dignity and the sinews of his lower back, Sophie spoke.

'We have not yet met,' she said to Kipper, inclining her head graciously, 'but I am Mr Hilliard's agent. Assuming that my client's safety will be of primary consideration, I can see no particular problem. Mr Hilliard may be playing an older character-part, but he would prefer to be viewed generally as a *leading* actor, fully able to cope with the demands of a more active role.'

And thus did he find himself standing nearly six yards above the studio floor ('Just a little bit further, Mr Hilliard, the eye-line's not quite there yet') with his arm muscles still trembling from the climb, and the props boy holding on to his belt, and below him the smirking faces of the crew – oh how they were enjoying this, damn them – and beneath him the edge of the tank, and the cabin roof. And there was Cerberus, gazing straight at him, his tail wagging so vigorously that his whole body was in motion, his paws treadling the roof in a dance of joy.

'Final checks, please,' called Kipper. 'Going for a take. Mr Hilliard, could you hold out your sausage, please?'

And of course there was a neigh of laughter from the rabble on the floor, and Kipper called for quiet, and on the word 'action' Ambrose extended the pathetic little rod and lowered the sausage towards Cerberus, and Cerberus leapt and woofed quite gratifyingly, and Kipper called 'Cut' and then 'Print'. There was a scattering of applause, followed by a shout of 'Three cheers for Mr 'illiard's nice little saveloy' and much filthy sniggering.

'Moving on,' called Kipper, 'Scene 303, crane shot, Scotchman firing at Stuka, could we have extras and Scotchman on board? Mr Best, I think you may also be in shot.'

Up in the tower, Ambrose shut his eyes and rested his forehead against one of the cool metal bars. 'A moment,' he said to the props boy who was still clutching his belt, 'just give me a moment.' Though he suspected he'd need a couple of lifetimes before he could forget the humiliation of the last ten minutes. *Nice little saveloy!* He opened his eyes again and saw a Scotchman pointing a gun at him.

'It's all right, Mr 'illiard,' said the man cheerfully. 'I'm just having a tiny wee practice, and in any case, they're only bl—'

The gun went off with a deafening bang and Ambrose started violently, and one of his feet slipped off the edge, and he lurched forward, and the props boy who was holding on to him lurched forward, and the tower, oh my God, the whole tower began to teeter and in that fraction of a second Ambrose could see the whole sequence, the slow obliquity and then the accelerating descent that would send him plunging on to the cabin roof of the *Redoubtable* with Cerberus beneath him and the whole weight of the tower above. '*Studio mourns death of performing dog. Actor dies too.*' And then there was a clang, and the tower stayed at a very slight angle for a second or two before righting itself with a judder.

'Lucky,' said the props boy, cheerfully. 'That big old lamp at the top caught on the gantry, dinnit? You all right there, Mr 'illiard?' Ambrose realized that he was clinging on to one of the uprights like a monkey on a stick, and it was yet another moment of indignity to add to today's list, and he was bone-tired, he was sick of the whole damn business, and he wanted someone to sit him down and bring him a cushion and a brandy and a nice slice of cake, and to shoo away the rotten old world for a while. Bastards, the lot of them.

It was halfway through the afternoon when Catrin spotted Buckley. He was standing on the other side of the studio holding a rock-cake in one hand and a cigarette in the other, and he caught her eye and raised the rock-cake in casual greeting, and then started to walk around the perimeter towards her. She felt stupidly nervous.

'How long have you been here?' she asked.

'Five minutes. Long enough to marvel yet again at the fact that the best part of a hundred people are getting paid to stand around drinking tea.'

'The lights are being adjusted, I think.'

Buckley took a bite of cake and grimaced. 'Rock by name . . .' he said, thickly. 'Gather I missed a bit of excitement this morning. Attempted assassination of Uncle Frank.'

'You missed him being sick behind the set as well. I think he's hungover.'

'Where did he find enough booze? I haven't had a hangover since January 1940.' He sighed gustily, sending a spray of crumbs down his tie. He looked, thought Catrin, he *sounded* like his old self.

'You don't usually come to studio,' she said, tentatively.

'And I don't usually go to the office on a Sunday, but I did today.'

'Oh.' It took her a moment to grasp the significance of the remark.

'Saw the Scotchman's line you wrote,' he said.

'Any good?'

'Middling. Did they shoot it?'

'Yes.'

'Do you know what a "bawbag" is?'

'No.'

'Well, let's hope the censor doesn't, either. Saw the other piece of dialogue you left as well.'

'Mmm.' The breath seemed to leave her. She couldn't look at him; she couldn't quite believe that she'd written it. 'What did you think?' she asked, staring at her hands.

'Bit slow.'

'Really?'

'And inconclusive. It's the sort of scene that ends with a slow fade.'

'Is that bad?'

'Arty. I wasn't wholly clear about what was going to happen next.'

'I wasn't very clear myself,' she said. She risked a glance at him: brilliantine, moustache, paunch, a currant on his jacket. No oil-painting. But then, she'd had enough of oil-paintings.

'Little Miss Blush is back, I see,' he said. 'So if I can rustle up a fiddler and a plate of whelks one evening soon, will you tell me the ending?'

She laughed, and put the back of her hand to her cheek and felt the unexpected heat of it.

'All right,' she said, and then there was a whistle blast and the usual shout for quiet and Buckley rolled his eyes.

'Off they go,' he muttered, 'murdering another one of our scenes. Which one is it?'

'312. Uncle Frank gets machine-gunned while untangling the propeller.'

Over luncheon, Ambrose had noticed Sophie's eye upon him – she'd been waiting, no doubt, for him to importune her about the promised role; if so, her wait had been in vain. He had sat in silence, indifferent alike to the food, to the prattle of the cast, to his very future. Misuse and derision had been his lot that morning; he had been dangled like a popinjay before the braying multitude, and the pain that lurked behind his eyes, the biliousness that prevented him from eating more than a single forkful of mock-duck in orange-substitute sauce, seemed to stem more from disgust at the world than from any indiscretion of the evening before. And in the afternoon, when filming recommenced, it was professionalism, solely professionalism, that guided his steps back to the sound-stage rather than to the nearest taxi-cab.

He lowered himself, at Kipper's request, into the tank beside the stern of the *Redoubtable*. He stood listening to a ten-minute discussion of the minutiae of the lighting rig while up to his nipples in water that was only just tepid. He submerged himself and mimed dexterous knifework before bobbing to the surface, alive but gravely wounded, and then did so a second time when there was discovered to be a hair in the gate, and a third when a bulb blew, and a fourth when something unspecified went amiss with the sound. He was hauled out of the tank and offered an upturned bucket to sit on. He was asked to climb back into the tank again. He held the knife towards camera for a close-up. Another bulb blew. He was hauled out for a second time and given a towel the texture of a doormat and a cup of cold cocoa and he endured the entire catalogue of ineptitude and negligence with nary a syllable of reproach; indeed, he scarcely noticed it at all.

Detachment. That was the word. It was as if he had never descended from the tower, and were still viewing the business of the studio from a great height. How petty it all seemed, how pointless – the scurrying crew, the gimcrack sets, the posturing and the strutting, the vastness of the enterprise, the vapidity of its purpose. This morning he had stood above it all and had felt the flimsy edifice tremble beneath his feet, and had glimpsed its paste-board heart. What did it matter, this play of shadows? What did any of it matter?

'Hilly, are you OK?' asked Lundback, when he too was summoned to the floor, and Ambrose, instead of objecting to the over-familiar contraction of his name, simply nodded.

'Rehearsal shortly, end of Scene 312,' called Kipper. 'Mr Hilliard, could we have you in the tank, please?'

Once again, he obeyed without demur. The camera was being lowered on its mechanical arm so that it hung just a yard or so above the water. Ambrose looked across at his reflection in the lens. A probable close-up, then, for Uncle Frank's final scene. Not that he cared two hoots.

'Say Hilly, can we practise the lines again?' asked Lundback, looking down at Ambrose from the rail of the *Redoubtable*. The deck behind him was packed with bodies: the sound-recordist; the woman from wardrobe; Cerberus curled on a piece of sacking, one anxious brown eye fixed on Ambrose; the continuity girl with her stool and clip-board and stop watch; the second and third ADs holding Uncle Frank's safety rope; Kipper in muttered conference with the director.

'Oh, very well,' said Ambrose. 'On "action" you'll climb down into the tank and support my head above the water, and then I'll say, "*I've dropped the knife.*" '

Lundback nodded. 'And I'll say "*You've done a FINE job, old timer.*" Only I'll say it real quiet, because I'll be close beside you.'

'Yes indeed,' said Ambrose. The loudest sound, by all the laws of drama, should be the rasp of Uncle Frank's breathing, the painful staccato of his next words: '*But I've not . . .*' He could put a wince in there, he thought, the merest tautening of the features; not that he gave the smallest fig about the scene. '*But I've not finished yet.*'

'OK,' said Lundback. 'And then I'll say "*You'll just have to leave it to ME.*" Only faster than that. And not saying the "*me*" so loud. And then there's only your lines left.'

'*Forgot you were an expert,*' supplied Ambrose – and perhaps at this point, for the transition from tragedy into humour which provided the climax of the scene, he could lift a hand above the surface and grasp, with feeble determination, Lundback's shoulder. '*Typical . . .*' a shuddering breath, maybe, and then just the hint of a wry smile, possibly captured in extreme close-up, though of course they could film the whole thing on a box brownie from the canteen for all he cared, '*. . . typical Yank.*' And then the bowline would tighten under his arms and he would be lifted out of the water, and that would be the end of the shoot for him, and he could walk away, he could shake the dust of artifice from his garments and learn to breathe a freer, truer air.

'Quiet, everyone,' shouted Kipper. 'Quiet. The director wants a script change, just a little tighten. We'll be cutting the last three lines, so after Hannigan says, "*You've done a fine job, old timer*", Uncle Frank will be pulled straight out of the water and Hannigan will start on his repairs of the propeller. All right? Everyone happy?'

And Ambrose felt suddenly winded, as if he'd received a blow to the solar plexus. He stared upward at the continuity girl, who was calmly crossing-out almost half a page of script, and he heard himself say 'No', and again, more loudly '*No.*'

Kipper peered over the rail, and Cerberus's nose appeared between his ankles. 'Sorry, Mr Hilliard, did you say something?'

And the distance between Ambrose and the studio seemed to telescope, and he was no longer an impassive observer but a participant, and he understood his task, he understood that he couldn't simply walk away from a quarter-century of knowledge and skill, he couldn't allow the wanton destruction of a well-shaped scene. He had to speak – he had to speak for the good of the film, for the cinema, for audiences everywhere. Effortlessly, he raised his voice to theatrical levels.

'I said no, it is not "all right". And no, I am not happy. And I demand to speak to the director about the proposed script changes.'

Catrin watched the third AD, half the age and a head taller than most of the crew, make a hesitant circuit of the studio floor, apparently looking for someone. It wasn't until he started heading straight towards her that she realized that the 'someone' was herself.

'You're the writer,' he said, his voice an uncertain waver, barely broken.

'I'm *a* writer,' she amended.

'Deny everything,' said Buckley, looking up from his *Daily Mirror*. He was sitting on a coil of rope, cup of tea beside him. 'Who's asking for writers?'

The youth glanced back at the water-tank, and lowered his voice confidentially. 'There's a bit of a row going on between Mr Hilliard and the director. Mr Hilliard is getting awfully worked up about line changes, and he's threatening not to do the scene at all unless something's done about it, and the continuity girl said that seeing as how one of the writers was actually in the studio for once, then perhaps we should make use of the fact, and Kipper told me to hurry off and fetch you.'

'What's the row about?' asked Catrin.

'Well, the director wanted to take out some dialogue because he says it interferes with the visual tension of the scene, and Mr Hilliard says if he does that, it'll affect the integrity of the story and—' He looked enquiringly at Buckley, who had given a snort.

'I shall translate,' said Buckley. 'The only time an actor ever uses a phrase like "integrity of the story" is when his own lines are being cut, and the words "visual tension" are a director's term for "you're spoiling my lovely pictures by overacting all over them". All we need now is for the cameraman to chip in about "the texture of the image" which means that he wants all the characters to blunder around in semi-darkness, and we'll have the full deck.'

'Well, anyway . . .' said the youth, rather desperately, turning to Catrin. '. . . I was told to see if I could get a writer to come up with a compromise.'

'I see.' She nodded, trying to appear willing; lodged in her memory was the previous ghastly occasion on which she'd spoken to Ambrose Hilliard about a script change. 'I'll do it.'

'No, I'll do it,' said Buckley. He waved a hand at her half-hearted protest. '*I'll* do it' he repeated, more firmly. 'This type of situation needs a bit of quick thinking – which you're perfectly capable of delivering – and a lorry-load of brazen, filthy, deceitful flattery, which you're not. You're a clever girl, but you can't tell a lie to save your life.'

'That's what you think,' said Catrin.

'So you fancy giving it a go?'

She grinned and shook her head. 'Not really. Thank you, Buckley.'

He gave her a wink, affectionate and more than a touch filthy, and ambled off, pausing beside the high wall of the tank in order to pat his pockets.

'Did I leave my Woodbines?' he called back to her, and she looked around towards the spot where he'd been sitting. There was no sign of his cigarettes. She turned back again, and as she did so, a movement caught her eye, and for a fraction of a second she thought that someone was diving from the very top of the scaffolding tower, and then she saw it was the lamp, the huge carbon lamp on its metal stalk, and it was gently, elegantly keeling over, the vast head swooning forward, the stalk leaving its socket, the whole of it dropping like a swollen rosebud on a stem, and it was so quiet, so quick, so graceful, that Catrin had hardly opened her mouth, had hardly begun to understand what she was seeing when the lamp hit the starboard bow of the *Redoubtable* with a noise like a bus exploding, and there was the groan of wood and a cracking sound, and the whole deck lurched forward and sideways and all the occupants, apart from the dog, fell off into the water, and a wave bounced across the width of the tank and slapped at the wooden wall and suddenly there was no wall on that side and a river was pouring through the breach and where Buckley had been standing there was nothing, there was no one, there was no one there at all . . .

FORTHCOMING ATTRACTIONS

The day was so warm that someone had prised away the boards that blocked one of the glassless windows of the twelfth-floor room. There was nothing to be seen through the narrow gap but the blue sky above Bloomsbury, and a pigeon who settled on the sill, keeping up a loud and persistent cooing.

Beside the contingent from Baker's, there were three Ministry of Information officials around the table, and a stenographer, and a tired-looking naval officer, the skin under his eyes like crumpled paper.

'Take no notice of me,' he said, when introductions were being made. 'I haven't the foggiest idea why I'm here,' and he gave Catrin a vague smile.

Rather than have to return it, she looked down at her hands. They were cold; they'd been cold all week, despite the weather. Her whole body felt chilled. She looked up again at Roger Swain, who had interviewed her nearly a year ago and whose hairline had retreated an inch or so since then.

'Let me just say,' he said, 'before we move on to the subject of this particular meeting, that I've taken a look at the initial report on the accident and whilst, obviously, it was a frightful tragedy, it seems to me a matter of extreme luck that it wasn't a great deal worse. Any number of people could have been standing at that end of the tank when the wall collapsed. Any number . . .' There was a pause; he looked towards the open window. 'Dreadful, all the same, an absolutely dreadful loss. Anyway, to the subject of the hour. Mr Baker?'

'I've just come from the cutting-room,' said Edwin Baker, grim but business-like, 'and they say they can't get around it, there's a hole in the story and at the moment there's nothing to fill it with – that propeller's got to get mended somehow.'

'Yes,' said Swain. 'The words "ha'p'orth of tar" do rather spring to mind. And have any ideas been forthcoming?'

'Not yet, no,' said Baker bluntly. He glanced at his writers, without reproach but without much expectation. Somewhere within the icy sludge of Catrin's brain, a half-thought stirred.

'And do we know the director's opinion?' asked Swain.

'I've been to the hospital . . .' Baker hesitated, his jaw moving from side-to-side in visible dissatisfaction. 'He's not making a great deal of sense at the moment. Bang on the head and all that, it's only been a few days . . . said he wants to re-shoot the whole thing with a different cast.'

One of the Ministry officials gave a huff of laughter, and Swain looked at him pointedly, before turning to Baker again.

'And you can't, for instance, shoot the missing scene in the lido with doubles of the characters?'

'We can't double both of them. Not at the same time. Lundback won't be off crutches for a month.'

'And the . . . what's his name? The old actor?'

'Hilliard. Another six weeks in plaster.'

Roger Swain sighed. 'I know that our chief's awfully keen about getting this picture ready for release. And of course, it's received a quite extraordinary amount of advance publicity over the last week. I know that may sound callous but it can't be gainsaid . . . Could you make use of the narrator again, perhaps?'

Baker nodded unenthusiastically. 'It'll probably come to that. Not an ideal ending to a thrilling picture though, is it? Distant shot of a boat and someone telling us what happened. Can't see punters queuing down the street for that.'

'Would it be . . . excuse me just a moment.' Swain stood and walked swiftly across to the window and clapped his hands, and the pigeon flew off with a clatter. 'Can't bear the creatures,' he said, returning to his seat. 'And it's very strange, there seem to be even more about than there used to be. God knows what they're eating.'

'Lime,' said Parfitt, loudly and unexpectedly. 'Lime in the exposed mortar.'

'Ah . . .' Swain paused, as if further pigeon lore might be forthcoming, but Parfitt's face had closed again.

'You were saying,' said Baker.

Swain shrugged. 'Oh, I was just wondering if we should bring a few more heads into the meeting. There's always a writer chappie or two hanging around the offices. Horribly ironic, isn't it, that the one person that we really need here is the one person we definitively can't have?'

And everyone except the naval officer looked at Catrin and Parfitt, or, rather, at the small gap between their chairs, as if the shade of Buckley might be hovering there, and if he *were*, thought Catrin – and she felt as if she'd been given a sudden sharp shove or an elbow in the ribs – if he *were*, then she could just imagine how he would react to the idea of Swain dragging a couple of random hacks into the discussion, a brace of weak-chinned varsity boys interfering with his script. She felt another jab of the elbow; go *on*, Mrs Taff. The half-thought thawed. She found that she'd raised her hand.

'Mrs Cole?' said Baker.

'I do have an idea.'

'Go on.'

'Rose could do it. Rose Starling could mend the propeller.'

Baker narrowed his eyes, as if perusing a balance sheet. 'Rose . . .' he said, doubtfully.

'After all, it's the Starling sisters' story, isn't it?' said Catrin. 'And she's on the stern already. She could call her uncle's name and climb into the water and – we could use a double for the uncle if he kept his head down, couldn't we? And he could be hauled out and then she could do the repair. And she's wearing a hat and dark clothes, isn't she, so it might not be too noticeable that she's not wet in the next scene . . . and maybe in another shot you could see the back of Hannigan's head too, maybe you could see her looking up at him and saying something.'

Beside her, Parfitt stirred. 'A gag?' he suggested. 'It'll need a gag.'

Baker looked at Swain, and then back at Catrin.

'We should go and talk it through with the cutter,' he said. 'See what he thinks.'

The naval officer remained at the table as everybody else got up to leave, and he caught Catrin's eye as she lit a cigarette.

'I'm afraid I wasn't very much help,' he said. 'I think I was supposed to be the maritime advisor.'

'It doesn't matter.' She held out the packet to him and he took one absently and let it droop between his fingers.

'So there was an accident, was there? In a film studio?'

'Yes,' she said. 'There was a lamp up near the roof, and it got loosened. It dropped on to a boat and one of the legs gave way.'

'The legs of the lamp?'

'The legs of the boat. It wasn't floating, you see, it was on stilts. And then one of the sides of the tank fell down.'

'A German tank?'

'A water-tank.'

He examined the cigarette, turning it over between his fingers as if he'd never seen one before. 'I thought the boat wasn't floating,' he said.

'It wasn't. But it looked as though it was floating.'

He nodded without comprehension.

'And someone was killed?' he asked.

She found that she couldn't answer that one.

'I'm sorry,' he said. 'A friend of yours, then?'

And she couldn't answer that either – couldn't frame the

words, couldn't think of how to define Buckley. She'd received no especial commiseration at his death, had merited no particular status in the mourning; what status could she have claimed? 'Buckley and Parfitt' had been an entity for twenty-odd years, and would last as long as their pictures were shown; 'Buckley and Catrin' had almost existed for twenty-odd minutes and had gone, now, for ever. Parfitt – poor Parfitt – had wept when he'd heard about the accident. Catrin had studied her own face and seen only bewilderment and a kind of outrage. She'd thought that her life had begun to follow a plot, but it had only been another incident in a series of incidents, one thing happening and then another, a romantic prologue jammed randomly between farce and tragedy.

'Are you coming, Mrs Cole?' called Edwin Baker from the corridor.

'I'm coming.' She nodded awkwardly at the naval officer.

'What's the title of your film?' he asked. 'So I can go and see it.'

'It doesn't have a title yet.'

'But is it a comedy? Or an action picture? Or a romance?'

She thought for a moment before she replied.

'It's a true story,' she said.

*

When he'd turned his ankle during the jousting sequence of *My Lady's Favour* (1924) Ambrose had been given his own room in a convalescent home beside Richmond Park. The bay window opposite his bed had afforded a view of rolling greensward, of groups of watchful deer among the spinneys.

From his current bed in men's orthopaedic, he could see Horace Crike, who'd tripped in the blackout and broken his ankle, Vic Shineman, who'd lost a leg when a parachute mine exploded opposite his shop, and Salvatore Cipriano, who was overspill from men's surgical, and who was awaiting the repair of a large hernia in his groin. Ambrose knew it was large, because Salvatore had showed it to him, flinging aside the covers one tedious afternoon to reveal a scrotum the size and shape of a boxing glove. 'Is agony,' he'd said, unnecessarily.

Five days on from the accident, Ambrose himself was in very little pain, unless one counted the mental anguish caused by his surroundings. What was driving him to utter distraction, however, was the incessant itching. The plaster cast extended in a rigid right-angle from his armpit down to his knuckles, and as it dried, a myriad tiny particles had started to shift and prick within it. Using his other hand, it was only possible to reach under the cast to scratch an inch or so of skin at either end. Unbearable. It was absolutely bloody unbearable.

Cecy had promised to bring in something that might help, and when visiting hour crawled round at last, he'd hoped that she'd be first into the ward as usual, but it was Vic Shineman's wife who led the charge, followed, surprisingly, by Sophie Smith.

'And how are you, Mr Hilliard?' she asked, arranging herself carefully on the visitor's chair.

'Beginning to feel very slightly better,' he said, 'thank you.'

'I am so glad. I telephoned the hospital yesterday and they said that you were doing as well as might be expected given your age and condition, so I was a little worried.'

'I see.'

'I won't stay very long, I don't want to tire you, but I needed to have a word about one or two rather important things.'

'Oh yes?'

'Before I forget—' She reached into her bag and took out a tissue-wrapped bunch of purple grapes and placed it on the bedside locker. *Grapes!* A gush of saliva filled his mouth; Good God, she must have gone to Harrods and paid a guinea at least for those. Almost involuntarily, he reached out and took one, felt the tug of the stalk, placed the fruit in his mouth, held the wonderful turgid weight of it on his tongue. He bit down, and was immediately disappointed: sour and full of pips.

'. . . rather fortunate,' Sophie was saying.

Ambrose ejected the pips into his hand. 'I'm afraid I missed that,' he said.

'The role that you were offered.'

'Which role?'

'The role that I was going to speak to you about on the last day of the studio. I wasn't sure, then, how you might respond, but now it all seems rather fortunate. Bearing in mind your indisposition.'

'And why's that?' he asked, warily. What part had she dredged up for him now? A buffoon in a bath chair? A crippled mute?

'Because you would be using your voice,' said Sophie. 'And only your voice.'

'You mean wireless?'

'No. I mean you would be providing the narration for the current film.'

'But I thought that the American character was going to be the . . .'

Sophie tilted her head very slightly.

'Oh Christ,' said Ambrose, revelation dawning. 'They want me to be Lundback.'

'Apparently you've been helping him with his lines, and your voices are a very good match.'

'They want me to do Lundback's acting for him.'

'And I have seen the script for the narration, and it's most eloquent and witty. They say it should be a notable feature of the film.'

'For which Lundback will get the credit.'

'And to compensate for that I shall be insisting that you be paid really rather well. I will also be ensuring that a taxi is provided for all your journeys to and from the dubbing suite, and that food considerably more substantial than a sandwich should be available for your luncheon.'

There was a long pause.

'Where's it being dubbed?' asked Ambrose.

'I believe in Dean Street.'

'The Maison Basque is in Dean Street.'

'I shall make a note of the fact.'

She sat with her gloved hands in her lap, very elegant and upright, the expression in her fine dark eyes faintly sardonic. She was clever, he realized with a jolt; far cleverer than her poor old brother – *dangerously* clever, the sort of cleverness that it would be best to keep in with. The old agency, with its woodwormed offices, was gone; Sophie would be re-building in steel.

'Thank you,' he said, rather mechanically. 'Those terms may be acceptable to me.' His arm, which he had forgotten about for a blessed minute or so, began to itch again.

'If you're not too tired,' she said, 'there is one other subject I'd like to discuss.'

'Oh yes?'

'It is Cerberus.'

'Is he well?'

'No, not very. He has stopped eating and he whines a great deal.'

'Have you taken him to a veterinary surgeon?'

'I believe he is pining for you, Mr Hilliard.'

Ambrose closed his eyes, heard again the crash of the lamp, felt the boat lurch, saw the others fall into the water, and a second later saw them whirl away as the far side of the tank disappeared and the pond became a mill-race. And the sole reason that he hadn't been dragged after the others, hadn't been tumbled and buffeted across the studio floor and through the scene-dock doors, was because he'd grabbed the propeller shaft with his right hand. He would thus have been the only one entirely uninjured had Cerberus not then jumped from the stern of the *Redoubtable*, all three stone of him landing squarely on Ambrose's extended arm. The pain had been so excruciating that he'd passed out and hit his head, and had come to ten minutes later to find the dog licking his face. The ambulance-woman had talked about nothing else – 'the little fellow brought you round, he did' – as if canine spittle were a famous restorative.

'He broke my elbow in two places,' he said to Sophie.

'He jumped to your rescue. Don't forget that he is a dog who is afraid of water.' She stood up and smoothed her skirt. 'I cannot pretend, Mr Hilliard, that I have any understanding of how this could have occurred, but the fact is that Cerberus loved my brother, and now he has transferred that love to you. He is, we could say, your legacy from Sammy, and of course it is extremely bad luck to refuse a legacy.'

She rested her gaze upon him, steady and implacable, and he understood, instantly, the nature of the bad luck in question: a dogless future was an agentless future. A tricky decision. He took a deep breath.

'I shall have to think about it,' he said. Sophie smiled.

All the men on the ward turned to watch her leave.

Cecy arrived a minute or two later. 'You will *never* guess why I'm late,' she said. 'I was passing a greengrocer's on the way to the station and what should I see but a—' She stopped speaking, her gaze fixed on the bunch of grapes on the bedside locker. 'Oh,' she said, in quite a different tone. 'Goodness. Don't those look nice.'

'My agent brought them, and as a matter of fact they're not.'

'No?'

'Bitter.'

'Oh, really?' Cecy looked slightly mollified. 'Well, I don't know if these are any better,' she said, taking another, smaller bunch from her bag. 'I had to queue for three-quarters of an hour to buy them. And I've brought the cuttings I promised you. Oh, and some marsh marigolds from the bottom of the garden, only a wild flower of course, but rather gay. Let me see if I can find a vase . . .' And she swept off again, exchanging little waves with the other occupants of the ward, smiling her toothy smile at the nurses.

'Next of kin?' they'd asked Ambrose, when he'd arrived at the hospital, and he'd tried, rather fuzzily, to recollect the location of his second cousin in Reigate, and had given them, instead, Cecy's address: The Ducklings, Thames Ditton. Peculiar thing, concussion.

He sifted through the cuttings she'd placed on the counterpane. *STUDIO HORROR: WRITER CRUSHED TO DEATH.* A photograph of Lundback on crutches surrounded by pretty nurses. *DUNKIRK EPIC WILL BE FINISHED, VOWS PRODUCER.* Another photograph of Lundback on crutches surrounded by pretty nurses. *DOG SAVES ACTOR.*

He pushed the pile of paper aside.

'Another lovely quiet night,' said Cecy, returning with a jug. 'Wouldn't it be marvellous if Mr Hitler has decided to go and bother another country instead? And don't these look madly cheerful?' She gave the flowers an admiring tweak.

'Very pleasant,' said Ambrose.

'So what did your agent say?' she asked, settling herself on the chair, and taking a piece of knitting out of her bag.

'Oh this and that. Spot of post-synchronization work for the current feature.'

'Anything coming up after that?'

'Not that I've heard of. You?'

'Ipswich hinting about a summer season. I've told them very firmly that it'll depend on whether or not my house guest is sufficiently recovered. No, really—' she said, as Ambrose began to protest. 'You may not be homeless, but you certainly can't manage to look after yourself in your current state, now can you? Besides, I'd rather hang on and see whether anything more interesting comes my way. I hear that British National are going to be adapting a novel by Mr Priestley, and, of course, I've just been in a play of his at Windsor . . .'

She paused, appearing to take a mesmerized interest in the ball of wool she was winding.

'Didn't you get a good notice?' asked Ambrose, taking his cue.

'Oh, just a little mention . . . you think it might be worth sending it to the casting director?'

'Undoubtedly.'

She nodded, pleased. For a while there was only the clack of her needles.

'Incidentally,' said Ambrose, scratching his knuckles, 'I may have to impose a second house guest upon you. I've managed to persuade my agent that Cerberus's place is by my side. As we've been through so much together.'

'Oh but that's *splendid*.'

'Yes.'

'And what a difficult conversation that must have been.'

He looked at her sharply but her expression was bland.

'Yes it was, rather,' he said.

He reached for the bunch of grapes she'd brought, and broke off one of them. It had a dimpled, senile look and a brown mark or two. He hesitated, turning it over between his fingers.

'Oh, I forgot,' said Cecy. 'I had a brainwave.' She reached into her bag and took out another knitting needle. 'An anti-itching solution. You should be able to reach almost anywhere with this,' and she mimed inserting it under the plaster cast and giving a vigorous scratch.

'Thank you,' said Ambrose. 'Very thoughtful.' Almost absently, he lifted the grape to his mouth.

'What's it like?' asked Cecy.

He bit into it, chewed, swallowed. Took another one.

'Surprisingly good,' he said.

*

August 1941

Dolly Clifford spotted Edith coming through the door of the Lyons Corner House, and waved her hand and shouted 'Cooeee! Over here! Long time no see!' and kept on waving her hand in a very deliberate fashion, so that there was no possible chance of Edith missing the engagement ring that glinted on her fourth finger.

'Canadian military policeman,' she said, as soon as Edith was within earshot. 'A sergeant!'

'And where did you meet him?' asked Edith, taking off her head-scarf.

'At a dance. Ooh, is your hair different?'

'I don't think so,' said Edith. 'It's started raining outside, maybe the ends have curled a bit.'

'Perhaps it's your lipstick, then. I've ordered tea and scones.'

'Thank you. So when did you get engaged?'

'Last month. He's called Robert but all his pals call him "Tiny".' She held up her finger so that Edith could admire the ring more closely. 'He wanted to get me a ruby but I told him that rubies were unlucky. My aunt had a ruby engagement ring and she'd only been married a week when her husband ran off with the next-door neighbour's daughter. They say sapphires are even worse.'

'It's very nice,' said Edith, peering at the diamond mote. 'And when are you getting married?'

'We haven't fixed a date yet. He always promised his mother

he'd tell her in person if he ever met someone, so it'll all depend on when he next gets home leave. Here—' She took a snapshot out of her handbag and Edith looked at the doughy, uncertain-looking man, his arm pinioned firmly in Dolly's. 'He owns a petrol station in Saskatchewan,' added Dolly. 'Well, his mother owns it really, but it'll be his one day.' She smiled with determined brightness. 'And how's your husband?'

'Arthur's very well.'

'Has he been sent abroad yet?'

'No. He was transferred. The army's setting up a catering corps, and they're taking men who've worked at that type of thing in civilian life,' and even saying the words was a pleasure, for they meant that rather than being torpedoed or sniped at or shelled or imprisoned or stung by mosquitoes, Arthur (at least for the time being) was in Aldershot debating tinned-meat requirements and the standardization of milk-to-cornflour proportions in the provision of custard to the forces, and these were things that he really and truly knew about, and the last time she'd seen him, nearly three weeks ago, she had detected about him a slight but definite air of assurance. The other men had nicknamed him 'Custard King', he'd told her. He'd seemed rather pleased by the soubriquet.

'And that must make you the Custard Queen,' he'd pointed out, and he'd bought her (by way of a crown) a maize-yellow Maltese cotton headscarf in La Mode in Acton High Street, just round the corner from her digs. She'd worn it to work the next day. It wasn't her usual choice of colour – it was rather startling, in fact – but the costume designer at Ealing had given her a long appraising look and said, 'Yes. It suits you', before shooing her off to the crowd room where thirty-five extras were waiting to be measured for Nazi uniforms for the new Will Hay picture. She'd worn the scarf every day since.

'And what's happened about the house?' asked Dolly, as the tea arrived.

Edith shook her head. 'Not very much, really. The site's

being cleared and Arthur's had to fill in an awfully long form. They've said he'll get government compensation, but not until after the war ends. Whenever that will be.'

'Next year,' said Dolly, with absolute conviction. 'My brother-in-law's neighbour's a barber and he was shaving a man who works in the – well, I shouldn't say, really, it's a hush-hush government place – but anyway he was telling my brother-in-law's neighbour that they're developing a new deadly weapon, a kind of glue that they'll drop on to the German forces. They're still working on it, but once it's ready, the whole war will be over in a weekend.'

'Well . . . good,' said Edith, somewhat inadequately.

'Did I tell you we're opening a Gallery of the Boffins at Tussaud's to celebrate scientific achievements of the Empire? I've been ironing an actual pair of R. J. Mitchell's trousers.'

Something about the phrase made Edith laugh, and Dolly stopped speaking and looked at her carefully.

'Now don't get offended,' she said, 'but do you think that your terrible experience in the Morrison shelter might have affected you in some way?'

'I suppose it might have done,' said Edith.

'Only you don't seem quite as . . . as *serious* as you used to be.'

'No?'

'No. Not that that's necessarily a bad thing.' She smiled at Edith, and Edith smiled back, and half-listened as Dolly related an anecdote about the Head of Moulds, and half-thought about the coming weekend, when Arthur would have two days' leave. She had designed and made herself a nightdress out of a remnant of plum-coloured sateen. She thought that he might rather like the result.

*

That summer it felt to Catrin as if time had slowed down. The raids had ceased, and with them the sirens, and now there was nothing to distinguish one week from another. London seemed half-empty, half-demolished, as shabby as its inhabitants. The war news was enervating; there was no progress or drama. She worked long hours, sometimes at Baker's, sometimes at the Ministry, and at night she slept badly. When she dreamed she often heard Buckley speaking, but she could never remember the sound of his voice when she awoke.

She tried to imagine what would have happened if he hadn't died. She saw the banter turning to friction, she saw them living and working together, she saw them arguing and quickly parting, she saw them talking for thirty years. She saw all the possible futures lined up alongside each other, untouched, sardines in a keyless tin.

Summer became autumn and there were still no raids. The treatment for the ARP film was rejected, rewritten, accepted and then placed in a pending tray somewhere in the Ministry of Information. Parfitt went to Gainsborough for six weeks to write jokes for the Crazy Gang, and then came back and slept through most of a month. Catrin ground out dialogue for a series of dull shorts about War Bonds. It rained incessantly. On a sodden September day, the gutter outside Baker's overflowed and an unexploded bomb was found lodged in the road gulley; that afternoon Catrin helped to carry a hundred and thirty-five boxes of paperwork around the corner to a temporary billet in Beak Street.

She was allocated half a table in a tiny basement room that was bathed in greenish light from a double row of glass bricks set in the pavement above her head. She tried to concentrate on a list of rewrites requested by the Ministry of Economic Warfare, but the door was opening and closing every five minutes as the office boy hauled more boxes into the room, and she gave up, eventually, and stared upwards instead at the shoes of passers-by as they slapped wetly across the glass ceiling. They seemed to have such purpose, such a sense of urgency. They knew where they were going.

'Last one,' said the office boy, plumping a stack of pasteboard files on to the table beside her and then exiting again. A sheaf of photographs slid from the top one, and Catrin caught at them before they could fall to the floor – glossy six-by-fours of Carl Lundback in his role as Hannigan, his signature, neat and rather schoolboyish, written across one corner. She looked through the other files in the stack and found signed portraits of Hadley Best, of Doris Cleavely and Angela Ralli-Thomas and of the dog, the latter stamped with a smudged paw-print.

She picked up the photograph of the twins again and studied it. They were wearing their sea-faring costume – knitted jumpers, trousers tucked into rubber boots, woollen hats, from which the odd curl escaped. They looked fresh and pretty and carefree, and she thought, for the first time in months, of the real twins, of Rose whispering fearfully behind a closed door, of Lily darting upstairs to fetch her treasured, tissue-wrapped, film-star photographs.

They should, of course – of *course* – be sent souvenirs of their very own (and pleasingly successful) film, as many souvenirs as she could muster, and she had begun to search through the chaos of boxes for an envelope when, quite suddenly, she thought of Lily's face and of what might happen if the twins' father were in the house when the postman came. She stood, hesitating, in the watery light, uncertain of what to do, and the uncertainty seemed to expand, to fill every nerve and hollow of her, so that she could no longer think beyond the next hour, or even the next minute, because every frame of the future seemed to require a decision of one sort or another, and she'd have to make those decisions on her own, and she didn't know whether she could, she didn't know if she were capable. And then Parfitt opened the door of the office, gave the jumbled interior a blood-shot stare and muttered, 'Ruddy coal-hole', and the uncertainty shrank again to a portable size.

'Parfitt,' she said, getting her breath back, 'do you have any idea how I could get a travel permit to go to Leigh-on-Sea?', and Parfitt, who seemed to lack curiosity in the way that some people lacked a sense of smell, replied, 'Tell Baker's secretary you're researching a short on fisher-folk for the Ministry of Agriculture, and ask her to send a chit to Home Security about it. Give it a title.'

'*Cockles and Mussels?*'

'That'll do.'

It took six weeks for the permit to come through, and she set off for the coast on a morning of numbing sleet. There were puddles in the carriages, and greatcoats dripping from the luggage racks. Catrin sat in a corner next to a Gurkha with a head-cold, and rubbed her frozen hands together and stared out of the window at a sky the colour of cocoa. The parcel of signed photographs was in her bag, wrapped in a piece of oil-cloth. Her plan was rudimentary: she would loiter on the pavement opposite the twins' house, hoping that one of them would spot her and sneak out. She was prepared to wait all day.

By the time that the local train reached Leigh-on-Sea, it was nearly eleven o'clock. The temperature had risen a little and instead of sleet there was heavy rain, and over the half-mile walk from the station, Catrin's shoes began to disintegrate, the uppers bagging, the cardboard in the insteps turning to fibrous porridge. She arrived in Whiting Walk at a slow shuffle, concentrating so hard on keeping the damn things on her feet that she nearly bumped into another pedestrian who had come to a sudden halt in front of her. It was an old man holding a string bag containing half a cabbage and a tin of butter beans, and he gave her an empty stare before letting himself in to one of the houses and closing the door. Number 15.

Catrin stood transfixed. The door was unchanged, the glass still missing from the occasion when a boot had been thrown at Rose, the gap still roughly patched with a section of tea chest. There was a movement in the front window, and she turned to see the man gazing out at her, cabbage still in hand. He was of average build, ordinary-looking, round-faced like his daughters, badly-shaven, his hair colourless and thinning; she'd expected to see something else, a monster, violence incarnate. He made a gesture at her – *go away*.

She took a step backward, and then crossed the road and looked round at the house again. He was still watching.

Behind her, a door opened. 'There's no point in waiting,' said a woman, scornfully, 'he won't talk to anyone about them.' She stood on the mat, arms folded. She was plump and pretty, her hair in stiff curls, her eyes like twin searchlights, missing nothing. She gave Catrin a quick head-to-foot inspection, dwelling on the leaking umbrella, the ruined shoes. 'You'll be from the papers,' she said, 'one of the weeklies.'

'No,' said Catrin, 'I'm a . . . a friend of Rose and Lily's'.

'Can't be much of a friend if you've come here looking for them. They've been gone six weeks.'

'Gone?'

'Joined the ATS. After the picture came out. Rose went along to the office in Southend and told them that if she could mend a boat engine she could certainly learn how to mend an army lorry, and so could her sister, and they got signed up straight away. Did a moonlight flit. You should have seen him when he found out. Went round the bend, the *bastard*.' The word was startling, dropping from that neat little mouth. Involuntarily, Catrin turned to look at Mr Starling again but the window was empty.

'He went all the way to the office to complain,' said the woman, with a glint of pleasure. 'They told him the girls were over twenty-one and he'd have to put up with it. Have you seen the picture?'

Catrin found herself shaking her head.

'It's still on at the Corona, up by the station.'

'Have *you* seen it?' asked Catrin.

'Course I have,' said the woman. 'Three times. It's our picture, isn't it? They're our girls.'

The hand-made banner outside the cinema read '*SEE YOUR LOCAL FILM STARS!*' and even on a Tuesday afternoon, the Corona was almost full. Catrin took her seat in the stalls and slipped off her shoes. She watched the end of a newsreel report about a Cossack dance display in Trafalgar Square, followed by a Food Flash urging her to eat more potatoes, and then the curtains closed briefly before opening again to show the Baker's logo, a loaf in the shape of the letter 'B'.

And what she had told the woman in Whiting Walk had almost been the truth, for although she *had* seen the picture before, it had been at the trade show in an auditorium stuffed with important business people, every seat filled, and she'd stood right at the back of the circle, beside the exit doors, and whether it had been the fault of the distance from the screen, or the tensions of the hour, or her own simple misery, the fact was that she'd scarcely been able to follow the plot. It had been nothing more than a collection of lines, each one hooked to a memory, so that she'd watched not the tale of the Starling sisters, but the ghost of her own story.

Now, as the Baker's logo dissolved into a shot of the gentle heaving sea off Badgeham Beach, and a voice somewhere in front of Catrin hissed, 'Wake up, mother, it's starting', and the violins on the soundtrack played the first notes of a shanty, she leaned forward and watched the title rise up out of the waves.

FORBIDDEN VOYAGE

And over the violins came the deep rich voice of Hannigan, '*I wasn't there at the beginning of the story . . .*'

And this time, in a cinema that smelled of damp coats and parma violets, where the dialogue was competing with the sound of someone shelling nuts in the row behind her, she could see beyond the script, could follow the twin threads of the plot as it moved between France and England, could duck as the Stukas roared overhead, could feel the release of tension as Rose Starling managed, at last, to untangle the propeller, could join in the scatter of applause as the *Redoubtable* reached home, as Hannigan spoke his final words over a panorama of the quayside ('and if this doesn't get the Yanks into the war,' Buckley had remarked, immodestly, 'then nothing will.'):

. . . like I said, I wasn't there at the beginning of the story, but you can bet your bottom dollar that I'm not leaving before the end. Because I know now that it has to be the right sort of ending, the sort of ending that's worth fighting for.

Someone in the front row gave a shrill whistle of approbation, and then the shot of the quayside was replaced abruptly with a screen that read

COULD PATRONS WHO HAVE SEEN
THE ENTIRE PROGRAMME
PLEASE LEAVE THE AUDITORIUM
TO MAKE ROOM FOR OTHERS.

No one moved. Catrin checked her watch; it was only half past two. She could see the whole thing over again and still have time to get back to London. After all, spending an entire afternoon at the cinema could be counted as an essential part of a screen-writer's job.

She glanced around at her fellow picture-goers, and felt a flicker of pride that they too wanted to stay.

It was a good film.

Some day she'd write one that was even better.

Acknowledgements

With thanks to Roy Ward Baker, Keith Barber, Pat Crosbie, Phyllis Dalton, Patricia Hayers, Mary Llewellyn, Julia McDermott, Peter Manley, Joe Marks, Myrtle French, Bernard Phillips and John Porter, all of whom were generous enough to share their memories of the era with me; to Barry Davis for his help with the Yiddish; to the incomparable staff of the BFI library – patient, knowledgeable, helpful and endlessly good-humoured; to Bill Scott-Kerr and Katie Espiner – it took me eight years, Bill, but I got there in the end – and to Georgia Garrett, for practically everything. Finally I want to thank Norman Longmate for writing *How We Lived Then*, which I first read when I was thirteen, and which awoke in me an abiding interest in the home front.

Crooked Heart

Lissa Evans

When Noel Bostock – aged ten, no family – is evacuated from London to escape the Blitz, he winds up in St Albans with Vera Sedge – thirty-six, drowning in debts. Always desperate for money, she's unscrupulous about how she gets it.

The war's thrown up all manner of new opportunities but what Vee needs is a cool head and the ability to make a plan. On her own, she's a disaster. With Noel, she's a team.

Together they cook up an idea. But there are plenty of other people making money out of the war and some of them are dangerous. Noel may have been moved to safety, but he isn't actually safe at all . . .

'Glorious. I loved every line of this book'
PAULA HAWKINS

'Darkly funny and deeply touching . . . it's a crooked journey, straight to the heart'
NEW YORK TIMES BOOK REVIEW

'Airy and bouncy as a good Victoria sponge . . . there's a great galloping joy in it'
INDEPENDENT

'Spirited, quirky characters and a devilish wit . . . Why is Lissa Evans not one of our best-known and best-loved authors?'
SUNDAY EXPRESS

'Touching and funny'
NICK HORNBY

'My book of the year'
JOJO MOYES

'Wonderfully vivid and eccentric'
THE TIMES

'Dazzling'
GUARDIAN

Petty Officer Marcus Luttrell joined the U.S. Navy in rch 1999 and became a combat-trained SEAL in January 2 2. After serving in Baghdad, he was deployed to Afghani- n in the spring of 2005. He was awarded the Navy Cross for nbat heroism in 2006 by President George W. Bush.

atrick Robinson is known for his bestselling U.S. Navy-based vels, and the autobiography of Admiral Sir Sandy Woodward, *C Hundred* Days, which he cowrote, was an international seller. He lives in England and spends his summers on e Cod, Massachusetts, where he and Luttrell wrote *Lone S vivor.*

LONE SURVIVOR

The Incredible True Story of Navy SEALs Under Siege

MARCUS LUTTRELL

WITH PATRICK ROBINSON

sphere

SPHERE

This edition published in 2014 by Sphere

16

First published in the United States of America in 2007
by Little, Brown and Company
First published in Great Britain in 2008 by Sphere
Reprinted 2008 (twice), 2009 (twice), 2011, 2013

A CIP catalogue record for this book
is available from the British Library.

ISBN 978-0-7515-5594-3

Map by George W. Ward

Typeset in Caslon by M Rules
Printed and bound in Great Britain by
Clays Ltd, St Ives plc

Papers used by Sphere are from well-managed forests
and other responsible sources.

Sphere
An imprint of
Little, Brown Book Group
Carmelite House
50 Victoria Embankment
London EC4Y 0DZ

An Hachette UK Company
www.hachette.co.uk

www.littlebrown.co.uk